Advance Praise for *The Unicorn Anthology*

"What a treasure trove! This anthology is filled with stories that will surprise, fascinate, and delight you. From an Arizona ghost town where souls
are healed to a medieval European forest to the middle of an elephant herd
in Persia, there are so many gems to be found!"
—Sarah Beth Durst, award-winning author of the Queens of Renthia series

"This slender but rich anthology compiled by Beagle and Weisman (*The
New Voices of Fantasy*) centers on the mythical beast for which Beagle is best
known, thanks to his classic novel *The Last Unicorn*. The 15 stories and one
poem reinterpret the unicorn myth across genre and style. Caitlín R. Kiernan's lesbian noir "The Maltese Unicorn" pits a hard-boiled rare book dealer
against a sorcerous femme fatale. In Jane Yolen's delicate "The Transfigured
Hart," a bookish boy and a horse-loving girl bond over a shared obsession
with a mysterious white woodland creature. Dave Smeds's "Survivor" in-
cludes elements of horror in its tale of a traumatized Vietnam vet, as does
Garth Nix's "The Highest Justice," in which a princess and a revenant queen
seek revenge with the help of a unicorn. Themes of innocence lost, first love,
and yearning for transcendence pervade all of the stories in this collection,
giving it a haunting and melancholy feel. Readers who love the mystery and
elegance of unicorns will find this a lovely homage."
—*Publishers Weekly*

"Unicorns are a rare and wondrous breed; fortunately for us, stories about
them are a little easier to find. Peter S. Beagle's new anthology contains a
marvellous collection of stories about the animal that probably never existed, but that we still can't stop dreaming about. Like the creature itself, the
stories are wild and wistful, graceful and glorious, kind and crazy. Everything we need to help us believe . . . in something worth believing in."
—Simon R. Green, author of *Night Fall* and *Blue Moon Rising*

"Between these pages you'll find tales that are as mysterious and arresting
as any creature of myth and legend. *The Unicorn Anthology* returned me to

the stories of writers I already loved and introduced me to the stories of writers I know I will come to love."
—Kevin Brockmeier, author of *A Brief History of the Dead*

"Well worth reading."
—*NY Journal of Books*

"Unicorns in literature are fascinating, evocative, mysterious, and elusive, and with *The Unicorn Anthology*, editors Peter S. Beagle—himself of unicorn fame—and Jacob Weisman invite continued appreciation of the legendary beast, drawing it beyond its familiar medieval framework."
—*Foreword*

Anthologies edited by Peter S. Beagle

"All 17 stories eschew all or most of the conventions of commercial fantasy. . . . Start reading and expect to enjoy."
—*Booklist* on *The Secret History of Fantasy*

"Set[s] out to rewrite our concept of fantasy, and with the help of some of the world's best writers, succeeds admirably."
—*The Agony Column* on *The Secret History of Fantasy*

"The stories are all, in many different ways, pleasures to read."
—*The Civilian Reader* on *The Secret History of Fantasy*

"An essential book not only for longtime followers of such intriguing stories but those who thought fantasy only took place in the completely imagined worlds of J. R. R. Tolkien."
—*Bookgasm* on *The Urban Fantasy Anthology* (with Joe R. Lansdale)

"An excellent collection of stories that showcases the best of urban fantasy (however you define it). Definitely a must-read!"
—*Interzone* on *The Urban Fantasy Anthology* (with Joe R. Lansdale)

"This is one of the best reprint anthologies of the year in terms of literary value, and you certainly get more than your money's worth of good fiction."
—*Locus* on *The Urban Fantasy Anthology* (with Joe R. Lansdale)

Anthologies edited by Jacob Weisman

★"This volume is a treasure trove of stories that draw equally from SF and literary fiction, and they are superlative in either context."
—*Publishers Weekly*, starred review on *Invaders*

"Playful and imaginative."
—*AV Club* on *Invaders*

"A superb batch of stories by literary authors who have invaded science fiction—and left distinct footprints behind."
—*Black Gate* on *Invaders*

★"This is an unbeatable selection from classic to modern, and each story brings its A game."
—*Publishers Weekly*, starred review on *The Sword & Sorcery Anthology* (with David G. Hartwell)

"Superbly presented . . . reignited this reader's interest."
—*SF Site* on *The Sword & Sorcery Anthology* (with David G. Hartwell)

"Hard and fast-paced fantasy that's strong from the first piece right through to the last."
—*Shades of Sentience* on *The Sword & Sorcery Anthology* (with David G. Hartwell)

"A marvelous mix of classics and rarely seen works, bibliophile's finds and old favorites . . . a treasury in every sense and a treasure!"
—Connie Willis, author of *Doomsday Book* and *To Say Nothing of the Dog* on *The Treasury of the Fantastic* (with David Sandner)

THE UNICORN ANTHOLOGY
Peter S. Beagle & Jacob Weisman, eds.

THE UNICORN
ANTHOLOGY

EDITED BY
PETER S. BEAGLE
AND JACOB WEISMAN

tachyon ◆ *san francisco*

Tachyon Publications LLC
1459 18th Street #139
San Francisco, CA 94107
(415) 285-5615
www.tachyonpublications.com
tachyon@tachyonpublications.com

Series Editor: Jacob Weisman
Project Editor: Jill Roberts

Print ISBN: 978-1-61696-315-6
Digital ISBN: 978-1-61696-283-8

Printed in Canada by Marquis

First Print Edition: 2019
9 8 7 6 5 4 3 2 1

CONTENTS

i.

Introduction

PETER S. BEAGLE

1.

The Magical Properties of Unicorn Ivory

CARLOS HERNANDEZ

14.

The Brew

KAREN JOY FOWLER

29.

Falling Off the Unicorn

DAVID D. LEVINE AND SARA A. MUELLER

45.

A Hunter's Ode to His Bait

CARRIE VAUGHN

61.

Ghost Town

JACK C. HALDEMAN II

74.

A Thousand Flowers

MARGO LANAGAN

98.

The Maltese Unicorn

CAITLÍN R. KIERNAN

130.

Stampede of Light

MARINA FITCH

144.
The Highest Justice
GARTH NIX

156.
The Lion and the Unicorn
A. C. WISE

161.
Survivor
DAVE SMEDS

188.
Homeward Bound
BRUCE COVILLE

199.
Unicorn Triangle
PATRICIA A. MCKILLIP

207.
My Son Heydari and the Karkadann
PETER S. BEAGLE

220.
The Transfigured Hart
JANE YOLEN

261.
Unicorn Series
NANCY SPRINGER

265.
About the Editors

INTRODUCTION
Peter S. Beagle

THE GREAT IRISH POET AND NOVELIST, James Stephens, whose work influenced my own far more—with every possible due respect—than Professor Tolkien's ever did—got so damn tired of being remembered only for his classic *The Crock of Gold* (which I discovered in high school) that he simply stopped writing novels at all. Spent the last twenty-five years of his life writing poetry and broadcasting on the BBC. Of Robert Nathan's thirty-odd novels, the only one still in print (thanks to Tachyon) is *Portrait of Jennie*, just as you'd likely have to dig to find any of Charles Jackson's books but *The Lost Weekend*—and that only because, like *Jennie*, it was made into a successful movie. Joe Haldeman continues to write just as notably as ever, but has told me that he's resigned to being recognized always as the author of *The Forever War*. My late Santa Cruz friend Jim Houston, who wrote several splendid novels about California and Hawaii (one day, surely, someone will film his *Snow Mountain Passage*, about the Donner Party), equally accepted having *Farewell to Manzanar*—written with his wife Jeanne, about her childhood years in the Japanese-American internment camps—as what he called "the family franchise." *Farewell to Manzanar* remains an award-winning TV movie (easily available online), and has been required reading in the majority of American high schools and colleges since its publication. I can't imagine it ever falling out of print.

Actors in a particularly popular role, in some ways, have it worse, of course. At least Eugene O'Neill's father, an actor who fed his family touring *The Count of Monte Cristo* across the country almost until he died, didn't have to deal with endless reruns. Leonard Nimoy's laudable denial, *I am not Spock*, was followed, some decades later—after a celebrated career as actor and director spent equally between movies, television and the theatre—by *I am Spock*. Christopher Lee was very proud of having played not only Sherlock Holmes but also Sherlock's "smarter brother" Mycroft (not to mention Dr. Fu Manchu); but to most viewers and fans he was forever Dracula. And glad to get it, as he said himself, "No Dracula . . . *who knows?*"

So it's become for me. *The Last Unicorn* isn't my favorite of my own books—for that matter, there will always be people who feel that I never wrote anything better than my first one, *A Fine & Private Place*—but without that damn unicorn, would so many people have discovered my ghosts, my poetic wanderers, my woman warriors, my ragtag wizards? To quote Christopher Lee, who knows?

I've tried to shuck off the beasts over the years, telling people about my longstanding offer to the late blessed Ursula Le Guin to trade my unicorns *en masse* even-up for her magnificent dragons. It was a mock-serious joke between us, on the rare occasions when we ran into each other, but it was serious enough as far as I was concerned. In 1968, when *The Last Unicorn* was published, I still didn't really think of myself as a career fantasist, even with *A Fine & Private Place*, "Come Lady Death," and "Lila the Werewolf" constituting my entire *oeuvre* to that point. And *The Last Unicorn* had been such an exhausting, frustrating horror to write (the only bits I remember enjoying were the incidental song lyrics, because writing songs is always a joy) that there was no way in the world that I was going back, ever, to that fairytale nightmare. Not a bloody chance, boy.

So I wrote *The Folk of the Air*, eighteen years later. It took me four drafts, and really should have gone through a fifth. There aren't any unicorns in that one; but by then I was living primarily off film and television screenwriting jobs, and I can tell you without the slightest fear of contradiction that there are no unicorns in Hollywood. Dragons, yes—unicorns no. None.

But I did at last go back to my unicorn and her world of kings and magicians and plain countryfolk, and beasts as legendary as herself. I went in the company of a valiant, aggravating nine-year-old girl named Sooz. And I'll be going back there again, because Sooz is seventeen now, and she has a journey to make—which I dread far more than she does, because she doesn't know any better. She never does. She just goes on.

It was Sooz who led me to embrace my Inner Unicorn Guy: that four-year-old who stood in front of his mother's elementary-school class (so family legend always had it) and told them all about unicorns. When the class ended, he said politely, "Goodbye—I'll come back sometime and tell you more about unicorns." Anyway, that's what my mother always told me.

Because of Sooz, who has only once taken *no* for an answer (that was from an aged, near-senile King Lir, whom she fell in love with), I've written stories about Chinese and Persian unicorns, a pregnant unicorn choosing to give birth on a rundown little farm in Calabria, a five-inch-high unicorn liberated from an ancient tapestry by Japanese magic, and trapped in an art gallery; even a unicorn in colonial Maine—a vision vouchsafed to a career con-artist named Olfert Dapper, who knows that he has no right in the world to the sight of it. Dr. Dapper (as he shamelessly titled himself) happens to be one of the two people to whom *The Last Unicorn* is dedicated. So I knew *something* back then, fifty years ago, even though I wasn't about to acknowledge it.

I've written about mermaids as well, not to mention giants and spooks and *dybbuks*—and even two dragons: one permanently pissed-off (at me, as it happens), and one soft-hearted dragon, who loves a princess as chivalrously as any knight. I have an old tenderness for all manner of shapeshifters (always wanted to be one, I guess); and a particular being of my own, called a *chandail*. And then there's the Shark God, his human wife, and his two troubled, demigod children. I'm proud of them all (especially Mrs. Eunice Giant, who declares indignantly to Jack, "I'm not either a monster! I'm big, yes, and I've got dietary needs, like you or anyone else!") Looking back, I love them all.

But the unicorns are . . . not special to me, not exactly, but something I've never had a word for. Olfert Dapper, of all people, hears it—or something as close to it as I can come—from a Puritan woman named Remorse Kirtley, citizen of a colonial settlement called No Popery, who has held a unicorn's head in her lap, and looked into its eyes.

"The unicorn set me free, can you understand me? Freed me from the world I have always been taught, and always believed, was the only world for a Christian soul. While I sat there and held him, he came into me— how else should I put it, dear Doctor?—he came into me and showed me the magic beyond poor, crabbed No Popery, the beauty beyond the sour singsong God of my worship . . ."

They are beautiful and mysterious, far past our understanding of either word. They have been, over the endless millennia, sometimes curious—even fatally so—about humans; sometimes—rarely, and only according to their own imagining of *that* word—generous. But they do not know love, and they are incapable of regret. Only one unicorn was ever born who could regret. It cannot be said to have served her well.

And perhaps that is why—speaking as a human being old enough to envy unicorns' freedom from such things—they still haunt the corners of my failing eyes, and of my dreams. Of all the beloved shadows, they remain, to paraphrase, of all things, the poignant old Rodgers & Hart song, "too beautiful to be true," leaving us all, as in the song, fools for beauty.

It's a little difficult for me to present an unbiased view of the stories included in this anthology, because so many are either by old friends of mine, like Patricia McKillip, Karen Joy Fowler and Nancy Springer, or people whose work I've admired for years, such as Garth Nix and Caitlín R. Kiernan. (I think "The Maltese Unicorn" just might be my favorite story of the collection. And I'm particularly delighted that its publication has raised money for Boon Lott's Elephant Sanctuary, among other wildlife charities. Elephants may not be unicorns, but they are magical in their own right, and splendid as well. Unicorns aren't splendid, or any other such word. As I've been trying to say through this foreword—indeed, through my entire odd career as the Unicorn Guy—at the last, there is no word to describe what a unicorn is. No word that *I* know, anyway.

THE MAGICAL PROPERTIES OF UNICORN IVORY

Carlos Hernandez

VOCATIONS DON'T GRANT VACATIONS. I'm supposedly on holiday in London when I get an offer no reporter could refuse: to see a unicorn in the wild.

I'm with my friend Samantha, hanging out at her dad's pub after a long night's clubbing, still wearing our dance-rumpled party dresses, dying to get out of our heels. Sam's father, Will, is tending bar tonight, so it's the perfect spot for late-night chips and hair-of-the-dog nightcaps. Plus, most of the clientele is over 50. We wouldn't have to spend all evening judo-throwing chirpsers. (And yes, this Latina's been in London a full eight days and has decided to adopt every bloody Britishism she hears. Deal.)

Or so we thought. Sam flicks her head toward a guy sitting alone, staring at us over his drink. He could be my dad, if my dad had forgotten to bring a condom to his junior prom. Short, stout, but really fit; looks like a cooper built his torso. The man's never heard of moisturizer. He's wearing a black pinstripe shirt with a skinny leather tie, black pleated pants and black ankle-boots. I am sure some cute sales girl had dressed him—because nobody who cared about him would've let him leave the house looking like dog's dinner.

And now—shit—I scrutinized him too long. He comes over, beer in hand.

"Ladies," he says.

"We're not hookers," says Sam. "I know these dresses might give a gentleman the wrong impression."

"Sorry to disappoint," I add, big smile.

"Right," he says, and turns on his heel.

"Hold on, Gavin," says Will, who's just pulled up with my Moscow Mule. "Don't let these two termagants scare you off. Make a little room for Gavin, Sam, will you?"

Gavin considers us a moment, then pulls up the stool next to Samantha and offers his hand. "Gavin Howard."

"Oh!" says Sam. She's suddenly unironically warm—a rare demeanor for her. "You're the forest ranger. Dad's told me about you. I'm Sam."

I put out my hand. "And I'm Gabi Reál."

"A pleasure," he says, then proceeds to purée my knucklebones—one of those insecure guys who has to try to destroy the other person's hand. Charming.

"This man's a national hero," Will says to me. "He's keeping our unicorns safe."

Now *that* is interesting. Back in the States, we've heard reports of unicorns appearing in forests throughout Great Britain. But in this age of photo manipulation it's hard to get anyone to believe anything anymore.

So I say as much: "Plenty of Americans don't think unicorns are real, you know."

"Oh, they're real, Ms. Reál," says Gavin, pleased with his wit. As if I hadn't heard that one 20 billion times.

"Americans," says Samantha. "You never think anything interesting could possibly be happening anywhere else in the world, do you?"

The Brits share a chuckle. I don't join in.

"We shouldn't insult our visitor," says Will. "I mean, if she were to tell us snaggletoothed pookahs started appearing in California, I suppose I'd want better proof than a picture." He leans to Gavin and adds, "Gabi's a reporter for the *San Francisco Squint*. Her column's called 'Let's Get Reál.' Two million read it every week, don't you know."

Gavin sizes me up like a squinting jeweler. "I'm all for reality. I have no patience for falsehood. I wish more people would 'get reál.'" His voice gets weirdly sincere.

I lean toward him and say, "Me too. My column's subtitle is 'Truth or Death.'" I smile and sip my Mule.

It's not the first time I've chirpsed to land an interview. Gavin drinks the rest of his beer but never takes his eyes off me. Neither do Will or the slightly-disgusted Sam, who sees exactly what's happening.

But screw her; a story's a story. Gavin sets down his glass and says the words I am longing to hear: "You know, I'm working the New Forest this weekend. If you'd like, it would be my pleasure to take you with me. You might just see a unicorn for yourself."

I thought this would make a nice fluffy piece for my column. I mean, unicorns!

Gavin—who is completely professional and hands-off, thank God—and I are having a delightful Sunday-morning hike through some less-traveled parts of the New Forest. It's everything an American could want of an English woods: fields of heath; majestic oaks and alders; rivers that run as slow as wisdom itself; and ponies! Thousands of ponies roaming feral and free like a reenactment of my girlhood fantasies.

Of course, that sets my Spidey-sense tingling. Wouldn't it be easy enough for rumors of unicorns to sprout up in a place with so many darling ponies ambling about?

This is what I am thinking when we come across a thick, almost unbroken trail of blood.

"Hornstalkers," Gavin says. And when he sees I'm not following: "Unicorn poachers. Of all the luck."

He calls it in on some last-century transceiver. HQ wants more information. They tell him to send me home and to follow the blood trail with extreme caution. "Do not attempt to apprehend them on your own," says HQ.

"Understood."

"I mean it, Gavin. Don't go showing off in front of your lady-friend."

"I said, 'Understood.'" He stows the transceiver and adds: "Wanker." And then to me he says, "Well, Gabi, it's poachers. Dangerous people. HQ says I'm supposed to send you home."

"Just try," I reply.

"Atta girl."

We hustle through the wilderness, following a grim trail of blood, snapped branches, hoofprints and bootprints. Gavin jogs ahead, while I do my best to keep up. He's a totally different person out here, absolutely in tune with the forest. He's half hound, loping with canine abandon through this forest, then stopping suddenly to cock his head to listen, sniff the air.

It's also clear he's used to running with a high-powered rifle in hand. He told me, as he strapped on its back-holster before we left his truck, that he was bringing it "just in case." So here we are.

He stops suddenly and crouches. I do too. From one of his cargo-pants pockets he pulls a Fey Spy, a top-of-its-class RC flying drone that looks like a green-gold robot hummingbird.

He tosses it into the air and it hovers, awaiting orders; using a controller/display-screen the size of a credit card, he sends the little drone bulleting into the forest.

I peer over Gavin's shoulder at the display and am treated to a fast-forward version of the terrain that awaits us. Gavin's a great pilot. The drone zooms and caroms through the woods with all the finesse of a real hummingbird.

And then we see them: the poachers, two of them. They wear balaclavas and camouflage jumpsuits, the kind sporting-goods stores love to sell to amateurs.

Between them walks a girl. A girl on a dog leash.

I'd judge her to be eight or nine. She's dressed for summer, tank-top and shorts and flip-flops; she's muddy to her ankles. Her head hangs, and her hair, the colors of late autumn, curtains her face. The collar around her neck is lined with fleece. (To prevent chafing, I presume? How considerate.) The leash seems mostly a formality, however, as it has so much slack that its middle almost dips to the ground.

"What the hell?" I whisper. "What's with the girl?"

Gavin, slowly and evenly, says, "Some hornstalkers believe that unicorns are attracted to virgin girls. So they kidnap one to help them in their hunt."

"What? You can't be serious."

Gavin shrugs. "One too many fairy tales when they were kids."

I can only imagine what is going through that poor girl's head. Kidnapping alone is already more evil than anyone deserves. But as a girl I loved horses, ponies, and especially unicorns. If unicorns had existed in our timeline when I was young, they would have dominated my every daydream. I can't imagine how scarred I would have been if I'd been forced by poachers to serve as bait. To watch them murder one right in front of me. Dig the horn out of its skull.

Gavin gives my wrist a fortifying squeeze. Then he hands me the RC controller, takes out his walkie-talkie and, as quietly as he can, reports what he's seen to HQ. I use the Fey Spy to keep an eye on the poachers. The group is moving forward cautiously. The girl's stooped, defeated gait fills me with dread.

Gavin has a conversation with the dispatcher that I can't quite make out. When he's done, he pockets the transceiver and looks at me. Then he holds out his rifle to me with both hands.

"This," he says, "is a Justice CAM-61X 'Apollo' sniper rifle. It has an effective range of 1,700 meters. It's loaded with .50 caliber Zeus rounds. They're less-lethal bullets. Bad guys get hit by these, they lose all muscular control, shit their pants, and take a nap. Then we just mosey up and cuff 'em."

I squint. "1,700 meters in a desert, maybe. You'd have to be halfway up their asses to get a clear shot, with all these trees."

He pats the rifle. "Not with these bullets, love. They're more like mini-missiles, with onboard targeting computers and everything. They can dodge around obstacles to reach their target. Especially," he emphasizes, "if we can create a virtual map of the forest between us and the target."

Lightbulb. "Which we can make with the Fey Spy."

He nods. "Listen, Gabi. That girl's in great peril. We're on the clock here. We can't wait for backup."

As a journalist, my ethics require me to remain disinterested when covering a story. Fuck you, journalistic ethics. "What you need me to do?"

He points at RC display/controller in my hand. "You any good flying one of these?"

"I'm a reporter. I make my living spying on people with drones."

Gavin smiles. Then: "I need you to fly the Fey Spy back to us, slowly and from high up in the canopy, so that it can map the forest between us and the poachers. Then fly it back over to them and keep them in the Fey Spy's field of vision. It'll automatically transmit the map of the forest to my rifle. Once it's done, it's as simple as bang bang bang. Everyone goes down."

I nod in agreement at first, before I realize this: "Wait. Bang bang *bang*? Three bangs? There are only two poachers."

His face goes green and guilty. "Well, we can't have the girl running scared through the forest. She could hurt herself."

I wait a second for the punchline, because he can't be serious. But of course he is. "Oh my God. Are you insane? You are not shooting the girl!"

"She'll just take a little nap."

"And shit her pants. You said she would shit her pants."

"She's not even wearing pants."

"Gavin!"

Gavin puts his finger to his lips.

"Sorry," I whisper.

"Look, if you've got a better idea, I'm all ears."

"I do," I say. "You shoot the poachers. I'll handle the girl."

Gavin's dubious. "That girl's undergone a severely traumatic sequence of experiences. I'm not sure a team of highly-trained psychologists could handle her right now."

"She'll be even more traumatized if you shoot her. Look, I admit it's not a great option. We just don't have any better ones. As soon as you have a lock on the hornstalkers, you take them out. I'll fly the Fey Spy to the girl and keep her entertained until backup arrives."

He's shaking his head. "What if she runs?"

"I'll go get her myself. She won't get far. She's in flip-flops."

He's about to argue, but decides against it. "Out of time," he sighs. "We do it your way. Don't fuck up."

"Don't miss."

Gavin aims the rifle ahead, looks into the scope with one eye, winks the other. I look back to the Fey Spy display-screen, catch up with my targets. They've barely moved at all. As if they're not sure what to do next. "I don't think these guys are pros," I say to Gavin.

"Unicorn horn is worth a mint," he says, his aim never wavering. "Every imbecile with a gun wants a piece of the action. Start flying the Fey Spy back to us."

I do, slaloming left and right through the forest in large swaths as I fly. It's a little over ten minutes before we make visual contact with our hummingbird robot.

"Good job," says Gavin, checking his rifle's readout. "We've almost got what we need. Fly the Fey Spy back over to them."

By the time I catch up with the poachers again, they are crouching behind a pair of trees, trying to peer into a hole the wounded unicorn must have punched through the forest as it fled. The girl stands next to the poacher with the metal leash around his wrist. She's as still as a Degas ballerina.

Within the space of a second Gavin fires two shots, and the two poachers simultaneously suffer seizures. They slap at their necks and fall to the ground, their guns tumbling away from them.

I hover in place; I want to see how the girl reacts.

She doesn't. She just stands above her handler. He is weakly reaching up to her. The leash is looped around his wrist, her neck. Her yellow-orange hair shields her face from me.

The poacher's hand finally drops. He's out. It suddenly occurs to me the girl must think he's dead. Jesus Christ: how much worse can we make things for her?

Gavin's already charging ahead to the forest to go truss up the poachers with zip-ties. He'll be there in a minute. All I need to do is keep her entertained until he gets there and make sure she doesn't—

—No! She slips the leash off the poacher's wrist and takes off running.

Here's an important safety tip for the kids at home. Do not go tearing as fast as you can through a moderately dense forest while also trying to fly a Fey Spy. You can't run and watch a screen and steer a robot at the same time. After my fourth stumble, I decide to go with the Fey Spy. It can move through the forest much faster than I can, and it will provide me her location via the map of the forest it's been creating this whole time.

It's the right choice. In less than three minutes, I find her. The Fey Spy flies into a small clearing where I witness a scene plagiarized from a medieval tapestry. The girl—the leash still around her neck—is kneeling in front of a horse. Huge and beautiful, chestnut-colored, male. He has folded his legs under him. He can barely keep his dipping head aloft. On his flank a bullet wound yawns; a slow lava-flow of blood gurgles out of the hole. Below it spreads a scabrous beard.

And, spiraling out from the horse's head, is a horn almost a meter long.

We have the Large Hadron Collider to thank for unicorns. Once the scientists at the LHC discovered they could make these adorable microscopic black holes, they couldn't resist doing it all the time. "They only last for microseconds," they said. "What harm could they do?" they asked.

How about destabilizing the membrane that keeps other universes from leaking into ours?

Think of our universe as some kid's crayon drawing on a piece of paper. Take that drawing, and place it on top of some other kid's. If nothing else happens, the drawing on top will hide the drawing beneath it. But now, take a spray bottle and spritz the drawing on top. Don't ruin it or cause the colors to run; just moisten it a little. As the paper gets wet, you'll be able to see hints of the picture that's underneath.

The numberless black holes created at the LHC "moistened" the paper on which our universe is drawn, allowing other universes to come peeking through.

Handwringers have announced the inevitable collapse of our universe but, so far at least, nothing so dramatic has happened. And in fact, a great deal of good has come of the LHC's experiments. Scientists have gained invaluable insights into how parallel universes work.

For instance, we now know that, in at least one alternate timeline, unicorns exist. And a few specimens have found their way into our neck of the multiverse.

Even before I entered the clearing, I could hear the girl calling out "Help! Is anybody there? Help us!" Not "Help me." "Help us."

So I enter the clearing slowly. The girl sits with the unicorn's head on her lap, petting its neck. Her face is a tragedy mask.

She asks me, with wounded voice, "Are you a hunter?"

I sit next to her. "My name's Gabrielle Reál. I'm a reporter."

"You're American?"

I nod. "I'm here to help you."

She feels safe enough to start crying in earnest. "Can you call my parents?"

"Help is on the way, sweetheart."

She cries and nods. "Can you help him?"

She means the unicorn. How to reply? I will not compound her future suffering with a lie—truth or death, remember?—but I don't want to heighten her present suffering by lecturing her about the stark realities of life and death. I finally settle on, "I can't. But I have a friend coming. He's a forest ranger. If anyone can help the unicorn, he can."

She nods, sniffles, redoubles her petting. The unicorn sighs, settles farther into her lap. I have to dodge his horn. It's even more amazing up close than any picture I've seen. It's a spiral of silver-gray, pitted and striated, covered with the nicks and flaws that come from a lifetime's use. It doesn't feel as cold as I expect; it's like reaching into a body and touching vital bone.

I should get us away from him, I know. This is a wounded wild animal; he can turn on us at any moment. But the truth is I don't want to move. I don't want this magnificent creature to die without knowing some comfort in his passing. It's a girlish, sentimental thought, I know. That doesn't make it any less authentic.

I scratch the unicorn's head. He moves slightly toward my hand, grateful. The girl rests her head on my arm, and together we pet him and weep.

Thousands of animals—elephants especially, but also walruses, rhinoceroses, and narwhals—are massacred every year for their horns and tusks. The demand for ivory continues with little abatement in China, Japan, Thailand, Indonesia, the Philippines, and other countries of that region. In spite of the bans and the international efforts to curb the ivory trade, poachers have no trouble finding deep-pocket buyers and government officials on the take.

In fact, the only thing that has seemed to be effective at slowing down the butchering of these animals has been the introduction of an even more desirable source of ivory into our universe. Unicorns.

Unicorn horn is said to possess all sorts of salubrious woo. It can detect and cure disease, anything from nosebleeds to lupus. It's a universal poison antidote. It can impart superhuman strength, speed, and/or intelligence; regenerate lost limbs; restore sight to the blind; recover sexual potency; reverse aging; raise the dead. Slice it, dice it, powder it, or keep it whole and use it as your magic wand—unicorn horn is good for what ails you.

Of course it has no such properties. But what science has learned already about unicorns is almost as wondrous. *Equus ferus hippoceros* seems to fit so well into our timeline's system of classification, there is reason to believe that it might actually have existed in our own universe at some point in our past, and that we may someday find indigenous unicorn fossils. Based on the specimens we have found so far, male unicorns seem to be up to 15% larger than the modern horse, females up to 10%. Their large skulls somewhat resemble those of large, extinct species from our Eocene era: save, of course, for the horns that spring from their heads.

A unicorn horn, much like a narwhal's, is actually a pair of repurposed canines that grow helically from the animal's palate and intertwine as they emerge from the forehead. Scientists believe that when the unicorn's ancestors switched from being omnivores to herbivores, evolution found other uses for their meat-tearing teeth. Defense against predators and mating displays are obvious assumptions, though neither has been observed as yet. They have been observed, however, using their horns as "fruit procurement appliances" (Gavin's words). And since the horn is actually two twisted teeth, it is sensitive to touch. Scientists are just beginning to hypothesize the various ways in which unicorns use their horns as sensory organs.

In short, the unicorn is an endlessly fascinating animal, one that not only has enriched our knowledge of our own natural world, but the natural world of at least one other timeline. It's scientifically priceless.

As I sit petting this dying unicorn, I wonder *Why isn't that enough? Why do we have to invent magical bullshit? They just got here, and we're hunting them to extinction based on lies.*

But then I grimly smile. Unicorns are not of our timeline. The few stragglers who have appeared here came by an LHC-induced accident. No matter what we do here, we can't erase them from existence in all universes. Even our folly, thank the gods, has limits.

Gavin cautiously enters the clearing. The rifle is holstered. He's walking in smiling, open-armed, crouching, cautious. He reminds me of Caliban.

"There they are," he says merrily. "Glad I finally found you. Now we can get you home safe and sound. So let's get a move on, right?"

Neither I nor the girl move. The girl's eyes are locked on Gavin, assessing. "Is that your friend?" she asks me.

"The forest ranger," I reply. "The bad men who kidnapped you are going to prison for a long time thanks to him."

She doesn't take her eyes off of him. "You said he could save the unicorn." Gavin shoots me a look.

"I didn't say he could definitely save him," I say. "I said if anyone could, he could. He's going to try."

"He can't just try. It has to work."

"There, now," says Gavin, coming over to us. He's picked up what's transpired between the girl and I and begins playing his part perfectly: he kneels down next to the unicorn and pats the beast's neck, looking at it nose to tail, examining it studiously. But you don't have to be a unicorn expert to know the beast's almost dead.

"Right," he says. "I'm going to have to perform a complicated bit of field surgery on this poor fellow. Gabi, my crew's half a klick south of here. You should head toward them with the little lady here."

"Come with me, sweetie," I say to the girl, standing and holding out my hand. "Let's get you back to your parents."

She doesn't look at me. "I want to stay," she says flatly.

"We have to let Mr. Howard do his work," I say. "He's the only chance the unicorn has. You want to help the unicorn, right?"

"Yes."

"The best way for us to help is to get out of the way."

She considers this, pets the horned horse more vigorously to help her think. Then—so, so carefully—she sets the unicorn's head on the ground, scoots her legs out from under. The unicorn is well beyond noticing such subtle gestures. Its black unmoving oculus reflects the clouds.

The girl rises and takes my hand. "Please do what you can," she says to Gavin.

Gavin opens a leather satchel of sharp instruments on the ground. They look a little crude for the fine cuts operations usually require. They look like tools for an autopsy: for sawing, hacking, flensing off. But maybe those are the tools unicorn field surgery necessitates. How would I know?

"Don't you worry," Gavin says to the girl. "I'll have Mr. Unicorn patched up in no time."

The support team is everything I could want from British rescuers. I'm offered tea and blankets and biscuits and a satellite phone. I call my editor and confess how I blew the story.

"Fuck journalistic ethics!" she says. Love that woman.

The support team does even better with the little girl. They've got her sitting on the tailgate of a pickup, drinking tea from a thermos, wrapped in a blanket she doesn't need. They washed her feet. A comfortingly overzealous Mary Poppins kneels behind her in the bed of the truck and brushes out her hair. The woman chats nonstop the entire time, a stream of solicitous chatter that, like all good white-noise machines, is threatening to put the blanketed girl to sleep.

But the girl wakes up immediately when Gavin rejoins us.

I have exactly one second to gather the truth from his body language. Then Gavin sees the girl scrutinizing him and muscles up a smile. He marches over to her with his elbows out, like he's about to start a musical number. "How are we doing? My people taking good care of you?"

"Yes."

"Did you talk to your mum and dad? I bet they were glad to hear your voice."

"Yes."

"Well, you'll be back with your family in a few hours."

"Did you save him?"

He had to know that question was coming, but in the moment he still finds himself unprepared to answer. "Well," he says slowly, looking down, "it wasn't easy." But then, looking at her conspiratorially: "But yes. I saved him."

"Really?" Her voice is chary.

Gavin clears his throat. "We had to pull a bit of a trick to pull it off. You see, unicorns really are magic in their own universe. But when they come here, suddenly they're as normal as any other horse."

"They're magical?"

"Sure they are, in their own time and place. Unicorns don't die or get sick or grow old in their own universe. Once I got him back to his rightful place, he healed up like that." Gavin snaps.

The girl blooms. "You can do that?"

"Sure I can. Can't I, team?"

"Yes. Oh, certainly. Do it all the time," says the team.

The girl is looking from face to face. She seems better. Finally she looks at me. "Is it true, Ms. Reál?"

"If Mr. Howard says so," I say before I can think about what I'm saying.

"Promise?"

Gavin's lying out his ass. It's not like there's some handy stargate we can push unicorns through to send them back to their universe. They're the first verifiable case we have of a living creature passing between timelines, but that may only be because, since they don't exist in this one, they were easy to identify. Millions of animals may be traveling back and forth between universes, or maybe just unicorns. Who knows? Certainly not us, not yet. We have zero idea how to send them back to their rightful reality.

So why am I not telling the girl all this?

Because doing so will gut her afresh. Because there's such a thing as mercy. Because she can learn what really happened later, when she's stronger: maybe even from me, if she happens to read this article. If you're reading this, P———, I'm so sorry. As a reporter, I'm supposed to be a steward of the truth. But as unheroic as it sounds, it's better to lie and stay alive. Way, way better.

I take P———'s hands and look her in the eye when I say, "Sweetie, I promise you, that unicorn is as alive as you and me."

THE BREW

Karen Joy Fowler

I SPENT LAST CHRISTMAS in The Hague. I hadn't wanted to be in a foreign country and away from the family at Christmastime, but it had happened. Once I was there I found it lonely, but also pleasantly insulated. The streets were strung with lights and it rained often, so the lights reflected off the shiny cobblestones, came at you out of the clouds like pale, golden bubbles. If you could ignore the damp, you felt wrapped in cotton, wrapped against breaking. I heightened the feeling by stopping in an ice cream shop for a cup of tea with rum.

Of course it was an illusion. Ever since I was young, whenever I have traveled, my mother has contrived to have a letter sent, usually waiting for me, sometimes a day or two behind my arrival. I am her only daughter and she was not the sort to let an illness stop her, and so the letter was at the hotel when I returned from my tea. It was a very cheerful letter, very loving, and the message that it was probably the last letter I would get from her and that I needed to finish things up and hurry home was nowhere on the page, but only in my heart. She sent some funny family stories and some small-town gossip and the death she talked about was not her own, but belonged instead to an old man who was once a neighbor of ours.

After I read the letter I wanted to go out again, to see if I could recover the mood of the mists and the golden lights. I tried. I walked for hours, wandering in and out of the clouds, out to the canals and into the stores. Although my own children are too old for toys and too young for grand-children, I did a lot of window-shopping at the toy stores. I was puzzling over the black elf they have in Holland, St. Nicholas' sidekick, wondering who he was and where he came into it all, when I saw a music box. It was a glass globe on a wooden base, and if you wound it, it played music and if you shook it, it snowed. Inside the globe there was a tiny forest of ceramic trees and, in the center, a unicorn with a silver horn, corkscrewed, like a narwhal's, and one gaily bent foreleg. A unicorn, tinted blue and frolicking in the snow.

What appealed to me most about the music box was not the snow or the unicorn, but the size. It was a little world, all enclosed, and I could imagine it as a real place, a place I could go. A little winter. There was an aquarium in the lobby of my hotel and I had a similar reaction to it. A little piece of ocean there, in the dry land of the lobby. Sometimes we can find a smaller world where we can live, inside the bigger world where we cannot.

Otherwise the store was filled with items tied-in to *The Lion King*. Less enchanting items to my mind—why is it that children always side with the aristocracy? Little royalists, each and every one of us, until we grow up and find ourselves in the cubicle or the scullery. And even then there's a sense of injustice about it all. Someone belongs there, but surely not us.

I'm going to tell you a secret, something I have never told anyone before. I took an oath when I was seventeen years old and have never broken it, although I cannot, in general, be trusted with secrets, and usually try to warn people of this before they confide in me. But the oath was about the man who died, my old neighbor, and so I am no longer bound to it. The secret takes the form of a story.

I should warn you that parts of the story will be hard to believe. Parts of it are not much to my credit, but I don't suppose you'll have trouble believing those. It's a big story, and this is just a small piece of it, my piece, which ends with my mother's letter and The Hague and the unicorn music box.

It begins in Bloomington, Indiana, the year I turned ten. It snowed early and often that year. My best friend Bobby and I built caves of snow, choirs of snowmen, and bridges that collapsed if you ever tried to actually walk on them.

We had a neighbor who lived next door to me and across the street from Bobby. His name was John McBean. Until that year McBean had been a figure of almost no interest to us. He didn't care for children much, and why should he? Behind his back we called him Rudolph, because he had a large, purplish nose, and cold weather whitened the rest of his face into paste so his nose stood out in startling contrast. He had no wife, no family that we were aware of. People used to pity that back then. He seemed to us quite an old man, grandfather age, but we were children, what did we know? Even now I have no idea what he did for a living. He was retired when I knew him, but I have no idea of what he was retired from. Work, such as our fathers did, was nothing very interesting, nothing to speculate on. We thought the name McBean rather funny, and then he was quite the skinflint, which struck us all, even our parents, as delightful, since he actually was Scottish. It gave rise to many jokes, limp, in retrospect, but pretty rich back then.

One afternoon that year Mr. McBean slipped in his icy yard. He went down with a roar. My father ran out to him, but as my father was helping him up, McBean tried to hit him on the chin. My father came home much amused. "He said I was a British spy," my father told my mother.

"You devil," she said. She kissed him.

He kissed her back. "It had something to do with Bonnie Prince Charlie. He wants to see a Stuart on the throne of England. He seemed to think I was preventing it."

As luck would have it this was also the year that Disney ran a television episode on the Great Pretender. I have a vague picture in my mind of a British actor—the same one who appeared with Haley Mills in *The Moon Spinners*. Whatever happened to him, whoever he was?

So Bobby and I gave up the ever-popular game of World War II and began instead, for a brief period, to play at being Jacobites. The struggle for the throne of England involved less direct confrontation, fewer sound effects, and less running about. It was a game of stealth, of hiding and escaping, altogether a more adult activity.

It was me who got the idea of breaking into the McBean cellar as a covert operation on behalf of the prince. I was interested in the cellar, having begun to note how often and at what odd hours McBean went down there.

The cellar window could be seen from my bedroom. Once I rose late at night and in the short time I watched, the light went on and off three times. It seemed a signal. I told Bobby that Mr. McBean might be holding the prince captive down there and that we should go and see. This plan added a real sense of danger to our imaginary game, without, we thought, actually putting us into peril.

The cellar door was set at an incline and such were the times that it shocked us to try it and find it locked. Bobby thought he could fit through the little window, whose latch could be lifted with a pencil. If he couldn't, I certainly could, though I was desperately hoping it wouldn't come to that—already at age ten I was more of an idea person. Bobby had the spirit. So I offered to go around the front and distract Mr. McBean long enough for Bobby to try the window. I believe that I said he shouldn't actually enter, that we would save that for a time when McBean was away. That's the way I remember it, my saying that.

And I remember that it had just snowed again, a fresh, white powder and a north wind, so the snow blew off the trees as if it was still coming down. It was bright, one of those paradoxical days of sun and ice, and so much light everything was drowned in it so you stumbled about as if there were no light at all. My scarf was iced with breath and my footprints were as large as a man's. I knocked at the front door, but my mittens muffled the sound. It took several tries and much pounding before Mr. McBean answered, too long to be accounted for simply by the mittens. When he did answer, he did it without opening the door.

"Go on with you," he said. "This is not a good time."

"Would you like your walk shoveled?" I asked him.

"A slip of a girl like you? You couldn't even lift the shovel." I imagine there is a tone, an expression, that would make this response affectionate, but Mr. McBean affected neither. He opened the door enough to tower over me with his blue nose, his gluey face, and the clenched set of his mouth.

"Bobby would help me. Thirty cents."

"Thirty cents! And that's the idlest boy God ever created. Thirty cents!!?"

"Since it's to be split. Fifteen cents each."

The door was closing again.

"Twenty cents."

"I've been shoveling my own walk long enough. No reason to stop."

The door clicked shut. The whole exchange had taken less than a minute. I stood undecidedly at the door for another minute, then stepped off the porch, into the yard. I walked around the back. I got there just in time to see the cellar light go on. The window was open. Bobby was gone.

I stood outside, but there was a wind, as I've said, and I couldn't hear and it was so bright outside and so dim within, I could hardly see. I knew that Bobby was inside, because there were no footprints leading away but my own. I had looked through the window on other occasions so I knew the light was a single bulb, hanging by its neck like a turnip, and that there were many objects between me and it, old and broken furniture, rusted tools, lawn mowers and rakes, boxes piled into stairs. I waited. I think I waited a very long time. The light went out. I waited some more. I moved to a tree, using it as a windbreak until finally it was clear there was no point in waiting any longer. Then I ran home, my face stinging with cold and tears, into our living room, where my mother pulled off my stiff scarf and rubbed my hands until the pins came into them. She made me cocoa with marshmallows. I would like you to believe that the next few hours were a very bad time for me, that I suffered a good deal more than Bobby did.

That case being so hard to make persuasively, I will tell you instead what was happening to him.

Bobby did, indeed, manage to wiggle in through the window, although it was hard enough to give him some pause as to how he would get out again. He landed on a stack of wooden crates, conveniently offset so that he could descend them like steps. Everywhere was cobwebs and dust; it was too dark to see this, but he could feel it and smell it. He was groping his way forward, hand over hand, when he heard the door at the top of the stairs. At the very moment the light went on, he found himself looking down the empty eyeslit of a suit of armor. It made him gasp; he couldn't help it. So he heard the footsteps on the stairs stop suddenly and then begin again, wary now. He hid himself behind a barrel. He thought maybe he'd escape notice—there was so much stuff in the cellar and the light so dim—and that was the worst time, those moments when he thought he might make it, much worse than what came next, when he found himself staring into the cracked and reddened eyes of Mr. McBean.

"What the devil are you doing?" McBean asked. He had a smoky, startled voice. "You've no business down here."

"I was just playing a game," Bobby told him, but didn't seem to hear.

"Who sent you? What did they tell you?"

He seemed to be frightened—of Bobby!—and angry, but that was to be expected, but there was something else that began to dawn on Bobby only slowly. His accent had thickened with every word. Mr. McBean was deadly drunk. He reached into Bobby's hiding place and hauled him out of it and his breath, as Bobby came closer, was as ripe as spoiled apples.

"We were playing at putting a Stuart on the throne," Bobby told him, imagining he could sympathize with this, but it seemed to be the wrong thing to say.

He pulled Bobby by the arm to the stairs. "Up we go."

"I have to be home by dinner." By now Bobby was very frightened.

"We'll see. I have to think what's to be done with you," said McBean.

They reached the door, then moved on into the living room where they sat for a long time in silence while McBean's eyes turned redder and redder and his fingers pinched into Bobby's arm. With his free hand, he drank. Perhaps this is what kept him warm, for the house was very cold and Bobby was glad he still had his coat on. Bobby was both trembling and shivering.

"Who told you about Prince Charlie?" McBean asked finally. "What did they say to you?" So Bobby told him what he knew, the Disney version, long as he could make it, waiting, of course, for me to do something, to send someone. McBean made the story longer by interrupting with suspicious and skeptical questions. Eventually the questions ceased and his grip loosened. Bobby hoped he might be falling asleep. His eyes were lowered. But when Bobby stopped talking, McBean shook himself awake and his hand was a clamp on Bobby's forearm again. "What a load of treacle," he said, his voice filled with contemptuous spit. "It was nothing like that."

He stared at Bobby for a moment and then past him. "I've never told this story before," he said and the pupils of his eyes were as empty and dark as the slit in the armor. "No doubt I shall regret telling it now."

In the days of the bonnie prince, the head of the McBane clan was the charismatic Ian McBane. Ian was a man with many talents, all of which he had honed and refined over the fifty-odd years he had lived so far. He was a botanist, an orientalist, a poet, and a master brewer. He was also a very godly man, a paragon, perhaps. At least in this story. To be godly is a hard thing and may create a hard man. A godly man is not necessarily a kindly man, although he can be, of course.

Now in those days, the woods and caves of Scotland were filled with witches; the church waged a constant battle to keep the witches dark and deep. Some of them were old and haggish, but others were mortally beautiful. The two words go together, mind you, mortal and beautiful. Nothing is so beautiful as that which is about to fade.

These witches were well aware of Ian McBane. They envied him his skills in the brewery, coveted his knowledge of chemistry. They, themselves, were always boiling and stirring, but they could only do what they knew how to do. Besides, his godliness irked them. Many times they sent the most beautiful among them, tricked out further with charms and incantations, to visit Ian McBane in his bedchamber and offer what they could offer in return for expert advice. They were so touching in their eagerness for knowledge, so unaware of their own desirability. They had the perfection of dreams. But Ian, who was, after all, fifty and not twenty, withstood them.

All of Scotland was hoping to see Charles Edward Stuart on the throne, and from hopes they progressed to rumors and from rumors to sightings. Then came the great victory at Falkirk. Naturally Ian wished to do his part and naturally, being a man of influence and standing, his part must be a large one. It was the sin of ambition which gave the witches an opening.

This time the woman they sent was not young and beautiful, but old and sweet. She was everyone's mother. She wore a scarf on her hair and her stockings rolled at her ankles. Blue rivers ran just beneath the skin of her legs. Out of her sleeve she drew a leather pouch.

"From the end of the world," she said. "Brought to me by a black warrior riding a white elephant, carried over mountains and across oceans." She made it a lullaby. Ian was drowsy when she finished. So she took his hand and emptied the pouch into his palm, closing it for him. When he opened his hand, he held the curled shards and splinters of a unicorn's horn.

Ian had never seen a unicorn's horn before, although he knew that the king of Denmark had an entire throne made of them. A unicorn's horn is a thing of power. It purifies water, nullifies poison. The witch reached out to Ian, slit his thumb with her one long nail, so his thumb ran blood. Then she touched the wound with a piece of horn. His thumb healed before his eyes, healed as if it had never been cut, the blood running back inside, the cut sealing over like water.

In return Ian gave the witch what she asked. He had given her his godliness, too, but he didn't know this at the time. When the witch was gone, Ian took the horn and ground it into dust. He subjected it to one more test of authenticity. He mixed a few grains into a hemlock concoction and fed it to his cat, stroking it down her throat. The cat followed the hemlock with a saucer of milk, which she wiped, purring, from her whiskers.

Ian had already put down a very fine single malt whiskey, many bottles, enough for the entire McBane clan to toast the coronation of Charles Stuart. It was golden in color and ninety proof, enough to make a large man feel larger without incapacitating him. Ian added a few pinches of the horn to every bottle. The whiskey color shattered and then vanished, so the standing bottle was filled with liquid the color of rainwater, but if you shook it, it pearled like the sea. Ian bottled his brew with a unicorn label, the unicorn enraged, two hooves slicing the air.

Have you ever heard of the American ghost dancers? The Boxers of China? Same sort of thing here. Ian distributed his whiskey to the McBanes before they marched off to Culloden. Taken just before the battle, Ian assured them that the drink would make them invulnerable. Sword wounds would seal up overnight, bullets would pass through flesh as if it were air.

I don't suppose your Disney says very much about Culloden. A massacre is a hard thing to set to music. Certainly they tell no stories and sing no songs about the McBanes that day. Davie McBane was the first to go, reeling about drunkenly and falling beneath one of the McBanes' own horses. Little Angus went next, shouting and racing down the top of a small hill, but before he could strike a single blow for Scotland, a dozen arrows jutted from him at all points. His name was a joke and he made a big, fat target. His youngest brother Robbie, a boy of only fifteen years, followed Angus in like a running back, and so delirious with whiskey that he wore no helmet and carried no weapon. His stomach was split open like a purse. An hour later, only two of the McBanes still lived. The rest had died grotesquely, humorously, without accounting for a single enemy death.

When news reached home, the McBane wives and daughters armed themselves with kitchen knives and went in search of Ian. They thought he had lied about the unicorn horn; they thought he had knowingly substituted the inferior tooth of a fish instead. Ian was already gone, and with enough time and forethought to have removed every bottle of the unicorn brew and taken it with him. This confirmed the women's suspicions, but the real explanation was different. Ian had every expectation the whiskey would work. When the McBanes returned, he didn't wish to share any more of it.

The women set fire to his home and his brewery. Ian saw it from a distance, from a boat at sea, exploding into the sky like a star. The women dumped every bottle of whiskey they found until the rivers bubbled and the fish swam upside down. But none of the whiskey bore the unicorn label. Ian was never seen or heard from again.

"Whiskey is subtle stuff. It's good for heartache; it works a treat against shame. But, even laced with unicorn horn, it cannot mend a man who has been split in two by a sword stroke. It cannot mend a man who no longer has a head. It cannot mend a man with a dozen arrows growing from his body like extra arms. It cannot give a man back his soul."

The story seemed to be over, although Prince Charles had never appeared in it. Bobby had no feeling left in his hand. "I see," he said politely.

McBean shook him once, then released him. He fetched a pipe. When he lit a match, he held it to his mouth and his breath flamed like a dragon's. "What will I do to you if you tell anyone?" he asked Bobby. This was a rhetorical question. He continued without pausing. "Something bad. Something so bad you'd have to be an adult even to imagine it."

So Bobby told me none of this. I didn't see him again that day. He did not come by, and when I finally went over his mother told me he was home, but that he was not feeling well, had gone to bed. "Don't worry," she said, in response, I suppose, to the look on my face. "Just a chill. Nothing to worry about."

He missed school the next day and the next after that. When I finally saw him, he was casual. Offhand. As if it had all happened so long ago, he had forgotten. "He caught me," Bobby said. "He was very angry. That's all. We better not do it again."

It was the end of our efforts to put a Stuart on the throne. There are days, I admit, when I'm seeing the dentist and I pick up *People* in the waiting room and there they are, the current sad little lot of Windsors, and I have a twinge of guilt. I just didn't care enough to see it through. I enjoyed Charles and Diana's wedding as much as the next person. How was I to know?

Bobby and I were less and less friends after that. It didn't happen all at once, but bit by bit, over the summer mostly. Sex came between us. Bobby went off and joined Little League. He turned out to be really good at it, and he met a lot of boys who didn't live so near to us, but had houses he could bike to. He dumped me, which hurt in an impersonal, inevitable way. I believed I had brought it on myself, leaving him that day, going home to a warm house and never saying a word to anyone. At that age, at that time, I did not believe this was something a boy would have done.

So Bobby and I continued to attend the same school and see each other about in our yards, and play sometimes when the game was big and involved other people as well. I grew up enough to understand what our parents thought of McBean, that he was often drunk. This was what had made his nose purple and made him rave about the Stuarts and made him slip in his snowy yard, his arms flapping like wings as he fell. "It's a miracle," my mother said, "that he never breaks a bone." But nothing much more happened between Bobby and me until the year we turned sixteen, me in February, him in May.

He was tired a lot that year and developed such alarming bruises under his eyes that his parents took him to a doctor who sent them right away to a different doctor. At dinner a few weeks later, my mother said she had something to tell me. Her eyes were shiny and her voice was coarse. "Bobby has leukemia," she said.

"He'll get better," I said quickly. Partly I was asking, but mostly I was warning her not to tell me differently. I leaned into her and she must have thought it was for comfort, but it wasn't. I did it so I wouldn't be able to see her face. She put her arm around me and I felt her tears falling on the top of my hair.

Bobby had to go to Indianapolis for treatments. Spring came and summer and he missed the baseball season. Fall, and he had to drop out of school. I didn't see him much, but his mother was over for coffee sometimes, and she had grown sickly herself, sad and thin and gray. "We have to hope," I heard her telling my mother. "The doctor says he is doing as well as we could expect. We're very encouraged." Her voice wobbled defiantly.

Bobby's friends came often to visit; I saw them trooping up the porch, all vibrant and healthy, stamping the slush off their boots and trailing their scarves. They went in noisy, left quiet. Sometimes I went with them. Everyone loved Bobby, though he lost his hair and swelled like a beached seal and it was hard to remember that you were looking at a gifted athlete, or even a boy.

Spring came again, but after a few weeks of it, winter returned suddenly with a strange storm. In the morning when I left for school, I saw a new bud completely encased in ice, and three dead birds whose feet had frozen to the telephone wires. This was the day Arnold Becker gave me the message that Bobby wanted to see me. "Right away," Arnie said. "This afternoon. And just you. None of your girlfriends with you."

In the old days Bobby and I used to climb in and out each other's windows, but this was for good times and intimacy; I didn't even consider it. I went to the front door and let his mother show me to his room as if I didn't even know the way. Bobby lay in his bed, with his puffy face and a new tube sticking into his nose and down his throat. There was a strong, strange odor in the room. I was afraid it was Bobby and wished not to get close enough to see.

He had sores in his mouth, his mother had explained to me. It was difficult for him to eat or even to talk. "You do the talking," she suggested. But I couldn't think of anything to say.

And anyway, Bobby came right to the point. "Do you remember," he asked me, "that day in the McBean cellar?" Talking was an obvious effort. It made him breathe hard, as if he'd been running.

Truthfully, I didn't remember. Apparently I had worked to forget it. I remember it now, but at the time, I didn't know what he was talking about.

"Bonnie Prince Charlie," he said, with an impatient rasp so I thought he was delirious. "I need you to go back. I need you to bring me a bottle of whiskey from McBean's cellar. There's a unicorn on the label."

"Why do you want whiskey?"

"Don't ask McBean. He'll never give it to you. Just take it. You would still fit through the window."

"Why do you want whiskey?"

"The unicorn label. Very important. Maybe," said Bobby, "I just want to taste one really good whiskey before I die. You do this and I'll owe you forever. You'll save my life."

He was exhausted. I went home. I did not plan to break into McBean's cellar. It was a mad request from a delusional boy. It saddened me, but I felt no obligation. I did think I could get him some whiskey. I had some money, I would spare no expense. But I was underage. I ate my dinner and tried to think who I could get to buy me liquor, who would do it, and who would even know a fine whiskey if they saw one. And while I was working out the problem I began, bit by bit, piece by piece, bite by bite, to remember. First I remembered the snow, remembered standing by the tree watching the cellar window with snow swirling around me. Then I remembered offering to shovel the walk. I remembered the footprints leading into the cellar window. It took all of dinner, most of the time when I was falling asleep, some concentrated sessions when I woke during the night. By morning, when the sky was light again, I remembered it complete.

It had been my idea and then I had let Bobby execute it and then I had abandoned him. I left him there that day and in another story, someone else's story, he was tortured or raped or even killed and eaten, although you'd have to be an adult to believe in these possibilities. The whole time he was in the McBean house I was lying on my bed and worrying about him, thinking, boy, he's really going to get it, but mostly worrying what I could tell my parents that would be plausible and would keep me out of it. The only way I could think of to make it right, was to do as he'd asked, and to break into the cellar again.

I also got caught, got caught right off. There was a trap. I tripped a wire rigged to a stack of boards; they fell with an enormous clatter and McBean was there, just as he'd been for Bobby, with those awful cavernous eyes, before I could make it back out the window.

"Who sent you?" he shouted at me. "What are you looking for?"

So I told him.

"That sneaking, thieving, lying boy," said McBean. "It's a lie, what he's said. How could it be true? And anyway, I couldn't spare it." I could see, behind him, the bottles with the unicorn label. There were half a dozen of them. All I asked was for one.

"He's a wonderful boy." I found myself crying.

"Get out," said McBean. "The way you came. The window."

"He's dying," I said. "And he's my best friend." I crawled back out while McBean stood and watched me, and walked back home with a face filled with tears. I was not giving up. There was another dinner I didn't eat and another night I didn't sleep. In the morning it was snowing, as if spring had never come. I planned to cut class, and break into the cellar again. This time I would be looking for traps. But as I passed McBean's house, carrying my books and pretending to be on my way to school, I heard his front door.

"Come here," McBean called angrily from his porch. He gave me a bottle, wrapped in red tissue. "There," he said. "Take it." He went back inside, but as I left he called again from behind the door. "Bring back what he doesn't drink. What's left is mine. It's mine, remember." And at that exact moment, the snow turned to rain.

For this trip I used the old window route. Bobby was almost past swallowing. I had to tip it from a spoon into his throat and the top of his mouth was covered with sores, so it burned him badly. One spoonful was all he could bear. But I came back the next day and repeated it and the next and by the fourth he could take it easily and after a week, he was eating again, and after two weeks I could see that he was going to live, just by looking in his mother's face. "He almost died of the cure," she told me. "The chemo. But we've done it. We've turned the corner." I left her thanking God and went into Bobby's room, where he was sitting up and looking like a boy again. I returned half the bottle to McBean.

"Did you spill any?" he asked angrily, taking it back. "Don't tell me it took so much."

And one night, that next summer, in Bryan's Park with the firecrackers going off above us, Bobby and I sat on a blanket and he told me McBean's story.

We finished school and graduated. I went to IU, but Bobby went to college in Boston and settled there. Sex came between us again. He came home once to tell his mother and father that he was gay and then took off like the whole town burned to the touch.

Bobby was the first person that I loved and lost, although there have, of course, been others since. Twenty-five years later I tracked him down and we had a dinner together. We were awkward with each other; the evening wasn't a great success. He tried to explain to me why he had left, as an apology for dumping me again. "It was just so hard to put the two lives together. At the time I felt that the first life was just a lie. I felt that everyone who loved me had been lied to. But now—being gay seems to be all I am sometimes. Now sometimes I want someplace where I can get away from it. Someplace where I'm just Bobby again. That turned out to be real, too." He was not meeting my eyes and then suddenly he was. "In the last five years I've lost twenty-eight of my friends."

"Are you all right?" I asked him.

"No. But if you mean, do I have AIDS, no, I don't. I should, I think, but I don't. I can't explain it."

There was a candle between us on the table. It flickered ghosts into his eyes. "You mean the whiskey," I said.

"Yeah. That's what I mean."

The whiskey had seemed easy to believe in when I was seventeen and Bobby had just had a miraculous recovery and the snow had turned to rain. I hadn't believed in it much since. I hadn't supposed Bobby had either, because if he did, then I really had saved his life back then and you don't leave a person who saves your life without a word. Those unicorn horns you read about in Europe and Scandinavia. They all turned out to be from narwhals. They were brought in by the Vikings through China. I've read a bit about it. Sometimes, someone just gets a miracle. Why not you? "You haven't seen Mr. McBean lately," I said. "He's getting old. Really old. Deadly old."

"I know," said Bobby, but the conclusion he drew was not the same as mine. "Believe me, I know. That whiskey is gone. I'd have been there to get it if it wasn't. I'd have been there twenty-eight times."

Bobby leaned forward and blew the candle out. "Remember when we wanted to live forever?" he asked me. "What made us think that was such a great idea?"

I never went inside the toy store in The Hague. I don't know what the music box played—"Edelweiss," perhaps, or "Lara's Theme," nothing to do with me. I didn't want to expose the strong sense I had that it had been put there for me, had traveled whatever travels, just to be there in that store window for me to see at that particular moment, with any evidence to the contrary. I didn't want to expose my own fragile magic to the light of day.

Certainly I didn't buy it. I didn't need to. It was already mine, only not here, not now. Not as something I bought for myself, on an afternoon by myself, in a foreign country with my mother dying a world away. But as something I found one Christmas morning, wrapped in red paper. I stood looking through the glass and wished that Bobby and I were still friends. That he knew me well enough to have bought me the music box as a gift.

And then I didn't wish that at all. Already I have too many friends, care too much about too many people, have exposed myself to loss on too many sides. I could never have imagined as a child how much it could hurt you to love people. It takes an adult to imagine such a thing. And that's the end of my story.

If I envy anything about McBean now, it is his solitude. But no, that's not really what I wish for either. When I was seventeen I thought McBean was a drunk because he had to have the whiskey so often. Now, when I believe in the whiskey at all, I think, like Bobby, that drinking was just the only way to live through living forever.

FALLING OFF THE UNICORN

David D. Levine and Sara A. Mueller

S AILING IN SLOW MOTION above the sand of the arena floor, Misty thought "This is going to hurt."

Just a moment ago she'd been in the saddle, nudging Vulcan through a shoulder-in, concentrating on moving the unicorn's right back hoof toward his left shoulder, getting him used to working in this building. It was new, still smelled of paint, and was making all the animals edgy.

And then some moron in the stands had lit up a goddamn cigarette.

Misty's spur caught on the saddle as Vulcan whirled out from under her, alabaster coat and flaxen mane blurring past her eyes. She couldn't get her hip under her and hit the ground on her left knee. It did hurt—it hurt like a sumbitch. She gasped from the pain, pulling in a breath full of shavings and manure dust as she rolled away from Vulcan's sharp cloven hooves. The last thing she needed was an enraged four-hundred-pound unicorn stepping on her head.

Somewhere in the stands, she could hear her groom Caroline shouting. There was shouting all around, and the metal voice from the announcer's booth called out "Loose unicorn, Harry, close the gate!" No one wanted a Persian stud running loose on the fairgrounds.

Misty kept one arm wrapped around her throbbing knee and the other over her head, but she could still see Vulcan rearing and pounding the rail with his iridescent hooves, making the hollow steel ring and tipping his head sideways to lunge through the rails with the double-edged spiral of his horn. His scream of rage echoed in the high hollow ceiling as he struggled to reach the offending smoker. Caroline pushed the stupid addict toward the exit, bellowing "Whoa, Vulcan! God-dammit, *whoa!*"

And the stupid beast whoa'd. He dropped right to his feet and gave a self-satisfied snort, pleased and proud that he'd defended his rider from the vicious cigarette. Misty rocked, holding her knee. Damn idiot animal. Caroline vaulted over the rail, dropped the six feet to the arena floor, and caught Vulcan's reins. Crisis controlled.

Misty tried to sit up as the announcer cleared the arena. Brighter pain stabbed in her knee; it felt full of white-hot glass shards. She pushed herself up on her arms, spitting and snorting out sand and the ground-up shreds of old sneaker soles. Caroline walked Vulcan over, the animal placidly lipping her dark buzz-cut as if to say "Did I do good, boss?"

Caroline crouched down and cradled Misty's knee in her hands, sliding her thumbs across the top of the kneecap. Only six weeks older than Misty, Caroline had always looked after her like a beloved little sister. She whispered under her breath, and a brief tingle of investigative magic slipped through the crackle of pain. "Can't tell how bad it is, but it's not broken. Think you can get up, blondie?" Though she kept her words light, concern tightened the skin around her eyes.

"I'd rather not."

Caroline gave a little smirk and hauled Misty to her good foot.

"Ow!" Misty leaned hard on Caroline and hopped to keep her balance. That was a mistake—the injured knee screamed with pain at the jolt. "Sonofa—" But she bit off the curse, sucking air through her teeth and blinking hard. There were a lot of things that unicorn riders weren't supposed to do, and one of them was swear out loud, especially not in front of an entire arena full of riders who'd love to see her disqualified.

Double especially not in front of Mary Frances Schwartz, the only other girl here with a real shot at the Nationals. Mary Frances was a barracuda in a double-A bra, five years younger than Misty's seventeen and almost as tall. She'd be too tall to ride Persians next year, unless she turned out to be a "teeny little freak" like Misty. She sidled her own unicorn Angel over, threateningly close to Vulcan, who laid his ears back and arched up at the other stud. "Are you all right?" she asked with nearly authentic sympathy.

"It's so sweet of you to ask," Misty ground out through clenched teeth. At least two reporters were taking notes, so she couldn't say what she was really thinking. She put one arm over Caroline's shoulder and the other over Vulcan's saddle, clutching the saddle horn as the three of them hobbled slowly out of the arena to the stable.

It took them almost ten minutes to cover the hundred yards to their stalls, Misty leaning into the lithe strength of Caroline's body. Vulcan was limping too; maybe he'd hurt himself attacking the rail. The dusty fairground was painfully bright after the mercury-lit dimness of the arena.

Once they reached the shade of the stall, Caroline eased Misty onto a shrink-wrapped sawdust bale. Misty sighed and rested her head in the soft hollow of Caroline's neck, smelling clean sweat and the cotton of her shirt collar. "Thank you," she said, and squeezed her hand.

Caroline squeezed back for a moment, then pulled away and turned back to Vulcan. Misty felt a childish urge to pout—Vulcan had to be secured in his stall, but the knee didn't hurt as much when she held Caroline's hand.

Caroline unbuckled Vulcan's bridle, replacing it with a halter cross-tied to each side of the open stall door. You never let that horn loose around people if you could help it. Once the unicorn was secured, Caroline brought Misty an ice pack from the trailer. "I told your mother those damn spurs were going to be trouble."

"Since when does she listen to either of us?" Misty sucked in a breath as Caroline laid the ice pack over the ruined knee of her pink Wranglers. She didn't want to let on just how much it hurt. "Anyway, it wasn't the spurs, it was me. You'd never have lost your seat." Caroline had grown too tall to show unicorns, but on a horse she was a study in long-limbed grace.

"I'm just the groom, shorty."

Misty gave Caroline a mock glare. "I'm gonna hit five feet this year, you wait and see."

"Dream on." Caroline crouched by Vulcan's front leg, inspecting the suspect hoof. "Looks like you've got a bruised hoof there, son."

"Seriously, Caro, it should be you out there on Vulcan, not me. You trained him, after all. I just sit on him. He's the proverbial push-button pony."

"I'm too tall, and you know it. I can ride 'em, I just don't look good on 'em." She picked up Vulcan's bruised foot and cupped it between her hands for a moment, muttering a healing charm like a prayer whispered in a lover's ear. Vulcan let his head hang in the cross-ties, eyes half closed as the magic flowed through his injured hoof.

"Even if you can't ride professionally, you could be a real trainer, in a real stable! Jack Thornton would hire you in a minute if he could. Why do you hang around this one-unicorn outfit?"

Caroline rose and busied herself with Vulcan's girth, not looking at Misty. "I like it here."

"Where's *here?* Caro, we're *nowhere*. Mom treats you like a servant, I know as well as you do that you haven't had a raise in three years, and we've been to the Nationals, what, five times?"

"But you still haven't won."

As if I cared. But she didn't say it . . . it would hurt Caroline so much. She'd worked so hard, put up with so much, all for Misty's sake; the least Misty could do in return was to make sure she got the accolades that would come from training a national champion unicorn.

Then Vulcan growled and tossed his head in the cross-ties. That meant some other stud was nearby, or . . .

Misty's mother announced her presence with a sandpaper screech of "I leave for *ten minutes* and what the hell happens!" She was already decked out in her Professional Show Mother outfit of white leather blazer, white leather skirt, and white Tony Lama boots—everyone on the circuit called her The Great White when she wasn't in earshot—but a chic silk turban concealed her bleached hair.

"I'm fine, Mother. Thanks for asking." Misty wondered if her mother's voice hurt her own ears, after all the vodka Bloody Marys she'd consumed when Misty had qualified for the finals last night.

"Let me see that knee." She grabbed Misty's calf, making big bright spots dance across Misty's vision, and yanked off the ice pack. The knee had swollen out to the limits of Misty's jeans. "These'll have to be cut off, I suppose. At least you had the sense not to practice in your competition outfit."

32

Caroline's eyes widened and she dropped the saddle unceremoniously onto its rack. "Misty! You didn't tell me it was that bad!" She knelt down in front of Misty and peered at the taut cloth. "We need to call the doctor."

Mother whirled on her. "No doctors! If some milksop gives her painkillers, she'll blow the blood test." She turned back to Misty, pointing with one pearl-manicured finger. "This is probably our last chance at the Nationals, and you are not going to wimp out on me."

Angry little lines appeared around Caroline's mouth, but Misty cut her off before she could say something that would get her fired. "I'll be fine, Mother." But she was looking at Caroline. "We'll wrap it and ice it and it's only one more class. I can stay on him for ten minutes."

"That's right. You are getting on that animal tonight, you are riding that class, and you are going to win it. I haven't busted my ass dragging you all over the countryside this year for nothing!"

Vulcan's ears went back at the rising shriek and he growled, strained against the cross-ties, digging with his hooves in the hard-packed dirt of the stall. Caroline said, "We're making Vulcan nervous, Mrs. Bell. We should get Misty into the trailer and elevate that knee."

"You do that." She glanced at her watch, encrusted with pink diamonds. "Oh God, now you've made me late. Look, I'm meeting Harvey to talk about your publicity photos over lunch, and then I'm going to get my hair done. I'll see you at the gate at seven." She strode out toward the parking lot, calling over her shoulder, "And I'd better not get another call from the show office!"

Misty looked around for the ice pack and saw it lying in the dirt, just out of her reach. "Can you get that for me?" Caroline leaned over and retrieved it, her lips pressed together in a hard white line. "Go ahead and say it," Misty prompted.

"Why bother? All it would do is make you have to defend her. And hearing you defend her is worse than watching how she treats you."

Misty sighed. She didn't know which would be worse—arguing with Caroline, or admitting that she had a point. "She's my mother, Caroline."

"Only genetically. Now let's get you inside. Can you hop, or do you want me to carry you?"

"I'll hop." But even straightening up was agony, and Misty didn't protest when Caroline carefully scooped her up, one arm warm behind her shoulders and the other under her thighs. Misty opened the trailer door and Caroline set her down on the bed in the back.

Misty looked down at the toes of her pink ropers, dreading the thought of pulling them off. "If we cut those, Mother will kill me."

"Let me try." Caroline worked one hand up Misty's pant leg to her calf. She cupped the heel of the boot in her other hand and started to ease it off. Misty gasped in pain, but a moment later the boot slipped off. "Good girl. Now the other one."

But when both boots and the socks were off the situation got even scarier. Misty's left foot was as white as her mother's leather skirt. "It's the swelling," Caroline said. "It's cut off the circulation. We have to get those jeans off."

Pulling the jeans down was absolutely out of the picture. Caroline went to the kitchen cabinet and came back with a pair of shears. Misty trembled, but said nothing as Caroline began to work her way up the outside seam. When she reached the knee, the scissors burned like ice against the hot skin and Misty bit her lower lip hard. Then, as the fabric parted, she thought she might faint from relief as the pressure released.

Caroline paused, her hand warm on Misty's inner thigh, after she had cut well past the knee. "They've got to come all the way off sooner or later. Do you want me to keep cutting?"

Misty's heart thudded in her throat, and she had to swallow before she could reply. "Might as well," she managed faintly.

Caroline seemed to be having trouble speaking as well, but she took a deep breath and resumed cutting. The cold scissor blades crept along Misty's thigh, and she felt the tip slip under the elastic of her panties. "Um, you got more than the jeans there."

"Sorry," Caroline squeaked, then cleared her throat and readjusted the scissors. "Sorry," she repeated in a more normal tone.

The bunched fabric at Misty's hip was awkward to get past. Then she had to wiggle out of her belt, and even with the belt gone the heavily layered waistband was a formidable obstacle. But Caroline sawed through it, and finally Misty was free. Both of them were panting from the effort. "Well, here I am, a seventeen-year-old virgin with no pants," Misty quipped in a trembling attempt at humor. "I bet there's a thousand boys who'd love to be you right now."

Caroline licked her lips. "Uh. Yeah." And she glanced up at Misty, her brown eyes half-hidden by her eyebrows, her face gone all serious. Misty swallowed, but returned Caroline's gaze for a long, awkward moment. Caroline was bent over her in the confined space, her calloused hand pressed between Misty's thighs. Misty had seen Caroline in nothing but a bra and panties plenty of times, living in the same trailer with her for what felt like a thousand shows. They'd been best friends since they were both eight, but she'd never wondered before what Caroline's skin felt like.

Then Caroline broke the contact to look down at Misty's knee. "Shit, girl. You aren't going to be standing up on this any time soon, much less getting on a unicorn." She was right. The knee was the size of a cantaloupe and an evil mix of purple and black.

Tears pinched at the back of Misty's throat. "I've got to, Caroline. I've just got to." If Misty didn't ride tonight, her mother would unleash her wrath on the nearest available object, and that was Caroline. Mother would make sure she never worked again.

Caroline sat back on her haunches, leaning her back against the bad imitation woodgrain of the wall. "I don't see how."

Misty licked her lips. "What about that healing touch of yours? It works on Vulcan."

"That's just a little hedge witchery. I don't practice on *people*! I don't have any experience, I don't have a license . . . hell, I wouldn't even do it on myself!"

"But Caroline, back in the arena . . ."

"I completely missed how badly you were hurt. If I mess up your knee healing it, they'll have to do surgery to put it right! You could be out of commission for six months!"

"So? Six *hours* is enough to lose our shot at the Nationals. I won't let my stupid mistake mess up your career."

"Screw my career!"

"Please, Caroline!" She reached out and took Caroline's hand. "Please."

Caroline didn't pull away. Her hand was very warm and moist in Misty's; her long strong fingers almost overwhelmed Misty's tiny delicate ones. "Okay," she said at last. "But only if it's what *you* want. Not your mother."

Do what you think is right.

Misty held Caroline's hand tighter. "This is what I want."

The two of them rearranged themselves in the tiny space so that Caroline could lay both hands on Misty's knee. They were trembling. Misty put her hands over Caroline's. "It's okay," she said. "I trust you."

"I know. But if I hurt you . . ."

"If you do, it'll be because I asked you to."

Caroline nodded and took a deep breath. Then she began to murmur, words as soft and convoluted as the inside of a unicorn's ear. At first Caroline's hands were cool on the heat of the injured knee, but then they began to warm—a deep thrumming warmth that resonated in Misty's bones. The heat of the injury was absorbed in that warmth, the shards of hot glass cooling and softening as Misty's knee relaxed back to normal. It was like music—the harsh jangled vibrations caught up and subsumed in the melody of Caroline's magic—a melody woven of Caroline's hands and her soft voice. It echoed low in Misty's belly. Misty sighed and closed her eyes.

As the swelling subsided, the warmth spread up Misty's leg and across her torso until it reached her heart and flowed to every part of her. She felt the rhythm of Caroline's words in her own pulse—each stronger for the other's presence.

"Misty. . . ?"

Caroline never called Misty by name . . . "blondie," "shorty," but never, ever "Misty." She opened her eyes.

Caroline was looking at her with bottomless dark eyes. Her hands were wrapped around Misty's knee, almost reverently. She was trembling again, and a sheen of sweat glistened on her face. "Misty . . . are you all right?"

"Better than all right." She leaned forward and slid her hands around the back of Caroline's neck, sliding forward until their bodies meshed. "Caroline . . ."

Caroline began to pull away. "I don't want to hurt you."

"This is what I want." And she kissed her.

Misty drifted slowly awake to Caroline's warm clean smell and the softness of her breast against Misty's cheek. The whole length of Caroline's long lean body was fitted smoothly against her, skin touching skin, and her arms enclosed Misty with gentle protectiveness. Misty sighed in contentment . . . but when she moved, like hitting the sand in the arena, it was going to hurt. Caroline would wake up, and the moment would be over, and Misty couldn't stand the thought of it.

The general public had a lot of misconceptions about unicorns, but the virginity trip was the real deal. Unicorns didn't share. The women around them were their herds, and they would brook no competition or threat to those they loved. Anyone not a virgin who tried to mount a unicorn was taking her life in her hands.

Misty's career was over.

Caroline's arms tightened around her. Holding on. Misty tipped up her head to look at Caroline's face, and saw tears in her eyes.

In all the years they'd lived together in trailer after trailer, Misty had never seen Caroline cry. No matter what cruel, horrible thing Mother said to her, Caroline pinched her lips together and sucked it down.

Misty brushed the tears off Caroline's cheek. "Don't cry, Caroline. It's okay."

Caroline squeezed her eyes shut and buried her face in Misty's hair. "It's *not* okay," she whispered, her voice broken. "I've ruined your whole life."

"It's only my life so far." Misty shifted so she could look Caroline in the eye. "And you didn't do anything to me. I'm the one who started it, remember? I think I've wanted this for a long time, even if I didn't know that until today." And she kissed her—trying to show Caroline that it really was all right, even though she wasn't sure herself.

Caroline kissed back with a desperate edge she hadn't shown before. She tasted of salt. She smelled of Misty.

Misty stroked Caroline's hair, gentling her down from desperation and murmuring vague reassurances. "We'll be all right. We'll be all right."

"How?" Caroline's voice was muffled against Misty's breast. "What do we do now?"

Misty took a deep breath. "Right now we're going to get up and take Vulcan a drink. He's been tied out there for three hours without any water. Then we're going to both get through the shower before Mother shows up."

"And then what?"

"I'll handle Mother. She's not your problem any more."

Caroline swallowed. "Okay. I'll take care of Vulcan while you hit the shower." She gave a rueful little smile. "Too bad there isn't room for both of us at once." Then she kissed Misty on the neck and slid out of bed, leaving a cold vacancy behind.

Once she was alone, Misty gathered the sheets into a wad in her lap, hunching herself into a tiny ball and rocking back and forth.

Her career was over.

No more trophies. No more spotlight. No more photographers. No more reporters watching her.

Imagine that.

No more having to act twelve. No more biting back what she wanted to say because it wasn't "nice." No more of Mother dressing her in fucking *pink* Wranglers.

And no more Caroline.

Even if she couldn't train unicorns any more, Caroline could make a perfectly good living working with horses. Once she realized what Misty had done to her, she wouldn't want to hang around a short, skinny ex-unicorn-rider who'd cost her a good job.

Misty'd always tried not to think about what would happen when she couldn't ride anymore. The very few riders who didn't grow up and get married became trainers, living like sisters in a closed monastic order. That never had been attractive to Misty before—she didn't have the patience for training—and it sure as hell wasn't an option now.

She didn't want to pop out babies for some goat-roper, and she didn't want to move to Dallas and marry the rich son of one of Daddy's friends.

She wanted Caroline.

But she didn't want Caroline to see her like this. She dried her eyes on a corner of the sheet, pulled herself together, and headed for the shower.

Three minutes later the water was turning lukewarm, and Misty shut it off to leave a little for Caroline. She poked her head out of the closet of a bathroom. Caroline hadn't come in yet.

How long could it take to get a pail of water?

Heart in her throat, Misty yanked a clean pair of jeans out of the drawer and struggled to pull them up her damp legs. Had Vulcan mauled her? Caroline was the best, but she'd never dealt with unicorns in a less-than-virginal state before. Misty fumbled with the buttons on her shirt as she headed for the door, afraid she'd find Caroline bleeding into the sawdust on the stall floor, but as she put her hand on the latch the door opened under it. It was Caroline.

"What took you so long?" Misty shouted. "I thought you were dead!"

Caroline pushed Misty gently back and closed the door firmly behind her. "Misty, maybe it doesn't count."

"What?"

"What we did. I'm not sure it *matters*."

"Well it mattered to me!"

"Me too, but I meant *Vulcan*."

"Oh." Misty paused. "Huh?"

"He was really snappish, but he let me water him and feed him."

"What do you mean 'snappish'?"

"He growled a lot, and pushed me into the wall, and he tried to bite me twice. But he could just be pissed at being locked up all day."

"Did you try to get on him?"

"I . . ." Caroline looked down. "No."

"Did you even take off the cross-ties?"

Caroline shook her head and didn't look up. "No. Didn't have the guts."

Misty sat down hard on the dinette bench. She didn't know what to think . . . didn't know if she could afford to hope . . . didn't even know if she *wanted* to hope.

And then came a familiar screech of "Misty!" The door slammed open, revealing Misty's mother beaming in carnivorous glee. "Misty, you'll never guess!"

Misty's heart tried to climb up her throat. "Mother!" she squeaked.

But Mother was on a roll, and didn't notice that half the buttons on Misty's shirt were in the wrong buttonholes. "Mary Frances Schwartz got herself gored!"

Caroline paled. "Omigod!"

Misty said "Is she okay?"

"Oh, she's at the hospital, I'm sure she'll be fine. The point is, *she can't ride*! Probably not for months! And with her out of the way, all you have to do is not fall off the stupid animal again, and we'll win the Nationals!"

She grabbed Misty by the cheeks and pinched hard. "We'll win!" she sing-songed, bouncing on the balls of her feet. "We'll get our first National championship!"

Misty couldn't keep the image of little Mary Frances torn open and bleeding out of her mind. It was too close to what she'd visualized happening to Caroline. "How did it happen?"

"The stupid little tart kissed a boy. Can you believe it?" She shook her head, and over her shoulder Misty saw Caroline's face drop into an expression of anxiety and dismay. "Now look, we have to get you into your outfit right away. There are going to be lots of photographers waiting in the warm-up arena and my little angel will have to be *perfect*." She turned to Caroline. "And so does Vulcan, so *you'd* better get to work instead of loitering around the trailer." But her habitual nastiness lacked its usual edge—blunted by the thought of Misty's ensuing triumph. She began to fuss at Misty's hair. "What, you've only just showered?" She made a sound of tried patience.

Caroline didn't move. She just stared as though she was afraid she'd never see Misty alive again.

Without turning, Misty's mother said "I thought I told you to get to work."

Caroline blew a shaky kiss to Misty and headed for the barn. Misty opened her mouth to call Caroline back, to say "Don't go," but Mother started to unbutton Misty's shirt.

"Good God, child, you're all crooked!"

In her panic over Caroline, Misty hadn't had time to put on a bra. She snatched the front of her shirt closed, backing toward the bedroom. "I can dress myself, Mother."

"Well, you can't prove it by me! Now hurry up, we have to do your hair."

Misty shut the folding door and swallowed her heart back down to its proper position. Her show outfit was hanging on the wall in its protective bag, and the white hat with its pink rhinestone hatband was still in its box on the shelf. She dressed in a daze, more out of habit than conviction.

What could she say? What could she do? What *should* she do? Would Vulcan even let her mount? She wasn't sure which she feared more—Vulcan's horn or her mother's tongue. At least if Vulcan attacked her she'd be dead.

At last she emerged, fully decked out in gleaming white and glittering pink. Her mother looked up from polishing Misty's pink ropers. "There's my angel!"

Misty thought she might throw up.

Her mother took her by the shoulders and looked seriously into her face. "You're gonna make me so proud."

Misty wanted to say "Let's just get this over with." But she put on the best smile she could muster and said, "Thanks."

Caroline had Vulcan saddled and ready to go. He tossed his head and sidled, ears back and lips taut. Misty reached out to stroke his neck and he snapped at her. "Easy," she crooned, but he twitched away from her touch.

Misty's mother cast a disgusted eye at Vulcan. "What on earth is wrong with that animal?" He growled and snapped at her. Mother backed away and turned to Caroline. "You keep him under control, do you hear me?"

"Yes, ma'am." She didn't sound at all certain.

Mother turned back to Misty, her face aglow, and squealed, "I'll see you in the ring!"

Once Misty's mother had left, Vulcan sniffed and snuffled Misty all over. She was used to that—she was covered in hairspray and powder for the show ring—but today his examination seemed more intrusive, more urgent. "What do you think, big fella?"

He snorted, which wasn't exactly an answer.

Caroline said, "Don't do this, Misty. Mary Frances got gored just for *kissing* a boy."

"You're not a boy." She reached for Caroline's hand, but before she could touch her Vulcan tossed his head and growled. "Whoa! Easy, boy!"

Working together, with pats and whispers and lumps of beef jerky, they managed to get him calmed down a bit. Eventually he let Misty rub his ears and scratch at the base of his horn.

"I don't know . . ." Misty said, stroking Vulcan's warm cheek. "Maybe he's just a little out of sorts. I think . . . I think I could ride him."

"And you could get killed trying." Caroline's eyes glistened. "I don't want to lose you!"

"You won't." Misty drew herself up to her full four-foot-eleven. "Not ever. But I have to do this, Caro. I have to try." She started walking.

After a moment Caroline followed, with Vulcan in tow.

They walked Vulcan up to the gate and checked in with the gate steward. He winked and gave them a thumbs-up. Misty smiled weakly back at him.

"Good luck." Caroline's voice was trembling as she handed Misty the reins.

Their fingers met briefly on the reins, and Misty stood abruptly up on tiptoe to kiss Caroline on the cheek. Caroline looked surprised, then a smile spread across her face. The expression made Misty's throat close up and her heart turn over. Flashbulbs stabbed through the semi-dark at them.

Caroline turned toward the stands, stroking her kissed cheek as she walked away.

Misty stood alone in the crowd of unicorns and riders, waiting in the shadow beneath the announcer's booth. A pall of apprehension hovered over them, riders pale and unicorns skittish—the usual pre-class jitters amplified in the wake of Mary Frances' accident. No one spoke.

The loudspeaker boomed and the first rider walked her unicorn out into the floodlights' scrutiny to mount in front of the judge. One by one they trickled away, in ascending order of points for the year, until only Misty remained.

"And finally," roared the announcer, "with four hundred and eighty-seven points, Miss Misty Bell and B. R. Vulcan's Golden Hammer!"

The gate steward swung the gate open and smiled at her.

Vulcan gently nudged her shoulder with his muzzle. They had done this hundreds of times, and he knew the routine. They should move forward into the glare of the arena.

And she knew. She knew that she could ride him.

She licked her lips and took one step forward. And stopped.

The announcer's voice came again. "Miss Misty Bell. Two minutes."

The gate steward looked at her quizzically. Vulcan reached under the brim of her hat to touch her face with his muzzle. His breath was sweet with oats and alfalfa.

All she had to do was walk in, mount, ride this class, and she would win it.

And then she'd win the Nationals, and next year she'd be back here doing it again. And every year after that, as long as her mother's ambition held out.

Her mother's ambition. Not hers.

"Scratch," she said quietly.

"Beg your pardon, Miss Bell?" said the gate steward.

"Close the gate, Harry."

And the ring steward closed the gate, giving the judge a go-ahead wave.

Misty turned and led Vulcan away from the lights of the show ring and out into the peaceful darkness of the fairgrounds. Behind her, the announcer's voice called out, "Miss Bell scratches." A mutter of consternation and curiosity ran through the stands, but she just kept walking, putting one pink boot in front of the other, in no particular hurry as she headed back through the evening to the barn.

Her mother caught up to her in the fringes of the barn lights, her face half-lit like a bright half moon. *"How can you do this to me?"* she screeched, face dark with rage above the white leather of her Show Mother suit.

"I'm not going to ride tonight, Mother," she said, her boots firm on the packed earth. She'd expected to be afraid, but she wasn't.

"Listen, little girl . . ."

"I'm not a little girl, Mother. That's the point."

Caroline pounded up behind Misty's mother. "What happened? Wouldn't he let you mount?"

Misty's mother froze, staring at Misty with dawning understanding and rage. "You. Little. Slut." She clenched her fists, and Vulcan growled a warning. "Who was it?" she hissed.

"That's none of your business."

Misty's mother whirled on Caroline. "You were supposed to watch her! How can you let this happen after all I've done for you?"

Caroline opened her mouth, but Misty cut her off. "You've never done anything for her, you platinum-plated bitch."

Misty's mother gawped at Misty, sputters and gasps of frustrated fury choking in her throat.

"You should go back to the hotel, Mother. Have a drink. We'll talk about it in the morning. And my knee's fine, thanks for asking."

"We'll see how fine you are with no money, you ungrateful little whore."

"Good night, Mother."

Left with nothing else to do, Misty's mother stalked stiff-backed toward the parking lot. Misty felt the muscles in the small of her back unclench.

Caroline could only stare. "Misty . . . what did you do?"

"I . . ." Misty slumped. "I think I just got you fired. Oh, Caroline . . . I'm sorry."

"I won't have any problem finding another job—Jack Thornton's been begging me for two years. But what about you? She's your mother!"

"I couldn't let her treat you like that any more. If I hadn't done something, neither of us would ever have gotten away."

"Misty, what'll you do?"

Misty shrugged, shook her head and couldn't make herself not smile. "I dunno. Maybe Jack Thornton'll let me shovel stalls for him or something." She put her foot in the stirrup and swung up into Vulcan's saddle. He purred and reached around to nuzzle her boot. "I'm going for a ride to clear my head. Will you still be here when I get back?"

Caroline squeezed Misty's knee. "You know it, shorty."

Misty pulled off the pink-rhinestoned hat and flung it into the darkness. Then she nudged Vulcan with her knee, and as they ambled down the quiet aisle between the barns, she shook her hair loose into the cool of the evening.

A HUNTER'S ODE
TO HIS BAIT

Carrie Vaughn

"You're sure she's untouched?"

"For God's sake yes. She's just a girl."

Duncan took the girl's face in his hands, tilted her head back, pried apart her lips and had a look at her teeth. Her frightened gaze darted between him and her mother. "Doesn't mean anything. There are whores younger than her."

She was twelve or thirteen, small and thin for her age but healthy—good teeth, straight back. In a year or so, with a few good meals in her, she'd be a beauty with golden hair and clear eyes.

Her mother stood a few steps away, wringing her hands and trying to maintain a business-like lack of expression. "I've heard men pay more for virgins."

"You heard right," Duncan said. "But you already agreed to my price. I'll take her." He tossed the pouch of silver at the woman. It landed at her feet, and she hurried to pick it up. Her husband was dead and she had eight other children to feed.

He went to where he'd tied his horse to a fence post. "Get your cloak, girl, and come on."

Barefoot, she stood in the dirt in front of the hovel and didn't move. "I don't have a cloak."

"Eleanor, go on." Her mother gestured, brushing her away like she was a wild dog.

She still didn't move, so Duncan picked her up and set her at the front of his saddle. He mounted behind her, wheeled his horse around, and rode off without a backward glance. She didn't struggle or cry at all, which worried him at first. Perhaps she was an idiot child.

Then she said, "What's a whore?"

He considered how to answer. The less she knew about such things the better, so he said nothing.

He kept her steady with an arm across her shoulders, and she was limp in his grasp.

In three days they reached the wilds of Northumbria, plunging straight into a forest of twisted oak. What few local folk there were would not enter the place because they said it was haunted. Duncan made camp in a glade where a spring flowed clear. He set the girl on the ground and left her huddled in the crook formed by an immense protruding root. He'd bought a cloak for her, and boots.

Late that afternoon, just before dusk, he took her to a glen dipped in the shadow of a hill. He carried his longbow, a quiver of arrows with varnished shafts, and his sword. He set about building a blind, a crawl space shadowed with leaves and branches that allowed a view of the whole clearing. The girl watched him with her wide, blue eyes and slack, numb face.

He bade her sit on a grassy hillock. She began to tremble, clutching the edges of her cloak and hugging herself. For a moment he doubted. What was he doing, paying silver for a slip of flesh and then dragging the poor girl out here? The prize, remember the prize. This would work.

"Don't be frightened," he said, putting a hand on her shoulder. "I'll be over there. Sit quietly, and the beast will appear. When it does, calm it."

"What beast?"

"You'll see."

He left her and went to his blind.

Wind shivered through the trees, sending autumn leaves raining.

One landed on the girl's cloak, and she brushed it off. Duncan held his bow with an arrow notched and watched all around the glen. Every whisper of leaves he took for footsteps.

Her fear passed with the time. She scratched at the dirt with a stick, played with the edges of her cloak. She started humming a country jig, a little off-tune. Over the next few days, Duncan kept the girl warm and fed, and she never complained.

After a week of sitting in the cold, the creature came.

It stepped out of the trees, out of the twilight mist, head low to the ground and nostrils quivering. A silver shadow in the form of a horse, seemingly made of mist itself. The long, spiral horn growing from its forehead reflected what little light remained in the world and seemed to glow.

The girl's gasp carried all the way to Duncan's blind. The unicorn's head lifted, ears pricked forward hard, and he feared that she'd startle the thing away. But no, her scent was strong, and its instinct was powerful. Instead of cringing in fear, she got to her knees and reached toward it with both hands, whispering to it.

It leaned toward her, like a horse would to a bucket of grain. It made careful, silent steps, not even rustling the fallen leaves. Its thick mane fell forward, covering its neck. It huffed quick breaths at her, stretching forward to sniff at her fingers. The girl cupped her hands. The unicorn rested its muzzle on her palms and sighed.

Duncan shot his arrow, striking the creature's neck.

It screamed, a piercing wail, and reared straight up like it might fly. Duncan shot again and hit the crook of its throat, where the head joined the neck. Twisting in midair, it tried to leap back to the shelter of the woods, crying with strained breaths. After one stride it fell, chest plowing into the earth, head and horn still raised. Groaning, it rolled to its side.

He didn't know how much it would take to kill it. The stories were vague on that point. Heart racing, Duncan drew his sword and approached. The thing shuddered, sighed quietly, the sound of air leaving a bellows. He sprang at it, driving his blade into its side, through its heart, but it didn't move again. Dark stains ran from all three wounds, matting the hair of its mane and coat.

His hands were trembling. He'd done it. Bracing his foot against the unicorn's ribs, Duncan pulled out the sword, stumbling back and dropping it. Its horn was a foot long. Worth a fortune. He took his hunting knife, and it occurred to him that no one would believe where the horn came from if he didn't take the whole head.

Belatedly, he looked at the girl.

She huddled on the ground, covering her head with her hands. Slowly, her face emerged. She stared at the dead unicorn, blood congealing on its side.

"You did well," he said, attempting gentleness. His voice shook.

This was another part he had not thought to plan for—what would she do after? He expected sobbing. But she merely gathered her cloak around her and got to her feet. She seemed older, wrapped in the gloom of the forest, mist-glow turning her hair silver.

She stepped to the body, knelt by its head, and pressed her hand to its cheek. Quickly, she drew away. "It's already cold."

"It's just a beast," he said. "Just a hunt."

He started cutting, and she moved out of the way. As he cut the final strand of muscle joining the head to the neck, the body began to shrivel, drying up, turning to dust, blowing away piece by piece. The girl put her hands in it, clutching the ash-like powder and opening her empty hands as it faded to nothing.

"It was beautiful," she said.

Eleanor gave a final tug on the cord that secured the bundle to the pack horse. The mass of it was awkward, wrapped tight in oilskin. A long, thin piece jutted out, lying flat along the horse's flank. It was the head of their ninth unicorn.

She'd grown like a weed the last five years. Regular meals worked wonders. Duncan kept her fed, and she put on weight, developing healthy curves and roses in her cheeks. He bought a horse for her, along with the pack horse. They made quite the little company now, a world of change from when he stalked the woods alone.

She scratched the pack horse's ear and went to kick dirt on the last embers of their campfire. "Do we ride far tonight?"

"Yes. I'd like to cross the border without guards watching. And—these woods are angry, I think." It was spring, but the trees still looked like skeletons, black shapes against the sky, reaching for him. He'd made a habit of killing magic, old magic, and he found himself looking over his shoulder more and more these days. "Will you be all right?"

"Of course." She said it sharply, but when he looked, she was smiling, watching him as she tightened her saddle's girth.

Of course she'd be all right, living wild in the wood and traveling like a bandit as she had. He avoided civilization as much as possible, kept her away from towns with their taverns, from people who might say a corrupting word. She was still pure; the unicorns still came to her.

They left the road before they reached the border and cut overland, picking their way through the ruins of the old Roman wall. No one saw them, and they stopped before dawn to rest.

In two days they reached their destination, where a wealthy lowland chieftain bought the horn, then opened his hall for a feast in honor of the hunter. Duncan relented. They wouldn't stay long.

Eleanor, wearing a simple gown of green wool, hair tied up in a braid, stood with him, untroubled by the great hall, the gold, the rich folk, and the stares. She had never been very excitable, but there was more to it than that. She was a creature of nature and didn't know to be wary here. She stood calmly, chin lifted, meeting every gaze that came to rest on her, refusing to be cowed by the noble company. She only gave a nod to the chieftain himself. They all saw she was proud, haughty even, and a wild beauty showed through with that pride. How had she learned to carry herself so, this waif from the hovel?

She glanced at him out of the corner of her eye and smiled.

He hadn't trimmed his beard or combed his hair to appear before the chieftain. His clothes were clean at least, but they were still hunting clothes, leather breeches and jerkin. And he, who slew unicorns, owed them no obeisance.

Then he knew: she'd learned by watching him.

That evening, he allowed himself more ale than he usually drank, to help chase away the shadows lurking at the edges of his thoughts. Sitting at the high table with the chieftain's men, he listened to conversation play around him. He only answered when someone spoke his name and woke him from his reflections.

"Duncan. The lord has given you a quarter of his wealth for that horn. You could live nobly on that."

"I hunt again in the morning," he said.

Laughing, the courtier said, "But why? You're rich, aren't you?" Several times over in fact, but he kept the money hidden. "You've a beautiful woman at your beck and call—"

Before Duncan could turn on the man to correct him of this notion, an older fellow with a white beard leaned over. "He doesn't do it for the wealth. That's what you don't understand. He does it for the power, to be able to turn his nose up at lords."

"And the girl?" the overloud courtier said. "Don't tell me you've never even touched her."

"You fool, of course he hasn't," said the older one. "She's the bait."

Across the hall, Eleanor was dancing with the chieftain's youngest son, a handsome lad of twenty with far more charm than Duncan liked. She didn't know the steps, and he was teaching her. She stumbled—Duncan had never in the last few years known her to stumble. The boy caught her waist, and she laughed. Then he took her hand and raised it to his lips.

Duncan set down his mug and climbed around the table.

He marched across the hall directly toward Eleanor and the boy, scattering the figures of the dance. The fiddler stopped playing, the drummer lost his beat, and the whole hall fell silent. Folk cleared a space for him.

Planting a hand on the young lord's chest, Duncan shoved him away and stood between him and Eleanor. He didn't say a word, only glared, and the boy backed into to the protection of the crowd.

Duncan put his hand on the back of Eleanor's neck and turned her toward the door.

"Never even think of it," he said, hissing into her ear.

"What are you—"

"If he gets what he wants from you, you become useless to me."

She ducked out of his grasp. "It was only a kiss—"

"A kiss leads to other things."

He'd said too much already. How much longer would he be able to keep her? "Go to the stable. Get our horses ready. We ride out tonight."

"Duncan, there's no reason to ride out. We've a warm place to sleep tonight. A roof, for God's sake."

"We ride out tonight."

So, wrapped in cloaks and huddled in their saddles against a cold drizzle, they spent the night on the road.

Eleanor rode behind him, and her silence bothered him. He kept looking over his shoulder to make sure she was still there.

"What did he say to you?" he said.

"Who?"

"That boy."

"He told me I was pretty."

"What else?"

"What's the matter with you?"

"What else?"

She gave a long-suffering sigh, then let hoofbeats fill the silence before answering. "He asked me if I ever felt like I was betraying them. He could not believe that I would draw a creature of magic to me, then betray it."

"Well? Is that how you feel?"

"I don't know. I don't think I want to do this forever. I think I would like to marry someday."

"What do you know about marriage?"

"It's what men and women do, isn't it?"

He was so very, very close to losing her. Perhaps he should just let her go. "Men like that don't marry girls like you, so you can stop thinking of it."

"I didn't say I'd like to marry *him*. Though—I've heard men pay more for virgins."

He might have said a hundred things to that, but he refused to be taunted.

A couple dozen strides of silence later, Eleanor said sullenly, "You may own me, Duncan, but you're not my father, so don't pretend to be."

More hoofbeats, more silence, then Duncan said softly, "You earned your way free a long time ago, Eleanor." He didn't think she heard him.

Eleanor let her hair hang loose, draping in waves down her shoulders and back. She wore a blue gown the color of sky at twilight and went barefoot. As she matured, becoming more comfortable in her own skin, she attracted older unicorns, ones not so easily enticed, the ones with the longest horns.

They might wait for weeks before drawing one close. During that time

Eleanor would wander through the woods, walking, singing, making her presence known. Duncan followed, moving softly and staying hidden. Once, he'd had to stay downwind of a unicorn who followed Eleanor for five days before finally revealing itself and coming to her hand.

He never struck until the unicorn touched her, thus losing its will to flee.

This time it took three days to lure the beast. Eleanor walked into a clearing, knelt, and picked flowers, humming to herself. The unicorn emerged from the trees behind her. She paused—perhaps she felt its breath on her neck—but she didn't turn around. She kept humming, picking flowers until she had a small bouquet. Duncan crouched in the shelter of a thicket and waited.

The unicorn, a broad, muscular beast with a horn almost two feet long, stepped around her, sniffing her. She didn't move, she was in its power—with its horn leveled at her, it could stab her at any moment. So she waited until it stopped before her, then slowly offered it her flowers. It reached and brushed them with its lips.

A cry, like the whinny of a horse sounded through a trumpet, rang through the forest. On the opposite side of the clearing from Duncan, a white shape hurdled the underbrush and thundered toward Eleanor and the unicorn. It snorted with each stride.

This creature, this second unicorn, was at least eighteen hands tall, a titan that shook the ground as it galloped. Its blazing horn must have been three feet long, the longest Duncan had ever seen.

Tossing its head, it raced at Eleanor's unicorn and rammed it flank-to-flank, shoving it away from her. The newcomer screamed again, rearing at its fellow, which cried in answer and spun out of the way, tearing the soil with black hooves. The monster drove it off, and it raced into the forest.

The monster's mane shook, white hair cascading over satin shoulders. As it turned to follow the other, it let fly a kick with all the power of those massive hindquarters.

Eleanor had backed away from the fight, but not out of range of those hooves. Struck, she flew back, lifted bodily and sent sprawling on the bracken.

"Eleanor!" Duncan burst from his hiding place just as the unicorn fled with the same rolls of thunder with which it had arrived.

She was curled on her side, coughing and gasping for breath. He left his longbow and sword behind and crouched by her, gingerly touching her arm and fearing how broken she might be.

"Eleanor, speak. Where are you hurt? Tell me." He touched her face, ran his hand to her neck and felt a rapid pulse.

"I'm all right," she said, wheezing, brushing his hands away and trying to sit up. "Lost my breath is all."

His hand went to her side to help her up, and she cried out and flinched away. Her breathing started to come in panicked gasps.

"Sit back. Breathe slow. Good." He helped her lie back against a tree and prodded her side. The pain came mostly in her ribs. Cracked, he wagered. She wasn't coughing blood, she could feel all her limbs. She'd come away lucky.

He made camp there and fetched a bucket of water from a cold stream. He came to where she lay curled up, favoring her injury.

"Strip," he said. "I'll have to wrap those ribs."

"What?"

"Take off your dress."

She blushed, crossing her hands over her chest. Then, a half-smile dawning on her lips, she gave him a look that made *him* blush.

"Yes, sir," she said and began unlacing her gown.

He pointedly did not stare at her breasts as he bandaged her torso. When had she gotten breasts? They weren't much, just large enough to fill a man's hand, and yet—he was not staring.

"What was that thing?" she asked, gritting her teeth as he pulled the cloth tight. "It didn't even notice me."

"A legend among legends. An old brute of a unicorn. Filled with rage and jaded to the scent of virgins."

"Like you," she said, sitting half-naked before him.

He tied off the bandage, giving it an extra tug that made her squeak.

"It's been watching us for some time," he said. "Perhaps—perhaps it is time I quit this game."

He helped her settle by the fire to rest, and he cooked their supper. They ate in silence. He put away the dishes, saw to their horses, and brought back his bedroll.

Eleanor watched him across the fire.

"We could catch it," she said.

"You don't just catch a beast like that. It is a god among unicorns, and we've inspired its wrath."

"You're afraid."

He grunted a denial and looked away. Not afraid—he'd spent more nights alone in wilderness most folk dared not travel in daylight than he had under roofs. He could buy any man, lord or commoner, that he chose. He made way for no one. He did not fear. But he was getting old, finding himself wishing for some of the roofs he had shunned. Perhaps that was nearly the same as fear.

Eleanor wouldn't understand, young imp that she was. Her eyes were bright, her face clean of wrinkles of age and worry. Her time in the wild had made her luminous.

"I think I can tempt an old brute of a unicorn."

"A beast like that sees nothing but its own fury."

She moved to his side of the fire, wincing and pressing her hand to the bandage as she crawled. She sat close to him; they had not been so close since he carried her before him on his saddle.

She touched his face. Not pressing, she held her palm lightly against his cheek, just enough to brush the edge of his beard. She was trembling a little, unsure of the gesture. Her brow furrowed, her expression anxious and waiting. Then, she kissed him.

Her lips felt as soft and clean as she looked. Her breath brushed his cheek, sending warmth across his face, through all his blood.

He dared not move, lest he frighten the creature away.

When he did not react, she ran her hand up his cheek, tangled her fingers in his hair, and kissed him more firmly. She was clumsy, her nose jutting into his, her balance on her knees wavering.

He took her face in both his hands and taught her how to kiss properly.

He almost gave in, and she almost let him, but his hand went from her breast to clutch her bandaged side and she gasped and flinched away. Giggling, she curled up in his arms, head resting on his chest.

"See? I can tempt an old brute."

He brushed his fingers through her fine hair, touching her as he went, ear, neck, shoulder.

"I never intended to make a whore of you," he said softly.

She pulled away and looked at him. "You've done it from the first, using me to make your money, haven't you?"

He chuckled sadly. She was right, after all. "You've become too worldly for this hunt."

"Not yet. We have one more unicorn to catch."

It would be best to leave it. But even if he never entered another forest for the rest of his days, that old beast would haunt him. That prize, that challenge, the three-foot horn—that was how he should end his hunting days. And the time was now: Eleanor had reached the peak of her maidenhood, unsurpassed beauty, her innocence still intact but ready to burst, a rose at the height of her bloom. Perhaps the old beast wouldn't be able to resist her. After all, five years of nothing but pure thoughts notwithstanding, only a cracked rib made him resist.

"Why do you want to do this?" he asked.

"The usual reasons: money, fame. Because it is the profession to which I was apprenticed and I have no choice."

"Then I set you free. Here and now, I have no hold over you, and moreover I will give you half of what we have earned these past years. I will not ask you to act as bait for the old one. So, will you leave?"

"No. I will hunt the old one."

"Why?"

She hesitated before answering, pursing her lips and looking around at trees and sky. "The power," she said finally. "The power I have over them. A girl like me—there's no other power I could have, is there?"

Heart pounding, he thought, *There is another power you have.*

They waited for Eleanor's ribs to heal before searching out the old one. They left their horses behind, took a minimum of gear, and traveled deeper into the northern woods than they ever had before.

Tracking unicorns, it was no good looking for hoof prints or broken twigs for signs of their passing. They left no prints. One searched for other evidence: a pool of water that should have been brackish, but was clear and fresh; a patch of grass greener than the foliage around it, where one of them had slept. Then, catching unicorns was more like fishing than hunting. Once a place they frequented was found, there was nothing to do but set the bait and wait.

They caught a glimpse of it after they had been looking for a week. Eleanor—watched by Duncan, who perched in a tree a hundred paces away—sat alone in a sunny clearing, brushing her hair. The beast, a fierce buck as large and thick as an oak tree, moved toward her, silently for all its bulk. Its thick mane and tail rippled, its coat shone like silver.

Duncan watched it pass to the edge of the clearing, but it did not enter. It circled, watching Eleanor. She looked up only when she heard its breath snort. When she did, it turned and galloped away.

Eleanor didn't eat much at supper that evening. "I think I'm afraid of it," she said, not meeting Duncan's gaze. "It sees into my heart, sees I'm proud. I can't fool it."

"Do you want to leave off?"

"No. Fear will pass."

The next day, clouds covered the sky. The day after, a drizzle set in, a long cold rain promising to last for days. They wrapped their cloaks tight around them and found sheltered hillocks in which to spend the nights. Eleanor said she caught glimpses of the old one twice, watching them through trees from far away.

"Who's hunting who, I wonder?" Duncan said, frowning.

A week later, at twilight, when the rain-damp sky was a breath away from falling to darkness, Eleanor stopped Duncan with a hand on his chest.

"Let me go on ahead," she said. "Circle 'round to that thicket, watch from there."

"You think he's there?"

"I think he's waiting for me."

He grabbed her hand and kissed her fingers before striking off.

A clearing lay where she had pointed him. He saw nothing, but crouched hidden, bow strung and arrow ready, and waited.

A moment later, Eleanor approached. She had left behind her pack, cloak, and boots, and unbound her hair. Her linen dress was quickly becoming soaked, clinging to her until every part of her slim frame showed: the line of her waist, slope of hip, the matched curves of her breasts. Her hair, darker when wet, dripped down her shoulders and back, framing her face, slick with rain.

Wandering into the glade, she seemed like a creature of mist, a nymph from a tale, one of the watery maids who pulled men under lakes to their deaths. Being soaking wet did not detract from her grace; she stepped lightly, lifting her skirt away from her feet, and stood tall. She looked up at the sky and smiled.

A snorting breath, loud as a roar, preceded the old unicorn's charge into the clearing. He ran at her, legs pumping, head lowered so its horn aimed for her heart. Duncan almost let fly his arrow, knowing he could never hit it as it ran but fearing for Eleanor.

She stood her ground. She didn't move. Just smiled a little and waited.

A mere stride away from her, the unicorn slid to an abrupt stop, hind end gathered underneath it, front legs lifted, and shook its head, brandishing the horn.

Eleanor crouched, lowering herself on bent knees, and raised her arm to the beast, offering her hand. She showed herself submissive, the lesser of the two.

The unicorn shook his head, his obsidian eyes flashing. He seemed torn, straining forward even as he resisted, as if pressing against a barrier. The beast stepped back, pranced in place, then spun away. He did not flee, but trotted a circle around her. She circled with him, her hand outstretched, fingers splayed, waiting for a chance when he might brush against them. While he came close—drifting in tighter and tighter circles, then suddenly leaping out to the edge of the clearing again, like a child playing around a bonfire—he never let her touch him.

All the while, Eleanor smiled a soft, wondering smile.

It was a game, this teasing and dodging. They must have played it for an hour. Sometimes the unicorn stopped and seemed ready to step toward her, head bowed, tamed. Then he reared and jumped away, and Eleanor laughed. At this, his ears pricked forward, his neck arced, and he seemed pleased to hear her.

Duncan watched from the thicket, his cold hands gripping his bow and notched arrow, his face flushed.

The unicorn moved toward her, hot breaths coming in clouds of mist.

His back stood a good deal taller than Eleanor; his head towered above her. He came close enough for his breath to wash over her lifted face, but he still would not cross the last stride to her arms.

So she played the tease, and backed away from him.

"I'm pure as starlight, dear one. Touch me."

She pulled at the laces closing the neck of her gown. She separated the front edges, enough to show breast but not nipple. She stretched her arms back, so that at any moment the gown might fall off her shoulders completely, but it didn't, and she shook back her hair. The unicorn stretched his neck toward her, but she stayed just out of reach.

Duncan bit his lip. He dared not shift, though he was hard, pressed painfully against his breeches. Blood pounded through his crotch. He willed his hands to remain steady.

Her feet and legs were caked with mud, the hem of her gown black with the stuff, even though she held it off the ground. She was wet as a drowned kitten, but smiling and shining, moving a slow dance like she was born to this damp world—as innocent as the rain. Rain which gave life, and which flooded and drowned. *This*, he thought, *was why men paid more for virgins.*

The old unicorn was also aroused.

She had him then. She got to her knees, as she had done instinctively that first time, and offered him her cupped hands. With deliberate steps he came to her, lowered his head until his whiskers brushed her fingers, and licked her palms with a thick pink tongue.

Duncan loosed his arrow.

Pierced through the throat, the unicorn screamed. He reared, becoming a tower of a beast, as tall as some of the trees. Duncan jumped from his blind and shot again and again. One arrow hit his chest, another his shoulder, but still the beast kept to his feet. Duncan thought the monster would turn and run, and he would have to track him until he dropped. But the unicorn stayed, kicking and rearing, pawing over and over again the ground where Eleanor had been.

She'd ducked away, crouching at the edge of the clearing; Duncan saw enough to know she was safe. He got one more shot away before the unicorn charged him. He drew his sword and managed a slice at him as he passed. The edge nicked his chest, drawing a little blood, but the unicorn didn't slow. He turned on his haunches, throwing a rain of mud behind him, and attacked. Neck arched, horn aimed, the unicorn ran at him. Duncan stumbled back and raised his sword to block.

He couldn't hold his own against the sheer force of the beast's movement. The unicorn pressed forward, his body a battering ram with his horn at the fore, and Duncan could only rush to escape, making token parries with his sword.

The unicorn got beside him and with a swipe of his head knocked Duncan over. He sprawled in the mud, and as he got to his knees the unicorn charged again, striking him as he turned away. The blow wrenched his shoulder and spun him around. Setting his will, he got to his feet and looked for the next attack—the unicorn was coming at him again, making a running start, ready to impale him on that prized, impossible horn.

He opened his hands—his sword was gone. He'd lost his bow as well.

He waited until the last moment to dodge, to keep the unicorn from swerving to stab him anyway, and again the beast's bulk shoved him over. With the wind knocked out of him, he was slower to rise this time. He heard the thunder of hot breaths coming closer.

Eleanor screamed. "Here I am! It's me you want!" She stood in the middle of the clearing, arms at her sides.

The unicorn stopped in a stride and turned to Eleanor, his betrayer. With a satisfied snort, he trotted at her, neck arced, horn ready.

"Eleanor, no," Duncan would have said, if he'd had the breath for it.

She got to her knees—putting herself too low for the beast to stab her comfortably. He'd have had to bring his nose nearly to his chest. So he had to crush her with his hooves. Duncan stumbled in the mud, hoping to get to her in time.

The unicorn reared, preparing to bring all his weight and anger down on Eleanor.

In a heartbeat, she stepped underneath him and raised Duncan's sword, which she'd hidden beside her.

She held it in place underneath his heart, and he came down on the point. For a split second he hung there, and it looked like she was holding him up with the sword. Blood rained down on her from the wound. Then he fell straight onto her, and they crumpled together.

Finally, too late, Duncan found his feet. The unicorn was dead. Its body lay on its side, a mound in the center of the clearing.

"Eleanor," he panted with each breath. He approached its back, his heart pounding in his throat. Blood streamed from the body, filling in puddles and footprints. He saw no movement, heard no cries.

He went around the great unicorn's head, twisted up from its neck, the horn half-buried in mud.

And there was Eleanor, streaked with blood and dirt, extricating herself from the unicorn's bent legs.

"Eleanor!" He slid into the mud beside her and touched her hair, her shoulders, her arms. He helped her wipe the grime from her face. "Are you hurt? Are you well?"

"I got away. I'm only a little bruised. But you—" She did the same, pawing him all over for signs of injury. His twisted shoulder hurt to move, but he could move it. All his limbs worked. He could draw breath. He would live. They both sighed.

Smiling, she took his hands.

"No more unicorns, Duncan. If you want me, I'm yours. And if you won't have me, I'll leave and find someone who will."

He swallowed her with kisses until she laughed. Then he took her, there in the rain and the mud, against the carcass of the unicorn.

GHOST TOWN

Jack C. Haldeman II

The clapped-out pickup almost made it to the gas station. I had to get out and push it the last fifty yards. It had been making suspiciously fatal sounds for the last couple of days, and the trail of oil it was leaving in the dusty road was not reassuring.

That I was broke and hadn't pulled a con in almost a week didn't improve my frame of mind as I huffed and sweated the piece of junk off the road and onto the hard-packed dirt of the gas station lot. A man sitting in a rocker on the station's porch watched me without moving to help. He was wearing faded jeans and a beat-up straw hat. His eyes showed no interest in me one way or another.

I leaned against the hood, catching my breath. What a dismal place to break down, stuck in the wilds of Arizona or maybe New Mexico. I wasn't sure exactly where I was. It all looked the same to me: hot, dusty, and not a civilized thing in sight.

The town didn't even rate a stop light. It was just a crossroads in the middle of a desert nowhere; one gas station with a whole lot of junked cars out back, a feed store, a place that looked like it was a combination grocery, restaurant, and bar. There were a few other buildings, but they were mostly boarded up and abandoned. The empty buildings didn't look much better than the occupied ones. Everything in sight was tilted one way or another, with sagging roofs and collapsing porches.

A faint breeze lifted a loose corner on the tin roof of the gas station. It slapped sharply again and again, echoing out over the desert quiet, but the man on the porch didn't seem to notice or care.

I walked over and climbed the warped wooden steps. There was a waist-high metal drink cooler at one end of the porch. I opened it, and the water was dark and cold, with large chunks of ice floating in it along with cans of soft drinks. I pulled out my handkerchief, soaked it in the ice-cold water, and wiped my face. Then I grabbed a can of Dr Pepper and cracked the top.

"Fifty cents," said the man.

I turned to him, and he still wasn't looking at me, just staring down the road that ran dusty and straight from here to forever without a turn. He might have been thirty, he might have been sixty. His face was as dry and parched as the land I'd been sputtering through for the last few days.

"In the can," he said.

Next to the cooler, an old coffee can had been nailed to the wall. There were maybe ten quarters in the bottom. I added two more, leaving me roughly six dollars to my name, and went over, leaned against the porch railing directly in front of the man, and took two long pulls on the soda.

He had to look up at me, and he did. His eyes were deep blue, and he had the look of a man who shaved with a cheap razor. He didn't say anything, just looked. I finished my drink. He still hadn't said anything.

"Busted down," I said. He didn't reply.

"Quit on me," I added.

He nodded, but otherwise didn't move.

"Think you could take a look?" I asked.

"I suppose," he said. When he got up, I wasn't sure if it was him or the chair creaking. He walked slowly to the truck and popped the hood.

"This here is a dead truck," he said. "Thrown a rod through the engine block, you did. Look right down here."

I looked but I couldn't tell anything. It was just engine pieces and oil. All I know about cars is how to scam people out of the titles, which key to put in the dash, and where the gas goes.

"Can you fix it?" I asked.

He snorted and shook his head. "Said it was *dead*. I did. And I mean what I say."

Things looked bad, but the truck was no great loss. I'd only had it a couple of months. Conned it off a widow-woman someplace in West Texas. Got her name out of the local paper, and all it took was a fake smile and the old Bible switch. I kicked the tires.

"Let you have it for two thousand," I said. "Don't feel like messing with it anymore. I'm a busy man, and ain't got time for automotive problems."

"Not interested," he said, slamming the hood.

"Fifteen hundred," I said. "You could part it out for that, easy."

He looked in the driver's window. "Cheap AM radio," he said. "No FM, no tape, no a/c. Give you ten dollars."

"An even thousand," I said. "Look at the tires."

Twenty minutes later, as I pulled my duffel bag out of the back, he had the title to the truck, and I had fifty dollars.

"You look like a man of taste," I lied. "A man like you ought to have a good watch. I've got my father's Rolex in my bag. Give you a good price on it."

He just snorted and went back to his chair on the porch. I crossed the street in search of a cold beer.

It took a minute for my eyes to adjust to the dark bar, which was simply two large rooms, one a restaurant and the other a lounge of sorts, attached to the general store. I use the word *lounge* loosely, as it was mostly a collection of odd clutter, a few booths, two overstuffed sofas, a beat-up bar with mismatched stools along one end, and a distinct lack of illumination. Well, I'd been in a lot worse. I dropped my bag on the floor by the bar and took one of the stools.

A young man was playing rotation pool by himself, and two men and a woman were sitting in a booth, nursing glasses of draft beer. The shelves behind the bar were littered with junk. Odd rusted farming tools sat next to katchina dolls and masks covered with feathers. A polar bear carved out of ivory sat between a ceramic Buddha and what appeared to be an African tribal mask. Not exactly the kind of junk I'd expected in a nowhere place like this.

The barmaid came out of the kitchen in back, wiping her hands on a towel. She was tall and slender, with blue eyes, and dark hair that seemed to be going in a thousand directions all at once. A few braided strands fell to each side of her face, tightly encased within beads of stone and silver.

"Hi," she said, with a friendly smile. "What can I get you?"

"Draft beer," I said. "It's dry out there."

"Oh, you get used to it," she said as she pulled the tap. "It's not so bad. You just passing through?"

"Guess so," I said. She was wearing a sleeveless tank top and a necklace with about a thousand little things hanging from it. Amid the general clutter, I could see a turquoise bear, an arrowhead, and a small silver unicorn. She drew the beer the way I like it, without much head, and as I set a five-dollar bill on the counter and took that first cold sip, she drew up a stool on the other side of the bar and sat down.

"Not much here to hold a person," I said. "All I've seen for the last three or four days is dust, cactus, and mountains that seem to hang on the horizon and never get any nearer."

"Oh, it's beautiful country," she said, fingering a small crystal of quartz that hung from her necklace. "And those mountains are sacred, you know; at least to some people."

"Couldn't prove it by me," I said. "They just look like something that's between me and where I want to be."

"And what place would that be?" she asked, with a smile. "Where would a man like you be headed?"

"Someplace else," I said, taking another hit of beer. "Where the action is."

"There's action here," she said. "Though probably not what you're looking for."

"I don't know what I'm looking for," I said honestly, finishing my beer and waiting while she drew another. "But I'm pretty sure it's not *here*." Her bracelets flashed as she pulled the beer. She wore several. Some were silver and turquoise, one was a simple copper band, others were strings of beadwork.

She set my beer down and locked her blue eyes with mine. "My name's Joline," she said. "Most people call me Jo. What's yours?"

"Mark Rogers," I said automatically, for some reason giving her my *real* name, something I never do with passing strangers. Dumb move.

I was rattled by the slip, and looked away. A good con man doesn't leave tracks like that.

"You seem to be a woman who appreciates fine jewelry, Jo," I said. "I've got a nice Rolex watch that used to belong to my dad. He left it for me in his will, but I've got no use for something so fancy. I could give you a good price on it."

I pulled one of the cheap imitations out of my duffel and set it between us. She gave me a hard look.

"It'd make a fine present for that special man in your life," I said, giving her my best fake smile.

She picked the five-dollar bill up off the counter and made change for the two beers, pushing it toward me and leaning back.

"No special man," she said, still looking hard. Then she cracked the slightest of smiles. "So, where'd you *really* get that watch, Mark?"

"Mexico," I said. "Bought twenty of them off a man in Tijuana. He wanted fifteen bucks apiece. We haggled. I was going to go five, but we settled on five-fifty. He said the extra fifty cents was for his kids."

"Did you believe him?" she asked. "About the kids?"

"Yes," I said, blushing. For a man who's pulled so many scams, you'd think I wouldn't have been pulled in by such an obvious ploy. But there'd been something about him; I don't know, but I *did* believe him. What a sucker!

She looked at me for a second, then turned and cracked the top on a tall can of beer. Handed it to me. "Let's take a walk," she said.

I reached to pick up my duffel bag. "You can leave that," she said.

"I'll carry it," I said, slinging the strap over my shoulder. A man like me can't be leaving sixteen imitation Rolex watches around where someone could steal his livelihood. I reached for my change on the bar.

"That'll be safe," she said firmly. I nodded and left it where it was.

"I'll watch the till," said the kid at the pool table as he sank the eleven ball. "I anticipate a real rush of customers," he added with a laugh, taking aim on the twelve.

"Thanks, Mike," Jo said. "This way."

I followed her through the kitchen, heavy with the smell of chilis, fried meat, and freshly baked bread. She gave one pot a stir, tasted the spoon, and turned down the gas. The screen door slammed behind us, and I was looking at a scene straight out of the '60s.

A wide dirt path, or maybe it had once been a narrow road, curved out from the back steps. It was heavily rutted and scarred. But what flashed me back were all the mismatched dwellings that lined the path.

I hadn't seen such a mishmash of funked-out, burned-out architecture since *Life* magazine, or maybe it was *People*, ran a photo spread on hippie communes back when I was a kid. No two places looked alike. The only thing they had in common was that they were all deserted and all falling apart. That didn't stop crazy Jo from *waving* at them as we walked down the path, her bracelets and—I now noticed—anklets, flashing in the late afternoon sun.

There were wrecked adobe houses and ruined log cabins. They sat beside disintegrating geodesic domes and caved-in sod huts that were nestled up next to rotting frame shanties and rusting travel trailers. A collapsed teepee leaned against something unidentifiable, apparently a home of sorts once made out of mud and sticks. All the hollow windows stared at us like the eyes of blind men, and it gave me the creeps. Jo didn't seem to mind, and she whistled and waved to them as she led me down the path, as though the empty windows were full of friends she was greeting. I was following a bedbug crazy woman, for sure.

At the end of the path was a small corral; hard-packed dirt with a few struggling weeds, surrounded by a collapsed fence of weathered junk lumber and dried tree limbs. Tumbleweeds were caught in the fence, and there was a pitiful swaybacked burro in the middle, pawing at the dirt and brushing flies off with its tail.

"Isn't this beautiful?" Jo asked, sitting on a rock. "This is my favorite place in the world."

I didn't know what to say, so I just shook my head. It looked like a dump to me.

"This place is magic," she said. "There are legends surrounding this area that go back to the beginning of time. The Indians considered it sacred ground. The Spanish built a mission here. It's a touchpoint to the spirit world. Can you feel it?"

"No," I said truthfully.

She smiled, fingering the unicorn around her neck. "It takes time," she said. "If the time is right, you will see. Your heart must be ready."

I could *see* all right, but what I *saw* was a mangy animal, a lot of desert, and some barren mountains off in the distance.

"So tell me about your father," she said. "The one that didn't leave you that fake Rolex in his will."

Which story to tell? I had several, all lies. In one, my father was a war hero. In another, he played baseball for the New York Yankees. Or he was a stock car driver, a successful surgeon, a missionary in Africa, it all depended on the situation.

"He died in prison," I said, and couldn't believe that the words were coming out of my mouth. "A riot or something. I was, I guess, about fifteen. He robbed gas stations, and sometimes liquor stores. I never got to see much of him. He was either traveling or in jail."

The burro had come over, and she was petting the sorry beast.

"My mother split when I was two. Mostly I was raised by my aunt and uncle. My Uncle Dan did occasional second-story work, stealing jewelry and cash, stuff like that. He hardly ever got caught, and he had a good lawyer. My aunt was into welfare fraud. She got about ten checks a month under different names. They treated me okay as long as I kept running scams and bringing in some cash. I mean, they didn't beat me all that much."

I looked away from Jo. How could I be saying this? The truth was a door I thought I'd closed a long time ago. I focused on the mountains in the distance. If I squinted just a bit, one of them looked a little like an eagle half-turned away from us.

"You ever been married, Mark?" she asked.

"Twice," I said. "Not very long either time. The first was a big mistake; we were too young. The second—Mary was her name—well, I was just bad to her. She was okay and tried hard, but I just didn't have it in me."

"What didn't you have in you?"

"I dunno," I said. "Love, compassion; whatever you want to call it, I fell short. She needed a stable life, and I had a bad case of the wanders. She was good to me, though. Better than I deserved."

"Life started in a place like this," she said, reaching down for a handful of sand and letting it trickle slowly through her fingers.

"Pardon?"

"Africa," she said, looking off into the distance. "Probably wasn't too different from this place. It was a harsh beginning, but we've come a long way since then. I think the heat's elemental, kind of like we were forged in some big furnace. Eventually we all come back. I think that once in our lives we find a place like this, and if our heart is clean, we'll see the magic. Do you still love her?"

"Mary?" The shift caught me unawares. For some reason, I'd been thinking about lions. "I guess I do. I don't know. She's somewhere in California, last I heard. Bakersfield. I try not to think about her too much. It was a long time ago, and we were different people."

"Some Indian tribes think we came from a spirit world. Some say it was from a cave not far from here. Others say we came from the sky. I like legends. Mostly I like them because they can *all* be true. It's a vast universe, and there's room for all kinds of things. What's important is what is in your *heart*. Did you always want to be a con man?"

I shrugged my shoulders. "It's what I know, I guess. Oh. I finished high school all right, and even sat in on a couple of junior college classes. Mostly art classes. But my uncle, he didn't see much use for that, and as long as I was staying at his house, I had to pull my own weight. I did okay."

"It gets cold here, too," she said. "Bitter cold. That's elemental, too. The Inuits believe that all animals have spirits and should be treated with respect, even when it is necessary to kill them for food. Are you hungry?"

Polar bears. Walrus. Flat tundra, harsh and cold.

"I guess I am," I said.

"Good," she said, hopping off the rock. "I'll put you to work and you can earn your dinner."

Walking back down the path to the restaurant, I was embarrassed at having told Jo so much. It wasn't like me at all to reveal so much of myself to anyone, much less to someone I hardly knew. My duffel bag was getting heavier. I wished I'd left it.

Someone must have been working on the lawns in front of the broken-down houses while we were at the corral. They looked a lot neater. It was only after we walked in the back door to the restaurant that I realized that I hadn't seen the buildings when I'd come into town.

Jo put me to work scrubbing pots and doing dishes. For a nowhere place, they served a lot of dinners. I didn't see most of the customers, since I was working in back, but once in a while someone would wander through the kitchen and talk to Jo or me. Everyone seemed to know everyone else. It was like a neighborhood bar and restaurant, except that there was no neighborhood.

There was no shortage of kids, though. It seemed like there were always one or two underfoot. They didn't seem to bother Jo, and she chatted with them as she cooked. They seemed to like her a lot.

One of the kids, her name was Donna, took a real interest in my rose tattoo. She was shy about it at first, but then I showed her how I could flex my arm and make the stem move. She thought that was great fun, and kept bringing her friends back into the kitchen to see it.

We kept busy all night. I enjoyed the work, and the chili Jo made was outstanding. The easy friendliness of the people coming back into the kitchen to visit made it seem like one big family. The time passed quickly, and I was surprised when Jo started closing down.

We sat in the quiet bar and talked for what seemed like hours. I told her things I'd never told anyone else. I even showed her my sketch book and she didn't laugh.

She said I had a lot of natural talent, and, with a little training, I could be a professional-level artist. I was embarrassed, but secretly pleased.

It wasn't like I was just jabbering. She really *listened* to what I said, like it was important. Not that is *was*, really; I was just telling her about how I grew up.

Jo said I could sleep on one of the sofas in the bar, and she brought in some sheets and a pillow. After she had gone, I looked in the cash register. It was full of money. She trusted me more than I trusted myself.

I closed the register and fell asleep, surrounded by all the ghostly artifacts that lined the walls of the bar.

The next morning. I followed my nose into the kitchen, where a pot of coffee was brewing. There was a note from Jo, saying that she'd gone to help a neighbor whose cow was having a difficult delivery. I poured a cup of coffee and went out the back door. I expected to feel bad for having said so much about myself the night before, but the truth was, I felt fine.

It was cool outside, the air was clear and sharp. As I walked down the path to check out that moth-eaten burro, the row of buildings didn't seem nearly as broken-down as they had the day before. I guess I was getting used to them.

I stopped short at the end of the path. The corral was gone, and in its place was a lush green field. A beautiful chestnut stallion was grazing in the middle, and looked up curiously when I dropped my coffee cup. He came over, stopping about three feet away from me.

Impossible! I reached out to touch him, and he casually stepped aside. I bent down and pulled up several sprigs of grass. They seemed real enough. I chewed on one, and it *tasted* like grass. It was all too strange. I put the grass in my shirt pocket.

As I hurried back down the path, I thought I saw a shadow move in a window of one of the adobe houses.

Jo had not returned, and I was the only one around. All the junk in the bar suddenly seemed ominous, as if each piece had a sinister story attached to it, and I started thinking about all the horror stories I'd read and all the *Twilight Zones* I'd watched on T.V. I was looking at my duffel bag and thinking about getting *out* of this crazy place before something horrible happened, when someone knocked on the door to the general store part of the building.

A man and a woman with three children stood outside the door. Their car was behind them, a rusted-out wreck loaded down with what must have been all their worldly belongings. Mattresses and a rocking chair were strapped to the roof.

"Sorry, we're closed," I said.

"Please, sir," said the man. "Milk for the children. I have one dollar." He slowly unbuttoned the front pocket on his frayed jeans jacket and pulled out a carefully folded dollar bill. He held it out for me to see.

I opened the door.

The man went over to the double glass doors where the drinks were kept. For one dollar, he might be able to get two small cartons of milk. I wondered how far that would get him. As he read the prices on the milk, the woman and their three kids—a boy and two girls—stood by the register.

"Daddy's got work in Mesilla," said the young boy proudly. "We're going to live in a real house this time."

"Hush, Danny," said the woman. "Don't bother the man." She looked up at me and smiled shyly. "Kids . . ." she said.

The woman was dressed plainly, in old, but neat and clean, clothes. A scarf around her neck was held in place by a beadwork pin, decorated with small feathers.

"That's a nice pin," I said.

"I made it for Mama," said one of the girls, holding the woman's hand tightly. "The last school we went to had an art class. It was fun, but we had to leave."

"I do like that pin," I said. "I couldn't talk you into trading it for some groceries, could I?"

I saw hope flash through the woman's face, but she covered it well, and looked down at her daughter. "That would have to be Lisa's decision," she said. "I can't trade a gift."

"Would it be enough for a jar of peanut butter and some crackers?" the girl asked.

I nodded. "And a little more," I said.

"Give him the pin, Mama. I can make you *another* one now that I know how. And they'll probably have an art class at the school in Mesilla. It's a big place, and I *love* peanut butter."

I had to send them back three times to get more groceries. They filled four bags, and I slipped a twenty-dollar bill down in the bottom of one of the bags, so that they wouldn't find it until later. When they left, I put the CLOSED sign back in the window and went into the dark bar.

The pin looked good on a shelf next to a carved piece of driftwood. I picked up my duffel bag.

"Some con man *you* are," said Jo, with a gentle laugh, from the darkness. "Five cents' worth of beads and a few chicken feathers for all that food!"

"I was going to leave you money for it," I said. "How long have you been here?"

"Long enough. And you know I don't care about the money."

"I was fixing to leave," I said. "This place does strange things to me."

"It does nothing but bring out what is *already* there," she said. "And I want to show you something before you go."

She turned and went through the kitchen. I set my duffel bag down and followed her out the back door.

There was magic in the air. The houses along the path shimmered and shifted as we walked past them. I held out the blades of grass.

"I found these," I said.

"You found more than that," she said. "Look."

We had reached the end of the path. An impossibly white unicorn stood in the middle of a field lush with wildflowers. It walked up to Jo and nuzzled her hair. She turned to me and smiled.

"Everyone comes to a place like this once in their lives," she said. "If your heart is right, you will recognize it for what it is. If your soul is hardened, you will pass it by and never know."

She walked over to me and kissed my cheek. Then she went back to the unicorn, and, with a fluid movement, pulled herself onto its back. They looked perfect together, as if they were one animal.

"Gook luck, Mark Rogers," she said. "You have found your path. To walk it or not is *your* decision."

She nudged the unicorn, and it turned to the right, rearing up slightly and then breaking into a gallop across the lush field of grass, which now seemed to stretch unbroken all the way to the distant mountains.

Smoke was curling from the first adobe house I passed on my way back. An old couple sat on the front porch. They waved to me and called my name. I waved back to them, as I did to all the others who lived in this place of spirit.

I got a ride with the first car passing through, driven by a heavyset man with a red beard. The back seat was full of sample cases, so I crammed my duffel down at my feet.

"Thanks," I said, settling in.

"No problem," he said, putting the car in gear. "I like to have someone to talk to. Besides, that looks like a nowhere place to be stuck looking for a ride."

"It has its good points," I said

"Not for me. I'm a traveling salesman, and I've seen a thousand one-horse towns like that. Not worth bothering with. No profit there. What do you do when you're not hitching rides?"

"I'm studying to be an artist," I said. I looked back over my shoulder, and, as I watched, the houses behind the restaurant wavered and faded from view. The pasture was gone. Nothing but sand.

"Say, fellow, you don't have the time, do you? I've got an appointment scheduled in Flagstaff and my watch is broke."

I reached down into my duffel and pulled out one of the watches. The battery was still good, and it was keeping time. I passed it to him.

"Nice watch," he said. "Rolex, isn't it? Wish I had one, but I bet they cost a bundle."

I paused for a moment.

"No," I said. "It's just a cheap imitation. Keep it. I appreciate the ride."

Somewhere I could feel doors slamming. But, at the same time, other doors were opening.

"Thanks," he said. "So, how far are you going?"

"Bakersfield," I said, after a moment. "I'm going all the way to Bakersfield."

A THOUSAND FLOWERS

Margo Lanagan

I WALKED AWAY FROM THE FIRE, in among the trees. I was looking for somewhere to relieve myself of all the ale I'd drunk, and I had told myself, goodness knows why, in my drunkenness, that I must piss where there were no flowers.

And this, in the late-spring forest, was proving impossible, for whatever did not froth or bow with its weight of blossoms was patterned or punctuated so by their fresh little faces, clustered or sweetly solitary, that a man could not find any place where one of them—some daisy closed against the darkness, some spray of maiden-breath testing the evening air—did not insist, or respectfully request, or only lean in the gloaming and hope, that he not stain and spoil it with his leavings.

"Damn you all," I muttered, and stumbled on, and lurched on. The fire and the carousing were now quite a distance behind me, no more than a bar or two of golden light among the tree-trunks, crossed with cavorting dancers, lengthened and shortened by the swaying of storytellers. The laughter itself and the music were becoming part of the night-forest noise, a kind of wind, several kinds of bird-cry. My bladder was *paining* me, it was so full. Look, I could trample flower after flower underfoot in my lurching—I could *kill* plant after plant that way! Why could I not stop, and piss on one, from which my liquids would surely drip and even be washed clean again, almost directly, by a rain shower, or even a drop of dew plashing from the bush, the tree, above?

It became a nightmare of flowers, and I was alone in it, my filth dammed up inside me and a pure world outside offering only innocents' faces, pale, fresh, unknowing of drunkenness and body dirt, for a man to piss on— which, had he any manners in him at all, he could not do.

But don't these flowers grow from dirt themselves? I thought desperately. *Aren't they rooted in all kinds of rot and excrements, of worm and bird and deer, hedgehog and who knows what else?* I scrabbled to unbutton my trousers, my mind holding to this scrap of sense, but fear also clutched in me, and flowers crowded my eyes, and breathed sweetness up my nose. I could have wept.

It is all the drink, I told myself, *that makes me bother this way, makes me mind.* "Have another swig, Manny!" Roste shouted in my memory, thumping me in the back, thrusting the pot at me with such vigour, two drops of ale flew out, catching my cheek and my lip with two cool tiny blows. I gasped and flailed among the thickening trees. They wanted to fight me, to wrestle me down, I was sure.

I made myself stop; I made myself laugh at myself. "Who do you think you are, Manny Foyer," I said, "to take on the whole forest? There, that oak. That's clear enough, the base of it. Stop this foolishness, now. Do you want to piss yourself? Do you want to go back to the fire piss-panted? And spend tomorrow's hunt in the smell of yourself?"

I propped myself against the oak trunk with one hand. I relieved myself most carefully against the wood. And a good long wash and lacquering I gave it—aah, is there any better feeling? I stood and stood, and the piss poured and poured. Where had I been keeping it all? Had it pressed all my organs out to the sides of me while it was in there? I had not been much more than a piss-flask—no wonder I could scarce think straight! Without all this in me, I would be so light, so shrunken, so comfortable, it might only re-quire a breath of the evening breeze to blow me like a leaf back to my fellows.

As I shook the very last droplets into the night, I saw that the moon was rising beyond the oak, low, in quite the wrong place. Had I wandered farther than I thought, as far as Artor's Outlook? I looked over my shoulder. No, there still was firelight back there, as if a house-door stood open a crack, showing the hearth within.

The moon was not the moon, I saw. It gave a nicker; it moved. I sidled round the tree very quietly, and there in the clearing beyond, the creature glowed in the starlight.

Imagine a pure white stallion, the finest conformed you have ever seen, so balanced, so smooth, so long-necked, you could picture how he would gallop, easy-curved and rippling as water, with the mane and tail foaming on him. He was muscled for swiftness, he was *big* around the heart, and his legs were straight and sound, firm and fine. He'd a grand head, a king's among horses, such as is stitched upon banners, or painted on shields in a baron's banquet hall. The finest pale velvet upholstered it, with the veins tracing their paths beneath, running his good blood about, warming and enlivening every neat-made corner of him.

Now imagine that out of that fine forehead, just as on a shield, spears a battle-spike—of narwhal-horn, say, spiraling like that. Then take away the spike's straps and buckles, so that the tusk grows straight from the horse's brow—*grows*, yes, from the skull, sprouts from the velvet brow as if naturally, like a stag-antler, like the horn of a rhinockerous.

Then . . .

Then add magic. I don't know how you will do this if you have not seen it; I myself only saw it the once and bugger me if I can describe it, the quality that tells you a thing is bespelled, or sorcerous itself. It is luminosity of a kind, cool but strong. All-encompassing and yet very delicate, it trickles in your bones; slowly it lifts the hairs on your legs, your arms, your chest, in waves like fields of high-grown grass under a gentle wind. And it thins and hollows the sounds of the world, owl hoots and rabbit scutters, and beyond them it rumors of vast rustlings and seethings, the tangling and untangling of the workings of the universe, this giant nest of interminable snakes.

When something like this appears before you, let me tell you, you must look at it; you must look at nothing else; your eyes are pulled to it like a falcon to the lure. Twinned to that compulsion is a terror, swimming with the magic up and down your bones, of being seen yourself, of having the creature turn and lock you to its slavery forever, or freeze you with its gaze; whatever it wishes, it might do. It has the power, and you yourself have nothing, and *are* nothing.

It did not look at me. It turned its fine white head just a touch my way, then tossed its mane, as if to say, *How foolish of me, even to notice such a drab being!* And then it moved off, into the trees at the far side of the clearing.

The rhythm of its walking beat in my muscles, and I followed; the sight of it drew me like pennants and tent-tops on a tourney-field, and I could not but go after. Its tail, at times, braided flowers into itself, then plaited silver threads down its strands, then lost those also and streamed out like weed in brook-water. Its haunches were pearly and moony and muscular. I wanted to catch up to its head and ask it, ask it . . . What impossible thing could I ask? And what if it should turn and answer—how terrible would that be? So, all confusion, I stumbled after, between the flowers of the forest, across their carpet and among their curtains and beneath their ribbons and festoons.

We came to a streamside; the creature led me into the water, stirring the stars on the surface. And while I watched a trail of them spin around a dimple left by his passing, he vanished—whether by walking away, or by leaping up and becoming stars himself, or by melting into the air, I could not say, but I was standing alone, in only starlight, my feet numb and my ankles aching with the water's snow-melt cold.

I stepped out onto the muddy bank; it was churned with many hoof-prints, all unshod that I could distinguish. There was no magic anywhere, only the smell of the mud and of wet rock, and behind that, like a tapestry behind a table, of the forest and its flowers.

Something lay higher up the bank, which the horse had fetched me to see. It was a person's body; I thought it must be dead, so still did it lie.

Another smell warned me as I walked closer on my un-numbing feet, on the warm-seeming mud, where the trampled grass lay bruised and tangled. It was not the smell of death, though. It was a wild smell, exciting, something like the sea and something like . . . I don't know, the first breath of spring, perhaps, of new-grown greenness somewhere, beckoning you across snow.

It was a woman—no more than a girl—and indecent. Lace, she wore, lace under-things only, and the lace was torn so badly about her throat that it draggled, muddily, aside and showed me her breast, that gleamed white as that horse's flank, with the bud upon it a soft round stain, a dim round eye.

Where do I begin with the rest of her? I stood there stupidly and stared and stared. Her storm-tossed petticoats were the finest weavings, broiderings, laces I had seen so close. Her muddied feet were the finest formed, softest, whitest, pitifullest feet I had laid eyes on in my life. The skirts of the underclothes were wrenched aside from her legs, but not from her thatch and privates, only as far as the thigh, and there was blood up there, at the highest place I could see, some dried and some shining fresher.

Her hair, my God! A great pillow of it, a great swag like cloth, torn at the edges, ran its shreds and frayings out into the mud. It was dark, but not black; I thought in proper light it might show reddish lights. Her face, white as milk, the features delicate as a faery's, was cheek-pillowed on this hair, the open lips resting against the knuckle and nail of one thumb; in her other hand, as if she were in the act of flinging it away, a coronet shone gold, and with it were snarled a few strands of the hair, that had come away when she tore the crown from her head.

I crouched a little way from this princess, hissing to myself in awe and fright. I could not see whether she breathed; I could not feel from here whether she was warm.

I stood and tiptoed around her, and crouched again, next to the crown. What a creation! I had never seen such smithing or such gems. You could not have paid me enough to touch the thing, it gave off such an atmosphere of power.

I was agitated to make the girl decent. I have sisters; I have a mother. They would not want such fellows as those back at the fire to happen on them in such a state. I reached across the body and lifted the lace, and the breast's small weight fell obedient into the pocket and hid itself. Then, being crouched, I waddled most carefully down and tried to make sense of the lace and linen there, not wanting to expose the poor girl further with any mistaken movement of the wrong hem or tatter. I decided which petticoat-piece would restore her modesty. I reached out to take it up with the very tips of my fingers.

A faint step sounded on the mudded grass behind me. I had not time to turn. Four hands, strong hands, the strongest I had ever felt, caught me by my upper arms, and lifted me as you lift a kitten, so that its paws stiffen out into the air searching for something to grasp.

"We have you." They were soldiers, with helmets, with those sinister clipped beards. They threw me hard to the ground away from the princess, and the fence they formed around me bristled with blades. Horror and hatred of me bent every back, deformed every face.

"You will die, and slowly," said one, in deepest disgust, "for what you done to our Lady."

They took me to the queen's castle, and put me in a dungeon there. Several days, they kept me, on water-soup and rock-bread, and I was near despair, for they would not tell me my fate nor allow me to send word to any family, and I could well imagine I was to spend the rest of my days pacing the rough cell, my brief time in the colorful out-world replaying itself to madness in my head.

Guards came for me, though, the third day. "Where are you taking me?" I said.

"To the block, man," said one.

My knees went to lily-stalks. The other guard hauled me up and swore. "Don't make trouble, Kettle," he told his fellow. "We don't want to bring him before them having shitted himself."

The other chuckled high, and slapped my face in what he doubtless thought a friendly way. "Oh no, lad, 'tis only a little conference with Her Majesty for you. A little confabulation regarding your misadventures." Which was scarcely less frightening than the block.

From the stony under-rooms of the castle, up we went. The floor flattened and the walls dried out and we passed the occasional terrifying thing: a suit of armour from the Elder Days; a portrait of a royal personage in silks bright as sunlit water, in lace collars like insect wings; a servant with a tray with goblets and decanter so knobbed and bejeweled you could scarce tell what they were.

"Here's the place," said the humorous guard, as we arrived at a doorway where people were waiting, gentlemen hosed and ruffed and cloaked, with shining-dressed hair, and two abject men about to collapse off that bench, they leaned so spineless and humiliated.

The guards let us straight in, to a room so splendid, I came very close to filling my pants. It was all hushed with the richest tapis, and ablaze with candles, and God help me, there was a throne, and the queen sat upon it, and at the pinnacle of all her clothing, all her posture, above her bright, severe eyes and her high forehead filled with brains, a fearsome crown nestled so close in her silvering reddish hair, it might have grown into place there. Under her gaze, my very bones froze within me.

"Give your name and origins," said the guard, nudging me.

"My name is Manny Foyer, of Piggott's Leap, Your Majesty."

"Now bow," the guard muttered.

I bowed. Oh, my filthy boots were sad on that bright carpet! But I would rather look on them than on that royal face.

"Daughter?" The queen did not take her attention from my face.

I gaped. Was she asking me if I *had* a daughter? Why would she care? Had she confused me with some other offender?

But a voice came from the shadows, beside, behind the throne. "I have never seen him in my life. I don't know why he has been brought here."

The queen spoke very slowly and bitterly. "Take a *close* look, daughter."

Out of the shadows walked the princess, tall and splendidly attired, her magnificent hair taken up into braids and knots and paddings so elaborate, they almost overwhelmed her little crown. Her every movement, and her white, fine-modelled face, spoke disdain—for me, for her mother, for the dignitaries and notables grouped about in their bright or sober costumes, in their medals and accoutrements or the plainer cloaks of their own authority.

She circled me. Her gown's heavy fabrics rustled and swung and shushed across the carpet. Then she looked to her mother, and shrugged. "He is entirely a stranger to me, Madam."

"Is it possible he rendered you insensible with a blow to your head, so that you did not see his face?"

The princess regarded me, over her shoulder. She was the taller of us, but I was built stockier than her, though almost transparent with hunger at this moment.

"Where is my constable? Where is Constable Barry?" said the queen impatiently, and when he was rattled forth behind me, "Tell me the circumstances of this man's arrest."

Which he did. I had my chance to protest, when he traduced me, that I had not touched the lady, that I had only been adjusting her clothing so that my fellows would not see her so exposed. I thought I sounded most breathless and feeble, but while the constable continued with his story I caught a glance from the princess, that was very considering of me, and contained some amusement, I thought.

There was a silence when he finished. The queen dandled my life in her hands. I was near to fainting; a thickness filled my ears and spots of light danced at the edges of my sight.

"He does not alter your story, daughter?" said the queen.

"I maintain," said the magnificent girl, "that I am pure. That no man has ever touched me, and certainly not this man."

The two of them glared at each other, the coldest, most rigid-faced, civilized glare that ever passed between two people.

"Free him," said the queen, with a tiny movement of her finger.

Constable Barry clicked his tongue, and there was a general movement and clank of arms and breastplates. They removed me from that room—I dare say I walked, but truly it was more that they wafted me, like a cloud of smoke that you fan and persuade towards a chimney.

They put me out the front of the castle, with half a pound-loaf of hard bread to see me home. It was raining, and cold, and I did not know my way, so I had quite a time of it, but eventually I did find my road home to Piggott's, and into the village I tottered late next day.

My mam welcomed me with relief. My dad wanted my word I had done no wrong before he would let me in the house. My fellows, farm men and hunters both, greeted me with such ribaldry I scarce knew where to look. "I never touched her!" I protested, but however hard I did, still they drank to me and clapped my back and winked at me and made unwholesome reference. "White as princess-skin, eh, Manny?" they would say, or, "Oh, he's not up for cherry-picking with us, this one as has wooed royalty!"

"Take no notice, son," Mam advised. "The more you fuss, the longer they will plague you."

And so I tried only to endure it, though I would not smile and join in their jesting. They had not seen her, that fine girl in her amussment; they had not been led to her through the flowering forest by a magical horse with a horn in its head; they had not quailed under her disdain, or plumped up again with hope when she had looked more kindly on them. They had not been in that dungeon facing their death, nor higher in the palace watching the queen's finger restore them to life. They did not know what they spoke of, so lightly.

I thought it all had ended. I had begun to relax and think life might return to being more comfortable, the night Johnny Blackbird took it into his head to goad me. He was a man of the lowest type; I knew even as I swung at him that Mam would be disgusted—Dad also—by my having let such an earwig annoy me with his crawlings. But he had gone on and on, pursuing me and insisting, full of rude questions and implications, and I was worn out with being so fecking noble about the whole business, when I had never asked to be led away and put beside a princess; I had never wanted picking up by queen-people and bringing into royal presences; most of all I had not wanted, not for a moment, to touch even as much of her clothing as I touched, of that young lady, let alone her flesh. I had never thought a smutty thought about her, for though she were a beauty she were much too imposing for a man like me to do more than bow down before, to slink away from.

Anyway, once I had landed my first thump, to the side of Blackbird's head, the relief of it was so great, I began to deliver on him all the blows and curses I had stored up till that moment. And hard blows they were, and well calculated, and curses that surged like vomit from my depths, so sincere I hardly recognized my own voice. He called pax almost straight away, the little dung-piece, but I kept into him until the Pershron twins pulled me off, by which time his face was well colored and pushed out of shape, the punishment I'd given him.

After that night people left me alone, and rather more than I wanted. They respected me, though there was the smell of fear, or maybe embarrassment— bad feeling, anyhow—in their respect. And I could not jolly them out of it, having never been that specimen of a jolly fellow. So I tended then to gloom off by myself, to work when asked and well, but less often to join the lads at the spring for a swim, or at the Brindle for a pot or two.

We were stooking early hay when the soldiers came again. One moment I was easy in the sunshine, watching how each forkful propped and fell; the next I came aware of a crowding down on the road like ants at jam, and someone running up the field—Cal Devonish it was, his shirt frantic around him. As soon as he was within the distance of me he cried, "They are come for you, Manny!" And I saw my death in his face, and I ran too.

The chase was messy and short. I achieved the forest, but I was not long running there before my foot slipped on a root, then between two roots, and the rest of my body fled over it and the bone snapped, above my ankle. I sat up and extricated myself, and I was sitting there holding my own foot like a broken baby in both my hands, knowing I would never run again, when the soldiers—how had they crossed the hayfield so fast?—came thundering at me out of the trees.

"What have I done?" I cried piteously. They wrenched me up. The leg-pain shouted up me, and flared off the top of my head as screams. "'Tis no less true now, what I said, than it was in the spring!"

"Why did you run, then," said one of them, "if you are so innocent?" And he kicked my broken leg, then slapped me awake when I swooned from the pain.

Up came Constable Barry, his face a creased mess of disgust and delight. "You *filth*." He spat in my face; he struck me to the ground. "You animal." He kicked me in my side, and I was sure he broke something there. "Getting your spawn upon our princess, spoiling and soiling the purest creature ever was."

"But I never!"

But he kicked me in the mouth, then, and thank God the pain of that shatterment washed straight back into my head, and wiped his ugly spittle-face from my sight, and the trees and the white sky behind it.

Straight up to the foot of the tower he rode, the guard. He dismounted jingling and untied a sacking bag from his saddle. It was stained at the bottom, dark and plentifully.

"You have someone in that tower, I think, Miss," he says to me. "A lady?"

"We do." I could not tear my gaze from the sack.

"I'm charged to show her something, and take her response to the Majesty."

"Very well," I said.

He followed me in; I conveyed his purpose to Joan Vinegar.

"Oh yes? And what is the thing you're to show?" And she stared at the bag just as I had, knowing it were some horror.

"I'm to show the leddy. I've no instructions to let anyone else see."

"I'll take you up." Joan was hoping for a look anyway. So was I. He was mad if he thought we would consent to not see. Nothing ever happened here; we were hungry for events, however grim.

Up they went, and I walked back outside, glanced to my gardening and considered it, then followed my musings around to the far side of the tower, under the arrow-slit that let out of the lady's room.

It was a windless day, and thus I heard clearly her first cry. If you had cared about her at all, it would have broke your heart, and now I discovered that despite the girl's general lifelessness, and her clear stupidity in getting herself childered when some lord needed her purity to bargain with, I did care. She was miserable enough already—what had he brought to make her miserabler?

Well, I knew, I knew. But there are some things you know but will not admit until you have seen them yourself. The bag swung black-stained before my mind's eye, a certain shape, a certain weight, and the lady cried on up there, not in words but in wild, unconnected noises, and there were thuds, too, of furniture, a crash of pottery. I drew in a sharp breath; we did not have pots to spare here, and the lady knew it.

I hurried back to the under-room. Her shrieks sounded down the stairs, and then the door slammed on them, and the man's boots hurried down, and there he was in the doorway, a blank, determined look on his face, the bag still in his hand, but looser, only held closed, not tied.

He thrust it at Joan as she arrived white-faced behind him. "Bury this," he said.

She held it away from her skirts.

"I'll be off," he said.

"You'll not sleep, sir, or take a bite?" said I.

"Not with that over me." He looked at the ceiling. We could hear the lady, but not down the stairs; her noise poured out the arrow-slit of her room, and bounced off the rocks outside, and in at the tower door. "I would sooner eat on a battlefield, with cavalry coming on, both sides."

And he was gone. Joan and I could not move, transfixed by the repellent bag.

"She has gone mad," I said.

"For the moment, yes," said Joan, as if she could keep things ordinary with her matter-of-fact tone.

We exchanged a long look. She read my question and my fear; she was not stupid. "Outside," she said. "We don't want to sully our living-place wi' this. Fetch the spade."

We stepped out in time for a last sight of the horseman a-galloping away into the trees. The grey light flared and fluttered unevenly, like my heartbeats. Joan bore the bag across the yellow grass, and I followed her into the edge of the forest, where we had raised the stone for old Cowlin. Joan sat on Cowlin's stone. She leaned out and laid the bag on the grass. "Dig," she said, pointing. "Right there."

She did not often order me about, only when she was very tired or annoyed, but I did not think to question her. I dug most efficiently, against the resistance of that bastard mountain soil, quite different from what we had managed to rot and soften into the vegetable garden. The last time I had dug this was for Cowlin's grave, and the same sense of death was closed in around us, and of the smallness of our activity among the endless pines, among the endless mountains.

While I dug, Joan sat recovering, her fingers over her mouth as if she would not let words out until she had ordered them better in her head. Every time I glanced at her she looked a different age, glistening a wide-eyed baby the once, then crumpled to a crone, then a fierce matron in her full strength. And she would not meet my eye.

"There," I said eventually. "'Tis done." The mistress's wails in the tower were weakening now; you might imagine them whistles of wind among the rocks, had your very spine not attuned itself to them like a dowser's hazel-rod bowing towards groundwater.

Joan sprang up. She brought the bag. She plunked it in my digging. Then she cast me a look. "You'll not be content 'til you see, will you?"

"No."

"It will haunt your dreams, girl."

"I don't care," I said. "I will *die* if you don't show me."

"I will show you, then." And with her gaze fixed brutal on my face she flicked back the corner of the sacking.

I looked a long time; I truly looked my fill. Joan had thought I would squirm and weep, maybe be sick, but I did not. I'd seen dead things before, and beaten things.

"It is her lover," I said. "The father of her bab," I added after some more of looking.

Joan did not answer. Who else would he be?

I touched him, his hair, his cold skin; I closed the eyelid that was making him look out so frightening. I pressed one of the bruises at his jaw. I could not hurt him; I could push as hard as I liked. But I was gentle. I felt gentle; there is nothing like the spectacle of savagery to bring on a girl's gentleness.

"I am astounded she recognized him," I said.

"Oh, she did," said Joan. "In an instant."

I looked a little longer, turned the head to both sides and made sure I saw all there was to see. "Well, for certain he don't look very lovable now."

"Well, he was once. Listen to her noise, would you?"

I glanced behind me, as if I might be able to see the thin skein of it winding from the window. One last glance at the beaten head, at the mouth—that had been done with a boot-toe, that had—to fix the two of them together in my mind, and then I laid him in the sacking in the ground, and I put the cloth over his face and then some of the poor soil on top of that, and proceeded to hide him away.

Joan Vinegar woke me, deep that night. "Come, girl, it is time for midwifery."

"What?" Muzzily I swam up from my dream. "There are *months* to go yet."

"Oh no there ain't," she said. "Today has brought it on, the sight of her man. She is in the throes now."

"What should I do?" I said, frightened. "You have not had time to show me."

"Assist, is all. Just do as I tell. I must get back to her. Bring all the cloths you can find, and a bowl and jug of water." And she was gone.

I rose and dressed and ran barefoot across the grass and rocks to the tower. The silence in the night, the smaller silence in the tower; the parcels of herbs opened on the table; the bowl and jug there, ready for me to fill; the stove a crack open, with the fire just woken inside—all of a sudden I was awake, with the eeriness of it, with the unusualness, with the imminence of a bab's arriving

Up I went with my bringings, into the prison-room. It was all cloth and candlelight up there, the lady curled around herself on the creased bed. She looked asleep, or dead, as far as I could see from my fearful glances. The fire was built up big, and it was hotter in here than I had ever known it, hotter than it ought to be, for the lady was supposed to enjoy no comforts, but find every aspect of her life here a punishment.

Joan took the cloths from me, took the jug and bowl. "Make up a tea," she said, "of just the chamomile, for now. Lots of blooms, lots of leaves, about a fifth what is in my parcel there, in the middling pot."

"No," murmured the lady, steeling herself for a pain, and Joan almost pushed me outside. I hurried away. I had only heard screams and dire stories of childbed, and the many babs brought healthy from its trials had done nothing to counter my terror of it.

Down in the lower room I went to work, with Joan's transmitted voice murmuring in the stairway door, wordless, like a low wind in a chimney. I tidied the fire and put the pot on, then sat with the stove open and my face almost in the flames, drinking of their orange-ness and stinging heat, listening for a sound from the lady above, which did not come; she must noise loudly for her dead man, but stay stalwart for babbing, it seemed. They are a weird folk, the nobility; they do nothing commonsensically.

I took up the tea, and Joan told me the next thing to prepare, and so began the strange time, that seemed to belong neither to night nor to day, but to happen as an extremely slow and vivid dream. Each time I glanced in at the door the lady would be somewhere else, but motionless—on the bed, crouched beside it, bracing herself against the chimney breast, her hair fallen around her like a cloak, full of snarls and tangles. Joan would hurry at me, as if I must not be seeing even as much as I saw. She would take what I had brought, and instruct me what next she needed. Downstairs was all smells and preparations—barley mush with honey and medicine-seeds crushed into it, this tea and that, from Joan's store of evil-smelling weeds, warmed-over soup for all of us, to sustain us in our various labors.

The fear came and went. Had I a task to do, I was better off, for it took my whole mind to ensure in my tiredness that I performed it right. When I was idle by the stove with Joan murmuring in the stairs, that was worse, when I could not envisage what awfulness might be happening up there, when only the lady's occasional gasp or word, pushed out of her on the force of a birth pain, stoked up my horrors. "Girl?" Joan would come to the door and say down the stairs, not needing to raise her voice. And then my fear would flare worst, at what I might glimpse when I went up, at what I might hear.

Then a new time began, and I could avoid the room no longer. Joan made me bring up the chair from the kitchen, and sit on it, and become a chair of sorts myself, with the lady's arms hooked over my thighs, my lap full of her hair. "Give her a sip," Joan would say, or, "Lift the hair off her neck and fan her there; she is hot as Hades." And in between she would be talking up into the lady's face, crouched before us, and though she was tired and old and aproned, I could see how she once must have been, and how her man might still desire her even now, her kind, fierce face, her living, watching eyes, her knowing what to do, after child after child after child of her own. She knew how to look after all of us, the laboring lady and the terrified girl assisting; she knew how to damp those two great forest fires, grief and fear, contain them and stop them taking over the world; she was in her element, doing what she was meant to do.

In the middle of one of the pains the lady reared, and there was a rush and a gush, and Joan exchanged sodden cloth for dry, out of sight there, under the lady's nightgown. She looked up exultant, over the bump of the baby. "That's your waters popped," she said. "Not long now, love-a-do."

I was almost in a faint, such a strong scent billowed out from the soaked cloth beside us, from the lady herself. Jessamine, I thought. No, elderflower. No—but as fast as I could name the flowers, the scent grew past them and encompassed others, sweet and sharp, so different and so strong my mind was painted now with scattered pinks, now with blood-black roses and with white daphne.

"Oh," I whispered, and drank another deep breath of it, "I can almost *taste* the sweetness!"

The lady's head lolled to the side; released from the pain, she faded into momentary sleep, her face almost rapturous with the relief. Beyond her Joan held the nightgown out, and watched below, shaking her head. "What is coming?" she said softly. "What is coming out of you, lovely girl?"

"A little horse," said the lady in her sleep. "A little white horse."

"Well, that will be a sight." Joan laughed gently, and arranged her cloths beneath.

What came, four pains and pushes later, was of course not a horse, but a child—but a child so strange, a horse might almost have been less so. For the child was white—not white in contrast to Moorish or Mongol or African prince, but white like a lily, white like the snow, like the moon, entirely without color, except . . . He was a boy-child, and the boy spout on him was tipped with wrinkled green like a bud, and the boy-sacks on him—a good size for one so small—were also green, and darker, like some kind of fruiting, or vegetable.

He was small, he was unfinished, he did not live long. Joan gave him into the lady's arms, and I sat behind her on the floor and supported her, and over her shoulder I watched as he took a few pained breaths of the sweet, heated air, and then took no more, but lay serene. He was barely human, barely arrived; he was an idea of a person that had not got quite properly uttered, not properly formed out of slippery white clay; and yet a significance hovered all round him quite disproportionate to his size. He smelled divine, and he looked it, a tiny godlet, precise in all his features, delicate, pale, powerful like nothing I had seen before, like nothing I have seen since.

"What is that on his forehead?" I said. Perhaps all newborns had it, and I was ignorant.

Joan shrugged, touched the crown of his tiny head. "Some kind of carbuncle?"

The lady held him better to the light.

"It looks like a great pearl there," I said. "Set in his skin. It has a gleam."

"Yes, a pearl," said the lady distantly, as if she had expected no less, and she kissed the bump of it.

Joan gave her a cloth, and she wrapped him, her hands steady, though I had begun to cry behind her, and were dripping onto her shoulder.

There was business to deal with—a body that has birthed needs to rid itself of all sorts of muck, and be washed, and dressed cleanly, and laid in a clean bed to rest, and it can only move slowly through these things. We proceeded calmly, Joan saying what I should do, task after simple task, and always I was aware of the little master, in his wrappings there, by the fire as if to keep his small deadness warm, and the dance we were doing around him, in his sweet air, in the atmosphere of him.

When she was abed the lady asked for him, and the three of us sat there in a row very quiet, and she held him, unwrapped, lying along her up-propped thighs. Quite lifeless, he was, quite bloodless, with the scrap of green cord hanging from his narrow belly; he ought to have looked pitiful, but I could feel through the lady's arm against mine, through the room's air, through the *world*, that none of us pitied him.

"He looks so wise," I whispered. "Like a wise little old man."

"Wise and wizened," said the lady. I have never known anyone so tranquil and strong as this lady, I thought. Whoever she was, all I wanted that night was to serve her forever, me and Joan together in that tower, bonded till death by this night's adventure, by the bringing of this tiny lad to the world, and the losing of him from it.

In the morning the flower-scent was gone; the fire had died, the tower was cold, and the air felt rotten with grief. *He will haunt your dreams*, Joan had told me, of that lover's head, but in fact he filled my waking mind, so well remembered in all his details that it was as if a picture of him—his ragged neck-flesh, the turned-up eye—went before me, painted on a cloth, wherever I went, to the well or the woods or wherever. And when he was not there, his son, pale as a corpse-candle, floated before me instead.

The lady gave the bab into Joan's hands, a tight-wrapped, tiny parcel, banded and knotted with lengths of her own hair. "Oh, of course!" I said when Joan brought it down the stair. "So that he always has his mam around him! And such a color, so warm!"

She laid him on the table. "So we've more digging to do, for him and the other birth-leavings. It is best to bury those, with proper wordage and herbery."

"How is she?" I said timidly. I was unnerved that our bond was gone, that we were three separate people again.

"Resting," said Joan. "Peaceful."

Then I must have looked very lost and useless, because she came to where I sat on the bench, and stood behind me with her hands on my shoulders, and she held me together while I cried into my apron, and "There, there," she said, and "There, there," but calmly, and patiently, as if she did not expect me ever to stop, but would stand quiet and radiant behind me, however long I took to weep myself dry.

I sent the girl home. She was in too much distress to be much use to me, and I could not let her near the lady. I thought it odd—she had hardly been squeamish at all when that head was brought in. I had had hopes for her. But the bab undid her, whether its birth or its death or its strangeness, or the fact that its mam shed no tears over it, but sank straight back away into the stupor we were used to, as if she had never been childered, as if she had never raved and suffered over her man's death.

With the rider who brought supplies and took the girl away, I sent a message to Lord Hawley, that the mistress was delivered of a dead child, and what were we to do now? For my contract with him had only specified up to the birth, but now that the bab was gone, could not some other woman, without midwifing skills, be brought to the task of guarding my lady? For though I could use the good money he was paying, I felt a fraud here now, when there were plenty of childered women in my own village to whom I could be truly useful, rather than playing nursemaid here.

For answer he sent money, money extra upon what he had promised, as if the death of the bab had been my doing and he wanted to show me favor for it. And he bid me stay on, while they sorted themselves out at court about this state of affairs. I could see them there in their ruffs and robes, around their glasses of foreign wine, discussing: ought they to humiliate the lady with further exile, or ought they allow her back, instead to be constantly reminded of her sullied state by the faces and gestures of others?

And so I stayed nursemaid. Although there were only the two of us now, I kept to my contracted behavior and did not keep company with my prisoner, but only attended her health as long as that was necessary, and made and brought her meals, emptied her chamberpot, and tended her small fire. I was under orders to speak to her only when spoken to, and to resist any attempt she might make to engage me in conversation, but had I obeyed them we would have passed our days entirely in silence, so to save my own sanity I kept to my practice after the birth of greeting the lady when I entered, and she would always greet me back, so that we began each day with my asserting that she was a lady and her acknowledging that I was Joan Vinegar, which otherwise we might well have forgot, there being nothing much else to remind us.

A month and a half we lived together, the lady and me in our silences, the mountain wastes around us. The lord's man came with his foodstuffs and more money, with no accompanying message. He told me all the gossip of court, sitting there eating bread and some of the cheese and wine that he himself had supplied, and truly it was as if he spoke of animals in a menagerie, so strange were their behaviors, so high-colored and passionate. He filled the tower-room with his noise and his uniform. I was so glad when he went and left us in peace again that I worried for myself, that I was turning like that one upstairs, entirely satisfied with nothing, with watching the endless parade of my own thoughts through my head.

I stood, with the man's meal-crumbs at the far end of the table, and a cabbage like a great pale-green head at the near, and the gold scattered beside it that I could not spend, for how much longer yet he had not said. She was silent upstairs. She had maintained her silence so thoroughly while the man was here, he might have thought me a hermit, hired only to do my prayers and observances for sake of the queen's health, not to attend any other human business. And none of this made sense, not the gold, or the cabbage, or the smell of the wine-dregs from the cup, or the disturbance his cheerful voice had wrought on the air of the usually silent room, but all flew apart in my senses like sparrows shooed from a seeded field, in all directions, to all quite different refuges.

My lady's womb ceased its emissions from the birth, and paused awhile dry. Then came a day when she requested cloths for her monthly blood. I wondered, as I brought them, then later as I washed them, whether this was good or bad, this return to normal health. Would Hawley have preferred—would he have showered me with yet more gold?—if she had died in expelling her child, or thereafter from some fever of childbed? Had I been supposed to understand that she was not to return alive from this exile? Had I failed in an unstated duty?

"Well, she is as *good* as dead," I said to myself, rinsing the scrubbed cloth and watching the pink cloud dissipate down the stream. "If you ask me."

Dreams began to trouble me. Often I dreamed of the dead child. Sometimes he lived, and made wise dreamish utterance that carried no sense when I repeated it to myself in the morning. Sometimes he died, or fell to pieces as he came out of his mother, or changed to a plant or a fleeing animal on emerging, but always these dreams were filled with the scent of him, maddening, unplaceable, all flowers and fruits combining, so strong it seemed still to linger in the room even after I woke, and slept again, and woke again in the morning, so tantalizing that several times I hunted on my hands and knees in the meadow around the cottage for the blossom that might be the source, that I might carry it about with me and tantalize myself further with the scent.

I woke very suddenly from one of these dreams, and lay frightened in the night, washes of color flowering forth onto the darkness with the surprise of the wakening to my heart and blood. My hearing was gone so sensitive, if one of my grandchildren had turned over in his sleep back home, I think I would have heard it. Outside a thud sounded, and another, earthen, and then another; a horse was about, not ridden by anyone, but perhaps it had pulled itself loose when tied to browse, and now wandered this unfruitful forest and had come upon our meadow in its hunger.

When I had tamed my heart and breath, I left my bed and quietly opened the cottage door, to see whether the animal was wild or of some worth. I dare say I had it in mind how useful a horse would be, if it were broken and not too grand, how I might add interest to my dreary life here with excursions, with discoveries of towns within a day's ride of the tower. I might spend a little of my gold there; I might converse with sellers and wives. Figures and goods and landscapes flowed across my imaginings, as I stepped out into the cold night, into the glare of the stars, the staring of the moon.

The air was thick with the flower-scent of the dead boy-child—such a warm, summery smell, here in autumn's chills and dyings! The horse stood white—a stallion, he was—against the dark forest. He was down the slope from the tower. He had raised his head and seemed to gaze at the upper window.

"Perhaps you are too splendid," I whispered, but I fetched the rope anyway, and tied a slip-loop. Then across the meadow I crept, stepping not much faster than a tree steps, so as not to frighten the horse away.

At a certain point my breathing quieted and the night breeze eased to where the low noise issuing from my lady's window reached me. That rooted me to the meadow-ground more firmly, her near-inhuman singing, her crooning, broken now and then with grunts and gutturals, something like triumphant laughter.

I have often been thought a witch myself, with my ugly looks and my childbedding, but I tell you, I have never evoked any such magic as shivered under that fine horse's moonlit hide, as streamed off it in the night, fainting me with its scent and eluding my eye with its blown blooms and shining threads. And I have never cast such a spell as trailed out that window on my mistress's, my charge's, song, if song it were. It turned my bones to sugar ice, I tell you, my mind to sweet syrup and my breath to perfume.

And then among her singing another sound intruded, with no voice to it, no magic, no song. It was an earthly sound: stone scraped on stone, heavily, and surreptitious somehow.

Then I knew what she was about, with her mad singing, with her green-tipped baby, with her caring so little for the shame of the queen's name and family. And I ran—more, I *flew*—across the meadow grasses and around to the tower door. I must be quiet, or she would hurry and be gone before I reached her; I must be quick!

I took the prison-room key from under its stone and managed to open the tower door silently. I sped up the stairs, put the key in the lock and turned it, with its usual squeaks and resistance. From inside, loud now, undisguised, came the grinding, the push, of stone on stone.

"My lady!" I forced the stiff key around.

More grinding. Then, and as I flung myself into the room, the stone the girl had loosened from the arrow-slot—months of labor in the night, it would have taken her!—thudded down into the meadow at the foot of the tower.

"My lady, no!"

She darkened the hole with her body, for the moments it took me to cross the room. My fingertip brushed the hem of her nightgown. Then moonlight and starlight whitened my reaching hand.

"Madam!" I screamed to the waiting horse, but through my scream I heard the impact of the lady below, the crack of breaking bone.

"Madam, no! What have you done?"

I pressed myself to the arrow-slot, peering down. The horse stepped up the grass, and I gasped. He bore a fine long spiraling horn on his brow, like some animals of Africa, anteloupes and such. I could smell him, the sweet ferocious flower-and-fruitishness of him, so powerfully that I was not surprised—I did not gasp again—when my lady appeared, walking across the meadow, not limping as she ought, or nursing any injury that I could see. And when she embraced him, he bowing his head to hold her slight body against his breast, and crooking his knee to further enclose her, the rightness and the joy of it caught me in belly and groin, like a birth-pain and a love pang together, and I drank of the sight as they each seemed to be drinking of the other, through their skins, through his coat and her clothing, from the warmth they pressed into being between them.

She held and held him, around his great neck, her fingers in his mane; she murmured into him, and rubbed her cheek on the nap of him and kissed him; she reached along his shoulder and the muscles there, holding him to her, and no further proof was needed than that embrace, and the sight of her lifted face, and the scent in my nostrils of all that lived and burgeoned, that the two of them were lovers and had loved, that the little green-tipped boy had been issue of this animal and this maiden, that the carbuncle on the boy's brow had been the first formings towards his own horn, that I had been witness to magic and marvels. The world, indeed, was a vaster and much mysteriouser place than queens and god-men would have us believe.

My mistress led the horse to the tree-stump I used for chopping kindling on. She mounted him from there, and rode him away. I shook my head and clutched my breast to see them, so nobly did he move, and so balanced was

95

her seat to his movement—they were almost the one creature, it was clear to me.

And then they were gone. There was nothing below but night-lit meadow, giving onto black forest. Above, stars sang out blindly in the square of air where my lady had removed the stone. The prison-room was empty; the door yawned; the window gaped. Everything felt loose, or broken. The sweetness slipped out of the air, leaving only the smell of the dead fire, and of cold stone.

I left the door ajar, from some strange notion that my lady might return, and require to imprison herself again. I walked down the stairs I had so lately flown up. Slowly I crossed the lower room to the other gaping door, and stepped out into the meadow. Brightly colorless, it was, under the moonlight, the grass like grey straw, the few late flowers leaning or drooping asleep.

I rounded the tower. There she was, her head broken on the fallen stone. I scarce could believe my eyes. I scarce could propel myself forward, surprise had frozen so thickly around the base of my spine, where all the impulses to walk begin, all the volitions.

"My lady, my lady!" I *fell* to my knees rather than knelt to them. How little she was, and fine, and pale! How much more delicate-crafted are noble ladies, aren't they?, than us countrywomen all muscled for fieldwork and family life! But even my thick skull could not have prevailed against that stone, and from that height. Blood had trickled from her eye-corner, and her nose and mouth, and poured through her hair; now she seemed glued blackly to the stone, staring to the forest, watching herself ride away.

This is the end of my story. I told a different one to Lord Hawley when I walked out of the mountains, and bought myself a strong little bay mare to ride to the palace and give my information. My lord—I had not seen him in person before—was small, and his furs and silks and chains and puffed-out sleeves made him seem as wide as he was tall. He listened to my tale most interestedly, and then he released me from my contract, paying it out in full though I had four months to serve yet, and adding to that amount the sum I had paid for the mare, and double the sum I had outlaid for bed and food to visit him, so that I should not arrive home at all out of pocket. He gave me a guard to protect me and my moneys all the way to Steeping

Dingle; that guard, in time, was to marry my youngest, little Ruth, and sire me four grandsons and three granddaughters.

I had no reason to complain of my treatment by the queen's house; every royal man gave me full courtesy and respect. And though I was sworn to secrecy over the whole affair, the fact that I had had royal dealings, as evidenced by my return with the guard, did much for my standing, and from that time on I made a tidier living bringing out babies than all the other good-women combined, in my village and throughout the surrounding country.

THE MALTESE UNICORN

Caitlín R. Kiernan

New York City (May 1935)

IT WASN'T HARD TO FIND HER. Sure, she had run. After Szabó let her walk like that, I knew Ellen would get wise that something was rotten, and she'd run like a scared rabbit with the dogs hot on its heels. She'd have it in her head to skip town, and she'd probably keep right on skipping until she was out of the country. Odds were pretty good she wouldn't stop until she was altogether free and clear of this particular plane of existence. There are plenty enough fetid little hidey holes in the universe, if you don't mind the heat and the smell and the company you keep. You only have to know how to find them, and the way I saw it, Ellen Andrews was good as Rand and McNally when it came to knowing her way around.

But first, she'd go back to that apartment of hers, the whole eleventh floor of the Colosseum, with its bleak westward view of the Hudson River and the New Jersey Palisades. I figured there would be those two or three little things she couldn't leave the city without, even if it meant risking her skin to collect them. Only she hadn't expected me to get there before her. Word on the street was Harpootlian still had me locked up tight, so Ellen hadn't expected me to get there at all.

From the hall came the buzz of the elevator, then I heard her key in the lock, the front door, and her footsteps as she hurried through the foyer and the dining room. Then she came dashing into that French Rococo nightmare of a library, and stopped cold in her tracks when she saw me sitting at the reading table with al-Jaldaki's grimoire open in front of me.

For a second, she didn't say anything. She just stood there, staring at me. Then she managed a forced sort of laugh and said, "I knew they'd send someone, Nat. I just didn't think it'd be you."

"After that gip you pulled with the dingus, they didn't really leave me much choice," I told her, which was the truth, or all the truth I felt like sharing. "You shouldn't have come back here. It's the first place anyone would think to check."

Ellen sat down in the armchair by the door. She looked beat, like whatever comes after exhausted, and I could tell Szabó's gunsels had made sure all the fight was gone before they'd turned her loose. They weren't taking any chances, and we were just going through the motions now, me and her. All our lines had been written.

"You played me for a sucker," I said, and picked up the pistol that had been lying beside the grimoire. My hand was shaking, and I tried to steady it by bracing my elbow against the table. "You played me, then you tried to play Harpootlian and Szabó both. Then you got caught. It was a bonehead move all the way round, Ellen."

"So, how's it gonna be, Natalie? You gonna shoot me for being stupid?"

"No, I'm going shoot you because it's the only way I can square things with Auntie H., and the only thing that's gonna keep Szabó from going on the warpath. *And* because you played me."

"In my shoes, you'd have done the same thing," she said. And the way she said it, I could tell she believed what she was saying. It's the sort of self-righteous bushwa so many grifters hide behind. They might stab their own mothers in the back if they see an angle in it, but that's jake, cause so would anyone else.

"Is that really all you have to say for yourself?" I asked, and pulled back the slide on the Colt, chambering the first round. She didn't even flinch . . . but, wait . . . I'm getting ahead of myself. Maybe I ought to begin nearer the beginning.

As it happens, I didn't go and name the place Yellow Dragon Books. It came with that moniker, and I just never saw any reason to change it. I'd only have had to pay for a new sign. Late in '28—right after Arnie "The Brain" Rothstein was shot to death during a poker game at the Park Central Hotel—I accidentally found myself on the sunny side of the proprietress of one of Manhattan's more infernal brothels. I say *accidentally* because I hadn't even heard of Madam Yeksabet Harpootlian when I began trying to dig up a buyer for an antique manuscript, a collection of necromantic erotica purportedly written by John Dee and Edward Kelley some time in the Sixteenth Century. Turns out, Harpootlian had been looking to get her mitts on it for decades.

Now, just how I came into possession of said manuscript, that's another story entirely, one for some other time and place. One that, with luck, I'll never get around to putting down on paper. Let's just say a couple of years earlier, I'd been living in Paris. Truthfully, I'd been doing my best, in a sloppy, irresolute way, to *die* in Paris. I was holed up in a fleabag Montmartre boarding house, busy squandering the last of a dwindling inheritance. I had in mind how maybe I could drown myself in cheap wine, bad poetry, Pernod, and prostitutes before the money ran out. But somewhere along the way, I lost my nerve, failed at my slow suicide, and bought a ticket back to the States. And the manuscript in question was one of the many strange and unsavory things I brought back with me. I've always had a nose for the macabre, and had dabbled—on and off—in the black arts since college. At Radcliffe, I'd fallen in with a circle of lesbyterians who fancied themselves witches. Mostly, I was in it for the sex . . . but I'm digressing.

A friend of a friend heard I was busted, down and out and peddling a bunch of old books, schlepping them about Manhattan in search of a buyer. This same friend, he knew one of Harpootlian's clients. One of her *human* clients, which was a pretty exclusive set (not that I knew that at the time). This friend of mine, he was the client's lover, and said client brokered the sale for Harpootlian—for a fat ten-percent finder's fee, of course. I promptly sold the Dee and Kelley manuscript to this supposedly notorious madam who, near as I could tell, no one much had ever heard of. She paid me what I asked, no questions, no haggling, never mind it was a fairly exorbitant sum. And on top of that, Harpootlian was so impressed

I'd gotten ahold of the damned thing, she staked me to the bookshop on Bowery, there in the shadow of the Third Avenue El, just a little ways south of Delancey Street. Only one catch: She had first dibs on everything I ferreted out, and sometimes I'd be asked to make deliveries. I should like to note that way back then, during that long, lost November of 1928, I had no idea whatsoever that her sobriquet, "the Demon Madam of the Lower East Side," was anything more than colorful hyperbole.

Anyway, jump ahead to a rainy May afternoon, more than six years later, and that's when I first laid eyes on Ellen Andrews. Well, that's what she called herself, though later on I'd find out she'd borrowed the name from Claudette Colbert's character in *It Happened One Night*. I was just back from an estate sale in Connecticut, and was busy unpacking a large crate when I heard the bell mounted above the shop door jingle. I looked up, and there she was, carelessly shaking rainwater from her orange umbrella before folding it closed. Droplets sprayed across the welcome mat and the floor and onto the spines of several nearby books.

"Hey, be careful," I said, "unless you intend to pay for those." I jabbed a thumb at the books she'd spattered. She promptly stopped shaking the umbrella and dropped it into the stand beside the door. That umbrella stand has always been one of my favorite things about the Yellow Dragon. It's made from the taxidermied foot of a hippopotamus, and accommodates at least a dozen umbrellas, although I don't think I've ever seen even half that many people in the shop at one time.

"Are you Natalie Beaumont?" she asked, looking down at her wet shoes. Her overcoat was dripping, and a small puddle was forming about her feet.

"Usually."

"Usually," she repeated. "How about right now?"

"Depends whether or not I owe you money," I replied, and removed a battered copy of Blavatsky's *Isis Unveiled* from the crate. "Also, depends whether you happen to be *employed* by someone I owe money."

"I see," she said, as if that settled the matter, then proceeded to examine the complete twelve-volume set of *The Golden Bough* occupying a top shelf not far from the door. "Awful funny sort of neighborhood for a bookstore, if you ask me."

"You don't think bums and winos read?"

"You ask me, people down here," she said, "they panhandle a few cents, I don't imagine they spend it on books."

"I don't recall asking for your opinion," I told her.

"No," she said. "You didn't. Still, queer sort of a shop to come across in this part of town."

"If you must know," I said, "the rent's cheap," then reached for my spectacles, which were dangling from their silver chain about my neck. I set them on the bridge of my nose, and watched while she feigned interest in Frazerian anthropology. It would be an understatement to say Ellen Andrews was a pretty girl. She was, in fact, a certified knockout, and I didn't get too many beautiful women in the Yellow Dragon, even when the weather was good. She wouldn't have looked out of place in Flo Ziegfeld's follies; on the Bowery, she stuck out like a sore thumb.

"Looking for anything in particular?" I asked her, and she shrugged.

"Just you," she said.

"Then I suppose you're in luck."

"I suppose I am," she said, and turned towards me again. Her eyes glinted red, just for an instant, like the eyes of a Siamese cat. I figured it for a trick of the light. "I'm a friend of Auntie H. I run errands for her, now and then. She needs you to pick up a package and see it gets safely where it's going."

So, there it was. Madam Harpootlian, or Auntie H. to those few unfortunates she called her friends. And suddenly it made a lot more sense, this choice bit of calico walking into my place, strolling in off the street like maybe she did all her shopping down on Skid Row. I'd have to finish unpacking the crate later. I stood up and dusted my hands off on the seat of my slacks.

"Sorry about the confusion," I said, even if I wasn't actually sorry, even if I was actually kind of pissed the girl hadn't told me who she was right up front. "When Auntie H. wants something done, she doesn't usually bother sending her orders around in such an attractive envelope."

The girl laughed, then said, "Yeah, Auntie H. warned me about you, Miss Beaumont."

"Did she now. How so?"

"You know, your predilections. How you're not like other women."

"I'd say that depends on which other women we're discussing, don't you think?"

"*Most* other women," she said, glancing over her shoulder at the rain pelting the shop windows. It sounded like frying meat out there, the sizzle of the rain against asphalt, and concrete, and the roofs of passing automobiles.

"And what about you?" I asked her. "Are *you* like most other women?"

She looked away from the window, looking back at me, and she smiled what must have been the faintest smile possible.

"Are you always this charming?"

"Not that I'm aware of," I said. "Then again, I never took a poll."

"The job, it's nothing particularly complicated," she said, changing the subject. "There's a Chinese apothecary not too far from here."

"That doesn't exactly narrow it down," I said, and lit a cigarette.

"Sixty-five Mott Street. The joint's run by an elderly Cantonese fellow name of Fong."

"Yeah, I know Jimmy Fong."

"That's good. Then maybe you won't get lost. Mr. Fong will be expecting you, and he'll have the package ready at five-thirty this evening. He's already been paid in full, so all you have to do is be there to receive it, right? And Miss Beaumont, please try to be on time. Auntie H. said you have a problem with punctuality."

"You believe everything you hear?"

"Only if I'm hearing it from Auntie H."

"Fair enough," I told her, then offered her a Pall Mall, but she declined.

"I need to be getting back," she said, reaching for the umbrella she'd only just deposited in the stuffed hippopotamus foot.

"What's the rush? What'd you come after, anyway, a ball of fire?"

She rolled her eyes. "I got places to be. You're not the only stop on my itinerary."

"Fine. Wouldn't want you getting in Dutch with Harpootlian on my account. Don't suppose you've got a name?"

"I might," she said.

"Don't suppose you'd share?" I asked her, and took a long drag on my cigarette, wondering why in blue blazes Harpootlian had sent this smart-mouthed skirt instead of one of her usual flunkies. Of course, Auntie H.

always did have a sadistic streak to put de Sade to shame, and likely as not this was her idea of a joke.

"Ellen," the girl said. "Ellen Andrews."

"So, Ellen Andrews, how is it we've never met? I mean, I've been making deliveries for your boss lady now going on seven years, and if I'd seen you, I'd remember. You're not the sort I forget."

"You got the moxie, don't you?"

"I'm just good with faces is all."

She chewed at a thumbnail, as if considering carefully what she should or shouldn't divulge. Then she said, "I'm from out of town, mostly. Just passing through, and thought I'd lend a hand. That's why you've never seen me before, Miss Beaumont. Now, I'll let you get back to work. And remember, don't be late."

"I heard you the first time, sister."

And then she left, and the brass bell above the door jingled again. I finished my cigarette and went back to unpacking the big crate of books from Connecticut. If I hurried, I could finish the job before heading for Chinatown.

She was right, of course. I did have a well-deserved reputation for not being on time. But I knew that Auntie H. was of the opinion that my acumen in antiquarian and occult matters more than compensated for my not-infrequent tardiness. I've never much cared for personal mottos, but maybe if I had one it might be, *You want it on time, or you want it done right?* Still, I honestly tried to be on time for the meeting with Fong. And still, through no fault of my own, I was more than twenty minutes late. I was lucky enough to find a cab, despite the rain, but then got stuck behind some sort of brouhaha after turning onto Canal, so there you go. It's not like the old man Fong had any place more pressing to be, not like he was gonna get pissy and leave me high and dry.

When I got to Sixty-Five Mott, the Chinaman's apothecary was locked up tight, all the lights were off, and the "Sorry, We're Closed" sign was hung in the front window. No big surprise there. But then I went around back, to the alley, and found a door standing wide open and quite a lot of fresh blood on the cinderblock steps leading into the building. Now, maybe I was the only lady bookseller in Manhattan who carried a gun, and maybe I wasn't. But times like that, I was glad to have the Colt tucked snugly inside its shoulder holster, and happier still that I knew how to use it. I took a deep breath, drew the pistol, flipped off the safety catch, and stepped inside.

The door opened onto a stockroom, and the tiny nook Jimmy Fong used as his office was a little farther in, over on my left. There was some light from a banker's lamp, but not much of it. I lingered in the shadows a moment, waiting for my heart to stop pounding, for the adrenaline high to fade. The air was close, and stunk of angelica root and dust, ginger and frankincense and fuck only knows what else. Powdered rhino horn and the pickled gall-bladders of panda bears. What the hell ever. I found the old man slumped over at his desk.

Whoever knifed him hadn't bothered to pull the shiv out of his spine, and I wondered if the poor s.o.b. had even seen it coming. It didn't exactly add up, not after seeing all that blood drying on the steps, but I figured, hey, maybe the killer was the sort of klutz can't spread butter without cutting himself. I had a quick look-see around the cluttered office, hoping I might turn up the package Ellen Andrews had sent me there to retrieve. But no dice, and then it occurred to me, maybe whoever had murdered Fong had come looking for the same thing I was looking for. Maybe they'd found it, too, only Fong knew better than to just hand it over, and that had gotten him killed. Anyway, nobody was paying me to play junior shamus, hence the hows, whys, and wherefores of the Chinaman's death were not my problem. *My* problem would be showing up at Harpootlian's cathouse empty-handed.

I returned the gun to its holster, then I started rifling through everything in sight—the great disarray of papers heaped upon the desk, Fong's accounting ledgers, sales invoices, catalogs, letters and postcards written in English, Mandarin, Wu, Cantonese, French, Spanish, and Arabic. I still had my gloves on, so it's not like I had to worry over fingerprints. A few of the desk drawers were unlocked, and I'd just started in on those, when the phone perched atop the filing cabinet rang. I froze, whatever I was looking at clutched forgotten in my hands, and stared at the phone.

Sure, it wasn't every day I blundered into the immediate aftermath of this sort of foul play, but I was plenty savvy enough I knew better than to answer that call. It didn't much matter who was on the other end of the line. If I answered, I could be placed at the scene of a murder only minutes after it had gone down. The phone rang a second time, and a third, and I glanced at the dead man in the chair. The crimson halo surrounding the switchblade's inlaid mother-of-pearl handle was still spreading, blossoming like some grim rose, and now there was blood dripping to the floor, as well. The phone rang a fourth time. A fifth. And then I was seized by an over-whelming compulsion to answer it, and answer it I did. I wasn't the least bit thrown that the voice coming through the receiver was Ellen Andrews'. All at once, the pieces were falling into place. You spend enough years doing the step-and-fetch-it routine for imps like Harpootlian, you find yourself ever more jaded at the inexplicable and the uncanny.

"Beaumont," she said, "I didn't think you were going to pick up."

"I wasn't. Funny thing how I did anyway."

"Funny thing," she said, and I heard her light a cigarette and realized my hands were shaking.

"See, I'm thinking maybe I had a little push," I said. "That about the size of it?"

"Wouldn't have been necessary if you'd have just answered the damn phone in the first place."

"You already know Fong's dead, don't you?" And, I swear to fuck, nothing makes me feel like more of a jackass than asking questions I know the answers to.

"Don't you worry about Fong. I'm sure he had all his ducks in a row and was right as rain with Buddha. I need you to pay attention—"

"Harpootlian had him killed, didn't she? And you *knew* he'd be dead when I showed up."

She didn't reply straight away, and I thought I could hear a radio playing in the background. "You knew," I said again, only this time it wasn't a query.

"Listen," she said. "You're a courier. I was told you're a courier we can trust, elsewise I never would have handed you this job."

"You didn't hand me the job. Your boss did."

"You're splitting hairs, Miss Beaumont."

"Yeah, well, there's a fucking dead celestial in the room with me. It's giving me the fidgets."

"So how about you shut up and listen, and I'll have you out of there in a jiffy." And that's what I did, I shut up, either because I knew it was the path of least resistance, or because whatever spell she'd used to persuade me to answer the phone was still working.

"On Fong's desk, there's a funny little porcelain statue of a cat."

"You mean the Maneki Neko?"

"If that's what it's called, that's what I mean. Now, break it open. There's a key inside."

I *tried* not to, just to see if I was being played as badly as I suspected I was being played. I gritted my teeth, dug in my heels, and tried *hard* not to break that damned cat.

"You're wasting time. Auntie H. didn't mention you were such a crybaby."

"Auntie H. and I have an agreement when it comes to free will. To *my* free will."

"*Break the goddamn cat,*" Ellen Andrews growled, and that's exactly what I did. In fact, I slammed it down directly on top of Fong's head. Bits of brightly painted porcelain flew everywhere, and a rusty barrel key tumbled out and landed at my feet. "Now pick it up," she said. "The key fits the bottom left-hand drawer of Fong's desk. Open it."

This time, I didn't even try to resist her. I was getting a headache from the last futile attempt. I unlocked the drawer, and pulled it open. Inside, there was nothing but the yellowed sheet of newspaper lining the drawer, three golf balls, a couple of old racing forms, and a finely carved wooden box lacquered almost the same shade of red as Jimmy Fong's blood. I didn't need to be told I'd been sent to retrieve the box—or, more specifically, whatever was *inside* the box.

"Yeah, I got it," I told Ellen Andrews.

"Good girl. Now, you have maybe twelve minutes before the cops show. Go out the same way you came in." Then she gave me a Riverside Drive address, and said there'd be a car waiting for me at the corner of Canal and Mulberry, a green Chevrolet coupe. "Just give the driver that address. He'll see you get where you're going."

"Yeah," I said, sliding the desk drawer shut again and locking it. I pocketed the key. "But sister, you and me are gonna have a talk."

"Wouldn't miss it for the world, Nat," she said and hung up. I shut my eyes, wondering if I really had twelve minutes before the bulls arrived, and if they were even on their way, wondering what would happen if I endeavored *not* to make the rendezvous with the green coupe. I stood there, trying to decide whether Harpootlian would have gone back on her word and given this bitch permission to turn her hoodoo tricks on me, and if aspirin would do anything at all for the dull throb behind my eyes. Then I looked at Fong one last time, at the knife jutting out of his back, his thin gray hair powdered with porcelain dust from the shattered "Lucky Cat." And then I stopped asking questions and did as I'd been told.

The car was there, just like she'd told me it would be. There was a young colored man behind the wheel, and when I climbed in the back, he asked me where we were headed.

"I'm guessing Hell," I said, "sooner or later."

"Got that right," he laughed and winked at me from the rearview mirror. "But I was thinking more in terms of the immediate here and now."

So I recited the address I'd been given over the phone, 435 Riverside.

"That's the Colosseum," he said.

"It is if you say so," I replied. "Just get me there."

The driver nodded and pulled away from the curb. As he navigated the slick, wet streets, I sat listening to the rain against the Chevy's hard top and the music coming from the Motorola. In particular, I can remember hearing the Dorsey Brothers, "Chasing Shadows." I suppose you'd call that a harbinger, if you go in for that sort of thing. Me, I do my best not to. In this business, you start jumping at everything that *might* be an omen or a portent, you end up doing nothing else. Ironically, rubbing shoulders with the supernatural has made me a great believer in coincidence.

Anyway, the driver drove, the radio played, and I sat staring at the red lacquered box I'd stolen from a dead man's locked desk drawer. I thought it might be mahogany, but it was impossible to be sure, what with all that cinnabar-tinted varnish. I know enough about Chinese mythology that I recognized the strange creature carved into the top—a *qilin*, a stout, ant-lered beast with cloven hooves, the scales of a dragon, and a long leonine tail. Much of its body was wreathed in flame, and its gaping jaws revealed teeth like daggers. For the Chinese, the qilin is a harbinger of good fortune, though it certainly hadn't worked out that way for Jimmy Fong. The box was heavier than it looked, most likely because of whatever was stashed inside. There was no latch, and as I examined it more closely, I realized there was no sign whatsoever of hinges or even a seam to indicate it actually had a lid.

"Unless I got it backwards," the driver said, "Miss Andrews didn't say nothing about trying to open that box, now did she?"

I looked up, startled, feeling like the proverbial kid caught with her hand in the cookie jar. He glanced at me in the mirror, then his eyes drifted back to the road.

"She didn't say one way or the other," I told him.

"Then how about we err on the side of caution?"

"So you didn't know where you're taking me, but you know I shouldn't open this box? How's that work?"

"Ain't the world just full of mysteries," he said.

For a minute or so, I silently watched the headlights of the oncoming traffic and the metronomic sweep of the windshield wipers. Then I asked the driver how long he'd worked for Ellen Andrews.

"Not very," he said. "Never laid eyes on the lady before this afternoon. Why you want to know?"

"No particular reason," I said, looking back down at the box and the qilin etched in the wood. I decided I was better off not asking any more questions, better off getting this over and done with, and never mind what did and didn't quite add up. "Just trying to make conversation, that all."

Which got him to talking about the Chicago stockyards and Cleveland and how it was he'd eventually wound up in New York City. He never told me his name, and I didn't ask. The trip uptown seemed to take forever, and the longer I sat with that box in my lap, the heavier it felt. I finally moved it, putting it down on the seat beside me. By the time we reached our destination, the rain had stopped and the setting sun was showing through the clouds, glittering off the dripping trees in Riverside Park and the waters of the wide gray Hudson. He pulled over, and I reached for my wallet.

"No ma'am," he said, shaking his head. "Miss Andrews, she's already seen to your fare."

"Then I hope you won't mind if I see to your tip," I said, and I gave him five dollars. He thanked me, and I took the wooden box and stepped out onto the wet sidewalk.

"She's up on the eleventh," he told me, nodding towards the apartments. Then he drove off, and I turned to face the imposing brick and limestone façade of the building the driver had called the Colosseum. I rarely find myself any farther north than the Upper West Side, so this was pretty much *terra incognita* for me.

The doorman gave me directions, *after* giving me and Fong's box the hairy eyeball, and I quickly made my way to the elevators, hurrying through that ritzy marble sepulcher passing itself off as a lobby. When the operator asked which floor I needed, I told him the eleventh, and he shook his head and muttered something under his breath. I almost asked him to speak up, but thought better of it. Didn't I already have plenty enough on my mind without entertaining the opinions of elevator boys? Sure, I did. I had a murdered Chinaman, a mysterious box, and this pushy little sorceress calling herself Ellen Andrews. I also had an especially disagreeable feeling about this job, and the sooner it was settled, the better. I kept my eyes on the brass needle as it haltingly swung from left to right, counting off the floors, and when the doors parted, she was there waiting for me. She slipped the boy a sawbuck, and he stuffed it into his jacket pocket and left us alone.

"So nice to see you again, Nat," she said, but she was looking at the lacquered box, not me. "Would you like to come in and have a drink? Auntie H. says you have a weakness for rye whiskey."

"Well, she's right about that. But just now, I'd be more fond of an explanation."

"How odd," she said, glancing up at me, still smiling. "Auntie said one thing she liked about you was how you didn't ask a lot of questions. Said you were real good at minding your own business."

"Sometimes I make exceptions."

"Let me get you that drink," she said, and I followed her the short distance from the elevator to the door of her apartment. Turns out, she had the whole floor to herself, each level of the Colosseum being a single apartment. Pretty ritzy accommodations, I thought, for someone who was *mostly* from out of town. But then I've spent the last few years living in that one-bedroom cracker box above the Yellow Dragon, hot and cold running cockroaches and so forth. She locked the door behind us, then led me through the foyer to a parlor. The whole place was done up gaudy period French, Louis Quinze and the like, all floral brocade and Orientalia. The walls were decorated with damask hangings, mostly of ample-bosomed women reclining in pastoral scenes, dogs and sheep and what have you lying at their feet. Ellen told me to have a seat, so I parked myself on a *récamier* near a window.

"Harpootlian spring for this place?" I asked.

"No," she replied. "It belonged to my mother."

"So, you come from money."

"Did I mention how you ask an awful lot of questions?"

"You might have," I said, and she inquired as to whether I liked my whiskey neat or on the rocks. I told her neat, and set the red box down on the sofa next to me.

"If you're not *too* thirsty, would you mind if I take a peek at that first," she said, pointing at the box.

"Be my guest," I said, and Ellen smiled again. She picked up the red lacquered box, then sat next to me. She cradled it in her lap, and there was this goofy expression on her face, a mix of awe, dread, and eager expectation.

"Must be something extra damn special," I said, and she laughed. It was a nervous kind of a laugh.

I've already mentioned how I couldn't discern any evidence the box had a lid, and I supposed there was some secret to getting it open, a gentle squeeze or nudge in just the right spot. Turns out, all it needed was someone to say the magic words.

"*Pain had no sting, and pleasure's wreath no flower*," she said, speaking slowly and all but whispering the words. There was a sharp *click* and the top of the box suddenly slid back with enough force that it tumbled over her knees and fell to the carpet.

"Keats," I said.

"Keats," she echoed, but added nothing more. She was too busy gazing at what lay inside the box, nestled in a bed of velvet the color of poppies.

She started to touch it, then hesitated, her fingertips hovering an inch or so above the object.

"You're fucking kidding me," I said, once I saw what was inside.

"Don't go jumping to conclusions, Nat."

"It's a dildo," I said, probably sounding as incredulous as I felt. "Exactly which conclusions am I not supposed to jump to? Sure, I enjoy a good rub-off as much as the next girl, but . . . you're telling me Harpootlian killed Fong over a dildo?"

"I never said Auntie H. killed Fong."

"Then I suppose he stuck that knife there himself."

And that's when she told me to shut the hell up for five minutes, if I knew how. She reached into the box and lifted out the phallus, handling it as gingerly as somebody might handle a stick of dynamite. But whatever made the thing special, it wasn't anything I could see.

"*Le Godemichet maudit*," she murmured, her voice so filled with reverence you'd have thought she was holding the devil's own wang. Near as I could tell, it was cast from some sort of hard black ceramic. It glistened faintly in the light getting in through the drapes. "I'll tell you about it," she said, "if you really want to know. I don't see the harm."

"Just so long as you get to the part where it makes sense that Harpootlian bumped the Chinaman for this dingus of yours, then sure."

She took her eyes off the thing long enough to scowl at me. "Auntie H. didn't kill Fong. One of Szabó's goons did that, then panicked and ran before he figured out where the box was hidden."

(Now, as for Madam Magdalena Szabó, the biggest boil on Auntie H.'s fanny, we'll get back to her by and by.)

"Ellen, how can you *possibly* fucking know that? Better yet, how could you've known Szabó's man would have given up and cleared out by the time I arrived?"

"Why did you answer that phone, Nat?" she asked, and that shut me up, good and proper. "As for our prize here," she continued, "it's a long story, a long story with a lot of missing pieces. The dingus, as you put it, is usually called le Godemichet maudit. Which doesn't necessarily mean it's actually cursed, mind you. Not literally. You *do* speak French, I assume?"

"Yeah," I told her. "I do speak French."

"That's ducky, Nat. Now, here's about as much as anyone could tell you. Though, frankly, I'd have thought a scholarly type like yourself would know all about it."

"Never said I was a scholar," I interrupted.

"But you went to college. Radcliffe, class of 1923, right? Graduated with honors."

"Lots of people go to college. Doesn't necessarily make them scholars. I just sell books."

"My mistake," she said, carefully returning the black dildo to its velvet case. "It won't happen again." Then she told me her tale, and I sat there on the récamier and listened to what she had to say. Yeah, it was long. There *were* certainly a whole lot of missing pieces. And as a wise man once said, this might not be schoolbook history, not Mr. Wells' history, but, near as I've been able to discover since that evening at her apartment, it's history, nevertheless. She asked me whether or not I'd ever heard of a Fourteenth-Century Persian alchemist named al-Jaldaki, Izz al-Din Aydamir al-Jaldaki, and I had, of course.

"He's sort of a hobby of mine," she said. "Came across his grimoire a few years back. Anyway, he's not where it begins, but that's where the written record starts. While studying in Anatolia, al-Jaldaki heard tales of a fabulous artifact that had been crafted from the horn of a unicorn at the behest of King Solomon."

"From a unicorn," I cut in. "So we believe in those now, do we?"

"Why not, Nat? I think it's safe to assume you've seen some peculiar shit in your time, that you've pierced the veil, so to speak. Surely a unicorn must be small potatoes for a worldly woman like yourself."

"So you'd think," I said.

"Anyhow," she went on, "the ivory horn was carved into the shape of a penis by the king's most skilled artisans. Supposedly, the result was so revered it was even placed in Solomon's temple, alongside the Ark of the Covenant and a slew of other sacred Hebrew relics. Records al-Jaldaki found in a mosque in the Taurus Mountains indicated that the horn had been removed from Solomon's temple when it was sacked in 587 BC by the Babylonians, and that eventually it had gone to Medina. But it was taken from Medina during, or shortly after, the siege of 627, when the Meccans invaded. And it's at this point that the horn is believed to have been given its ebony coating of porcelain enamel, possibly in an attempt to disguise it."

"Or," I said, "because someone in Medina preferred swarthy cock. You mind if I smoke?" I asked her, and she shook her head and pointed at an ashtray.

"A Medinan rabbi of the Banu Nadir tribe was entrusted with the horn's safety. He escaped, making his way west across the desert to Yanbu' al Bahr, then north along the al-Hejaz all the way to Jerusalem. But two years later, when the Sassanid army lost control of the city to the Byzantine Emperor Heraclius, the horn was taken to a monastery in Malta, where it remained for centuries."

"That's quite a saga for a dildo. But you still haven't answered my question. What makes it so special? What the hell's it *do*?"

"Maybe you've heard enough," she said, and this whole time she hadn't taken her eyes off the thing in the box.

"Yeah, and maybe I haven't," I told her, tapping ash from my Pall Mall into the ashtray. "So, al-Jaldaki goes to Malta and finds the big black dingus."

She scowled again. No, it was more than a scowl; she *glowered*, and she looked away from the box just long enough to glower *at* me. "Yes," Ellen Andrews said. "At least, that's what he wrote. al-Jaldaki found it buried in the ruins of a monastery in Malta, and then carried the horn with him to Cairo. It seems to have been in his possession until his death in 1342. After that it disappeared, and there's no word of it again until 1891."

I did the math in my head. "Five hundred and forty-nine years," I said. "So it must have gone to a good home. Must have lucked out and found itself a long-lived and appreciative keeper."

"The Freemasons might have had it," she went on, ignoring or oblivious to my sarcasm. "Maybe the Vatican. Doesn't make much difference."

"Okay. So what happened in 1891?"

"A party in Paris, in an old house not far from the *Cimetière du Montparnasse*. Not so much a party, really, as an out and out orgy, the way the story goes. This was back before Montparnasse became so fashionable with painters and poets and expatriate Americans. Verlaine was there, though. At the orgy, I mean. It's not clear what happened precisely, but three women died, and afterwards there were rumors of black magic and ritual sacrifice, and tales surfaced of a cult that worshipped some sort of dae-monic *objet d'art* that had made its way to France from Egypt. There was an official investigation, naturally, but someone saw to it that *la Préfecture de Police* came up with zilch."

"Naturally," I said. I glanced at the window. It was getting dark, and I wondered if my ride back to the Bowery had been arranged. "So, where's Black Beauty here been for the past forty-four years?"

Ellen leaned forward, reaching for the lid to the red lacquered box. When she set it back in place, covering that brazen scrap of antiquity, I heard the *click* again as the lid melded seamlessly with the rest of the box. Now there was only the etching of the qilin, and I remembered that the beast has sometimes been referred to as the "Chinese unicorn." It seemed odd I'd not thought of that before.

"I think we've probably had enough of a history lesson for now," she said, and I didn't disagree. Truth be told, the whole subject was begin-ning to bore me. It hardly mattered whether or not I believed in unicorns or enchanted dildos. I'd done my job, so there'd be no complaints from Harpootlian. I admit I felt kind of shitty about poor old Fong, who wasn't such a bad sort. But when you're an errand girl for the wicked folk, that shit comes with the territory. People get killed, and worse.

"It's getting late," I said, crushing out my cigarette in the ashtray. "I should dangle."

"Wait. Please. I promised you a drink, Nat. Don't want you telling Auntie H. I was a bad hostess, now do I?" And Ellen Andrews stood up, the red box tucked snugly beneath her left arm.

"No worries, kiddo," I assured her. "If she ever asks, which I doubt, I'll say you were a regular Emily Post."

"I insist," she replied. "I really, truly do," and before I could say another word, she turned and rushed out of the parlor, leaving me alone with all that furniture and the buxom giantesses watching me from the walls. I wondered if there were any servants, or a live-in beau, or if possibly she had the place all to herself, that huge apartment overlooking the river. I pushed the drapes aside and stared out at twilight gathering in the park across the street. Then she was back (minus the red box) with a silver serving tray, two glasses, and a virgin bottle of Sazerac rye.

"Maybe just one," I said, and she smiled. I went back to watching River-side Park while she poured the whiskey. No harm in a shot or two. It's not like I had some place to be, and there were still a couple of unanswered questions bugging me. Such as why Harpootlian had broken her promise, the one that was supposed to prevent her underlings from practicing their hocus-pocus on me. That is, assuming Ellen Andrews had even bothered to ask permission. Regardless, she didn't need magic or a spell book for her next dirty trick. The Mickey Finn she slipped me did the job just fine.

So, I came to, four, perhaps five hours later—sometime before midnight. By then, as I'd soon learn, the shit had already hit the fan. I woke up sick as a dog and my head pounding like there was an ape with a kettledrum loose inside my skull. I opened my eyes, but it wasn't Ellen Andrews' Baroque clutter and chintz that greeted me, and I immediately shut them again. I smelled the hookahs and the smoldering *bukhoor*, the opium smoke and sandarac and, somewhere underneath it all, that pervasive brimstone stink that no amount of incense can mask. Besides, I'd seen the spiny ginger-skinned thing crouching not far from me, the eunuch, and I knew I was somewhere in the rat's maze labyrinth of Harpootlian's bordello. I started to sit up, but then my stomach lurched and I thought better of it. At least there were soft cushions beneath me, and the silk was cool against my feverish skin.

"You know where you are?" the eunuch asked; it had a woman's voice and a hint of a Russian accent, but I was pretty sure both were only affecta-tions. First rule of demon brothels: Check your preconceptions of male and female at the door. Second rule: Appearances are fucking *meant* to be deceiving.

"Sure," I moaned and tried not to think about vomiting. "I might have a notion or three."

"Good. Then you lie still and take it easy, Miss Beaumont. We've got a few questions need answering." Which made it mutual, but I kept my mouth shut on that account. The voice was beginning to sound not so much feminine as what you might hear if you scraped frozen pork back and forth across a cheese grater. "This afternoon, you were contacted by an associate of Madam Harpootlian's, yes? She told you her name was Ellen Andrews. That's not her true name, of course. Just something she heard in a motion picture—"

"Of course," I replied. "You sort never bother with your real names. Anyway, what of it?"

"She asked you to go see Jimmy Fong and bring her something, yes? Something very precious. Something powerful and rare."

"The dingus," I said, rubbing at my aching head. "Right, but . . . hey . . . Fong was already dead when I got there, scout's honor. Andrews told me one of Szabó's people did him."

"The Chinese gentleman's fate is no concern of ours," the eunuch said. "But we need to talk about Ellen Andrews. She has caused this house serious inconvenience. She's troubled us, and troubles us still."

"You and me both, bub," I said. It was just starting to dawn on me how there were some sizable holes in my memory. I clearly recalled the taste of rye, and gazing down at the park, but then nothing. Nothing at all. I asked the ginger demon, "Where is she? And how'd I get here, anyway?"

"We seem to have many of the same questions," it replied, dispassionate as a corpse. "You answer ours, maybe we shall find the answers to yours along the way."

I knew damn well I didn't have much say in the matter. After all, I'd been down this road before. When Auntie H. wants answers, she doesn't usually bother with asking. Why waste your time wondering if someone's feeding you a load of baloney when all you gotta do is reach inside his brain and help yourself to whatever you need?

"Fine," I said, trying not to tense up, because tensing up only ever makes it worse. "How about let's cut the chit chat and get this over with."

"Very well, but you should know," it said, "Madam regrets the necessity of this imposition." And then there were the usual wet, squelching noises as the relevant appendages unfurled and slithered across the floor towards me.

"Sure, no problem. Ain't no secret Madam's got a heart of gold," and maybe I shouldn't have smarted off like that, because when the stingers hit me, they hit hard. Harder than I knew was necessary to make the connection. I might have screamed. I know I pissed myself. And then it was inside me, prowling about, roughly picking its way through my conscious and unconscious mind—through my soul, if that word suits you better. All the heady sounds and smells of the brothel faded away, along with my physical discomfort. For a while I drifted nowhere and nowhen in particular, and then, then I stopped drifting . . .

. . . Ellen asked me, "You ever think you've had enough? Of the life, I mean. Don't you sometimes contemplate just up and blowing town, not even stopping long enough to look back? Doesn't that ever cross your mind, Nat?"

I sipped my whiskey and watched her, undressing her with my eyes and not especially ashamed of myself for doing so. "Not too often," I said. "I've had it worse. This gig's not perfect, but I usually get a fair shake."

"Yeah, usually," she said, her words hardly more than a sigh. "Just, now and then, I feel like I'm missing out."

I laughed, and she glared at me.

"You'd cut a swell figure in a breadline," I said, and took another swallow of the rye.

"I hate when people laugh at me."

"Then don't say funny things," I told her.

And that's when she turned and took my glass. I thought she was about to tell me to get lost, and don't let the door hit me in the ass on the way out. Instead, she set the drink down on the silver serving tray, and she kissed me. Her mouth tasted like peaches. Peaches and cinnamon. Then she pulled back, and her eyes flashed red, the way they had in the Yellow Dragon, only now I knew it wasn't an illusion.

"You're a demon," I said, not all that surprised.

"Only a quarter. My grandmother . . . well, I'd rather not get into that, if it's all the same to you. Is it a problem?"

"No, it's not a problem," I replied, and she kissed me again. Right about here, I started to feel the first twinges of whatever she'd put into the Sazerac, but, frankly, I was too horny to heed the warning signs.

"I've got a plan," she said, whispering, as if she were afraid someone was listening in. "I have it all worked out, but I wouldn't mind some company on the road."

"I have no . . . no idea . . . what you're talking about," and there was something else I wanted to say, but I'd begun slurring my words and decided against it. I put a hand on her left breast, and she didn't stop me.

"We'll talk about it later," she said, kissing me again, and right about then, that's when the curtain came crashing down, and the ginger-colored demon in my brain turned a page . . .

. . . I opened my eyes, and I was lying in a black room. I mean, a *perfectly* black room. Every wall had been painted matte black, and the ceiling, and the floor. If there were any windows, they'd also been painted over, or boarded up. I was cold, and a moment later I realized that was because I was naked. I was naked and lying at the center of a wide white pentagram that had been chalked onto that black floor. A white pentagram held within a white circle. There was a single white candle burning at each of the five points. I looked up, and Ellen Andrews was standing above me. Like me, she was naked. Except she was wearing that dingus from the lacquered box, fitted into a leather harness strapped about her hips. The phallus drooped obscenely and glimmered in the candlelight. There were dozens of runic and Enochian symbols painted on her skin in blood and shit and charcoal. Most of them I recognized. At her feet, there was a small iron cauldron, and a black-handled dagger, and something dead. It might have been a rabbit, or a small dog. I couldn't be sure which, because she'd skinned it.

Ellen looked down, and saw me looking up at her. She frowned, and tilted her head to one side. For just a second, there was something undeniably predatory in that expression, something murderous. All spite and not a jot of mercy. For that second, I was face-to-face with the one quarter of her bloodline that changed all the rules, the ancestor she hadn't wanted to talk about. But then that second passed, and she softly whispered, "I have a plan, Natalie Beaumont."

"What are you doing?" I asked her. But my mouth was so dry and numb, my throat so parched, it felt like I took forever to cajole my tongue into shaping those four simple words.

"No one will know," she said. "I promise. Not Harpootlian, not Szabó, not anyone. I've been over this a thousand times, worked all the angles." And she went down on one knee then, leaning over me. "But you're supposed to be asleep, Nat."

"Ellen, you don't cross Harpootlian," I croaked.

"Trust me," she said.

In that place, the two of us adrift on an island of light in an endless sea of blackness, she was the most beautiful woman I'd ever seen. Her hair was down now, and I reached up, brushing it back from her face. When my fingers moved across her scalp, I found two stubby horns, but they weren't anything a girl couldn't hide with the right hairdo and a hat.

"Ellen, what are you doing?"

"I'm about to give you a gift, Nat. The most exquisite gift in all creation. A gift that even the angels might covet. You wanted to know what the unicorn does. Well, I'm not going to tell you, I'm going to *show* you."

She put a hand between my legs and found I was already wet.

I licked at my chapped lips, fumbling for words that wouldn't come. Maybe I didn't know what she was getting at, this *gift*, but I had a feeling I didn't want any part of it, no matter how exquisite it might be. I knew these things, clear as day, but I was lost in the beauty of her, and whatever protests I might have uttered, they were about as sincere as ol' Brer Rabbit begging Brer Fox not to throw him into that briar patch. I could say I was bewitched, but it would be a lie.

She mounted me then, and I didn't argue.

"What happens now?" I asked.

"Now I fuck you," she replied. "Then I'm going to talk to my grandmother." And, with that, the world fell out from beneath me again. And the ginger-skinned eunuch moved along to the next tableau, that next set of memories I couldn't recollect on my own . . .

. . . Stars were tumbling from the skies. Not a few stray shooting stars here and there. No, *all* the stars were falling. One by one, at first, and then the sky was raining pitchforks, only it *wasn't* rain, see. It was light. The whole sorry world was being born or was dying, and I saw it didn't much matter which. Go back far enough, or far enough forward, the past and future wind up holding hands, cozy as a couple of lovebirds. Ellen had thrown open a doorway, and she'd dragged me along for the ride. I was *so* cold. I couldn't understand how there could be that much fire in the sky, and me still be freezing my tits off like that. I lay there shivering as the brittle vault of heaven collapsed. I could feel her inside me. I could feel *it* inside me, and same as I'd been lost in Ellen's beauty, I was being smothered by that ecstasy. And then . . . then the eunuch showed me the gift, which I'd forgotten . . . and which I would immediately forget again.

How do you write about something, when all that remains of it is the faintest of impressions of glory? When all you can bring to mind is the empty place where a memory ought to be and isn't, and only that conspicuous absence is there to remind you of what cannot ever be recalled? Strain as you might, all that effort hardly adds up to a trip for biscuits. So, *how do you write it down?* You don't, *that's* how. You do your damnedest to think about what came next, instead, knowing your sanity hangs in the balance.

So, here's what came *after* the gift, since le *Godemichet maudit* is a goddamn Indian giver if ever one was born. Here's the curse that rides shotgun on the gift, as impossible to obliterate from reminiscence as the other is to awaken.

There were falling stars, and that unendurable cold . . . and then the empty, aching socket to mark the countermanded gift . . . and *then* I saw the unicorn. I don't mean the dingus. I mean the *living creature*, standing in a glade of cedars, bathed in clean sunlight and radiating a light all its own. It didn't look much like what you see in storybooks or those medieval tapestries they got hanging in the Cloisters. It also didn't look much like the beast carved into the lid of Fong's wooden box. But I knew what it was, all the same.

A naked girl stood before it, and the unicorn kneeled at her feet. She sat down, and it rested its head on her lap. She whispered reassurances I couldn't hear, because they were spoken as softly as falling snow. And then she offered the unicorn one of her breasts, and I watched as it suckled. This scene of chastity and absolute peace lasted maybe a minute, may two, before the trap was sprung and the hunters stepped out from the shadows of the cedar boughs. They killed the unicorn, with cold iron lances and swords, but first the unicorn killed the virgin who'd betrayed it to its doom . . .

. . . and Harpootlian's ginger eunuch turned another page (a ham-fisted analogy if ever there was one, but it works for me), and we were back in the black room. Ellen and me. Only two of the candles were still burning, two guttering, half-hearted counterpoints to all that darkness. The other three had been snuffed out by a sudden gust of wind that had smelled of rust, sulfur, and slaughterhouse floors. I could hear Ellen crying, weeping somewhere in the darkness beyond the candles and the periphery of her protective circle. I rolled over onto my right side, still shivering, still so cold I couldn't imagine being warm ever again. I stared into the black, blinking and dimly amazed that my eyelids hadn't frozen shut. Then something snapped into focus, and there she was, cowering on her hands and knees, a tattered rag of a woman lost in the gloom. I could see her stunted, twitching tail, hardly as long as my middle finger, and the thing from the box was still strapped to her crotch. Only now it had a twin, clutched tightly in her left hand.

I think I must have asked her what the hell she'd done, though I had a pretty good idea. She turned towards me, and her eyes . . . well, you see that sort of pain, and you spend the rest of your life trying to forget you saw it.

"I didn't understand," she said, still sobbing. "I didn't understand she'd take so much of me away."

A bitter wave of conflicting, irreconcilable emotion surged and boiled about inside me. Yeah, I knew what she'd done to me, and I knew I'd been used for something unspeakable. I knew *violation* was too tame a word for it, and that I'd been marked forever by this gold-digging half-breed of a twist. And part of me was determined to drag her kicking and screaming to Harpootlian. Or fuck it, I could kill her myself, and take my own sweet time doing so. I could kill her the way the hunters had murdered the unicorn. But—on the other hand—the woman I saw lying there before me was shattered almost beyond recognition. There'd been a steep price for her trespass, and she'd paid it and then some. Besides, I was learning fast that when you've been to Hades' doorstep with someone, and the two of you make it back more or less alive, there's a bond, whether you want it or not. So, there we were, a cheap, latter-day parody of Orpheus and Eurydice, and all I could think about was holding her, tight as I could, until she stopped crying and I was warm again.

"She took *so much*," Ellen whispered. I didn't ask what her grandmother had taken. Maybe it was a slice of her soul, or maybe a scrap of her humanity. Maybe it was the memory of the happiest day of her life, or the ability to taste her favorite food. It didn't seem to matter. It was gone, and she'd never get it back. I reached for her, too cold and too sick to speak, but sharing her hurt and needing to offer my hollow consolation, stretching out to touch . . .

. . . and the eunuch said, "Madam wishes to speak with you now," and that's when I realized the parade down memory lane was over. I was back at Harpootlian's, and there was a clock somewhere chiming down to three a.m., the dead hour. I could feel the nasty welt the stingers had left at the base of my skull and underneath my jaw, and I still hadn't shaken off the hangover from that tainted shot of rye whiskey. But above and underneath and all about these mundane discomforts was a far more egregious pang, a portrait of that guileless white beast cut down and its blood spurting from gaping wounds. Still, I did manage to get myself upright without puking. Sure, I gagged once or twice, but I didn't puke. I pride myself on that. I sat with my head cradled in my hands, waiting for the room to stop tilting and sliding around like I'd gone for a spin on the Coney Island Wonder Wheel.

"Soon, you'll feel better, Miss Beaumont."

"Says you," I replied. "Anyway, give me a half a fucking minute, will you please? Surely your employer isn't gonna cast a kitten if you let me get my bearings first, not after the work-over you just gave me. Not after—"

"I will remind you, her patience is not infinite," the ginger demon said firmly, and then it clicked its long claws together.

"Yeah?" I asked. "Well, who the hell's is?" But I'd gotten the message, plain and clear. The gloves were off, and whatever forbearance Auntie H. might have granted me in the past, it was spent and now I was living on the installment plan. I took a deep breath and struggled to my feet. At least the eunuch didn't try to lend a hand.

I can't say for certain when Yeksabet Harpootlian set up shop in Manhattan, but I have it on good faith that Magdalena Szabó was here first. And anyone who knows her onions knows the two of them have been at each other's throats since the day Auntie H. decided to claim a slice of the action for herself. Now, you'd think there'd be plenty enough of the hellion cock-and-tail trade to go around, what with all the netherworlders who call the Five Boroughs their home away from home. And likely as not, you'd be right. Just don't try telling that to Szabó or Auntie H. Sure, they've each got their elite stable of "girls and boys," and they both have more customers than they know what to do with. Doesn't stop them from spending every waking hour looking for a way to banish the other once and for all—or at least find the unholy grail of competitive advantages.

Now, by the time the ginger-skinned eunuch led me through the chaos of Auntie H.'s stately pleasure dome, far below the subways and sewers and tenements of the Lower East Side, I already had a pretty good idea the dingus from Jimmy Fong's shiny box was meant to be Harpootlian's trump card. Only, here was Ellen Andrews, this mutt of a courier gumming up the works, playing fast and loose with the loving cup. And here was me, stuck smack in the middle, the unwilling stooge in her double-cross.

As I followed the eunuch down the winding corridor that ended in Auntie H.'s grand salon, we passed doorway after doorway, all of them opening onto scenes of inhuman passion and madness, the most odious of perversions, and tortures that make short work of merely mortal flesh. It would be disingenuous to say I looked away. After all, this wasn't my first time. Here were the hinterlands of wanton physical delight and agony, where the two become indistinguishable in a rapturous *Totentanz*. Here were spectacles to remind me how Doré and Hieronymus Bosch never even came close, and all of it laid bare for the eyes of any passing voyeur. You see, there are no locked doors to be found at Madam Harpootlian's. There are no doors at all.

"It's a busy night," the eunuch said, though it looked like business as usual to me.

"Sure," I muttered. "You'd think the Shriners were in town. You'd think Mayor La Guardia himself had come down off his high horse to raise a little hell."

And then we reached the end of the hallway, and I was shown into the mirrored chamber where Auntie H. holds court. The eunuch told me to wait, then left me alone. I'd never seen the place so empty. There was no sign of the usual retinue of rogues, ghouls, and archfiends, only all those goddamn mirrors, because no one looks directly at Madam Harpootlian and lives to tell the tale. I chose a particularly fancy looking glass, maybe ten feet high and held inside an elaborate gilded frame. When Harpootlian spoke up, the mirror rippled like it was only water, and my reflection rippled with it.

"Good evening, Natalie," she said. "I trust you've been treated well?"

"You won't hear any complaints outta me," I replied. "I always say, the Waldorf-Astoria's got nothing on you."

She laughed then, or something that we'll call laughter for the sake of convenience.

"A crying shame we're not meeting under more amicable circumstances. Were it not for this unpleasantness with Miss Andrews, I'd offer you something—on the house, of course."

"Maybe another time," I said.

"So, you *know* why you're here?"

"Sure," I said. "The dingus I took off the dead Chinaman. The salami with the fancy French name."

"It has many names, Natalie. Karkadann's Brow, *El consolador sangriento,* the Horn of Malta—"

"*Le Godemichet maudit,*" I said. "Ellen's cock."

Harpootlian grunted, and her reflection made an ugly dismissive gesture. "It is nothing of Miss Andrews. It is mine, bought and paid for. With the sweat of my own brow did I track down the spoils of al-Jaldaki's long search. It's *my* investment, one purchased with so grievous a forfeiture this quadroon mongrel could not begin to appreciate the severity of her crime. But you, Natalie, you know, don't you? You've been privy to the wonders of Solomon's talisman, so I think, maybe, you are cognizant of my loss."

"I can't exactly say what I'm cognizant of," I told her, doing my best to stand up straight and not flinch or look away. "I saw the murder of a creature I didn't even believe in yesterday morning. That was sort of an eye opener, I'll grant you. And then there's the part I can't seem to conjure up, even after golden boy did that swell Roto-Rooter number on my head."

"Yes. Well, that's the catch," she said and smiled. There's no shame in saying I looked away then. Even in a mirror, the smile of Yeksabet Harpootlian isn't something you want to see straight on.

"Isn't there always a catch?" I asked, and she chuckled.

"True, it's a fleeting boon," she purred. "The gift comes, and then it goes, and no one may ever remember it. But always, *always* they will long for it again, even hobbled by that ignorance."

"You've lost me, Auntie," I said, and she grunted again. That's when I told her I wouldn't take it as an insult to my intelligence or expertise if she laid her cards on the table and spelled it out plain and simple, like she was talking to a woman who didn't regularly have tea and crumpets with the damned. She mumbled something to the effect that maybe she gave me too much credit, and I didn't disagree.

"Consider," she said, "what it *is*, a unicorn. It is the incarnation of purity, an avatar of innocence. And here is the *power* of the talisman, for that state of grace which soon passes from us each and everyone is forever locked inside the horn, the horn become the phallus. And in the instant that it brought you, Natalie, to orgasm, you knew again that innocence, the bliss of a child before it suffers corruption."

I didn't interrupt her, but all at once I got the gist.

"Still, you are only a mortal woman, so what negligible, insignificant sins could you have possibly committed during your short life? Likewise, whatever calamities and wrongs have been visited upon your flesh *or* you soul, they are trifles. But if you survived the war in Paradise, if you refused the yoke and so are counted among the exiles, then you've persisted down all the long eons. You were already broken and despoiled billions of years before the coming of man. And your transgressions outnumber the stars."

"Now," she asked, "what would *you* pay, were you so cursed, to know even one fleeting moment of that stainless, former existence?"

Starting to feel sick to my stomach all over again, I said, "More to the point, if I *always* forgot it, immediately, but it left this emptiness I feel—"

"You would come back," Auntie H. smirked. "You would come back again and again and again, because there would be no satiating that void, and always would you hope that maybe *this* time it would take and you might *keep* the memories of that immaculate condition."

"Which makes it priceless, no matter what you paid."

"Precisely. And now Miss Andrews has forged a copy—an *identical* copy, actually—meaning to sell one to me, and one to Magdalena Szabó. That's where Miss Andrews is now."

"Did you tell her she could hex me?"

"I would never do such a thing, Natalie. You're much too valuable to me."

"*But* you think I had something to do with Ellen's mystical little counterfeit scheme."

"Technically, you did. The ritual of division required a supplicant, someone to *receive* the gift granted by the unicorn, before the summoning of a succubus mighty enough to affect such a difficult twinning."

"So maybe, instead of sitting here bumping gums with me, you should send one of your torpedoes after her. And, while we're on the subject of how you pick your little henchmen, maybe—"

"*Natalie*," snarled Auntie H. from someplace not far behind me. "Have I failed to make myself *understood*? Might it be I need to raise my voice?" The floor rumbled, and tiny hairline cracks began to crisscross the surface of the looking glass. I shut my eyes.

"No," I told her. "I get it. It's a grift, and you're out for blood. But you *know* she used me. Your lackey, it had a good, long look around my upper story, right, and there's no way you can think I was trying to con you."

For a dozen or so heartbeats, she didn't answer me, and the mirrored room was still and silent, save all the moans and screaming leaking in through the walls. I could smell my own sour sweat, and it was making me sick to my stomach.

"There are some gray areas," she said finally. "Matters of sentiment and lust, a certain reluctant infatuation, even."

I opened my eyes and forced myself to gaze directly into that mirror, at the abomination crouched on its writhing throne. And all at once, I'd had enough, enough of Ellen Andrews and her dingus, enough of the cloak and dagger bullshit, and definitely enough kowtowing to the monsters.

"For fuck's sake," I said, "I only just met the woman this afternoon. She drugs and rapes me, and you think that means she's my sheba?"

"Like I told you, I think there are gray areas," Auntie H. replied. She grinned, and I looked away again.

"Fine. You tell me what it's gonna take to make this right with you, and I'll do it."

"Always so eager to please," Auntie H. laughed, and the mirror in front of me rippled. "But, since you've asked, and as I do not doubt your *present* sincerity, I will tell you. I want her dead, Natalie. Kill her, and all will be . . . forgiven."

"Sure," I said, because what the hell else was I going to say. "But if she's with Szabó—"

"I have spoken already with Magdalena Szabó, and we have agreed to set aside our differences long enough to deal with Miss Andrews. After all, she has attempted to cheat us both, in equal measure."

"How do I find her?"

"You're a resourceful young lady, Natalie," she said. "I have faith in you. Now . . . if you will excuse me," and, before I could get in another word, the mirrored room dissolved around me. There was a flash, not of light, but of the deepest abyssal darkness, and I found myself back at the Yellow Dragon, watching through the bookshop's grimy windows as the sun rose over the Bowery.

There you go, the dope on just how it is I found myself holding a gun on Ellen Andrews, and just how it is she found herself wondering if I was angry enough or scared enough or desperate enough to pull the trigger. And like I said, I chambered a round, but she just stood there. She didn't even flinch.

"I wanted to give you a gift, Nat," she said.

"Even if I believed that—and I don't—all I got to show for this *gift* of yours is a nagging yen for something I'm never going to get back. We lose our innocence, it stays lost. That's the way it works. So, all I got from you, Ellen, is a thirst can't ever be slaked. That and Harpootlian figuring me for a clip artist."

She looked hard at the gun, then looked harder at me.

"So what? You thought I was gonna plead for my life? You thought maybe I was gonna get down on my knees for you and beg? Is that how you like it? Maybe you're just steamed cause I was on top—"

"Shut up, Ellen. You don't get to talk yourself out of this mess. It's a done deal. You tried to give Auntie H. the high hat."

"And you honestly think she's on the level? You think you pop me and she lets you off the hook, like nothing happened?"

"I do," I said. And maybe it wasn't as simple as that, but I wasn't exactly

I pondered this. "I don't know. What do you think?"

Corey grinned, a sudden, gap-toothed smile. "Yeah, he did. The best one."

"What do you think Willy named—?"

"Teacher!" someone wailed.

I turned. A group of kids ran toward me in geese formation. The girl in the lead scrabbled to a stop. "Teacher," she said, "Kevin threw my softball over the fence!"

Kevin slid to a halt. "Can I help it if Gabby can't catch?"

"First things first," I said. "Where did it go over the fence?"

Kevin and Gabby pointed, then glared at each other. I sighted down their fingers . . . to the far corner and the rainbow woman.

A child stood beside her, a boy with a buzz—Josue Hernandez. I'd had him two years ago. He stood beside her, intent on her hands as they skipped like pebbles across her lap.

An image seared through me: *Josue resting his head in the woman's lap. He dissolved like steam—*

By the time the image faded, I was halfway across the field, the gaggle of students squawking behind me. I froze five feet from Josue and the woman. Josue seemed . . . faded, as if he'd been stonewashed. His eyes were no longer chocolate dark, but faint as a shadow on sun-dried mud. He gazed at the woman's hands.

Long and slender, her hands were crosshatched with tiny nicks. She wore porcelain thimbles on her left thumb and forefinger. She wielded a golden needle with her right, embroidering something onto her skirt with a dark thread. I stepped closer. Her lap glittered as if appliquéd with mirrors. I took another step. No, not mirrors—tiny unicorns that sparkled like distant stars. The newest one, a dull, black unicorn on a field of green, lacked its horn. The woman's hands stopped. I looked up—

"Ms. Scibilin! Ms. Scibilin!" someone yelled. "Gabby threw Kevin's shoe over the fence!"

Little hands dragged me to the fence and pointed out the ball, embedded in a pumpkin, and the shoe, dangling from a bare guide wire. When I turned back to the woman, she and Josue were gone.

———

I walked onto the playground and scanned the field as I had every day for the past week. There was no sign of the woman. I frowned, disappointed. Juanita Vargas, the principal, had promised to call the police next time the woman set foot on the school grounds.

Even if she couldn't remember Josue or the girl.

Corey fell in step beside me. We'd shared three more books after school—two on dogs and one on magic tricks. He'd taken home the magic book.

"I figured out the Kleenex trick," he said. "How to make it disappear? But I can't get the penny one."

"That's a tough one," I said. "I'll help you with it after school."

He grinned at me. I smiled back, then did a quick survey of the field.

A chill wind whistled across the playground, rearranging the fallen leaves. A string of girls threaded their way between Corey and me, chasing orange and gold maple leaves. I scanned the play structures, lingering on a possible fight, then circled slowly. A football game skirmished along the edge of the field. Beyond the grass-stained players, Corey leaned against the fence, watching the woman.

I snatched at Gabby's wrist as she walked by. "Gabby," I said. "Go to the office and tell Ms. Vargas I need her to make that phone call. *Now.*"

Corey inched closer to the woman.

My chest constricted. I ran toward Corey. I glanced at the woman. She had another child with her, not what's-his-name, Josue, but a blonde second grader, one of Kristy's. Amanda Schuyler. The woman looked up, and even at that distance, I could swear she was looking at me—

"Ms. Scibilin! Watch out!"

Three hurtling bodies tackled me in the end zone. They tumbled over the top of me, then scrambled away. "Teacher, are you all right?" someone said.

I spat out a mouthful of grass. "I'm fine."

I swayed to my feet, then sat down abruptly. I knew if I glanced at the corner, Amanda and the woman would be gone.

I limped into the office an hour after the last bell. Panic muted the pain. The police had found nothing, no bits of thread, no embroidery needles, no matted grass. I'd sent them to Kristy's class to talk to Amanda Schuyler. Kristy told them she didn't have an Amanda Schuyler and never had. . . .

I winced, lowering myself into the secretary's chair. I went through the roll sheets, then the emergency cards. I even hobbled over to the filing cabinet and searched the cumulative folders. According to the Cayuga Elementary School records, Josue Hernandez and Amanda Schuyler did not exist. Not even in their siblings' cum files.

I struck the filing cabinet with my fist.

Juanita poked her head into the office. "You okay?"

"Fine," I muttered. I slipped Jason Schuyler's cum folder back in place, then slammed the filing cabinet.

Juanita studied me. "They hit you pretty hard. You're going to Doctors on Duty."

"I'm fine, Juanita. Really—"

She raised two elegantly penciled eyebrows. "District'll foot the bill if you go now. Something shows up later, you'll need a paper trail."

I hesitated. She was right, but—

"You're going," she said. She jangled her keys. "Come on. I'll drive."

Juanita insisted I drape my arm around her neck as we crept slowly down the front steps. I hunched deeper into my jacket, hoping no one was watching. "Juanita," I said in a low voice, "it's just a bruise. I'll be stiff for a few days, then it'll disappear."

Juanita grunted under my weight. "Could be fractured."

Fractured. I grimaced. "Great."

We passed the potted rosemary. Corey peeked between its branches, his face pale in the shadows. He bit down on his lower lip and withdrew.

I twisted my head to try to catch another glimpse of him. This is where I needed to be. With Corey, not in some clinic. "Juanita, I'm fine, really. It's just a bruise—"

Juanita stopped. She eyed me coolly. "I'm not worried about your leg. I'm worried about your head."

My cheeks flamed. My head—because no one else remembered Amanda Schuyler.

No fractures, leg or skull, just a bruise the size of a cantaloupe. Between the wait, the exam—complete with X-rays—and Juanita's unwillingness to release me unfed, it was almost seven when I made it back to the school. I waited until Juanita sped away, then got out of my car and limped up the steps. I searched behind the rosemary. No Corey, but tucked between the planter and the wall was the book of magic tricks.

Corey veered away from me when he walked into the classroom next morning. Head down, he put his backpack in his cubby and shuffled to his desk.

At one point Lily, the girl seated next to him, opened his desk and took his crayons. "Lily," I said. "Put those back and ask Corey if you may borrow them."

"He's not here—" Lily sat up, startled. Her eyes grew as round as slammers when she saw Corey. Backing away, she dropped his crayons.

Corey sat quietly, hands folded in his lap.

Within an hour, the class had forgotten him again.

It took me several minutes to find Corey when I went out for lunch recess.

He huddled ten feet from the woman. No one stood beside her this time. Her hands lay still in that colorful expanse of glittering unicorns. I imagined the one she'd been working on while the dark-haired boy hovered over her. I tried to recall the boy's name or face, but all I could remember was that dull, black embroidery amid the stellar unicorns.

I limped toward them. Girls. There had been two girls, too. But I could remember nothing but a sense of them, like perfume lingering in a closed room.

Corey took a step toward the woman. Her face tilted toward him. She seemed to be talking to him, coaxing him—

I gasped at the image: *Corey resting his head in the woman's lap, fading like mist in sunlight to become—*

I stared at Corey and the woman, not daring to shift my gaze. As if by watching them, I could keep that little head from lowering itself to that glittering field.

The woman's hands nested in her lap. Corey leaned into the fence; it bowed behind him like a hammock.

Gritting my teeth, I pushed myself to a lunging jog. The bruise throbbed along my hip. I cupped my hands to my mouth and called.

Corey flinched at the sound of his name, but refused to look at me. He stepped closer to the woman and knelt before her. She reached to pull his head into her lap. . . .

I lumbered toward them, tensing against the pain. Three, four yards and I'd be there. Sucking in a deep breath, I shouted, "Corey, get away from her!"

He snapped upright, swinging to look at me. The woman touched his leg. She murmured something. He glared at me, then bent toward her. The woman ran her fingers through his hair—

I grasped him by the arm. The woman pulled her hand back, plucking a lock of his ginger hair.

"Corey," I said. I dragged him away, reaching out to steady him with my other hand. With a growl, he wrenched away from me and ran toward the buildings. I sagged with relief, then turned on the woman. "Who are you?" I said. "What do you want—?"

She was gone.

I knelt beside the rosemary, parting its branches. "Corey?"

Reaching behind the planter, I patted the landing. I withdrew my dust-covered fingers.

I sat next to the planter. Late afternoon closed around me. "I have a special book for you," I said, hoping he was within hearing. The shadows deepened. I glanced at my watch. Four fourteen. "It's about dogs," I said. If I stayed too late and he refused to come out of hiding, he'd miss his dad. "Corey, I'm sorry about yesterday," I said. "Ms. Vargas took me to the doctor. By the time I got back, you were gone." I glanced at my watch again. Four thirty-five. A car pulled up to the curb. I sat up. A teenage couple got out and strolled across the front lawn, arm in arm. "Corey," I said. "I'm going.

I don't want you to miss your dad." I pulled the book on Samoyeds from my book bag. "I'll leave this for you," I said. "Behind the planter. I'll see you tomorrow, okay?"

I arrived at school early the next morning, to see if Corey had taken the book. A shoe peeped from the planter's shadow. Puzzled, I squatted beside the rosemary. Corey curled around the planter, his backpack tucked under his head. His mouth hung slack, his eyes were closed. My heart lurched. I reached in and touched him. He murmured, then jerked awake, eyes wide.

I wound my arms around him and pulled him out. I hugged him. The chill of him seeped through my sweater. I smoothed the hair from his face. "Corey, have you been here all night?"

He nodded.

The breath went out of me. "Your father. . . ?"

He looked at me blankly. "Father?"

"My God," I whispered. I held him tight, rocking him. "What has that woman done?"

I had to look up his father in the phone book. Corey's emergency card was gone. So was his cumulative file. When Mr. Ferris answered, he had no idea who I was. "There must be some mistake," he said curtly. "I don't have a son—"

"But Corey—"

"Corey," he said. His voice grew wistful. "That was my grandfather's name." The curtness returned. "Sorry. Wrong Ferris." He hung up.

I weighed the receiver in my hand, then set it down. I went into the nurse's office. Corey huddled under a pile of blankets. I sat next to him. "Hungry?" I said.

He shook his head.

Peggy breezed in, glanced at Corey, yanked open the medicine cabinet. She took out a bottle of lotion. "New student?" she said.

Corey had worked his way to the end of the line by the time I led my students into the classroom. The boy just ahead of him shut the door in his face as if he weren't there. I opened the door and, taking his hand, led him inside.

When I took roll, his name wasn't listed. I flipped through the old roll sheets. According to these, he'd never been listed. I wrote him in and marked him "present."

During independent reading time, I walked over and crouched beside him. "She can't have you," I said. "I won't let her."

I kept him in during morning recess. I read to him; he stared out the window at the field. I moved my chair so that he had to look at me. "What did she promise you?" I said. "Where is she trying to take you?"

He turned away from me.

I touched his knee. "Corey?"

He slumped in his chair, staring at his desk.

The hair tickled along the back of my neck. On a hunch, I opened his desk. It was empty.

I followed him onto the playground at lunchtime. He ran across the field to the fence. I tried to keep up, but the bruise slowed me down. I gritted my teeth, trying to ignore the pain. He spurted ahead. The woman sat in the corner, waiting, her right hand raised slightly. A glint of gold winked between her fingers.

Corey stumbled to a stop in front of her.

"Leave him alone!" I shouted. "Leave them *all* alone!"

Neither Corey nor the woman turned.

I tripped, somehow caught myself. I winced, closing my eyes—

The image swept through me like a flash flood: *Corey, the boy, the two girls, countless other children, resting their heads in the woman's lap. One by one they blazed and disappeared like shooting stars, the only trace of them the bright unicorns on the woman's rainbow skirt—*

I forced my eyes open. Corey inched closer to the woman, his shins brushing her knee. The woman plunged the needle in and out of the cloth like a seabird diving through waves. I limped up to her, clenching and unclenching my hands.

Beneath the woman's needle, the outline of a unicorn was slowly taking shape on a field of blue, stitched in lusterless ginger thread. I searched the constellation of unicorns for the dull, black one, that other boy's, but couldn't find it. I finally located it on its field of green—now as bright as all the others.

Then a dull shape caught my eye. I took a step closer. Amid all the sparkling, prancing unicorns stood one small, brown horse on a field of blue.

Me.

I stood beside the rainbow woman. Her needle stitched the blue cloth with my hair, filling in the outline of the tiny unicorn. I knelt, my breath quick and shallow as I waited anxiously for her to finish. I would be someone. I would no longer be forgotten. I would become—

Corey dropped to his knees.

I tried to reel the image back, tried to remember. For Corey's sake. For mine.

I would become one of those gleaming unicorns that danced in her eyes.

I looked slowly from the woman's lap.

And trembled, that forgotten longing aching through me. Too frightened to take her in all at once, I started with her hair, that thick, manzanita-red mane that tumbled over her shoulders, then the perfect oval of her chin, the strawberry ripeness of her lips, the gentle slope of her nose. I steeled myself. Her eyes. . . .

Her eyes had no color—not even white or black. I gazed into them, knowing what I would find there when my own longing had peeled away the layers of this world: unicorns, tossing their heads, light spiraling down their horns. . . .

I held my breath. They were more beautiful than I remembered. And so many—herds of them, streaking through the woodlands like a meteor shower. My ears rang with the drum of their cloven hooves.

If this is what Corey wanted, to join these magnificent creatures, who was I to stand in his way? I took a step back.

Rage kindled in me. Who had stood in *my* way?

I froze. Mrs. Rodriguez.

Kneeling beside me, she had forced my head up so that I could no longer see the gold needle pierce the blue cloth. "An illusion, Mary," she said. "There is so much in the world, so many things to discover and explore and create. Don't give up everything for an illusion."

I fought her, fought her words and the urging of her hands as she forced me to look. . . .

I swallowed, my throat dry and tight. But if this was what Corey wanted, who was I to deny him?

I am no Mrs. Rodriguez.

I am no saint.

The unicorns wheeled and galloped before me, a stampede of light. Then one of the unicorns stopped and faced me.

It yearned toward me, its eyes overflowing with a terrible loneliness. Another unicorn stopped, and another, until at least a dozen stared back at me. The first unicorn's longing echoed from eye to eye.

Their sadness sickened me. Without looking away, I groped for Corey. My hand clasped his shoulder. I drew him to me, caging him with my elbows and cupping his chin in my hands. I raised his head. "Look, Corey," I said. "Look into her eyes. If this is what you want, I'll let you go. But be sure."

He squirmed. More unicorns stopped to gaze at us.

"I want to be like them!" he said.

"Look *hard* at them, Corey," I said, reluctant to fulfill my promise. "See how lonely they are?"

"And is it any different here?" the woman said, her voice as husky as woodsmoke. "You are lonely here, Corey. There you will have others of your kind."

I wet my lips. "Corey—"

The woman hissed. "Leave us, meddler. You have nothing to offer him."

"Nothing," Corey said. But the word trailed with doubt.

My heart pounded. What had Mrs. Rodriguez said? What had finally reached me?

But I couldn't find the words. Frantic, I lashed out. "What does *she* have to offer you? An illusion, Corey. A lie. It's not real. It's like the Kleenex trick—"

Corey strained against my arms. The unicorns loped away.

"Let him go," the woman said. "He is mine. You have nothing for him. Absolutely nothing."

I loosened my grip slowly. My voice cracked. "Maybe I don't, but this world does. I saw you, Corey. I wanted to be your friend. Other people will, too. And they'll want to see that Kleenex trick. They'll want to know what Willy named his new dog."

The unicorns returned, gazing at me intently.

"They'll chase leaves," I said. "They'll throw balls and shoes over the fence. Your father will pick you up and take you out for ice cream. And I can—I can teach you the penny trick."

Corey stood still as my arms fell away. The unicorns crept closer—

Their faces changed. Josue peered back at me, and Amanda and Heather. Jason from Peggy's class last year and Mindy from Kristy's class two years ago. More. Children I had never known. . . .

I doubled around the ache in my stomach. I had stopped trying and I had failed them, all of them. I had failed Corey.

The woman blinked. Her eyes became colorless once more.

Corey cried out. He grabbed me, burrowing under my arm, his breath hot and damp through my sweater. I clung to him, resting my cheek on his head. His hair smelled of rosemary. My gaze fell to the woman's hands.

She jerked the needle, snapping the thread. Dull and hornless, the ginger unicorn sank into a fold as she stood. "You've promised him much," she said. "Don't let him down."

She vanished.

Corey choked back a sob. His hands twisted the hem of my sweater. I held him with one arm. With my free hand, I fished a Kleenex from my skirt pocket. Footsteps stampeded toward us. I jerked to look. Unicorns. . . ?

Children.

"Ms. Scibilin! Ms. Scibilin!" a chorus of voices shouted. Small hands pulled at us, some patting me, some patting Corey. "What's wrong with Corey? Is Corey all right? Corey, you okay?"

"He's fine," I said.

Corey's chest shuddered with a deep breath. Tears beaded his lashes. I handed him the Kleenex. He stared at it a minute, then looked up at me.

Eagerness and wonder dwelt in those gray eyes. So did Mrs. Rodriguez. So did I.

He held up the Kleenex so that the other children could see it. "Want to see me make it disappear?" he said.

THE HIGHEST JUSTICE

Garth Nix

The girl did not ride the unicorn, because no one ever did. She rode a nervous oat-colored palfrey that had no name, and led the second horse, a blind and almost-deaf ancient who long ago had been called Rinaldo and was now simply Rin. The unicorn sometimes paced next to the palfrey, and sometimes not.

Rin bore the dead Queen on his back, barely noticing her twitches and mumbles and the cloying stench of decaying flesh that seeped out through the honey- and spice-soaked bandages. She was tied to the saddle, but could have snapped those bonds if she had thought to do so. She had become monstrously strong since her death three days before, and the intervention by her daughter that had returned her to a semblance of life.

Not that Princess Jess as a witch or necromancer. She knew no more magic than any other young woman. But she was fifteen years old, a virgin, and she believed the old tale of the kingdom's founding: that the unicorn who had aided the legendary Queen Jessibelle the First was still alive and would honor the compact made so long ago, to come in the time of the kingdom's need.

The unicorn's secret name was Elibet. Jess had called this name to the waxing moon at midnight from the tallest tower of the castle, and had seen something ripple in answer across the surface of the earth's companion in the sky.

An hour later Elibet was in the tower. She was somewhat like a horse with a horn, if you looked at her full on, albeit one made of white cloud and moonshine. Looked at sideways she was a fiercer thing, of less familiar shape, made of storm clouds and darkness, the horn more prominent and bloody at the tip, like the setting sun. Jess preferred to see a white horse with a silvery horn, and so that was what she saw.

Jess had called the unicorn as her mother gasped out her final breath. The unicorn had come too late to save the Queen, but by then Jess had another plan. The unicorn listened and then by the power of her horn, brought back some part of the Queen to inhabit a body from which life had all too quickly sped.

They had then set forth, to seek the Queen's poisoner, and mete out justice.

Jess halted her palfrey as they came to a choice of ways. The royal forest was thick and dark in these parts, and the path was no more than a beaten track some dozen paces wide. It forked ahead, into two lesser, narrower paths.

"Which way?" asked Jess, speaking to the unicorn, who had once again mysteriously appeared at her side.

The unicorn pointed her horn at the left-hand path.

"Are you sure—" Jess asked. "No, it's just that—"

"The other way looks more traveled—"

"No, I'm not losing heart—"

"I know you know—"

"Talking to yourself?" interjected a rough male voice, the only other sound in the forest, for if the unicorn had spoken, no one but Jess had heard her.

The palfrey shied as Jess swung around and reached for her sword. But she was too late, as a dirty bearded ruffian held a rusty pike to her side. He grinned, and raised his eyebrows.

"Here's a tasty morsel, then," he leered. "Step down lightly, and no tricks."

"Elibet!" said Jess indignantly.

The unicorn slid out of the forest behind the outlaw, and lightly pricked

145

him in the back of his torn leather jerkin with her horn. The man's eyebrows went up still farther and his eyes darted to the left and right.

"Ground your pike," said Jess. "My friend can strike faster than any man."

"I give up," he wheezed, leaning forward as if he might escape the sharp horn. "Ease off on the spear, and take me to the sheriff. I swear—"

"Hunger," interrupted the Queen. Her voice had changed with her death. It had become gruff and leathery, and significantly less human.

The bandit glanced at the veiled figure under the broad-brimmed pilgrim's hat.

"What?" he asked hesitantly.

"Hunger," groaned the Queen. "Hunger."

She raised her right arm, and the leather cord that bound her to the saddle's high cantle snapped with a sharp crack. A bandage came loose at her wrist and dropped to the ground in a series of spinning turns, revealing the mottled blue-bruised skin beneath.

"Shoot 'em!" shouted the bandit as he dove under Jess's horse and scuttled across the path toward the safety of the trees. As he ran, an arrow flew over his head and struck the Queen in the shoulder. Another, coming behind it, went past Jess's head as she jerked herself forward and down. The third was struck out of the air by a blur of vaguely unicorn-shaped motion. There were no more arrows, but a second later there was a scream from halfway up a broad oak that loomed over the path ahead, followed by the heavy thud of a body hitting the ground.

Jess drew her sword and kicked her palfrey into a lurching charge. She caught the surviving bandit just before he managed to slip between two thorny bushes, and landed a solid blow on his head with the back of the blade. She hadn't meant to be merciful, but the sword had turned in her sweaty grasp. He fell under the horse's feet, and got trampled a little before Jess managed to turn about.

She glanced down to make sure he was at least dazed, but sure of this, spared him no more time. Her mother had broken the bonds on her left arm as well, and was ripping off the veil that hid her face.

"Hunger!" boomed the Queen, loud enough even for poor old deaf Rin to hear. He stopped eating the grass and lifted his head, time-worn nostrils almost smelling something he didn't like.

"Elibet! Please . . ." beseeched Jess. "A little longer—we must be almost there."

The unicorn stepped out from behind a tree and looked at her. It was the look of a stern teacher about to allow a pupil some small favor.

"One more touch, please, Elibet."

The unicorn bent her head, paced over to the dead Queen, and touched the woman lightly with her horn, briefly imbuing her with a subtle nimbus of summer sunshine, bright in the shadowed forest. Propelled by that strange light, the arrow in the Queen's shoulder popped out, the blue-black bruises on her arms faded, and her skin shone, pink and new. She stopped fumbling with the veil, slumped down in her saddle, and let out a relatively delicate and human-sounding snore.

"Thank you," said Jess.

She dismounted and went to look at the bandit. He had sat up and was trying to wipe away the blood that slowly dripped across his left eye.

"So you give up, do you?" Jess asked, and snorted.

The bandit didn't answer.

Jess pricked him with her sword, so he was forced to look at her.

"I should finish you off here and now," said Jess fiercely. "Like your friend."

"My brother," muttered the man. "But you won't finish me, will you? You're the rightful type, I can tell. Take me to the sheriff. Let him do what needs to be done."

"You're probably in league with the sheriff," said Jess.

"Makes no odds to you, anyways. Only the sheriff has the right to justice in this wood. King's wood, it is."

"I have the right to the Middle and the Low Justice, under the King," said Jess, but even as she said it, she knew it was the wrong thing to say. Robbery and attempted murder in the King's wood were matters for the High Justice.

"Slip of a girl like you? Don't be daft," the bandit said, laughing. "Besides, it's the High Justice for me. I'll go willingly along to the sheriff."

"I don't have time to take you to the sheriff," said Jess. She could not help glancing back at her mother. Already there were tiny spots of darkness visible on her arm, like the first signs of mold on bread.

"Better leave me, then," said the bandit. He smiled, an expression that was part cunning and part relief beginning to appear upon his weather-beaten face.

"Leave you!" exploded Jess. "I'm not going to—What?"

She tilted her head, to look at a patch of shadow in the nearer trees.

"You have the High Justice? Really?"

"Who are you talking to?" asked the bandit nervously. The cunning look remained, but the relief was rapidly disappearing.

"Very well. I beseech you, in the King's name, to judge this man fairly. As you saw, he sought to rob me, and perhaps worse, and told his companion to shoot."

"Who are you talking to?" screamed the bandit. He staggered to his feet as Jess backed off, keeping her sword out and steady, aimed now at his guts.

"Your judge," said Jess. "Who I believe is about to announce—"

Jess stopped talking as the unicorn appeared behind the bandit, her horn already through the man's chest. The bandit walked another step, unknowing, then his mouth fell open and he looked down at the sharp whorled spike that had seemingly grown out of his heart. He lifted his hand to grasp it, but halfway there nerves and muscles failed, and his life was ended.

The unicorn tossed her head, and the bandit's corpse slid off, into the forest mulch.

Jess choked a little, and coughed. She hadn't realized she had stopped breathing. She had seen men killed before, but not by a unicorn. Elibet snorted, and wiped her horn against the trunk of a tree, like a bird sharpening its beak.

"Yes. Yes, you're right," said Jess. "I know we must hurry."

Jess quickly fastened her mother's bandages and bonds and rearranged the veil before mounting her palfrey. It shivered under her as she took up the reins, and looked back with one wild eye.

"Hup!" said Jess, and dug in her heels. She took the left-hand path, ducking under a branch.

They came to the King's hunting lodge at nightfall. It had been a simple fort once, a rectangle of earth ramparts, but the King had built a large wooden hall at its center, complete with an upper solar that had glass windows, the whole of it topped with a sharply sloped roof of dark red tiles.

A lodge and fort lay in the middle of a broad forest clearing, which was currently lit by several score of lanterns, hung from hop poles. Jess grimaced as she saw the lanterns, though it was much as she expected. The lodge was, after all, her father's favorite trysting place. The lanterns would be a "romantic" gesture from the King to his latest and most significant mistress.

The guards saw her coming, and possibly recognized the palfrey. Two came out cautiously to the forest's edge, swords drawn, while several others watched from the ramparts, their bows held ready. The King was not well-loved by his subjects, with good cause. But his guards were well-paid and, so long as they had not spent their last pay, loyal.

"Princess Jess?" asked the closer guard. "What brings you here?"

He was a new guard, who had not yet experienced enough of the King's court to be hardened by it, or so sickened that he sought to leave to return to his family's estate. His name was Piers, and he was only a year or two older than Jess. She knew him as well as a Princess might know a servant, for her mother had long ago advised her to remember the names of all the guards, and make friends of them as soon as she could.

"Oh, I'm glad to see you, Piers," sighed Jess. She gestured to the cloaked and veiled figure behind. It was dark enough that the guards would not immediately see the Queen's bonds. "It is my mother. She wished to see the King."

"Your Highness!" exclaimed Piers, and he bent his head, as did his companion, a man the other guards called Old Briars, though his name was Brian and he was not that old. "But where are your attendants? Your guards?"

"They follow," said Jess. She let her horse amble forward, so the guards had to scramble to keep alongside. "We came on ahead. My mother must see the King immediately. It is an urgent matter. She is not well."

"His Majesty the King ordered that he not be disturbed—" rumbled Old Briars.

"My mother must see His Majesty," said Jess. "Perhaps, Piers, you could run ahead and warn . . . let the King know we will soon be with him?"

"Better not, boy. You know what—" Old Briars started to say. He was interrupted by the Queen, who suddenly sat straighter and rasped out a single word.

"Edmund . . ."

Either the King's name, spoken so strangely by the Queen, or the desperate look on Jess's small, thin face made Old Briars stop talking and stand aside.

"I'll go at once," said Piers, with sudden decision. "Brian, show Their Highnesses into the *hall*."

He laid a particular stress on the last word, which Jess knew meant "Keep them out of the solar," the upper chamber that the King had undoubtedly already retired to with his latest mistress, the Lady Lieka— who, unlike Jess, actually was a witch.

They left the horses at the tumbledown stable near the gate. The King had not bothered to rebuild that. As Jess untied the Queen and helped her down, she saw Brian working hard to keep his expression stolid, to maintain the professional unseeing look all the guardsmen had long perfected. The King being what he was, the outer guards usually did not want to see anything. If they did want to watch, or even participate, they joined his inner retinue.

The Queen was mumbling and twitching again. Jess had to breathe through her mouth to avoid the stench that was overcoming spices and scent.

"Ed-mund . . ." rasped the Queen as Jess led her to the hall. "Ed-mund . . ."

"Yes, Mother," soothed Jess. "You will see him in a moment."

She caught a glimpse of Elibet as Brian stood aside to let them pass through the great oaken door of the hall. Piers was waiting inside, and he bowed deeply as they went in. He didn't notice the unicorn streaming in ahead, the smoke from the fire and candles eddying as she passed.

The King was seated at the high table as if he had been there all the time, though Jess could tell he had just thrown a richly furred robe of red and gold over his nightshirt. Lady Lieka, clad in a similar robe, sat on a low stool at his side, and poured a stream of dark wine into the King's jeweled goblet, as if she were some ordinary handmaiden.

None of the King's usual henchmen were with him, which suggested a very rapid descent from the solar. Jess could still hear laughter and talking above. The absence of courtiers and the inner guards could be a bad sign. The King liked an audience for his more ordinary deeds of foulness but preferred privacy when it came to mistreating his own family.

"Milady Queen and my . . . thoughtful . . . daughter," boomed out the King. "What brings you to this poor seat?"

He was very angry, Jess could tell, though his voice did not betray that anger. It was in the tightness in his eyes and the way he sat, leaning forward, ready to roar and hurl abuse.

"Ed-mund . . . " said the Queen, the word half a growl and half a sigh. She staggered forward. Jess ran after her, and took off her hat, the veil coming away with it.

"What is this!" exclaimed the King, rising to his feet.

"Edmund . . . " rasped the Queen. Her face was gray and blotched, and flies clustered in the corners of her desiccated eyes, all the signs of a death three days gone returning as the unicorn's blessing faded.

"Lieka!" screamed the King.

The Queen shambled forward, her arms outstretched, the bandages unwinding behind her. Flesh peeled off her fingers as she flexed them, white bone reflecting the fire- and candlelight.

"She was poisoned!" shouted Jess angrily. She pointed accusingly at Lieka. "Poisoned by your leman! Yet even dead she loves you still!"

"No!" shrieked the King. He stood on his chair and looked wildly about. "Get her away. Lieka!"

"One kiss," mumbled the Queen. She pursed her lips, and gray-green spittle fell from her wizened mouth. "Love . . . love . . ."

"Be calm, my dove," said Lieka. She rested one almond-white hand on the King's shoulder. Under her touch he sank back down into his high-backed chair. "You—strike off her head."

She spoke to Piers. He had unsheathed his sword, but remained near the door.

"Don't, Piers!" said Jess. "Kiss her, Father, and she will be gone. That's all she wants."

"Kill it!" shrieked the King.

Piers strode across the hall, but Jess held out one beseeching hand. He stopped by her side, and went no farther. The Queen slowly shambled on, rasping and muttering as she progressed toward the raised dais, the King and Lady Lieka.

"Traitors," whined the King. "I am surrounded by traitors."

"One kiss!" shouted Jess. "You owe her that."

"Not all are traitors, Majesty," purred Lieka. She spoke in the King's ear, careless of the Queen's pathetic faltering step up on the dais. "Shall I rid you of this relict?"

"Yes!" answered the King. "Yes!"

He turned to look the other way, shielding his face in his hands. Lieka took up a six-branched silver candelabra and whispered to it, the candle flames blazing high in answer to her call.

"Father!" screamed Jess. "One kiss! That's all she wants!"

Lieka thrust out the candelabra as the Queen finally made it onto the dais and staggered forward. The flames licked at dress and bandages, but only slowly, until Lieka made a claw with her other hand and dragged it up through the air, the flames leaping in response as if she had hauled upon their secret strings.

The Queen screeched, and ran forward with surprising speed. Lieka jumped away, but the King tripped and fell as he tried to leave his chair. Before he could get up, the Queen knelt at his side and, now completely ablaze, embraced him. The King screamed and writhed but could not break free as she bent her flame-wreathed blackened head down for a final kiss.

"Aaaahhhh!" the Queen's grateful sigh filled the hall, drowning out the final muffled choking scream of the King. She slumped over him, pushed him down into the smoldering rushes on the dais, and both were still.

Lieka gestured. The burning bodies, the smoking rushes, and the great fire in the corner pit went out. The candles and the tapers flickered, then resumed their steady light.

"A remarkable display of foolishness," the witch said to Jess, who stood staring, her face whiter than even Lieka's lead-painted visage. "What did you think to achieve?"

"Mother loved him, despite everything," whispered Jess. "And I hoped to bring the murder home to you."

"But instead you have made me Queen," said Lieka. She sat down in the King's chair. "Edmund and I were married yesterday. A full day after your mother's death."

"Then he knew . . ." said Jess stoically. It was not a surprise, not after all this time and the King's other actions, but she had retained some small hope, now extinguished. "He knew you had poisoned her."

"He ordered it!" Lieka laughed. "But I must confess I did not dare hope that it would lead to his death in turn. I must thank you for that, girl. I am also curious how you brought the old slattern back. Or rather, who you got to do it for you. I had not thought there was another practitioner of the art who would dare to cross me."

"An old friend of the kingdom helped me," said Jess. "Someone I hope will help me again, to bring you to justice."

"Justice!" spat Lieka. "Edmund ordered me to poison your mother. I merely did as the King commanded. His own death was at the Queen's hands, or perhaps more charitably by misadventure. Besides, who can judge me now that I am the highest in the land?"

Jess looked out the darkest corner of the hall, behind the dais.

"Please," she said quietly. "Surely this is a matter for the Highest Justice of all?"

"Who are you talking to?" said Lieka. She turned in her seat and looked around, her beautiful eyes narrowed in concentration. Seeing nothing, she smiled and turned back. "You are more a fool than your mother. Guard, take her away."

Piers did not answer. He was staring at the dais. Jess watched too, as the unicorn stepped lightly to Lieka's side, and gently dipped her horn into the King's goblet.

"Take her away!" ordered Lieka again. "Lock her up somewhere dark. And summon the others from the solar. There is much to celebrate."

She raised the goblet, and took a drink. The wine stained her lips dark, and she licked them before she took another draft.

"The royal wine is swee—"

The word never quite quit Lieka's mouth. The skin on her forehead wrinkled in puzzlement, her perfectly painted face crazing over with tiny cracks. She began to turn her head toward the unicorn, and pitched forward onto the table, knocking the goblet over. The spilled wine pooled to the edge, and began to slowly drip upon the blackened feet of the Queen, who lay beneath, conjoined with her King.

"Thank you," said Jess. She slumped to the floor, raising her knees so she could make herself small and rest her head. She had never felt so tired, so totally spent, as if everything had poured out of her, all energy, emotion, and thought.

Then she felt the unicorn's horn, the side of it, not the point. Jess raised her head, and was forced to stand up as Elibet continued to chide her, almost levering her up.

"What?" asked Jess miserably. "I said 'thank you.' It's done, now, isn't it? Justice has been served, foul murderers served their due portion. My mother even . . . even . . . got her kiss . . ."

The unicorn looked at her. Jess wiped the tears out of her eyes and listened.

"But there's my brother. He'll be old enough in a few years—well, six years—"

"I know father was a bad king, but that doesn't mean—"

"It's not fair! It's too hard! I was going to go to Aunt Maria's convent school—"

Elibet stamped her foot down, through the rushes, hard enough to make the flagstones beneath ring like a beaten gong. Jess swallowed her latest protest and bent her head.

"Is that a unicorn?" whispered Piers.

"You can see her?" exclaimed Jess.

Piers blushed. Jess stared at him. Evidently her father's outer guards did not take their lead from the King in all respects, or Piers was simply too new to have been forced to take part in the King's frequent bacchanalia.

"I . . . I . . . There is someone in particular . . . " muttered Piers. He met her gaze as he spoke, not looking down as a good servant should. She noticed that his eyes were a very warm brown, and there was something about his face that made her want to look at him more closely. . . .

Then she was distracted by the unicorn, who stepped back up onto the dais and delicately plucked the simple traveling crown from the King's head with her horn. Balancing it there, she headed back to Jess.

"What's she doing?" whispered Piers.

"Dispensing justice," said Elibet. She dropped the crown onto Jess's head and tapped it in place with her horn. "I trust you will be a better judge than your father. In all respects."

"I will try," said Jess. She reached up and touched the thin gold circlet. It didn't feel real, but then nothing did. Perhaps it might in daylight, after a very long sleep.

"Do so," said Elibet. She paced around them and walked toward the door.

"Wait!" cried Jess. "Will I see you again?"

The unicorn looked back at the Princess and the young guardsman at her side.

"Perhaps," said Elibet, and was gone.

THE LION
AND THE UNICORN

A. C. Wise

T HE MOMENT THEY SEE THE UNICORN BOY—the shine of his skin, the
pearlescent spiral of his horn, his silken hair pale as moonlight—they
want him. It's no wonder he prefers virgins. Their uncertainty makes their
plucking hands almost gentle. Some of them are even sweet. Afraid.

But even in them, the wanting does not wait long. And there is only
one answer to the wanting. It is not that he gives, but they take. Insistent
hands leave bruises in their wake, dropped petals scatterwhickering the
snow of his flesh. Hard, needful fingers tangle in his hair, pulling strands
free in blind ardour. Fingers press inside him, pushing, choking, wanting
without end.

Sometimes there is pleasure, but it is brief and accidental. The men and
women who come to his tapestried chamber, all woven with scenes of his
downfall, are not there for him. They come to sate themselves, scarcely
knowing they do. After, they wake, spent, dazed, wondering at the lost time.
They leave feeling full. Light settles like good wine in their bellies, and they
are happy for a time. Until the wanting comes round again and they find
themselves back at his door with hunger in their eyes.

This has always been the way, for as long as he can remember. For *almost*
as long as he can remember.

Brief snatches of memory creep from the corners of his mind at odd times, almost crueller than the hands and mouths that come for him at every hour. A pool with sweet water. Fruit, cool and crisp on his tongue. The soft whicker of his father's breath. A song his mother sang to him. Strong, calloused fingers on his brow, soothing fever as his horn pushed through his skin and he wailed like a child teething, not understanding the pain.

Although it was never spoken aloud, he knows his mother took his father against his will—thus is it always with their kind—and that she wept for it ever after. Overcome by wanting first, then grief afterward, blinded by desire and need. But unlike any other, she stayed, did her penance by remaining to guard his father from future wanting hands, and by raising his child.

There is no one to guard or protect him. Only a thin chain—fine as sunlight—bound around his ankle and chafing his skin, running to a ring of iron bolted to the floor. Sometimes, he thinks he hears footsteps pause just outside his door. Hope and fear bloom in these moments, but in the end, neither is fulfilled. The door does not open, and he is left alone.

Slender as it is, the chain binding him will not break for him. He has cut his hands trying. So there is only this room, the silken hangings, the soft pillows his face is pressed into to stifle tears and cries. Beyond these tapestry-hung walls, he knows nothing of this place, save there are other beasts here. He hears their cries sometimes—a peacock's mourn, the howl of a lonely wolf, something vast and dark snuffling in sorrow through the halls.

At least he cannot bear a child to the monsters who come for him with ravenous hands. At least his mother had the foresight and courage to smother his sister before she drew her first breath, in the instant she followed him from the womb.

The unicorn boy wakes from a fever of lips and teeth and tongues all tearing at him to a different kind of heat. His skin flushes from moonlight to dull mother-of-pearl, hair matted in sweat. And still they come for him. He whimpers low, too weak to protest, but the hands that part the hangings of his bed don't immediately reach for him.

Through the shine of sickness, he sees blunted nails, torn, bloodied to their beds. The fingers are strong, rough when they touch his brow, but they do not tug at him. They drag a wet cloth over his too-hot skin, skirting his horn in a way that makes him shudder. A face leans into his, yellow-eyed, breath smelling of carrion, hair brambled wild to frame it all.

"Who?" He has never seen her before.

She smiles, not a kind thing, showing broken teeth. Blunted, like her nails. Broken by force, to tame her. He knows all this in a heartbeat; he knows what it is to be shattered and chained.

Bells decorate her tangled tresses, circle her wrists, and her ankles below the tattered hem of her robe. Yet she made no sound in her approach, makes none now as she refreshes the cloth and lays it on his brow. Seeing him looking, her grin widens, showing more of the shattered stumps of her teeth, the meaty-darkness of her maw.

"Once upon a time, my children wove bells in my hair to honour me. They placed cinnamon in my mouth. I was a queen, a sorceress, a warrior. I was fierce sunlight scouring desert sands and stripping men's flesh from their bones as the day wound down."

A scar crosses her left eye, leaving it milky. She smoothes more water over his skin. He shivers as it dries, cold, and the chain around his ankle chimes in answer. In a deft movement, she snaps one of the bells from the bracelet at her wrist, holding it out to show the clapper broken.

"Here, they made me wear bells to warn them of my approach, so I could not sneak up on them and take their life by force."

She raises her arms, makes a little step, a turn; all her bells are silenced. Her expression is sly a moment longer, wicked light, curved as a sickle moon, sliding through her eyes. Then her expression sobers, posture softened and turned inward once more.

"I have spent time in the slave pits, been forced to fight battles not my own. I bear scars not of my choosing."

"And now?" the unicorn boy asks, mouth dry.

"I am old and forgotten. They think me harmless. They tell me you are sick and send me to care for you."

"Why?"

"Monsters must see to monsters, the beautiful and the horrid."

She sits, uninvited, on the edge of his bed. He flinches from her heat and smell, from the memory of hands and wanting.

"You are scarce more than a mouthful." She smiles again, showing cracked teeth, wounded gums. "You would not fill my belly."

She leans in again, gaze raking him like coals. She touches the down of his mane, brushing it from his eyes.

"Would you learn to be terrible?" she asks.

The shine in her eyes frightens him. It shows the desert she described, ink-stained with shadows from the lowering sun, scattered with bones picked clean to leave meat-stink between her teeth. Once they curved wicked, strong, yellow like high noon.

"Beauty can be terrible, too," he says, voice scant a whisper.

His eyes flutter closed. What might his terrible beauty be? Not the relentless pound of daylight, but the subtle burn of the moon. Sliding, insidious, to turn desire against those who would claim him and leaving them drained. Even after all he has suffered, bruises patterning his skin, and the hollowness left in their wake, he does not think he could do it. His beauty cuts inward. He cannot give back what is given to him, what is taken. Where the lion roars and devours the day, the unicorn thinks only of the soft whicker of his father's breath, a scent like oranges, and his mother threading blossoms through a mane silver like his own.

"I want to run." He opens his eyes.

"How far can you run? How fast?" Her anger is for him, not at him; she can see as well as he that his soles are lily skin, not hardened hooves.

"As far and as fast as I can. I hope it is enough."

The lion whuffs, a breath that might be a laugh or only taking the scent of him. She presses the bell with its torn clapper into his palm, hard enough to dent the skin, hard enough almost to draw blood, and folds his fingers over it tightly. She picks up his thin golden chain, runs it over calloused pads before bringing it to her mouth.

"As do I. Run and tell my children of this place. Give them my token, and they will not devour you. Or . . ." she gives him another wicked smile, so he can see in her the ferocity, the youth stamped on her features, bright as a new-minted coin, just behind the tarnish of age. "Or, at least they will give you a fair head start. Tell them of this place as you run from their wicked teeth and snapping jaws. Tell them to come shatter its walls and burn it to the ground."

She bites, gnashing with torn teeth, blood slicking her chin. He sees her, blazing in this room, standing in his absence to snap at those wanting hands and rending as many as she can before they take her down. He is frightened of her and for her. Perhaps they are the same thing. The chain breaks. Hot breath, blood-scented, touches his flank. She growls low in her throat, bells not making a sound at her movements. He runs.

SURVIVOR

Dave Smeds

1967

G.I. Bob's Quality Tattoos the neon sign declared, luring customers through the Bay Area summer fog with a tropistic intensity. Tucked between a laundromat and an appliance repair shop in lower Oakland, the studio was the only place of business on the block open at that hour. Troy Chesley scanned right and left as if he were on patrol, dropping into a firefight stance behind a parked car as a thin, dark-skinned man strode up to the nearest intersection.

"Easy, man." Roger, Troy's companion, grabbed him by the collar and yanked him toward the door. "We ain't back in 'Nam *yet*."

Troy's cheeks flushed. He had been doing things like that all night. No more booze. It wasn't every grunt that got a furlough back to the mainland in mid-tour, even if it happened for the worst of reasons. The least he could do was stay sober enough to acknowledge he was out of the war zone.

Troy was no longer sure why he had let Roger talk him into this. Nabbing some skin art was one thing; doing it in such a seedy locale was another. He jumped as the little bell above the lintel rang, announcing their entrance.

A man appeared through the curtains at the back. "May I help you?" he asked.

The hair on the nape of Troy's neck stood on end. Or would have, except that his father had insisted on a haircut so that he would look like a proper military man for his mother's funeral. (*"Your lieutenant lets you look like that on the battlefield?"*) "Shit," he blurted, "It's a gook."

No sooner had the words left his mouth than he knew it was the wrong thing to say. Yet the tattooist merely blinked his almond eyes, shrugged, and said calmly, "No, sir. Nobody but us chinks here." He spoke with no more than a slight accent, and with an air that said he was used to the ill grace of soldiers.

"Sorry. Been drinking," Troy mumbled. But drunk or not, it wasn't like him to be *that* much of an asshole. For some reason he felt menaced. The man was such a weird-looking fucker. He appeared to be middle-aged, but in an odd, preserved sort of way. His shirt was highly starched and black, his skin dry as parchment, his fingertips so loaded with nicotine they had stained the exterior of his cigarette. He sure as hell wasn't G.I. Bob.

He had no tattoos on his own arms. What kind of stitcher never applied the ink to himself?

"Come on," Troy said, tugging Roger's sleeve. "Let's get out of here."

Roger slid free. "We came all this way, Chesley my boy. What's the matter? Are the guys in your unit pussies?"

Those were the magic words. Troy barely knew Roger—their connection was that they had shared a flight from Da Nang to Travis and, in seven hours, would share the return leg—but he was his buddy of the moment, and he couldn't let the man say he lacked balls. He was a God-damned U. S. of A. soldier heading back to finish up eight months more In Country.

"All right, all right," Troy muttered.

"Do you know what design you want?" the stitcher asked. When both young men shook their heads, he opened up his books of patterns. "How about a nice eagle? Stars and Stripes? A lightning bolt?" He opened the pages to other suggestions he thought appropriate. To Troy, he seemed to give off a predatory glee at the prospect of jabbing them with a sharp instrument.

In less than two minutes Roger pointed to his choice: a traditional "Don't Tread on Me" snake. The artist nodded, propped the book open on the counter for reference, and swabbed the infantryman's upper arm with alcohol. To Troy's amazement, he did not use a transfer or tracing of any sort. He simply drew the design, freehand, crafting a startlingly faithful copy. The needle gun began to whir.

The noise, along with Roger's occasional cussword, faded into the background. Troy turned page after page, but the designs did not call to him. It had finally struck him that he would be living with whatever choice he made. A sign above the photos of satisfied customers warned, A TATTOO IS FOREVER.

Whatever image he chose had to be right. It had to be him. He finished all the books: No good. They contained nothing but other people's ideas. He needed something he hadn't seen on anyone else's body.

It came to him clearly and insistently. "Can you do a unicorn?" Troy asked.

The artist paused, dabbing at Roger's wounded skin with a cloth. "A unicorn?" he asked, with the seriousness of a man who used powdered rhinoceros horn to enhance sexual potency.

"A mean son-of-a-bitch unicorn, with fire in its eyes and blood dripping from its spike." Troy chuckled. "That'd be hot, wouldn't it, Rodge?"

"That's affirmed," Roger said.

The stitcher lit a new cigarette, sucking on two at once, and blew a long, blue cloud. He closed his eyes and appeared to tune out the parlor and his customers. When he roused, he reached into a drawer and pulled out a fresh needle gun, its metal gleaming as if never before used. "Yes. I can do that. But only over your heart."

Troy blinked, rubbing his chest. He hadn't considered anywhere but his arm, but the suggestion had a strange appropriateness to it. "Yeah," he said. "Okay."

The artist pulled out a sketch pad and blocked in a muscular, rearing horse shape, added the horn, and then gave it the intimidating, man-of-war embellishments Troy had asked for.

"That's fabulous," Troy said. He bared his upper body and dropped into the chair that Roger had vacated.

The man pencilled the design onto Troy's left breast, with the unicorn's lashing tail at the sternum and the point of his horn jabbing above and past the nipple. He performed his work with a frenzied fluidity, stopping only when he reached for the needle gun.

"Point of no return," he said, which Troy thought odd, since he hadn't given Roger that sort of warning. It was at that moment he realized why the symbol of a unicorn had sprung to his mind. During the funeral, while the minister droned on, Troy had been thinking of an old book in which the hero was saved from death by a puff of a unicorn's breath.

His mind was made up. He nodded.

The needle bit. Troy clenched his teeth until his mouth tasted of metal. As the initial shock passed, he forced himself to relax, reasoning that tension would only worsen the discomfort. The technique worked. The procedure took on a flavor of timelessness not unlike watching illumination rounds flower in the night sky over rice paddies fifty klicks away. Detached, Troy watched himself bleed. He could handle anything, as long as he knew he was going to survive the experience. Wasn't that why he was there—proving like so many G.I.s before him how durable he was? To feel anything, even pain, was a comfort, with his poor mother now cold in her grave, with himself going back into the jungle hardly more than a target dummy for the Viet Cong.

To be able to spit at Death was worth any price.

"What the hell is *that?*" asked Siddens, pointing at Troy's chest.

The squad was hanging out in a jungle clearing a dozen klicks west of their firebase, enduring the wait until the choppers arrived to take them beyond Hill 625—to a landing zone that promised to be just as dull as this one. They had spotted no sign of the enemy for a week, a blessing that created its own sort of edginess.

Troy, bare from the waist up, held up the shirt he had just used to wipe the sweat from his forehead. The tattoo blazed in plain sight of Siddens—the medic—and PFC Holcomb, as they crouched in the shade of a clump of elephant grass.

"It's a unicorn," Troy said, wishing he had not removed the shirt. "You know, like, 'Only virgins touch me'?" He winced, too aware of being only nineteen. The joke had seemed so good when he thought of it, but in the past three weeks, the only laughing had been *at* him, not with him.

But Siddens did not laugh. "You got that back in the World?" he asked.

"Yeah."

The medic turned back to Holcomb, obviously continuing a conversation begun before Troy had wandered over to them. "See? Told you it had to be something."

Siddens and Holcomb were a study in contrast. Siddens was wiry, white, freckled, and gifted with a logic all his own. Holcomb was beefy, black, handsome, and spoke with down-home, common-sense directness. But Troy thought of them in the same way. Siddens was the kind of bandage-jockey a grunt relied on. Dedicated. He was determined to get to medical school, even if his family's poverty meant taking a side trip through a war. Holcomb was steady as a rock. He wrote home to his widowed mother and eight younger siblings back in Mississippi five times a week—he had a letter-in-progress in a clipboard in his lap at that moment.

Troy, who had dropped out of his first semester of college, and who had managed to write to his mother only three times between boot camp and her death, wanted to be like both these men.

"You guys want to let me in on this?" Troy asked.

Holcomb smiled and pointed at the tattoo. "Doug here thinks that's your rabbit's foot. Your four-leaf clover. Ain't nothing gonna touch you now."

Troy laughed. "What makes you think that?"

"We been watching you since you got back. Remember that punji pit you stepped into? How do suppose you landed on your feet without getting jabbed by even one of them slivers of bamboo?"

"Just lucky, I guess."

"And where you figure all that luck comes from?" Holcomb asked. "You were never that lucky before. Remember your first patrol? You be such a Fucking New Guy you poked yourself with your own bayonet. You slashed your ankle on that concertina wire."

Troy nodded slowly. The story of his life. Broken leg in junior high. Burst appendix at fifteen. Nobody had ever called him lucky. Little mishaps plagued him all the time.

But not for the past three weeks. Not since he had acquired the tattoo.

"Causality," Siddens intoned. "Everything happens for a reason. Remember Winston?"

Troy remembered Winston very well. When Troy was first assigned to the platoon, the corporal had been a short timer just counting the days until his DEROS. He used to meditate on which boot to put on first. Some mornings he started with the left, some days with the right. When he doubted his choice, he was jittery as a rabbit. On one patrol, his shoelace broke. His cheeks turned the color of ashes. A sniper wasted him that afternoon.

"He knew he was fucked," Siddens said. "Nothing could have saved him. You're just the opposite. You've got the magic right there on your chest. It's locked in. You're invulnerable, Bozo. You're immortal." His voice dropped. "And there isn't a damn thing you can do about it."

Troy rubbed his chest, frowning, wondering if the two men were just trying to mindfuck him. But Holcomb just nodded sagely, adding, "Some folks get to know whether their time a comin'. The rest of us, we just keep guessing."

Siddens was right. It was as if there were a force field around Troy. Even the mosquitoes and leeches stayed off him. When he and some other grunts from the platoon spent an R&R polishing their peckers in a Saigon whore-house, Troy was the only one who didn't need a shot of penicillin afterward.

Troy began leaving his shirt off, or at least unbuttoned, as often as possible, until he realized his tan was obscuring the tattoo, then he covered up again. He began to smile and make jokes. He even volunteered to be point man on patrols. At first the lieutenant let him, but later shitcanned the idea: Troy wasn't cautious enough.

Then, as the summer of '67 dribbled into late autumn, the North Vietnamese began to get serious about the war. Suddenly the enemy's presence meant more than an occasional sniper, a punji pit, or a land mine in the road. It meant assaulting fortified bunkers in the face of bullets and heavy artillery.

As the whole Second Battalion was swept into the midst of the firefight in the hills surrounding Dak To, Troy huddled in a foxhole, trying to banish the noise of the bombs from his consciousness. A 500-pounder from a U.S. plane had accidentally wasted thirty paratroopers over on

Hill 875—"friendly fire"—trying to dislodge the NVA from their hilltop fortifications. A brown, sticky mass stained the crotch of his fatigue pants—it had been there for hours. Hunger gnawed at his stomach—no resupply had been able to reach them for two days. Over and over he repeated the words Siddens had told him: *"Don't worry. You got the magic."*

He so needed to believe.

Dusk was falling. Staff Sgt. Morris passed a hand signal back. The platoon was going to advance.

A cacophony of machine guns and grenades filtered through the vegetation ahead. Somewhere, other elements of the battalion needed help. Troy gripped his rifle tightly as he rose from his foxhole. Crouching, he joined Holcomb and Siddens. They sprinted forward a bit at a time, heading for the base of the next large tree.

Troy was consumed by the urge to shut his eyes and clap his hands to his ears. No sooner had he done so than the ground erupted in front of him. Blinking, ears ringing, he realized only after the fact what he had sensed.

"Incoming!" he shouted.

His yell came too late. The smoking crater was already there. He was covered with specks of heavy, red laterite clay. He whirled to his right. There, still upright, stood the pelvis and legs of Doug Siddens. The medic's upper body lay somewhere in the brush.

Troy spun to his left. Leroy Holcomb was trying to scoop his intestines back into his abdomen with his remaining arm. Troy caught him just as he fell. His buddy let out a sigh and went limp, his blood and life soaking into the ruptured soil. He didn't even have time to utter a last sentence.

Troy cradled Holcomb's head in his lap. Sgt. Morris was yelling—probably something about retreating to the holes—but the words sailed right past. Troy examined his arms, his legs, his torso. Not a single cut. He had been the closest man to the explosion, and all it had done to him was get him dirty.

"Who'd have thought those gooks could whup our asses like this?" muttered Warren Nance, the radio telephone operator.

Troy raised his finger to his lips. The RTO should not have been talking.

The jungle was fearsomely still, but that did not guarantee that the enemy had all fled.

The Battle of Dak To had ended suddenly. One moment the NVA were there, blasting with everything they had; the next moment they had melted into the earth, leaving the clean-up to the Americans. At present, Troy and the other survivors were scouring the jungle for the wounded and dead, a gory process that a Special Forces sharpshooter at the base camp had called, "Shaking the trees for dog tags" due to the unidentifiability of some of the remains.

After the adrenaline overdose of the past week, the quiet did not seem real to Troy. Coherent thought was impossible. He still touched himself here and there, confirming that no pieces were missing. He felt no victory, no elation, no horror, no fear. All he knew is that he was here. The only emotion he was sure of was relief: What was left of Siddens and Holcomb had been zipped into body bags and shipped off. The KIA Travel Bureau was the wrong way to leave Vietnam, but at least he knew they were no longer rotting on the ground a million miles from home.

Why them? were the words rolling over and over through his mind. *Why them and not me?*

Whenever he considered the question, his hand rose up and scratched the left side of his chest. Sometimes it almost felt as if the unicorn were rearing and stamping its feet. Today the impression was stronger than ever.

They came to a gully containing the body of a dead U.S. soldier, lying on his side. Flies crawled from his mouth and danced above the gaping wound in his back. As Nance bent to roll the corpse flat to check the tags, Sgt. Morris grabbed him by the radio and hauled him back two steps. "Hold it!" he hissed.

Morris knelt down, shifted a few leaves next to the front of the dead man, and uncovered a trip wire. "It's booby-trapped."

"Damn," Nance said. "Sure saved my ass, Sarge."

A burst from an AK-47 blistered the foliage around them. Nance jerked and fell.

"Down!" Morris yelled.

The squad hit the ground. Instantly half a dozen men trained their weapons in the direction from which the attack had come and began emptying their clips as fast as they could without melting their gun barrels.

Troy knew the bullets would continue to fly for minutes yet, even longer if the sniper were stupid enough to shoot back rather than play phantom. Meanwhile Nance was lying next to him, choking. A slug had torn through the back of the RTO's mouth.

What do I do? Troy thought. Nance was dying, and they had no medic; Siddens had not yet been replaced.

Troy's tattoo quivered violently. Abruptly the knowledge he needed came to him. He confirmed Nance's upper breathing passage was too damaged to be cleared. Surgeons would have to do that after the medevacs airlifted the wounded man to a field hospital.

Nance's skin was turning blue. Troy pulled out his knife, located the correct notch near his buddy's Adam's apple, and sliced. Holding the gash open with his finger, Troy nodded in satisfaction as air poured directly into Nance's trachea. The RTO's lungs filled.

The panic in Nance's pupils faded to mere terror. Sgt. Morris managed to get to the radio on Nance's back and used it to request a chopper. Troy sighed. His buddy would live.

And then, with brutal suddenness, he understood why he had felt so certain of a medical procedure he had never before attempted. A presence was hovering inside him. He had been aware of the sensation for days, whenever the tattoo stirred, but he had not realized what it was. All he had known was that, from time to time, he felt as though he were looking at the world with different eyes.

The presence was not always the same. There were two entities. The visits had begun the night Siddens and Holcomb had died.

His buddies had not left him, after all.

1972

Specks of red Georgia clay marred the knees of Troy's baseball uniform. He bent down and brushed with his hands, but the dirt clung. With an abruptness just short of frantic, he tried again.

"Chesley!" The booming voice came from the rotund, middle-aged man near the dugout. "Where do you think you are? Vietnam? Pitch the damn ball already!"

"Sorry, Angus," Troy called, straightening up.

Troy had made the mistake a few days back of telling Angus that a lapse of attention had been caused by thinking of the war. Now the old fart accused him of more of the same any chance he could.

Troy shrugged off both the insult and the distraction that had provoked it. The ball was cool and dry in his hand, a tool he knew how to use. He wound up and let fly. The batter, suckered by Troy's body language, swung high and missed. Strike two.

Angus nodded. That was the kind of quality he expected of a prospective pitcher. Troy tipped his cap at the talent scout. Everything under control.

Troy had been thinking of Vietnam, though. Specifically of a buddy named Arturo Rivas with whom he had served during his second tour.

"When I get out of this puto country, I'm going to do nothing but play baseball," Rivas said, huddling under a tarp. *Thanks to the monsoons, the platoon hadn't breathed dry air in four days.*

Troy noted his companion's ropy muscles and gracile hands and, with a friendliness borrowed from Leroy Holcomb, said, "You mean as a pro, don't you?"

Rivas shrugged and smiled. "Why not? My uncle, he played in the minors for five years, and I'm better than him." He winked, full of young man's bluster. Troy could tell he believed what he said.

"I want to see you get there," Troy responded with sincerity.

That was five weeks before Rivas lost three vertebrae and too many internal organs in a nameless village in the Central Highlands. He had been the last one. First Siddens and Holcomb, then Artie Farina, Stewart Hutchison, Dennis Short, and Jimmy Wyckoff. Seven men dead from bullets, mortar rounds, and claymores that could have, should have killed Troy.

Dirt on his pants. He could wash a million times, and never lose the traces of those men.

Troy wound up, reading the batter's desire for another sinker like the last one. Troy laid it in straight and fast. Strike three.

"I want to see you get there." When Troy had made that comment, it had

been intended merely as polite encouragement, but it had since gone beyond that. Arturo was with him. He guided Troy's arm through its moves, told him what the batters might be thinking, gave him speed when he ran around the bases. He was the one Angus was impressed with, the one the scout might reward with a contract.

The tattoo itched. *No,* Troy thought. *Not now.* But his wishes were ignored. The mindset of a pitcher vanished. Arturo had phased out. He was Troy Chesley again—an indifferent athlete with no real knack for baseball.

The new batter was waiting. Troy hesitated, drawing another of Angus's infamous glares. No choice but to pitch and hope for the best. He flung the ball toward the plate.

The gleam in the batter's eye said it all even before he swung. The crack of wood against leather echoed from one side of the stadium to the other. The ball easily cleared the left field fence.

The next few pitches were not much better. The batter let two go by wide and outside, then with a whack claimed a standing double. Luckily the player after that popped out to center field, sparing Troy any more humiliation.

That ended the three-inning mini-game. Angus and his assistants reconfigured the players into a brand new Team A and Team B. Troy waited by the dugout for his assignment, but it didn't come. As the other aspiring pros hit the turf or loosened their batting arms, Angus pulled Troy aside.

The scout spat a brown river of tobacco juice onto the ground. "I know you don't want to hear this," he said gruffly. "You've got talent, Chesley, but no consistency. One moment you're hot, the next you're a meathead. Until you can keep yourself in the groove, you might as well forget about this camp. Put in some time on your own, get the kinks out, and maybe I'll see you here next year."

Angus turned back to the diamond. His posture said that as far as he was concerned, Troy no longer existed.

Troy slapped the dust from his mitt and trudged into the locker room. Next year? Next year would be no different. No matter how hard he tried to keep Arturo Rivas at the forefront, sooner or later he, Troy, would re-emerge—he or one of the other six.

He was living a total of eight lives. Out there on the diamond, he had been Arturo, as intended. This morning while shaving Artie Farina had surfaced, and he had whistled a tune learned during a boyhood in Brooklyn, three thousand miles from where Troy Chesley had grown up. At least he thought it was Artie. Sometimes there was no way to really know. He simply *was* one guy or another, without any sort of command over the phenomenon, his only clue to the transition consisting of an itch or warmth or tingle in the area of his tattoo.

He opened his locker, took out his kit bag, and began shoving items within, changing out of his togs as he went. No shower. He wanted out of this place. Already he knew what he would feel the next time Arturo emerged—the shame, the disappointment, the anger. The ambient stink of sweat and anti-fungal powder attacked Troy's nostrils, making him crave clean air.

"I'm sorry," Troy whispered. "I tried."

How he had tried. This time with baseball, for Arturo. Last year in pre-med courses, aiming for the M.D. that Doug Siddens had wanted. In his biochemistry class he had sailed through the midterm, propelled by the mental faculties of a man determined to learn whatever was required to become a doctor. On the final, the unicorn remained as flat and dull as plain ink, and as mere Troy Chesley he scored a dismal thirty-two percent, killing his chance of a passing grade.

As he peeled away his shirt, the tattoo was framed in the small mirror he had mounted on the inside of his locker door. He touched it, as ever feeling as though, no matter how much it was under his skin, it wasn't truly part of him.

A good luck charm? Oh, he'd survived all right. Through the war without a scratch. He had all the life and youth he could ever have imagined. Seven extra doses. But as usual, the rearing shape gave him no clue what he was supposed to do with so much abundance.

1975

Troy's dented Pontiac Bonneville carried him out of New Orleans, across the Pontchartrain Causeway, through the counties of St. Tammany and Washington, and over the boundary into southern Mississippi. As he drove along country roads beside trees draped with Spanish moss and parasitic masses of kudzu, the sense of familiarity grew ever more intense, though he had never been to this part of the South.

He unerringly selected the correct turns, having no need to consult his map. His destination appeared through the windshield. Hardly a town at all, it was one of those impoverished, former whistlestop communities destined to vanish into the woods as more and more of its young men and women migrated to the cities with each generation. By all rights he should never have recalled the place name; it had been mentioned in his presence no more than twice, all those years ago.

There were two cemeteries, the first dotted with old family mausoleums and elaborate tombstones—a forest of marble. He went straight to the second, a modest but carefully maintained site overlooking a river. The caretaker stared at him as if he had never seen a white man on the grounds before, but he was polite as he directed Troy to the graves belonging to the Holcomb family.

Leroy's resting place was easy to find. Eight years of weather had not been enough to mute the engraving of the granite marker. A few wilted flowers lay in the cup. He lifted them to his nose, catching vestiges of aroma. Not yet a week old. After eight years, someone still remembered this particular dead man. That brought a tightness to his throat.

He had a fresh bouquet with him, but he placed it at the head of a nearby grave marked LIONEL HOLCOMB, 1919-1962.

"Rest in peace, Daddy," he whispered.

A woodpecker hammered in the oak tree on the river side of the graveyard. The air thrummed with an invisible chorus of insects that could never survive in the San Francisco Bay Area, where Troy had been raised. Seldom had he felt anything so real as the smell of the grass at his feet or the humidity sucking at his pores.

He turned and walked determinedly back to his car and drove into town. A block past the Baptist church, he pulled up at a house. The clapboard was peeling, but the lawn was mowed and the roof had been recently patched, showing that while no rich folk lived here, the occupants cared about the property.

Troy stepped up onto the porch. The urge to rush inside was next to overwhelming, but he stifled it. The body he inhabited was the wrong color, the wrong size. No matter what, part of him was always Troy Chesley, even when he didn't want it to be so. He knocked politely.

A stout Black woman in a flower-print dress opened the inner door and stared at him through the screen mesh, her eyes widening at his stranger's face.

Mama! I love you, Mama! Troy forced down the words in his mind and uttered the pale substitutions circumstances allowed. "Mrs. Holcomb?"

"That's me," she said.

I missed you, Mama. "My name is Troy Chesley. I served with your son Leroy in the war."

The woman lifted her bifocals out of the way and wiped her eyes. "Leroy," she said huskily. "He was my first-born, you know. Hard on an old widow to lose a son like that. What can I do for you, child?"

"I have a few questions, Ma'am. I was wondering . . . what kind of plans Leroy had? What he wanted to do with his life? What do you think he'd be doing right now, if he'd come back from over there?"

She shook her graying head firmly. "Now what you want to go asking me those kinds of things for? All that will just remind me he ain't here. The war is over, Mr. Chesley. Go on about your business and don't bother me no mo'." She shut the door.

"But—" Troy raised his hand to protest, but blank wood confronted him. *You don't understand, Mama. Troy's got all my chances.*

"I've got everybody's chances," he murmured as he turned, shoulders drooping, and stumbled back to his Pontiac.

1978

The bathroom mirror showed Troy a twenty-one-year-old self. No traces of the beer belly or the receding hairline his younger brother was developing. No need for the corrective lenses his sister had required when she reached twenty-five. His greet-the-day erection stood stiff as a recruit being screamed at by a drill sergeant: A kid's boner, there even when all he wanted to do was take a piss.

He was aging eight times slower than normal. He was thirty now, a point when other two-tour vets often looked forty-five. At least he *was* aging. That proved he wasn't literally immortal. Just as he wasn't totally invulnerable, or the razor wouldn't have nicked him the day before. He didn't think he could bear it if the tattoo didn't have *some* limits.

He showered, dried, and drifted into the living room/kitchenette wearing only a pair of briefs—the summer sun was already high, and the apartment had no air-conditioning. Slicing an apple and eating it a sliver at a time filled the next three minutes. The clock above the stove ticked: The heartbeat of the room.

So many years to live.

Troy pulled open the file cabinet in the corner of the room that served as his home office and ran his fingers across a series of manila folders marked with names. He pulled out one at random.

It turned out to be that of Warren Nance, the RTO whose life he had saved with the emergency tracheotomy. That is to say, the one Doug Siddens had saved using Troy's hands. Clippings dropped out onto the floor, covering the threadbare spots his landlord described as "a little wear and tear." He sat down cross-legged and glanced at them as he put them back in the folder.

Warren was a realtor these days. The first clipping was a Yellow Pages ad for his business, describing it as the largest in the Texas panhandle. A pamphlet of houses-for-sale listed Warren's name as agent more than two dozen times. The third item, a newspaper clipping, praised him for a large donation to help people with speech impediments.

A dozen files in Troy's cabinet told similar tales. Sgt. Morris was now an assistant county superintendent of schools. Crazy Vic Naughton, now clean-cut and much heftier than he had been in Vietnam, was a sports commentator for a television station.

The one thing the files did not contain was direct correspondence, save for a Christmas card or two. Troy had seldom attempted to contact old buddies; he had abandoned the effort altogether after the incident with Leroy Holcomb's mother. As happened throughout the veteran community, the connections he had established in Vietnam disintegrated within the milieu of the World, no matter how intense those ties had been in the jungle.

It worked both ways. Troy had received scores of letters during late '69 and early '70. All from guys still In Country. He barely heard from those men once they arrived stateside. As the saying in 'Nam went: "There it is." And there it was. Soldiers sitting in the elephant grass watching the gunships rumble by overhead needed to hold in their hands replies from someone who made it back, just to have written proof that it was *possible* to make it back. Once they came home themselves, they didn't want to be reminded of the war. Now, with North Vietnam the victor, the silence was even more entrenched. Troy saw no reason to disrupt the quiet, and many reasons not to.

But still he kept the files. The other drawer contained only seven, but they were inches thick, filled with all the information he could collect on Leroy, on Doug, on Arturo and the others who had died beside him. This morning that drawer remained locked. He was thinking about the men who had lived. The other survivors.

They were making something of themselves.

Here he sat. He didn't even have a savings account. He was employed as a short order cook at Denny's, a job he had had for two months and one he would probably quit before another two months had gone by. Where his buddies had found focus, he had found dissipation, his efforts spread too thin in too many directions.

Too many chances. Those other men knew the Grim Reaper would catch them sooner rather than later, so they got down to business before their youth and energy raced away. Troy was missing that urgency.

On the other side of the wall he heard the reverberation of feet landing on the floor beside the bed and padding into the bathroom. The toilet flushed. The shower nozzle spat fitfully into life, and a soprano voice rose in song above the din of the spray and the groan of the plumbing: "Carry On Wayward Son" by Kansas.

A hint of a smile played at the edges of Troy's lips. Troy let the folder in his hands close. He cleared the floor, stowed the materials in the file cabinet, and locked the drawer. Before sitting back down, he lowered his briefs and tossed them on the couch.

Maybe he could make some sort of progress after all.

Hardly had the thought coalesced in his mind than his chest began to itch. He scratched reflexively, fingernails tracing the outline of the unicorn. No. He would not let anyone surface. This was his moment. With a firm act of will, he drew his hand away, brought his attention back to the sound of faucets being shut off in the bathroom. The doorway to the bedroom seemed to grow larger and larger until his girl friend emerged wrapping a towel around her glossy brunette mane, her bare skin rosy from the effect of the hot water.

Scanning his naked body with an appreciative eye, she migrated forward with the boldness that had originally lured him into their relationship. He clasped her wrists, easing her down beside him and patiently thwarting her attempts to fondle him.

"Lydia, do you love me?"

She tilted her head, humming. "I will if you let go of my hands."

"I'm serious."

She blanched as the gravity of his tone sank in. "I . . . oh . . ." She hiccupped.

"I take it that's a yes?" he said as he released her wrists.

Head turning aside, arms hugging herself, and cheeks ablaze with uncharacteristic shyness, she nodded. "You weren't supposed to know, you fucker." He realized the drops on her face were not drips from her wet hair. "Not until you said it first."

"Will you marry me?" he asked.

Her nose crinkled, as if she were going to laugh or sneeze. She lay back on the ratty carpet and spread her legs. "You sure I can't distract you enough to make you forget you said that?"

"Not a chance," he said firmly. "Does that mean you're turning me down?"

"I'm . . . stalling." Her features hardened. "I don't want you to say one thing today, and another tomorrow, Troy. If you mean to follow through, then of course I'll marry you."

The puff of his pent-up breath almost made the walls shake. Shifting forward, he accepted her body's invitation.

1983

"You can't be doing this," Lydia said, yanking at the tag on his garment bag.

"Don't. You'll rip it." As he snapped his briefcase closed, she let go of the tag, spun, and marched to the window of their apartment. The Minneapolis/

St. Paul skyline stretched flat beyond her—the nearest mountain a billion miles over the horizon. They had moved here when she landed the hospital job, but after almost two years he still couldn't get used to the landscape. He wanted geographical features that could daunt the wind, and most especially slow the approach of the summer thunderstorms whose booms reminded him too much of artillery.

"Darling, we discussed this," he said. "I'll be back by suppertime tomorrow. It's a little late to change plans."

"You didn't even ask what I thought of the idea. You didn't even think about the budget when you bought the plane ticket." Lydia tugged the curtain to the side and frowned. "The taxi's here." She turned back, meeting him eye to eye, freezing him in place instead of tendering silent permission to pick up his luggage. "What is so important that you have to spend money we don't have?"

"We have the money."

"Barely. There are other things we could have done with that cash."

He sighed and, denying her spell, carried his things to the front door. "This is something I need to do. You act like I'm way out of line."

"You're going all this way for a guy you knew for a few months? Doesn't that strike you as little obsessive?" She patted her abdomen, highlighting the prominent evidence of pregnancy. "Don't you think you have bigger priorities at home right now? Christ, Troy, I feel like I'm living with a stranger sometimes. I don't know you right now. You're someone else."

Troy turned away before she could see his reaction. Her glare drilled a hole through the back of his head as he walked out the doorway, and the wound remained open throughout the ride to the airport, the liftoff, and the climb to cruising altitude. How he wanted to tell her: about the unicorn, about the seven lives he lived besides his own. Everything.

Even Stu wanted to tell her. That's who had emerged earlier in the week. Stewart Hutchison, his squad leader after Sgt. Morris had rotated to the safety of rear echelon duty. Stu understood Troy's needs the way Troy understood his.

He lowered the lunch tray and tried to write his explanation out in a note. He began by admitting that he had lied: This trip was not for a funeral. But when it came to speaking of all he had been holding in throughout their relationship, he kept crossing out the sentences, finally giving up when he noticed the woman seated next to him glancing at the paper.

He wasn't the person he needed to be in order to write it. Much as Stu tried to cooperate, the words had to be Troy's and Troy's alone.

After a troubled night in a motel room, he reached his exact destination: the stadium bleachers at Colorado State University, Fort Collins. He was among the throng gathered for the graduation of the class of '83. Patiently he waited as the university president announced the names, until he called that of Marti Hutchison, highest honors, Dean's List.

Stu had *had* to emerge this week. This was an event the man would certainly have attended had he not been killed in the Tet Offensive. Marti Hutchison had been a toddler when Stu enlisted, an action he had taken partly in order to support his young family. That day at the recruitment office the war had been only a spark no one believed would flare into an inferno. He had never expected to be removed so far from his child; that was not his concept of the right way to do things. A man needed to Be There, as he had said when he learned he had knocked up his high school girl friend and heard her suggest giving the baby up for adoption.

He was Being Here today. Troy kept his binoculars pointed at the freckled face until she reached the base of the podium and vanished into the sea of caps and gowns. The eyepieces were wet with tears as he lowered the glasses, and it felt like somebody was pushing at his rib cage from the inside. The sensation recalled an occasion when he had sat in a bunker all night, so scared of the incoming ordnance that his heart tried to leap out and hide under the floor slats with the snakes. Or was that something Stu had experienced?

It wasn't fear he was feeling now, though. It was pride. He let the emotion cascade through him, yielding fully, allowing his buddy to savor every particle of the joy.

A memory came to Troy hard and potent, one of those that he and Stu shared directly: *Stu was sitting next to him in the shade of a troop carrier, speaking fondly of his wife, who was due to rendezvous with him in the Philippines during a long R&R the sergeant had coming up.*

"*Gonna try for a boy.*" *He grinned.* "*On purpose, this time.*"

Troy shut his eyes tight, reliving the moment when the claymore wasted his buddy, ten days before that R&R came due. No boy. Perhaps Troy and Lydia's child could make up for that, though that was not something he could control. At least he had this much. He caught a glimpse of Marti over the heads of several female classmates—she was almost as tall as her father had been. Again came the heat to his eyes and the tightness to his throat.

"Do you feel it, Stu?" His murmurs were drowned by the din of the names continuing to boom from the loudspeakers, though to his right a grandmother in a hat and veil glanced at his moving lips with puzzlement. "It's for you, buddy. You gotta be in here, feeling this."

Stu felt it, indulged in it, and as a sharp throb hit Troy on the left half of his chest, the dead man slipped back into limbo.

A peace came over Troy, a faith that he had done what he was supposed to. Because of him, seven men had their own taste of immortality.

Lydia would rip his hide off him if he went on more trips soon. But there was so much more to do. He still had never been to the California/Oregon border, where Doug Siddens was from, nor to Artie Farina's old digs in Brooklyn, nor to . . .

Surely there was some way to balance it all.

1989

"Do you ever really feel anything for us?" Lydia asked.

The abrupt comment made Troy jump. He had been gazing at the clouds out of the windows of their rental suburban tract home, lost to the moment. He always seemed to be lost to the moment.

Outside, his daughter Kirsten, resplendent in ruffled skirts and pigtails for her final day of kindergarten, swung vigorously to and fro, fingers laced tightly around the chains, calling to him to watch her Go-So-High as he had promised to do when she headed for the back yard. Had that been thirty seconds ago, or several minutes?

"What do you mean?" He cleared his throat. "Of course I do."

"Do you?" Lydia hid her expression by stepping to the stove to remove the boiling tea kettle from the burner. "That's good." She said it deadpan, which was worse than overt sarcasm, because it implied a measure of faith still at risk upon the chopping block.

"What makes you ask such a question?" He wanted to let the subject drop, but somewhere he found the courage to listen to the answer.

"You let yourself trickle out in a million directions," Lydia said, reaching into a cabinet for the box of Mountain Thunder. She put two bags in her mug and poured the water. "But it's not because you don't know what discipline is. You make trips, you subscribe to all sorts of small newspapers, you make scrapbooks. You even hired a private detective that time—all to find out more about some guys in your past. If that isn't ambition, I don't know what is. But you don't apply yourself to what you've got right here."

Lydia's jaw trembled. "It's like you're not even you, half the time. You're a bunch of different people, and none of them are grown up. When you're in one of those moods, it's like Kirsten and I don't count. Are we just background to you?"

"I love you both," he said. "I'm just . . . not good at remembering to say so."

Lydia turned away, sipped her tea, and spat the liquid into the sink because it was far too hot. Testily, she waved toward the back yard. "Go push your child. You only have half an hour before you're supposed to go to that job interview."

"Oh. The appointment," he said. "Almost forgot."

"I know."

1991

As Operation Desert Storm progressed and U.S. ground troops poised on the border of Kuwait, Troy grew painfully aware of the frowns of the senior citizens at the park where he walked on afternoons when the temp agency failed to find work for him. Those conservative old men were undoubtedly wondering why someone as young as he wasn't over there kicking Saddam Hussein's ass, showing the world that America hadn't forgotten how to win a war. There was no way to explain the truth to them.

Just as there was no way to tell Lydia, not after all this time.

The day the Scud missile went cruising into a Jerusalem apartment building, Lydia emerged from the bathroom holding an empty tube of hair darkener, the brand Reagan had used during his administration. "Do you want me to get the larger size when I go to the store?"

"What do you mean? You're the only one who uses that stuff," he replied.

She blinked. "Me? I'm not the one going gray."

Troy swallowed his answer. No use confronting her. Four years younger than he, she was having a hard enough time dealing with her entry into middle age. She smeared on wrinkle cream every morning. She examined her body in the mirror each night after she undressed, bought new bras with greater support features, wore a one-piece bathing suit instead of a bikini so that the stretch marks below her navel would not show.

"Hey," he said consolingly, "it's all right, you know. It doesn't matter to me how you look."

Slowly she held up the tube to his face, her expression a fluctuating mix of anger and pity. "Troy, Troy, Troy—*this isn't even my hair color.* When are you going to stop playing these games?"

She had said it once too often. "It's not a game, Lydia." He choked back, not daring to say more. He regretted saying that much, but he couldn't let something so important be denigrated that way.

She tossed the empty tube across the room toward the general vicinity of the waste basket. "Troy, you're forty-four years old. No matter how well you maintain your looks, let's face it—you're getting old. I don't like it any better than you do, but there it is. I've put up with a lot of weird shit from you in thirteen years, but this little fantasy of yours has gone far enough. I think it's time you saw a therapist."

Troy just looked at her in stony silence. The unicorn reared and snorted, though if it heralded the arrival of one of the guys, the latter held back, letting Troy keep command.

"No?" Lydia asked. "All right then, try this: You move out. I've done what I can. You get help, you make some changes, then maybe you can come back." She whirled and stalked out of the room the way she had come.

Troy hung his head. He did not go to the bathroom door, did not try to get her to change her mind, though he knew that was what she was hoping for. She would give him a dozen more chances, if only he would promise to change. But how could he do that? The facts were the facts.

He dragged himself into the bedroom and began to pack a suitcase—just a few things, so that he could get out of the house. He would arrange to come back for other possessions when Lydia would not be home.

He did not want to leave. This was yet another casualty in his life, and he was tired of making up for a choice he had made when he was nineteen. When would he be through paying the price?

1995

July the fifteenth arrived in a blaze of heat and humidity that recalled the jungle. It was Saturday, one of the special days. He pulled up to the curb outside what had once been his home and honked the horn. Kirsten, a lean and spry eleven-year-old, bounded out to his car with a grin on her face.

She still idolized him. He gazed at her wistfully as she buckled her seat belts: Flat-chested, a bit under five feet tall, not yet one of those adolescents who had no time for parents. She would remain his girl child for another year or so.

Troy thought of all those times he had failed to be a good father. He used to fall asleep trying to read her books at bedtime. He would forget to pick her up after school. She always forgave him.

"Mom says I need to be back by ten," she reported.

"Good," Troy replied, drawing heavy, damp air into his lungs, letting the dose of oxygen lift his spirits. The deadline was later than ever; it was, in fact, Kirsten's weekend bedtime. "Is your mother feeling generous, or what?"

"I made a bet with her." Kirsten giggled. "She said you'd be late. I said you'd show up on time. She promised that if you did, I could stay out until ten."

He chuckled. Kirsten had, as usual, asked him to be on time when they had spoken over the phone on Friday, but he had to admit, most times he managed to be late no matter what.

They went to the lake for swimming and boating, then returned to town to pig out on pizza and Diet Coke.

"Mom always gets vegetables on pizza," Kirsten said with a scowl. She beamed as he ordered pepperoni, sausage, and Canadian bacon. One of the few good things about being a divorced father was that he didn't have to bother with the hard stuff like enforcing rules, helping with homework, taking her to the dentist. He got to be the pal.

They finished their evening at the bowling lanes, where Kirsten managed not to gutter a single ball, beating him two times out of three. She danced a little jig as she landed a strike in the final frame.

He hugged her, noting with regret that it was 9:30 PM. "Come on, Shortstuff. Let's get you home."

"I had a great time with you, Daddy."

Yes, Troy thought. It had been a good day. He felt like a real father. A competent, mature person, seeing to his offspring's needs. He had hope there would be more days like it. Leroy and Doug and the others emerged less and less as the years went on. What was the point of living in his body when they couldn't truly follow their paths? Troy actually found himself looking forward to the next decade or two, to seeing what sort of adult Kirsten would evolve into.

Chatting with his girl, he drove along the familiar streets toward Lydia's house, through intersections and around curves that were second nature to him. Three blocks from their destination, he stopped at a signal, waited for the green light, and when it came, pressed on the gas pedal to make a left hand turn.

Headlights blazed in through the righthand windows of the car, appearing as if out of nowhere. An engine whined, the noise changing pitch as the driver of the vehicle attempted to make it through a light that had already changed to red. Kirsten screamed. As fast as humanly possible, Troy shifted his foot from accelerator to brake. He had barely pressed down when metal slammed into metal.

Troy's car, hit broadside on the passenger side, careened across the asphalt, tires squealing, the other car clinging to it as if welded. Finally the motion stopped. Troy, hands frozen on the steering wheel, body still pressed against his door, looked sharply to his right and wished he hadn't.

Onlookers had to pull him away from his seat to keep him from uselessly trying to stanch Kirsten's bleeding. Numb, he finally let them drag him to the sidewalk. Nearby lay the dazed, yet intact, driver of the other car. The reek of alcohol rose from him like fumes from a refinery.

Troy had a bruise on his left shoulder and had sprained a wrist. That was all.

The way Troy saw it a day later, Kirsten had been a natural target. What better life essence to steal than that of the very young? The unicorn had probably had it in for her from the moment she was born.

He should never have called the tattooist a gook. The man had cursed him. For so many years, he had seen the unicorn at least partly as a blessing, when in fact the tattoo must have instigated all those deaths around him.

Causality. Everything happens for a reason.

The warnings had been there yesterday, but he had been blind to them. First there had been his uncharacteristic promptness. Then, Kirsten's smile in the bowling alley had reminded him all too much of Artie Farina grinning over a joke right at the moment the bullet struck him. Troy should never have kept his baby out late, should have taken her home in the daylight, before the drunk was on the road.

It was his fault. If not for the curse, reality would have taken a different path. The drunk would have come from the opposite direction, would have smashed into the driver's side of the car. Troy would have died, and his daughter would have lived.

It had been his fault in Vietnam as well. If he had taken the death assigned to him then, maybe all of his buddies would have lived.

He would not accept the devil's reward this time. He would not continue on, wandering through the decades, living glimpses of Kirsten's life, the one she would never live directly.

Blood seeped from the edges of the bandage on his chest. He pressed the gauze down, added another strip of tape from his shoulder to his rib cage. Pain radiated in pulses all the way down to his toes, but he paid it no more heed than he had when the stitcher's needle gun had impregnated him with ink back at G.I. Bob's.

He had been afraid, when he picked up the knife, that his skin could not be cut, that the invulnerability would apply. But it was done now, and the tears of relief dribbled down the sides of his face. Soon he would pick up the phone—to call Lydia, or contact the hospital directly. The docs could patch him up whatever way they wanted, recommend plastic surgery or let the scars form. All that mattered was that the tattoo was gone.

He had done the right thing, he told himself, wincing. He knew he could have scheduled laser surgery, could have gone to one of those parlors advertising tattoo removal. But it needed to happen before anything came along to change his mind. Now that he had found the courage, even one minute's delay would have been too much.

And it was working. He leaned toward his bathroom mirror, his reflection sharpening as he came within range of his nearsighted vision. There— little crow's feet radiated from the corners of his eyes. Gray roots showed like tiny maggots at the base of his hair. His joints ached, and his midriff complained of all the years held unnaturally taut and firm. He was back in the timeline, looking as if he had never left it. Tomorrow's dawn would mark the first time in twenty-eight years that he would wake up as Troy Chesley and no one else.

His breath caught. Over the bandage, he faintly detected a glow. It coalesced into a horselike shape with a spike protruding from its head. It hung there, letting him get a good look, then it sank into his body. As it did so, his spine straightened, his hair thickened, and an unholy vibrancy coursed through his bloodstream.

His newfound sense of victory drained away. The ordeal had not ended. Some part of him was still willing to do anything to have a suit of impenetrable armor. The marks upon him had long since gone beyond skin deep.

A tattoo was forever.

"No," he whispered. His hand flailed across the counter top until his fingers closed on the knife. "I won't let this go on." If cutting off the unicorn was not enough to destroy its power, there was another way, and he would take it. He raised the knife to his throat . . .

The weapon clattered to the floor. Troy stared at his image in the mirror. It had changed again. Though it was his same—youthful—face, his aspect now radiated an impression of intimidating, heroic size, as if he were looking at himself from the perspective of someone smaller and dependent.

"My God," he moaned.

The glow over his wound had done more than restore his immortality; it had brought an entity to the forefront. Troy reached toward the floor, willing his knees to bend, but they would not. The person possessing him would not allow a knife to point at the flesh of the man she had adored her whole brief life.

Leroy and Doug and Arturo and the others might have permitted him to consign them to oblivion. But this new one did not understand. She was frightened of death. Whatever shred of existence remained to her, she wanted to keep.

How could he deny her?

Troy stumbled into the second bedroom, lay down, and tucked up his knees. Overhead hung posters of cartoon characters. The coverlet was pink and trimmed with ruffles. He pulled Brown Bear off the pillow and hugged him close, beginning to cry as only an eleven-year-old, afraid of darkness and abandonment, could do.

HOMEWARD BOUND

Bruce Coville

J AMIE STOOD ON THE STEPS of his uncle's house and looked up. The place was tall and bleak. With its windows closed and shuttered, as they were now, it was easy to imagine the building was actually trying to keep him out.

"This isn't home," he thought rebelliously. "It's not home, and it never will be."

A pigeon fluttered onto the lawn nearby. Jamie started, then frowned. His father had raised homing pigeons, and the two of them had spent many happy hours together, tending his flock. The sight of the bird now, with the loss of his father still so fresh in his mind, only stirred up memories he wasn't ready to deal with yet.

He looked at the house again and was struck by an odd feeling: while this wasn't home, coming here had somehow taken him one step closer to finding it. That feeling had to do with the horn, of course; of that much, he was certain.

Jamie was seven the first time he had seen the horn hanging on the wall of his uncle's study.

"Narwhal," said his uncle, following the boy's gaze. "It's a whale with a horn growing out of the front of its head." He put one hand to his forehead and thrust out a finger to illustrate, as if Jamie were some sort of an idiot. "Sort of a sea-going unicorn," he continued. "Except, of course, that it's real instead of imaginary. I'd rather you didn't touch it. I paid dearly to get it."

Jamie had stepped back behind his father without speaking. He didn't dare say what was on his mind. Grown-ups, especially his uncle, didn't like being told they were wrong.

But his uncle *was* wrong. The horn had not come from a narwhal, not come from the sea at all.

It was the horn of a genuine unicorn.

Jamie couldn't have explained how he knew this was so. But he did, as surely—and mysteriously—as his father's pigeons knew their way home. Thinking of that moment of certainty now, he was reminded of those stormy nights when he and his father had watched lightning crackle through the summer sky. For an instant, everything would be outlined in light. Then, just as quickly, the world would be plunged back into darkness, with nothing remaining but a dazzling memory.

That was how it had been with the horn, five years ago.

And now Jamie was twelve, and his father was dead, and he had been sent to live with this rich, remote man who had always frightened him so much.

Oddly, that fear didn't come from his uncle. Despite his stern manner, the man was always quiet and polite with Jamie. Rather, he had learned it from his father. The men had not been together often, for his uncle frequently disappeared on mysterious "business trips" lasting weeks or even months on end. But as he watched his father grow nervous and unhappy whenever his brother returned, Jamie came to sense that the one man had a strange hold over the other.

It frightened him.

Yet as scared as he was, as sad and lonely over the death of his father, one small corner of his soul was burning now with a fierce joy, because he was finally going to be close to the horn.

Of course, in a way, he had never been apart from it. Ever since that first sight, five years ago, the horn had shimmered in his memory. It was the first thing he thought of when he woke up and the last at night when he went to sleep. It was a gleaming beacon in his dreams, reassuring him that no matter how cruel and ugly a day might have been, there was a reason to go on, a reason to be. His one glimpse of the horn had filled him with a sense of beauty and rightness so powerful that it had carried him through these five years.

Even now, while his uncle was droning on about the household rules, he saw it again in that space in the back of his head where it seemed to reside. Like a shaft of never-ending light, it tapered through the darkness of his mind, wrist-thick at its base, ice-pick sharp at its tip, a spiraled wonder of icy, pearly whiteness. And while Jamie's uncle was telling him the study was off-limits, Jamie was trying to figure out how quickly he could slip in there to see the horn again.

For once again, his uncle was wrong. No place that held the horn could be off-limits for him. It was too deeply a part of him.

That was why he had come here so willingly, despite his fear of his uncle. Like the pigeons, he was making his way home.

Jamie listened to the big clock downstairs as it marked off the quarter hours. When the house had been quiet for seventy-five minutes, he took the flashlight from under his pillow, climbed out of bed, and slipped on his robe. Walking softly, he made his way down the hall, enjoying the feel of the thick carpet like moss beneath his feet.

He paused at the door of the study. Despite his feelings, he hesitated. What would his uncle say, or do, if he woke and caught him here?

The truth was, it didn't matter. He had no choice. He had to see the horn again.

Turning the knob of the door, he held his breath against the inevitable click. When it came, it was mercifully soft. He stepped inside and flicked on his flashlight.

His heart lurched as the beam struck the opposite wall and showed an empty place where the horn had once hung. A little cry slipped through his lips before he remembered how important it was to remain silent.

He swung the light around the room and breathed a sigh of relief. The horn, the alicorn, as his reading had told him it was called, lay across his uncle's desk.

He stepped forward, almost unable to believe that the moment he had dreamed of all these years was finally at hand.

He took another step, and another.

He was beside the desk now, close enough to reach out and touch the horn.

And still he hesitated.

Part of that hesitation came from wonder, for the horn was even more beautiful than he had remembered. Another part of it came from a desire to make this moment last as long as he possibly could. It was something he had been living toward for five years now, and he wanted to savor it. But the biggest part of his hesitation came from fear. He had a sense that once he had touched the horn, his life might never be the same.

That didn't mean he wouldn't do it.

But he needed to prepare himself. So for a while, he simply stood in the darkness, gazing at the horn. Light seemed to play beneath its surface, as if there were something alive inside it—though how that could be after all this time, he didn't know.

Finally, he reached out to stroke the horn. Just stroke it. He wasn't ready, yet, to truly embrace whatever mystery was waiting for him. Just a hint, just a teasing glimpse, was all he wanted.

His fingertip grazed the horn, and he cried out in terror as the room lights blazed on, and his uncle's powerful voice thundered over him, demanding to know what was going on.

Jamie collapsed beside the desk. His uncle scooped him up and carried him back to his room.

A fever set in, and it was three days before Jamie got out of bed again.

He had vague memories of people coming to see him during that time— of a doctor who took his pulse and temperature; of an older woman who hovered beside him, spooning a thin broth between his lips and wiping his forehead with a cool cloth; and, most of all, of his uncle, who loomed over his bed like a thundercloud, glowering down at him.

His only other memories were of the strange dream that gripped him over and over again, causing him to thrash and cry out in terror. In the dream, he was running through a deep forest. Something was behind him, pursuing him. He leapt over mossy logs, splashed through cold streams, crashed through brambles and thickets. But no matter how he tried, he couldn't escape the fierce thing that was after him—a thing that wore his uncle's face.

More than once, Jamie sat up in bed, gasping and covered with sweat. Then the old woman, or the doctor, would speak soothing words and try to calm his fears.

Once he woke quietly. He could hear doves cooing outside his window. Looking up, he saw his uncle standing beside the bed, staring down at him angrily.

"Why?" wondered Jamie. "Why doesn't he want me to touch the horn?"

But he was tired, and the question faded as he slipped back into his dreams.

He was sent away to a school, where he was vaguely miserable but functioned well enough to keep the faculty at a comfortable distance. The other students, not so easily escaped, took some delight in trying to torment the dreamy boy who was so oblivious to their little world of studies and games, their private wars and rages. After a while, they gave it up; Jamie didn't react enough to make their tortures worth the effort on any but the most boring of days.

He had other things to think about, memories and mysteries that absorbed him and carried him through the year, aware of the world around him only enough to move from one place to another, to answer questions, to keep people away.

The memories had two sources. The first was the vision that had momentarily dazzled him when he touched the horn, a tantalizing instant of joy so deep and powerful that it had shaken him to the roots of his being. Hints of green, of cool, of wind in face and hair whispered at the edges of that vision.

He longed to experience it again.

The other memories echoed from his fever dreams and were not so pleasant. They spoke only of fear, and some terrible loss he did not understand.

Christmas, when it finally came, was difficult. As the other boys were leaving for home, his uncle sent word that urgent business would keep him out of town throughout the holiday. He paid the headmaster handsomely to keep an eye on Jamie and feed him Christmas dinner.

The boy spent a bleak holiday longing for his father. Until now, his obsession with the horn had shielded him from the still-raw pain of that loss. But the sounds and smells of the holiday, the tinkling bells, the warm spices, the temporary but real goodwill surrounding him, all stirred the sorrow inside him, and he wept himself to sleep at night.

He would dream. In his dreams, his father would reach out to take his hand. "We're all lost," he would whisper, as he had the day he died. "Lost, and aching to find our name, so that we can finally go home again."

When Jamie woke, his pillow would be soaked with sweat and tears.

The sorrow faded with the return of the other students and the resumption of a daily routine. Even so, it was a relief when three months later, his uncle sent word that he would be allowed to come back for the spring holiday.

The man made a point of letting Jamie know he had hidden the horn, by taking him into the study soon after his arrival at the house. He watched closely as the boy's eyes flickered over the walls, searching for the horn, and seemed satisfied at the expression of defeat that twisted his face before he closed in on himself, shutting out the world again.

But Jamie had become cunning. The defeat he showed his uncle was real. What the man didn't see, because the boy buried it as soon as he was aware of it, was that the defeat was temporary. For hiding the horn didn't make any difference. Now that Jamie had touched it, he was bound to it. Wherever it was hidden, he would find it. Its call was too powerful to mistake.

Even so, Jamie thought he might lose his mind before he got his chance. Day after day, his uncle stayed in the house, guarding his treasure. Finally, on the morning of the fifth day, an urgent message pulled him away. Even then, the anger that burned in his face as he stormed through the great oak doors, an anger Jamie knew was rooted in being called from his vigil, might have frightened someone less determined.

The boy didn't care. He would make his way to the horn while he had the chance.

He knew where it was, of course—had known from the evening of the first day.

It was in his uncle's bedroom.

The room was locked. Moving cautiously, Jamie slipped downstairs to the servant's quarters and stole the master key, then scurried back to the door. To his surprise, he felt no fear.

He decided it was because he had no choice; he was only doing what he had to do.

He twisted the key in the lock and swung the door open.

His uncle's room was large and richly decorated, filled with heavy, carefully carved furniture. Above the dresser hung a huge mirror.

Jamie hesitated for just a moment, then lay on his stomach and peered beneath the bed.

The horn was there, wrapped in a length of blue velvet.

He reached in and drew the package out. Then he stood and placed it gently on the bed. With reverent fingers, he unrolled the velvet. Cradled by the rich blue fabric, the horn looked like a comet blazing across a midnight sky.

This time, there could be no interruption. Hesitating for no more than a heartbeat, he reached out and clutched the horn with both hands.

He cried out, in agony, and in awe. For a moment, he thought he was going to die. The feelings the horn unleashed within him seemed too much for his body to hold. He didn't die, though his heart was racing faster than it had any right to.

"More," he thought, as images of the place he had seen in his dreams rushed through his mind. "I have to know more."

He drew the horn to his chest and laid his cheek against it.

He thought his heart would beat its way out of his body.

And still it wasn't enough.

He knew what he had to do next. But he was afraid.

Fear made no difference. He remembered again what his father had said about people aching to find their true name. He was close to his now. "No one can come this close and not reach out for the answer," he thought. "The emptiness would kill them on the spot."

And so he did what he had to do, fearful as it was. Placing the base of the horn against the foot of the massive bed, he set the tip of it against his heart.

Then he leaned forward.

The point of the horn pierced his flesh like a sword made of fire and ice. He cried out, first in pain, then in joy and wonder. Finally, the answer was clear to him, and he understood his obsession, and his loneliness.

"No wonder I didn't fit," he thought, as his fingers fused, then split into cloven hooves.

The transformation was painful. But the joy so far surpassed it that he barely noticed the fire he felt as his neck began to stretch, and the horn erupted from his brow. "No wonder, no wonder, no it's all wonder, wonder, wonder and joy!"

He reared back in triumph, his silken mane streaming behind him, as he trumpeted the joyful discovery that he was, and always had been, and always would be, a unicorn.

And knowing his name, he finally knew how to go home. Hunching the powerful muscles of his hind legs, he launched himself toward the dresser. His horn struck the mirror, and it shattered into a million pieces that crashed and tinkled into two different worlds.

He hardly noticed. He was through, and home at last.

"No," said a voice at the back of his head. "You're not home yet."

He stopped. It was true. He wasn't home yet, though he was much closer. But there was still more to do, and farther to go.

How could that be? He knew he was, had always been, a unicorn. Then he trembled, as he realized his father's last words were still true. There was still something inside that needed to be discovered, to be named.

He whickered nervously as he realized that all he had really done was to come back to where most people begin—his own place, his own shape.

He looked around. He was standing at the edge of a clearing in an old oak wood. Sunlight filtered through the leaves, dappling patches of warmth onto his flanks. He paused for a moment, taking pleasure in feeling his own true shape at last.

Suddenly he shivered, then stood stock still as the smell of the girl reached his nostrils.

The scent was sweet, and rich, and he could resist it no more than he had resisted the horn. He began trotting in her direction, sunlight bouncing off the horn that jutted out from his forehead.

He found her beneath an apple tree, singing to herself while she brushed her honey-colored hair. Doves rustled and cooed at the edges of the clearing. They reminded him of the pigeons his father had raised.

As he stood and watched her, every fiber of his being cried out that there was danger here. But it was not in the nature of a unicorn to resist such a girl.

Lowering his head, he walked forward.

"So," she said. "You've come at last."

He knelt beside her, and she began to stroke his mane. Her fingers felt cool against his neck, and she sang to him in a voice that seemed to wash away old sorrows. He relaxed into a sweet silence, content for the first time that he could remember.

He wanted the moment to go on forever.

But it ended almost instantly, as the girl slipped a golden bridle over his head, and his uncle stepped into the clearing.

The man was wearing a wizard's garb, which didn't surprise Jamie. Ten armed soldiers stood behind him.

Jamie sprang to his feet. But he had been bound by the magic of the bridle; he could neither run nor attack.

Flanks heaving, he stared at his wizard uncle.

"Did you really think you could get away from me?" asked the man.

"I have!" thought Jamie fiercely, knowing the thought would be understood.

"Don't be absurd!" snarled his uncle. "I'll take your horn, as I did your father's. And then I'll take your shape, and finally your memory. You'll come back with me and be no different than he was—a dreamy, foolish mortal, lost and out of place."

"Why?" thought Jamie. "Why would anyone want to hold a unicorn?"

His uncle didn't answer.

Jamie locked eyes with him, begging him to explain.

No answer came. But he realized that he had found a way to survive. Just as the golden bridle held him helpless, so his gaze could hold his uncle. As long as he could stare into the man's eyes, he could keep him from moving.

He knew, too, that as soon as he flinched, the battle would be over.

Jamie had no idea how long the struggle actually lasted. They seemed to be in a place apart, far away from the clearing, away from the girl, and the soldiers.

He began to grow fearful. Sooner or later, he would falter, and his uncle would regain control. It wasn't enough to hold him. He had to conquer him.

But how? How? He couldn't win unless he knew why he was fighting. He had to discover why his uncle wanted to capture and hold him.

But the only way to do that was to look deeper inside the man. The idea frightened him; he didn't know what he would find there. Even worse, it would work two ways. He couldn't look deeper into his uncle without letting his uncle look more deeply into him.

He hesitated. But there was no other way. Accepting the risk, he opened himself to his uncle.

At the same time, he plunged into the man's soul.

His uncle cried out, then dropped to his knees and buried his face in his hands, trembling with the humiliation of being seen.

Jamie trembled too, for the emptiness he found inside this man could swallow suns and devour planets. This was the hunger that had driven him to capture unicorns, in the hope that their glory could fill his darkness.

Then, at last, Jamie knew what he must do. Stepping forward, he pressed the tip of his horn against his uncle's heart.

He had been aware of his horn's healing power, of course. But this was the first time he had tried to use it. He wasn't expecting the shock of pain that jolted through him, or the wave of despair that followed as he took in the emptiness, and the fear, and the hunger that had driven his uncle for so long.

He wanted to pull away, to run in terror.

But if he did, it would only start all over again. Only a healing would put an end to the pursuit. And this was the only way to heal this man, this wizard, who, he now understood, had never really been his uncle, but only his captor. He had to be seen, in all his sorrow and his ugliness; seen, and accepted, and loved. Only then could he be free of the emptiness that made him want to possess a unicorn.

Jamie trembled as the waves of emptiness and sorrow continued to wash through him. But, at last, he was nearly done. Still swaying from the effort, he whispered to the man: "Go back. Go back and find your name. And then—go *home*."

That was when the sword fell, slicing through his neck.

It didn't matter, really, though he felt sorry for his "uncle," who began to weep, and sorrier still for the soldier who had done the deed. He knew it would be a decade or so before the man could sleep without mind-twisting nightmares of the day he had killed a unicorn.

But for Jamie himself, the change made no difference. Because he still was what he had always been, what he always would be, what a unicorn had simply been one appropriate shape to hold. He was a being of power and light.

He shook with delight, as he realized that he had named himself at last.

He turned to the wizard and was amazed. No longer hampered by mere eyes, he could see that the same thing was true for him—as it was for the girl, as it was for the soldiers.

They were *all* beings of power and light.

The terrible thing was, they didn't know it.

Suddenly, he understood. This was the secret, the unnamed thing his father had been trying to remember: that we are all beings of power and light. And all the pain, all the sorrow—it all came from not knowing this simple truth.

Why? wondered Jamie. *Why don't any of us know how beautiful we really are?*

And then even that question became unimportant, because his father had come to take him home, and suddenly he wasn't just a unicorn but all unicorns, was part of every wise and daring being that had worn that shape and that name, every unicorn that had ever lived, or ever would live. And he felt himself stretch to fill the sky, as the stars came tumbling into his body, stars at his knees and at his hooves, at his shoulder and his tail, and, most of all, a shimmer of stars that lined the length of his horn, a horn that stretched across the sky, pointing out, for anyone who cared to look, the way to go home.

UNICORN TRIANGLE

Patricia A. McKillip

I GET FLASHBACKS NOW AND THEN. What it was like. Then. Before. The moonlight a path of diamonds and ivory, suspended between the mist of trees whose names I knew, every one of them, as well as who had dropped what nut that made this tree, that meant this name. My watching eyes as dark as night, my pelt as sleek and perfect as the moon at full, my hooves and spiraling horn forged of that dream, that glittering. All the scents and secret whisperings: water, brambles opening flowers, sharpening thorns, bracken crumbling oh so slowly, a sift, a shift of a splinter of wood, a break of driest leaf spending a timeless moment edging apart, resettling itself like a dreamer fitting itself into sleep, into earth. The sound of the wings of the Luna moth fluttering toward that white fire, spellbound by the moon.

Then. I almost remember my name.

Then someone says a name, over and over, until I realize it must mean me.

Erin heaves a sigh, and squeezes air out of a pillow to wrestle it into its shroud. Case. Whatever.

"Jeez Louise, Lisa, I swear your brain lives in a different time zone."

That seems so likely, that different time zone, that I go there to test its truth. It is a step away, but farther, I guess, than anyone even close can see. A pillow brings me back, bouncing off my head.

"Lisa! We've got eight more rooms before check-in!"

Maybe so, but I suddenly flash back to the sorcerer's face, his final expression, the last he could ever say with it before he flung the spell out of himself with his dying breath—so strong it was even his fingernails splintered and his eyelashes fell out—and I was left standing alone, staring at the little, wicked smile frozen in his eyes. My horn, which had pierced his heart, turned to moon-mist and disappeared. So had my forelegs, my lovely hooves. I lost all balance, toppled forward into the rose of blood blooming out of his chest.

Now here I am, changing sheets, emptying little refrigerators of half-eaten chip dips, sloshing brushes around in the bathroom, vacuuming sand, tossing shells people had carried back to the room and then forgotten to pack. Over the balcony they go, despite Erin's protests. I haven't hit anybody yet.

Listen, I was trying to say when they discovered me in the brambles, when they asked my name. *List. Lis.*

So. That's what I've become.

I didn't know what language to speak those first words. I've been nearly everywhere in the world, though not entirely. Not, I think, in that ancient land where mountains have crumbled to the bone and tall, feisty, hornless creatures abound, whose young peep out of pouches on their bellies. Nor in the coldest places, though it is—or was—said that I swam in the sea. I tried that once, tangled in some sailor's dream of horns and unicorns. I didn't like it; I smelled brine for days, though it had only been a dream.

In other lands, I go disguised. I wear the face and features of the creatures they know as unicorn: it seems polite. In one, my horn might be colored like a rainbow; in another I have a beard, and my hooves are cleft. In yet another, I have scales like a lizard and my single horn branches like a tree. In some, I speak words of wisdom; in others, I just rage and bite. In those where I belong to earth and time, I am gorgeously ugly. In most, I am mostly seen in tale and memory. I am made of dreams, of thread, of colored ink. I am ancient yet unforgotten; everyone recognizes me and no one ever sees me.

Except the sorcerer.

I managed to get a few words right when I was found; the sorcerer's blood on me did the rest. They thought I'd tumbled into some blackberry brambles along the hillside below the hotel. They have never—not even Erin—decided what land I came from, what language I spoke when they found me, or even if my tongue is tangled by my slow wits or by my bad translation.

I see no point in trying to tell the truth.

Nobody knew what to do with me after they found me. I couldn't tell them: I had no idea, either. I understood them, but I could barely speak. I kept trying to find my balance, and falling over. *Where's the rest of me?* I asked, or tried to. I had just impaled a sorcerer through his heart with my horn; I was still enraged, still trembling with the exhausting battle to elude his sorcery. I wanted to run as far, as fast as I could down the bridge of light between the sea and the setting moon until that placid, ancient face calmed me. Instead I was tangled in hair and kept falling down. I had hands where my forehooves had been. I had seen enough humans to know that they weren't slender, graceful, pampered ladies' fingers, either. They could have heaved a sack of flour, or swung an ax. Hair the color of my vanished pelt, ivory and moonlight, tumbled out of my head and spilled over me like a cloak to my great, ungainly feet. It hid at least some of my unclothed skin, at which I stared in horror and fascination. As did others, until a modest young virgin tried to pull some morning glory vines over me.

He said, "Somebody call the police."

"Hospital," a woman said briefly. "Look at the blood on her."

"It's not mine," I said, or tried to; they looked at me with complete bewilderment. "It's the sorcerer's."

"Russian?" somebody guessed.

"Doesn't sound like my high school Spanish."

"Something Nordic?"

"It's more lilty—maybe French?"

A little girl, staring at me, pulled the finger out of her mouth and said, "It is the language of bells." She smiled at me, as though we shared a secret, and I wanted to kneel then and there and lay my head in her lap.

But.

There was more chatter, more of me falling over, more alarmed voices, then more vast, wailing alarms. The little girl vanished. As the hours passed,

I grew to understand the lights, the buildings, the uniforms, the things done to me, why they asked the questions they did, over and over, until I fell asleep and then fell off my chair, and woke up again to more of everything all over again.

They argued incessantly—yes, no, yes—about me: as in what to do with. I finally stopped listening, sat drooping in ugly garments and gave myself up to my memories, my yearnings, my overwhelming despair. I was a unicorn without a horn slumped in a chair, with no name and nowhere to go.

I had won the battle and lost my life. And I had not a star-glint of an idea why the sorcerer had attacked me. It was not the familiar human motive: to kill me and cut off my horn to use for cleaning sullied waters or detecting poison in unexpected places. The sorcerer had fought to his death when he could have run; he used his last breath to destroy us both.

Why? I wondered, in my morass of bewilderment, regret, pain for my lost limbs, my lost life. What had I ever done to him?

They prodded me; I got up. They asked yet more questions; I stared at them blankly, asking them why I should care. They moved, nudged me again; I followed. More talking, face to face, face to phone, more standing, more papers signed, more talking. Phones sang, gabbled, sang again. Then a voice on one of the tiny phones screeched like a raven and even I stood up a little straighter.

One of the uniforms took the phone. Every time he tried to speak, the voice again, like a hoof grating on rock, like wood tearing itself raggedly in two. Finally, he said the only words he was allowed: "Yes, ma'am."

The voice cooed like a dove in love and went still.

So here I am in the hundred-year-old beach hotel, changing sheets and bars of soap, and wondering what to do with myself. I've learned to form more useful words with my unfamiliar lips. Understanding words and those who spoke them was never the problem; I was around at the beginning of their language. I know what they want from me—a detailed human history from birth to here—and I haven't one to give them. For a long time, a time of full moons, bleak skies, tossing ships, new moons, warm rain, golden days, sandy footprints on the carpets, I even forgot to wonder whose trainwreck of a voice had brought me to that place.

Then the phone rings in a room Erin and I are cleaning; Erin answers it. "Yeah?" She listens, then hangs up and says to me, "Geegee wants you."

"Who?"

"Geegee. In the office. Now."

So I go. I don't have the slightest who Geegee is, nor do I care. Maybe, I think without hope, this Geegee will fire me, and I can spend the summer among the brambles, foraging for wild fruit, then lie me down in the lace of tide as the chill winds rouse, and let the sea drift me to the moon.

Nobody is behind the registration desk. The inner office door is open. I peer into that, and my heart tries to grow wings and fly.

The young girl's eyes meet mine, seeing me, knowing me. Only this time they are in a face with lines like a walnut shell, all rippling together as she smiles. She is a small bundle of old bones in skirts and various scarves and sweaters, sitting in a rocking chair by a window, her feet dangling above the floor.

She says my name.

I feel my bones try to rearrange themselves, trying to remember the shape they once knew. But, powerful as that voice she has is, it can't pull me out of what I have become. The lines on her face shift, hope and power blurring into rue.

"Dang," she says softly, while I scramble around for the pieces of my thoughts.

"Who—what—?"

"You can call me Geegee. Short for great-grandmother." She shrugs a little. "Not enough greats by a long shot, but who's counting?"

"You almost—"

"Almost is no better than not. No better at all."

"Who are you?" I ask, I plead, for I haven't seen such eyes, such knowledge, such recognition, anywhere else in this barren time where not even the moon remembers me.

She says nothing, just pats her knees, and I sink to mine, crawl to her, wrap my arms around her skirts, lean against her like some giant child finding solace in those ancient bones. She slides a hand down my head, pats my back.

"I've been waiting for you for a very long time," she says. "I was there with you when the sorcerer sent you into the future. I was the princess you never saw."

"Hah?" I say into her skirts. Then I am quiet, remembering again the smile of triumph in the sorcerer's dead eyes. I think, barely understanding myself: this future would explain that smile. Another word intrudes. I don't want to think about it; I just want to kneel there at the old woman's feet, feeling her stroke my hair.

Princess?

"He's not dead, you know," she says, and I feel my heart again, tightening this time, reforming itself, growing hard, harder on the outside, sealing the seething fury within. I lift my face, stare at her blindly. Surely she would not say that, she would never light that flame unless she knew. I feel my wildness rage against where my hooves should be, my horn.

"I killed him." I do not recognize my voice.

"There is a world," she says very gently, her hand on my forehead where the horn once was, "in which I am not old, and he is not dead." I hear myself make a noise in some language I do not know. Her fingers, warm and steady on my brow, quiet me. "I was foolish then. I made you into something more than wild and beautiful; my heart fashioned you into someone who did not exist. My heart wished you human, someone perfect, magical, who could love me. Silly girl, I was. Foolish princess. But no more foolish than the sorcerer, who looked at me and wanted me changed into someone who could love him. He could love only me; I could love only you. You stood between us, in his eyes. If you disappeared, he thought, my heart must turn to him. Together he and I turned you into some impossible creature who could never exist in any kind of peace." Her fingers brush down my cheek, slide beneath my chin, and draw my face up so that she can look into my eyes. "He didn't notice me watching, either, when he fought you. That was his mistake." I stare into hers, wondering if she could see beneath the pale human surface of mine to the midnight within. For an instant, I see the memory in her eyes: her youth and beauty, the dream that she had made of me.

But I am far, far older than she, and wilder than she could imagine. "Where is he?" I ask.

"It took me all this time to find him," she answers a bit impatiently, annoyed with herself. "All this time since you tumbled here. Of course I learned a few things, searching all those futures where you weren't."

I eye her silently, wondering. In the world the sorcerer had tossed me out of, I would have recognized the magic in her even before I ever saw the princess. But I'd never noticed that lovelorn maiden trailing hopelessly after me. Maybe, I realize, she hadn't been a budding sorceress then. Or a virgin, either, for that matter. Which, on the whole, was none of my business. But I wonder suddenly what she truly wanted from me.

So I ask her.

"Well, of course," she answers without surprise, "my passion for you had nothing much at all to do with love."

"Of course," I echo with bewilderment.

"I wanted to be you. All that power. All that beauty. Since you inspired me to be what I have become, I feel I owe you a bit of help." She pats my cheek, then stirs, hands on the rocker arms, rising, so that I am forced to let go of the safe-haven of her strength, her understanding heart. I move reluctantly; she adds, as I get to my feet, "That's why we need the sorcerer."

"I know I killed him," I protest. "I know I did."

Her mouth tightens; I glimpse the lightning glint of power in her eyes. "He is a wily one," she murmurs grimly. "He fled that body you killed on the flow of its last breath."

"Where is he?" I demand. "I'll—"

"You'll what?" she asks, reminding me, with a sweeping glance, of the awkward, unwieldy body he left me in. It had its weapons, I realize, an arsenal between my great feet and my big, hard head. Not a pretty thought, I know, but handy, so to speak.

She adds, maybe reading my mind, "We want him alive."

"We."

"We need him to undo with his own power what he has done to you. It is a twisted, tangled piece of work, that spell. But I have learned a thing or two, by now, and I can make him eat his words."

"How?" I ask incredulously.

"By giving him what he thought he wanted."

"You."

She gives me a tortoise-smile, thin-lipped, leathery. "Something like that. You'll see. You don't have a reason to hang around this place? No one to say farewell to?" I shake my head. "Neither do I. Say good-bye to Geegee."

"What is your name?" I wonder as she holds out her hand for mine. Then someone hits the bell at the reception desk, and the hotel, with Geegee still sitting in her rocker, fades away around us along with my question.

In that nameless place, I see again the dimensions of the princess's sorcery: how much she has learned since she shadowed me and I never noticed her, any more than I paid heed to what clung to my hooves and followed me everywhere. She changes into white fire, moonlight, foam-laced wave, midnight.

She becomes me.

And then she changes me.

And I, beautiful and virgin in any world, no words left in me of any language, can only follow her helplessly to watch her battle for my lost self.

MY SON HEYDARI
AND THE KARKADANN

Peter S. Beagle

N O, THEY ARE VANISHING NOW, the karkadanns; at least they are almost gone from this part of Persia. Which is a very good thing, and you'll find no one in the land to tell you otherwise. It is an especially good thing for a man master of the only working elephant herd north of Baghdad. If your business is felling trees and hauling them off to the river, to be rafted downstream to the lumber mill and turned into palaces, ships, furniture, what you will—then you are almost bound to come to me and my elephants. It has been my family's trade for four generations, and my eldest son, Farid, will make the fifth when I am gone. It is our place in the world. It is what we do.

And it is only in this generation—my generation—that we have found ourselves increasingly free of those monsters, those terrible horned demons, the karkadanns. You have never seen one, I assume? No, not likely, coming from Turkey as you do. All the same, you must surely have heard that they are huge creatures, easily the size of Greek bulls, with double hooves, tails like lions, hides like thick leather plates—and that *horn!* Six, even seven feet long they run; and with the power of that great body behind it, they can splinter a cedar or an oak into kindling. I saw it happen just so when I was a boy.

That same horn can also split an elephant like a dumpling. I have seen that happen too.

Why karkadanns hate elephants as particularly and intensely as they do, no scholar has ever been able to explain, not to my satisfaction. I still have nightmares about seeing two karkadanns charging down out of the hills they favor, bellowing that chilling challenge of theirs—like battle horns, only deeper, and with a more carrying tone—and watching helplessly as they went through my herd, slashing left and right, literally spitting elephants on their horns like kebabs, then hurling them aside and going on to the next poor picketed beast. The elephants almost never fought back, never even tried to run away. Elephants are very intelligent, you know, and perhaps their imaginations simply paralyzed them: they could see what was going to happen, see it so clearly that they could not move. I felt the same way, watching those karkadanns coming.

They trample farmers' fields too, without a thought, most especially during the mating season. The farmers plant extra crops for just that reason, hoping to salvage *something* after the beasts get through with their wheat or their corn, their arbors or their orchards. And as for guards—if you can hire any—or dogs, if you can keep them from tucking tail and fleeing at the first distant smell of a karkadann . . . well, why even discuss it? We lost men too, in those old days, as well as elephants.

The karkadann has no natural enemies. I am told that a thousand years ago, the dragons kept them within reasonable check; but, of course, in our human wisdom, we killed off the dragons in the egg and the nest, because they cost us a lamb or a goat now and again. So—of course—the karkadanns promptly ran wild, and we could only be grateful that at least they were not carnivores, like the dragons. That was our sole blessing, for all those thousand years.

No, we did have one thing else to thank the gods for in our prayers: the fact that karkadanns never drop more than one foal at a time. As many as two . . . no, it doesn't bear considering. Two to a birth, and they would own the country by this time. And other lands too, perhaps—who knows?

They are entirely vegetarian—though their two curving fangs imply otherwise—and entirely solitary by nature, except for those few weeks when they run mad with lust, and are then very nearly as likely to attack one another as they are elephants or humans. Even the females can be badly hurt during the rut; and more than once I have been gratified to encounter a pack of jackals feasting on the carcass of a karkadann bearing the marks of a comrade's brutal assault. All in all, an unlovely, unadmirable, and altogether detestable creature. And your fascination with it is a complete mystery to me.

But it would not be so to Heydari, my third son. You will meet him at dinner, Farid being away on business. Which is a pity, because I would like you to observe the difference between them. Farid is me in large, as you might say, being that much bigger and that much more ambitious—though not yet that much cleverer, though he thinks he is. I do not always *like* him, I suppose—do you like all *your* children all the time?—but I *understand* him, which is a comfort and a reassurance, and makes for a peaceful association. But Heydari. That Heydari.

You would never take them for brothers if you met them together. Heydari is small and slight, and much darker than Farid, and much less immediately charming. I think he makes a point of it, having seen Farid making friends everywhere, instantly, all his life. He has never been any use with the elephants, and we would be out of business in a month if I put him in charge of my accounts. Yet he is more intelligent than Farid—quite likely more intelligent than all the rest of us—but I cannot see that it has thus far done him much good. All the same, I confess to a feeling for him that I can neither explain nor defend. Especially not defend, not after the time he saved the life of a bloody karkadann.

How old was he? Thirteen or fourteen, I suppose; when else would you be that stupid, in exactly that way? As he told it in his own time— long after he *should* have told it—he found the creature high in those same foothills you came through, being drawn to it by the urgent calling of a ringdove; which, for reasons no one has ever fathomed, is the karkadann's only friend. As curious as any boy, he climbed after the bird and followed it to the entrance of a cave, where the beast lay bleeding its life away, and good riddance, through several deep wounds on its throat and flanks. It was barely breathing, he said, and the yellow eyes it tried to focus on him were seeing something else.

Like any man in this realm—any man but my son—I would either have helped the miserable monster on its way, or merely sat myself down and savored its passing. But not Heydari, not my softhearted, softheaded boy. He immediately set about fetching the karkadann water from a nearby spring, going back and forth to carry it in his cap. Apart from the stupidity of it, it was a risky matter as well, for the creature was in pain, and it lunged at him more than once with the last of its strength. He treated its injuries with what herbs he could find, and bound them with strips torn from his own clothes, while the ringdove perched on that murderous horn, cooing its approval. Then he went away, promising to return on the following day, but certain that he would find the karkadann dead when he did. I have said that he has never been of any practical use with the elephants, but he has been a kind boy from his childhood. An *idiot*, but always kind.

Well, he did return, keeping his word; and, unfortunately, the wretched beast was living yet. It was still unable to raise more than its head—which it did mostly to snap at him, even with one of those wicked fangs broken off halfway—but its wounds had stopped bleeding, and its breath was coming a bit deeper and more steadily. My son was greatly encouraged. He brought it more water, and fetched an armload or two of the fruits and vines that karkadanns favor, laying it all within reach in case the creature's appetite should revive. Then he sat close beside it, because he is a fool, and recited the old, old prayers and *sutras* most of the night before he went home.

And climbed back up the next day, and the day after that, to attend to that vile animal's recovery. Mind you, he told *us*, his own family, nothing of this—which, I must say, was the first intelligent thing he had done in the whole mad business. As many losses as we had endured over the years, in terms not merely of dead elephants, but taking into account the cost of workers, of lost time and equipment and the timber itself, we would all probably have fallen upon him and torn him to shreds. To be nursing a karkadann back to health, in order that it might continue slaughtering, destroying . . . you see, even now I am sweating and snarling with rage at my own son. Even now.

Now if this were a fairy tale out of the *Shahnameh*, the boy and the karkadann would become such fast friends that the monster would give up all its evil ways and turn to loving and aiding humanity, even against its own folk. Hardly. It did stop trying to kill Heydari, having finally connected his ministrations with its survival and recovery; but it permitted no liberties, such as petting or grooming—only the ringdove was permitted that sort of intimacy—and it would clearly have died itself before ever taking food from his hand. He tried to explain to me once why he could not help liking that quality in the beast.

"It was so *proud*, Father," he said. "No, it was not even a matter of pride— it was just what it was, and not about to yield a fraction of itself to anyone, whatever the cost. Yes, it was a dreadful creature, wicked and heartless like all the rest of its kind . . . but oh, it was magnificent too—splendidly terrible. Father, can you understand a little of what I am saying?"

Of course I hit him. You can't go around asking your father questions like that.

But that was later, well later. Meanwhile, he was caring for that karkadann every day—I should have been able to smell it on him; they smell like hay just starting to turn moldy—while the ringdove murmured smugly to them both, and his brothers were shouting for him to put his worthless self to some use cleaning the elephants' quarters. And now and then, so he told me, he would look up from his medicating and see those yellow eyes fixed on him, and he would wonder what the creature was thinking, what it *could* possibly be thinking at that moment. Which I, or any man with the sense of a bedbug, could have told him, but let that pass. What difference? Let it pass.

Finally, there came the day when Heydari made his way to the cave, and found the karkadann standing erect for the first time. It was grotesquely thin for its great size, and it seemed barely able to lift its head with that monstrous horn, but it stayed on its feet, swaying dazedly from side to side, and looking every moment as though it might crumple completely. Heydari clapped his hands and shouted encouragement, and the karkadann snarled in its chest and made a weak feint at him with the horn. The boy was wise enough to come no closer, but went off to find as much of the creature's preferred vegetation as he could carry in both arms. Then, as always, he simply sat down and watched it eat, rumbling evilly to itself. And as far as I can ever suppose, he was perfectly content.

At least, he was until Niloufar discovered them.

She was a shepherd girl, Niloufar—I knew her father well, as it happens.

When I think about it, it's a wonder she had a flock to tend, as many sheep as the old man slaughtered on the day she was born. He had six sons, which was more than enough for him when he thought about the battles to come over their inheritance, and the celebration of Niloufar's arrival lasted almost a week. So she was undoubtedly spoiled, treated like a princess from her birth, shepherdess or no; but she was actually quite a good girl, when all's said and done. A little bit of a thing, but pretty with it—Farid was already eyeing her, and so was Abbas, my second boy—but I am not sure that Heydari had even noticed her, or remembered her name, for that matter. She'd noticed him, though, or I'm more of a fool than he.

Her flock had winded the karkadann, of course, and were having none of it, but fled in panic to rejoin in the little valley below the cave. Niloufar left her two dogs minding them and—being just as idiotically inquisitive as my idiot son—climbed back up to the cave mouth, having heard a familiar voice there. She knew the smell of a karkadann as surely as any sheep, and she was afraid, but she kept coming anyway. The rest of her family are quite sensible.

The karkadann growled savagely as soon as it saw her, and made as though to charge. Heydari cried out, "*No!*" and the beast halted, being still so weak that it almost fell with the first steps. But Niloufar was mightily impressed with a boy who could make a karkadann obey, and she said, "Have you actually tamed it, then? I never heard of anyone doing such a thing, not even a wizard."

It was a great temptation to Heydari to say that he had indeed done this, but he was a truthful boy, even when he *should* lie, and he explained to Niloufar how he had found the karkadann near death and done what he could for it. This impressed her even more, for all that she feared and hated the creatures as much as anyone. And then . . . well, he is not a bad-looking boy, you know—favors his mother more than me, which is as well—and between one thing and another, she said, "I think you must be a remarkable person, and very brave," which is all any boy of his age cares to hear from a girl. And I am sure he found the wit somewhere to mumble that he thought she was a remarkable person too . . . and all this with that bloody karkadann rumbling and eyeing them, ready to spear them and toss them and trample them to rags, as kind as my Heydari had been to the thing. And I suppose one compliment led to another . . .

... and so they began meeting at the cave—always by chance, naturally—to sit solemnly together and eat their lunches, and watch the karkadann gaining strength every day. As great fools as they were, the pair of them, they knew just how dangerous the beast was, and how unchanged in its nature, for all that it owed its life to Heydari. But they were young, and stupidity is exciting when you are young. I remember better than I should.

As Heydari tells it, Niloufar was always the one asking, "But what will you do if one day it should suddenly turn on us? What is your plan?" That dreaming boy of mine with a plan—*there's* a notion for you!

But he had been thinking ahead, it turned out. Girls will have that effect on you. He said, "You and I are both quick—we will run in different directions. It cannot follow us both, and I will make certain that it follows me."

"And how will you do that?" she wanted to know. Smiling, I am sure, for what girl does not want to hear that a boy will risk his life to lure a monster away from her? "How *can* you be so sure that I will not be the one it pursues?"

To which Heydari answered her, "Because I did it a good turn. For such a creature as the karkadann, that is intolerable. It will seek to wipe away the stain on its pride along with me." Then Niloufar became genuinely frightened for him, which was doubtless exciting too, for both of them. It is exhausting, even *thinking* about the young.

So Niloufar watched over her father's sheep, and Heydari watched over the recovering karkadann; and both of them shyly watched over each other as best they knew how. I am sure she must have practiced chiding and warning him, as he must have copied me telling his mother to be quiet, in the name of all the gods, and let me *think*. I hope they did not reproduce us too closely, those children. It is uncomfortable, somehow, to imagine.

And then there was the ringdove. It is important not to forget the ringdove.

It must have had no family responsibilities, for it was there all the time, or the next thing to it. Now and then it would fly away for a little while, tending to its bird business, but it always returned within the hour. And it always perched on the karkadann's immense horn, and it always cooed the softest, gentlest melody, over and over; and the karkadann would always, sooner or later, close its yellow eyes and fall into as peaceful-seeming a sleep as you can imagine those creatures ever enjoying. Sometimes it would even lie down, Heydari said, and rest its head on its front feet, which are as much like claws as they are like hooves. It would even snore now and then, in the daintiest manner imaginable, like that teakettle we only bring out for company. "You know, the way Mother snores," he explained, and I cuffed him for it, even though she does.

Heydari sometimes dozed briefly, with his head on Niloufar's shoulder, but she herself never closed an eye in the presence of the karkadann. As she told me long afterward, it was not that Heydari trusted the creature any more than she, or that she was less fascinated by it than he was; rather, she liked knowing that he trusted *her* with his safety, his protection, which no one but a sheep had ever done before. At times her eyes would meet the karkadann's yellow glare, the one as unblinking as the other, and on a few occasions she spoke to it while Heydari slept. "Why are you what you are? Why do you and your folk have no friends, no companions—not even each other—but those birds? Is there truly nothing to you but hatred and rage and solitude? Why are you in the world at all?"

Girls ask questions like that. Sometimes they ask them of men.

The karkadann never showed any sign of interest or comprehension, of course, except for one moment, when Niloufar asked, "The song of the ringdove—does it run *so*?" and she imitated it in her throat, for she had an excellent ear for melody, like all her family, even all those boys. The karkadann made a strange, perplexed sound; it woke Heydari, who blinked from one to the other of them as Niloufar repeated the run of notes, again and again. The ringdove itself fluffed out its gray and blue-gray feathers, but remained asleep on the great horn, while the karkadann stamped its front feet, and the questioning rumble grew louder. But Niloufar kept singing.

Perhaps fortunately for my unborn grandchildren, Heydari put his hand over her mouth and held it there while he shouted at her. "Are you mad, girl? Do you think you are some sort of wizard, some sort of wise-woman? In another moment, you would have been decorating that horn like a flower, and there would have been nothing, *nothing*, I could do to save you. Get back to your accursed sheep if you are going to behave so!" I myself have never seen him so angry, but this is what Niloufar told me.

Another little girl would have burst into tears and flounced away—but looking slyly over her shoulder, expecting the boy to call her back. Not that one. She drew herself up to her full height, such as it is, and stalked out of the cave and down the hill without a backward glance. And no, Heydari did *not* call, though I am certain he wished to, very much. But he is as stubborn as I am—in that one way at least he is like me—so all he did was stare back at the growling karkadann, having some notion of stilling it with his eyes. And presently, for that reason or another, the beast did grow quiet, though it did not sleep again, for all the cooing of the ringdove. Neither did Heydari.

He did not leave the cave until Niloufar had driven her sheep homeward; nor did he even look to notice whether she had returned to the valley the next afternoon when he climbed to see to the karkadann. She did not come at all that day, nor the next, nor the next, when at last he *was* watching for her; and when at last he gave that up, he felt older than he was. And that *is* how we grow old, you know, waiting for whatever we insist we are not waiting for. I know this.

By and by, there was no question but that the karkadann was fully restored to wicked health, its wounds entirely healed, and its terrible strength revealed in even the smallest movement it made. It even left the cave to forage for itself, now and again, and to make its way to the spring for water. Yet it lingered on with Heydari, surely not out of need or affection, but as though it too were waiting for . . . something, some certain moment when it would know exactly what to do about this annoying, baffling little creature. Not that there was any mystery about what *that* was going to be. Karkadanns only do one thing.

Why Heydari continued to visit the cave and care for the creature . . . ah, if you ever solve that one, explain it to him before me, because he still can't say himself. The best he was ever able to tell me was that for him it was like dancing on the edge of a knife blade, or a great abyss, knowing that if you keep dancing there you will very likely fall to your death—but that if you *stop* dancing, you surely will. He said he was terrified every moment, but in a wonderfully calm way, if that made any sense to me. Which it did not, no more than anything he's ever done has made sense, but there you are. There's my son for you.

And after Niloufar stopped coming . . . oh, then nothing much really seemed to matter, living or dying. And there's a boy, if you like, any boy at all. It's a wonder any of them survive to father a new crop of idiots like themselves. He meant it, too. They all mean it. He said he almost wished the karkadann would make up its mind and kill him . . . but at the same time he could not keep from wondering, as he stared at it day after day, whether it might not have some sort of a weak spot, a vulnerable place under all that hide and power that no one had ever discovered. He imagined it being his legacy to Persia, and to me. Boys.

I wonder now and again whether the beast truly felt no gratitude at all toward my son. I have never known an animal—human beings excepted—to be totally incapable of showing some form of appreciation for a kindness. My wife has tamed a snake enough that it will come to her and take milk from her hand; Heydari himself took such care of a baby elephant when its mother was killed by a karkadann that to this day that enormous animal—Mojtaba, biggest male in my herd—follows him around, holding Heydari's hand with his trunk. And maybe there was some way in which Heydari, all the while knowing better, believed that the karkadann—*his* karkadann—would never, at the last, actually turn on him. Mind you, I say *maybe*.

Very well. There came one hot and cloudless afternoon when the air was so still you almost had to push your way through it, like a great sticky mass of old cobwebs. The karkadann had already been to the spring twice to drink, and now it half-crouched against the cave wall, eyes half-closed, growling to itself so deeply and softly that Heydari could barely hear the sound at all. The ringdove was perched, as ever, on the tip of its horn, its rippling murmur rasping at Heydari's nerves for the first time. He felt the way you feel when a storm is coming, even though it may yet be a day, or even two days, from reaching you: there is a *smell*, and there is a kind of stiff crackle, like invisible lightning, racing up and down your arms, and you have to think about each breath you take. He found that he was crouching himself, ready to spring in any direction; and at the same time—so he told me—thinking, as he studied the light and shadow playing over the brutal majesty of the beast's flanks and high shoulders, that if it had to be, now would be the time to go. Did you ever think such a thought when you were fourteen years old? I never thought anything like that.

But the boy isn't a total fool, not even then—not all the way through. When the yellow eyes seemed to have closed completely, under the influence of the ringdove's endless cooing, Heydari began edging toward the cave mouth on his haunches, inch by inch, watching the karkadann every moment. He's never said what instinct made him do it, only that it felt suddenly very close in the cave, what with that moldy-hay smell of the creature, and that birdsong going on and on, and he began to feel in need of fresh air. Another foot—two feet at most—and he would simply rise and walk out and down into the little valley . . . and perhaps Niloufar would be there, even though her sheep were not. Not, you understand, that he cared a rap about *that.*

And what finally tipped the balance—what woke the karkadann and set it at last *seeing* my son as it never had before—I don't imagine he or Niloufar or I will ever know. Heydari says it actually made that same odd puzzled sound before it charged, just as though it didn't know yet why it was being made to do this. Though I don't suppose that's true for a minute, and it wouldn't make any bloody difference if it were. It bloody *charged.*

Coming at him, absolutely silent, it looked twice as huge as it had just a moment before, for all that he had grown so used to the immensity of it in the cave. He shrieked, fell over backward, and rolled some way down the slope, stopping himself by grabbing at clumps of grass and stones. When he stumbled to his feet, the karkadann filled his entire horizon, poised at the cave mouth, staring down at him. It did not move for what he tells me is still the longest moment of his life. Once he said that it would almost have been worth dying on that horn like an elephant to know what was going through the beast's mind. I tried to hit him, but he ducked out of range.

He could see the great leg muscles gathering and swelling like thunderheads as the karkadann set itself, and he thought—or he *says* he thought—of his family, and how sad his mother would be, and how furious I would be, and wished he were safely home with us all. That's as may be; but I've always suspected he'd have been thinking of little Niloufar, and wishing he had had time and sense enough to make it up with her. I hope he was.

In a vague kind of way, he wondered where the ringdove had gotten to. It had flown up the moment the karkadann charged him, and he could not see it anywhere. A pity, for if there was anything in the world that soothed that devil-gotten creature at all, it was the song of the dove. The strange thing was that he could have sworn he still heard it somewhere. Perched in some tree, like enough, waiting patiently for the slaughter to be over, the same as always. Ringdoves aren't smart birds, but they aren't fools either.

Then the karkadann came for him.

He says he never heard the bellow. He says what he'll remember to his last day is—of all things—the sound of the stones of the hillside surging backward under the karkadann's clawed hoofs. That, and the ringdove, suddenly sounding almost in his right ear . . . and another sound that he knew he knew, but it shouldn't be there, it mustn't be there . . .

It was Niloufar. It was Niloufar, singing her perfect imitation of the ringdove's song—and it was Niloufar riding my big Mojtaba straight at the karkadann! Now, as I think I've made abundantly clear to you, there is no elephant in the *world* who will challenge a karkadann . . . except, perhaps, one who has lost his mother to such beasts, and who sees his adoptive mother in the same danger. Mojtaba trumpeted—Niloufar swears it sounded more like a roar than anything else—laid his big ears back flat, curled his trunk out of harm's way, and charged.

As nearly as I could ever make out from their two accounts, that double impossibility—a ringdove singing sweetly where there wasn't a ringdove, and an elephant half its size attacking head-on, with death in his red eyes— the karkadann must have been thrown off guard, unable either to halt or commit to a full rush, and too bewildered to do more than brace itself for Mojtaba's onslaught. Mad with vengeance or not, the elephant knew enough to strike at an angle that made the broken fang useless as a weapon, and he crashed into the karkadann with his full weight and power, knocking the beast off its feet for—doubtless—the first time in its life. Mojtaba's tusks— five feet long, both of them, if they're an inch—drove into its side, wrenched free, drove again . . .

But poor Niloufar, flattening herself in vain against the elephant's back, was knocked from her hold and hurled through the air. And the gods only know how badly she might have been hurt, if Heydari, my son, running as fast as though the karkadann were still behind him, had not managed to break her fall with his own body. She hit him broadside, just as Mojtaba had crashed into the karkadann, and they both went down together—both,

I think, unconscious for at least a minute or two. Then they sat up in the high grass and looked at each other, and of course that was the real beginning. I know that, and I wasn't even there.

Heydari said, "I thought I would never see you again. I kept hoping I would see your sheep grazing in the valley, but I never did."

And Niloufar answered simply, "I have been here every day. I am a very good hider."

"Do not hide from me again, please," Heydari said, and Niloufar promised.

The karkadann was dead, but it took the children some time to call Mojtaba away from trampling the body. The elephant was trembling and whimpering—they are *very* emotional, comes with the sensitivity—and did not calm down until Heydari led him to the little hill stream and carefully washed the blood from his tusks. Then he went back and buried the karkadann near the cave. Niloufar helped, but it took a very long time, and Heydari insisted on marking the grave. As well as that girl understands him, I don't think she knows to this day why he wanted to do that.

But I do. It was what he was trying to tell me, and what I hit him for, and likely still would, my duty as a father having nothing to do with understanding. The karkadann was magnificent, as he said, and utterly monstrous too, and he probably came as near to taming it as anyone ever has or ever will. And perhaps that was why it hated him so, in the end, because he had tempted it to violate its entire nature, and almost won. Or maybe not . . . talk to my idiot son, and you start thinking about things like that. You'll see—I'll seat you next to him at dinner.

No, we've never called them anything but karkadanns. Odd, a Roman fellow, a trader, he asked the same question a while back. Only other time I ever heard that word, *unicorn*.

THE TRANSFIGURED HART

Jane Yolen

The Sages say truly that two animals are in this forest: one glorious, beautiful and swift, a great and strong deer; the other an unicorn. . . . If we apply the parable of our art, we shall call the forest the body. . . . The unicorn will be the spirit at all times. The deer desires no other name but that of the soul. . . . He that knows how to tame and master them by art, to couple them together, and to lead them in and out of the forest, may justly be called a Master.

—from Abraham Lambsprink's
On the Philosophers' Stone,
a rare Hermetic tract

One

THE HART LIVED IN A THICKET close by a shimmering pool. He had been born in that thicket on a spring morning before the sun had quite gained the sky.

As soon as he was born, his mother had sensed something wrong. She licked off his birth wrapping. The sheaths fell off his hooves. But the doe nuzzled her fawn with a hesitant motion, puzzling out his peculiarity.

He was an albino, born weak and white on that clear spring day. His eyes were pink and his nose a mottled pink, too.

After a few minutes, the doe was satisfied. The fawn would live. He was different, but he would live.

So the white hart was born, and so he grew.

By the time he had reached his fifth year, and had dodged the pack of dogs that ran in the woods and, in season, the hunters as well, he was a wise and wily beast. He knew the best runs to the water. He could paw down the snow to the shoots that winter had left and find the sweet early spring grass.

No hunters in the area had actually identified the albino. Or if they had noticed a flash of white, they had not known him for what he was. For the white hart was a loner. He chose a solitary existence, never joining— even in the rutting season—the small herds that lived in Five Mile Wood.

He spent much of his time in the thicket of twenty-two trees close by the shimmering pool. And he lay, mute and gleaming, under a wild apple tree a good part of each day.

Two

Richard Plante was a loner, too. He had read a lot for a twelve-year-old. At first he read because he was so sick and there was nothing else to do in the great house where he lived, the only child among adults.

Richard read about giants and kings, about buried treasure and ghosts, about gods and heroes far away in place and time and some near enough for memory. His wall was papered with the lists of his reading, neatly arranged by subject and author in a secret code that only he understood.

Richard had read in his bed, mostly, since that was where he had seemed condemned to spend much of his early childhood. But even after he got better and was allowed to run about several hours a day and urged to play with children his own age, the reading habit stayed with him. He read in his bed, still, though his room was outfitted with two generous reading chairs with a table and lamp between them. And when he was pronounced entirely well from the rheumatic fever that had kept him in bed, the loner habit stayed with him, too.

Rather than being with other children when the adults urged him out of doors, Richard preferred to take a book and make his way deep into Five Mile Wood. When he could find a comfortable spot lined with soft leaves, a mossy place by a stream, an outdoor bed, Richard would lie down and read. He read in great gulps, devouring his books with an appetite his aunt would have preferred he show at the table. And he retained almost all that he read, his mind a ragbag of facts that he forced into mental lists.

After several hours had passed, Richard would tuck his book into his shirt and head for home. He would run the last hundred yards or so. That way he would be just enough out of breath to allow his aunt to assume he had been following doctor's orders and playing outdoors with neighborhood friends.

It was after dinner one evening that fall that Richard first saw the white hart by the shimmering pool. There was a splash in the water, and suddenly, in the fading light, he caught a glimpse of a white haunch, a flash of leg, a dart of head before the startled stag leaped into thick brush. But there was still enough daylight left for Richard to feel sure of what he had seen. A *unicorn*. What else but a unicorn was that silken swift and dazzling white?

Recognition, almost like a pain, burned in his heart. All the things that he had ever read about unicorns tumbled into his mind. That they had been confused with rhinoceroses. That sailors brought back narwhale tusks and said they came from unicorns. That the early Christians thought the unicorn a symbol of Christ. He especially remembered the line "And He was beloved like the son of the Unicornes," because once he had tried to put it into a song in his own off-key way.

Richard shook his head to clear it of the tag-ends of his readings. He disliked the sudden leaps that his mind sometimes took. They were so untidy. He was more comfortable when he could set things down straight, in ordered lists as his father had.

Something in the back of his brain was bothering him, though. Some piece of the puzzle did not fit.

He rehearsed the scene again. The flash of haunch, leg, head. The startling white in the fall setting. The spiraled horn.

No. That was it. He had seen no horn.

The shift back into an ordinary day was too much to bear. Richard tried to shake off the disappointment. He ordered his thoughts, trying to control them. Made a mental list and read it off carefully. And then he made another connection. A unicorn was probably related to a deer. And if that was so, then perhaps it lost its horn every year just like a deer and grew a velvety one anew. He didn't recall reading such a thing in any of his father's books. But what did that matter? The answer felt right, it *had* to be right. He would take the books out of the study again and reread them, all the books that mentioned unicorns.

For it *was* a unicorn—of that Richard was once again convinced.

He hurried back to the great house, eager to get to his father's book-lined library. The beat of his heart paced his steps, and when he ran into the house his aunt could only raise her pencil-arched eyebrows and breathe out a surprised "Well!"

Richard did not let his aunt's eyebrows or her frequent "Wells" bother him. It had been five years since she and her husband had become his guardians. And for four of those years Richard had been too ill to care about raised eyebrows. He had just floated in the sea of his bed, his books his raft.

"Well, hello," Richard said back now, in unconscious parody, as if bursting breathless into the house were a usual entrance for him.

"Well! You were out until dark," she said, eyebrows lifting again in a kind of greeting.

Richard said no more but went into his father's study. It was kept just as his father had left it. A gentle widowed scholar and teacher who had died as quietly as he had lived, Edward Plante had left only his book-lined study as a legacy for his boy. The house and everything else had gone as a sort of bribe to his younger brother and sister-in-law to take care of Richard. Whenever Richard felt tired or mean, he would think bitterly that the arrangement had worked very well. Hugh Plante and his wife had moved in just in time to give Richard into the hands of a doctor and to nurse him through his long days of sickness.

But most often Richard didn't feel mean, and lately less and less tired. Still, he had never quite gotten over a certain distrust of his aunt and uncle. He felt, in the deepest part of him, that they were there because of the house, and he was just another part of it, another part to be kept clean and polished and presentable.

In the study that was his but that he still called his father's, Richard went over to the middle shelf. It was the shelf he had practically learned by heart. Here were his favorite books. Folklore. Bestiaries. Collections of the Brothers Grimm and Asbjornsen and William Butler Yeats. Fables and the fabulous. It was all there, all waiting for him to unriddle.

He put his hand out and reached for his father's well-thumbed copy of Robert Graves's *The White Goddess*. Richard had not yet understood more than the smallest part of it. But he was sure it was great poetry and as he learned more he would understand more. He looked up *unicorn* in the index.

"Richard!" It was his aunt again. "Don't you ignore me, young man. Into a hot bath with you. Then bed. You might get sick all over again. Then where would you be?"

"Where would *you* be?" Richard thought. He knew where he would be—in bed. But what his Aunt Marcie really couldn't stand was the thought of all that waiting on him again. He had overheard her saying it to Uncle Hugh one day. And that's where she'd be, his aunt, who always seemed to intrude on him when he wanted to be private. She meant well, he tried to tell himself. It was just that she and his uncle seemed to consider silence a personal affront, an antisocial attitude on his part that they felt duty-bound to change. So they tried to surround him with spoken words. He much preferred the quiet of the printed page.

Reluctantly but obediently, Richard went upstairs. The hallway was dark and Richard remembered how he used to dread the trip upstairs when he was little, even when they carried him up trailing his quilt. He had to admit that he still felt a bit queasy about walking through the dark. And though he no longer woke at night shrieking, oppressed by the dark weight on his chest, he still felt safer in the light. Of course, he would never admit that to anyone, especially his aunt and uncle. He hardly liked to admit it to himself. So he squinted his eyes and barreled ahead, full tilt up the steps and into the bathroom. The contrasting glow of the lights was instantly comforting. He ran the bath as hot as he dared and sank down until only his nose showed. His body was underwater but his thoughts were still in the forest, where, with a flash of haunch and head, the unicorn danced on and on.

Richard knew what he must do. Morning, tomorrow being a Sunday, would give him plenty of time.

Three

Heather Fielding was an enjoyer. She enjoyed other people, she enjoyed her family, she enjoyed new places, she enjoyed old legends, and she enjoyed slipping off quietly by herself on an adventure.

Since she had been little, Heather had enjoyed going off alone. But she had an annoying habit of going too far and getting lost. After the third time the local police had been called out to find four-year-old Heather, the Fieldings began to keep a very careful eye on their only daughter. And even though she was now almost thirteen, she still had literally to sign out for an afternoon when she wanted to disappear. It meant leaving a detailed note on the bulletin board for her mother or three brothers. It was one of those many rules she had first resented and then found ways to make enjoyable. And so this day the bulletin board read:

> *Don't have time to really stop.*
> *Into Five Mile Wood on Hop.*

Hop was Heather's horse, an appaloosa gelding, gentle and undemanding, with a gray-dappled hide that looked as if it had been spotted by raindrops. His slow, loose-limbed pace fitted Heather's style. It gave her plenty of time to enjoy, to drink in the world as they ambled by.

The fall day Heather saw the white deer, the sky was overcast and threatening. This only heightened her enjoyment, for the woods always changed colors under a leaden sky. Little creatures began to creep out that might otherwise have hidden, terrified of the bright, revealing sun.

Heather reined in Hop and slid off his broad back. She allowed the horse to wander and graze, knowing he would not let her out of his sight.

Then she sat down by the shimmering pool. Strangely, it was new to her. In all her wanderings, she had never made the precise series of turns that led through the old apple orchard to here. It was a find. Heather breathed in the air. It was heavy, as heavy as the day. But that didn't make her feel unhappy. Nothing about this new discovery, this crystalline pool, blue and still, could make her feel sad.

She picked up a palm-size rock and flipped it over and over in her hand. It was cool and smooth; a faint gray-white line wormed its way across the rock's surface.

Heather flung the rock into the pool in order to watch the ripples. At the splash, another sound, a high whistling, started up from below the wild apple tree to her right.

There was an explosion of white head and flank. The dark hooves and horns were invisible against the brush, so gleaming white was the hide.

Heather leaped up at the same time, as startled as the deer.

"An albino," she breathed, and then was still. The beauty of the animal burned itself into her eyes. She blinked. The deer was gone. She closed her eyes. The image of the white hart seemed imprinted on the inside of her eyelids.

The animal's sudden, crashing flight broke across the stillness of the pond. As though a spell had been broken, the pond itself was ruffled by a breeze, and a hound bayed from far off. The mood changed. Heather felt it was impossible to stay any longer. But she repeated "an albino" to herself as she swung a leg over Hop's broad back.

She kept rehearsing the scene to herself and paid no attention to the road. The horse, without being guided, brought them both safely home.

Heather dismounted and settled Hop in the barn as if in a dream, for her thoughts were still back at the pool. Only the fact that her arms and legs knew the routine of feeding and bedding so well saved Hop from a long, cold, hungry night.

Entering the bright yellow kitchen, Heather was awakened by the smells. Saturday-night stew again. The famous Fielding leftover pot. As always on Saturday, they ate late, gathering in the scattered clan from the holiday tasks and events.

Heather debated telling of the pool. Usually her tongue ran ahead of her brain and she spoke without considering the consequences. Brian, her oldest brother, would often knot her long braids under her chin and say "You're tongue-tripping again." It might sound mean to someone outside the family, but Heather knew that Brian said it with affection.

Still, because the white hart had so captured her imagination, Heather hesitated about mentioning the pool to her family. The pool would lead them right to the white deer, and she could not tell them about that. Her brothers were all hunters. Nineteen, eighteen, and sixteen, they'd had guns as long as she could remember. A shudder went through her as she pictured the white hart, crumpled and bleeding, on the forest floor.

No, this was one time she could not say anything to the family. Not even to her father, Julian, whom she adored.

And glancing guiltily around the table at the faces of those people she most dearly and truly loved, Heather resolved herself to silence. In fact, she was so quiet throughout the meal, it was noticed.

"Come on, Heath, where's your tongue?" It was Brian.

Dylan added, "She must be sick."

"Am not."

"Are, too." It was Ian. They always argued.

"Am not."

"Then why are you so sickly silent?"

"I'm just thinking."

"Come on, Heath. You never think."

"Mama." It was a plea.

"Children, children. Her silence is a blessing. Why not give me a wholesale blessing," said Mrs. Fielding, not having to add that Heather was the brightest one of the lot and well they all knew it, though her school work never reflected it.

"Amen," said Julian Fielding with such a hearty sigh that they all had to laugh. Even Heather. They left her alone after that as they talked about the hunting season to come.

In her silence, with the conversation so ordinary and familiar eddying about her, Heather planned what to do. Tomorrow, after church, there would be plenty of time.

Four

When the striped rock hit the water, the white hart leaped from his bed without thought.

As he ran down the path, his body gleaming in the twilight, he looked like a statue in motion. Under his gleaming coat, the muscles rippled. The dark antlers, curving in a wide arch over his head, were a large, bony crown, all but invisible in the dusk. The brow tines were long and straight, and above them sprouted the bay tines, slightly curved. A third pair grew higher, with little fingers of horn on the spatulate tines.

The first fear gone, the white hart slowed down and began to feel hunger gnawing. Even though it was fall, there was still much rich food in the forest. Groves of young birch offered leafless shoots where he might browse, to grow fat against the coming winter. And there were acorns hidden in the mossy caves between the rocks or under the rotting leaves.

Far away, the hart could hear the baying of hounds. They were upwind, tracking some small animal across the meadow. It was a motley pack of farm dogs, led by a Scottish deerhound whose master never kept him tied. Abruptly, the baying stopped. The quarry was caught.

The hart knew the pack was too far away to fear, and so he kept up his search for food. But as he looked for the shoots and nuts, the sounds of water called to him. There was a small stream nearby, tumbling over rocks, into riffles and pools of standing water filled with fish.

The hart went over to the stream, through a chest-high stand of dried sunflower disks that rattled crisply as he passed. He looked up the stream and down, then walked in. Pushing against the current, he came at last to one of the pools that was deep enough for him to stand in and let the water swirl about his body.

He bathed then, going down first onto his knees and then rolling over, frightening the fingerlings and sending them fleeing in all directions.

Then he rose and walked out of the pool, upstream against the current, and onto the mossy bank. He shook himself all over and then rolled again, drying himself on the bank.

The hart stood up and raised his head, with its rack like a giant crown. He sniffed the air. There was no more danger. The intruders had left. Slowly he made his way back to the path, circled carefully for almost a mile, eating as he moved. But always he knew that he would return to the shimmering pool and his bed before morn.

Five

Richard woke up early enough to avoid his aunt and uncle. Sunday was their sleeping day. It was always a special day for Richard, too. He could have breakfast and the whole early morning to himself without their annoying questions.

For Aunt Marcie and Uncle Hugh always wanted to know *why*. Why don't you go out and play with other boys? Why can't you sit up straight at the table? Why do you read all the time? Why don't you ever want to talk about your father and mother? Why do you make those indecipherable lists? Why do you stare into space? Why? Why? Why?

All those questions were impossible to answer, because the only reasons Richard could give them, they refused to accept: I am just me. It's just the way I am. Just because. He wondered over and over how they could have known his father and not recognized that Richard had the same insatiable need to know, to understand, to study, to put bits of information in order. Richard wondered at their obtuseness. It was a good word, "obtuseness": dull and blunted. It seemed strange that his uncle should not be like his own brother, should not understand Richard at all. But then, they didn't really need to understand him, if they would just leave him alone. But they didn't leave him alone. They both kept asking Why? Why? Why? So Richard had stopped giving them his reasons, had virtually stopped talking to them beyond answering grunts at the breakfast and dinner table. And all they did was add a new question to their list: Why don't you talk to us? Why? Why? Why?

Richard went downstairs as quietly as he could, given the amount of clothes he had bundled on. If he was going to spend all day in the woods, he had to be sure to keep warm. Two pairs of socks, long johns, and two undershirts under his heaviest clothing. An extra sweater to carry along, just in case. Not to mention the jacket, mittens, scarf, and hat he was going to wear.

Breakfast was a quick snack of cheese and raisins. He packed a couple of peanut butter and apple jelly sandwiches in case, and stuck them in the jacket pocket. He did not know how long he would be gone. It might be all day. And if it *was* all day, he did not want his stomach talking to him in loud growls.

He did not even take a book, for he had sneaked down with a flashlight to his father's study after Uncle Hugh and Aunt Marcie had gone to bed. He had been up much of the night reading. He had read again all the references to unicorns in the folklore books. He had read from Ctesias, a Greek historian of the fourth century B.C. He had read a passage he had not understood at all in *The White Goddess* about a deer and a unicorn in the forest. He had checked *The Bestiary* by T. H. White and the encyclopedias of mythology. And he had even borrowed one of Uncle Hugh's hunting magazines from the bathroom bookshelf and read it.

He felt that he now knew what he needed to know about unicorns. He had taken notes on all that he had read. Neatly written on 3 x 5 cards in his private code, they were now in his jacket pocket, nestled next to one of the sandwiches. Facts. Legends. Lists. He was as organized as he could be for seeing and understanding the beast. Beyond that . . . the pain in his chest came swiftly as it sometimes did when he was excited, a quick burning that went as fast as it came. Beyond that, he did not plan, for he did not dare. What could one do with a unicorn? Look at it and long for it, and love it. It was enough for now.

The door clicked behind him quietly. As he walked down the road toward Five Mile Wood, he finished dressing. He buttoned his jacket and wrapped the maroon scarf loosely around his neck. An old stocking cap of bright red yarn fitted over his mousy hair and stopped just short of covering his ears. They were always difficult to cover, his ears—they stuck out so. The gloves were from two different pairs, one of green wool and one of tan leather. The mismatch of color and material bothered him, and he kept his eyes off his hands, but he could not help feeling the difference. He hadn't had time to make a more thorough search. He was afraid that his aunt and uncle would be getting up soon.

As Richard walked along, his breath came out in short, wispy gusts, clouds of panting. The morning seemed to dare him. He took the dare and began to jog along. He could feel the sandwiches keeping time, hitting his sides in a soggy rhythm.

When he got to the turnoff into the woods, he stopped and looked around. The road was clear. No one was in sight, for it was still too early for the main church traffic. The Sunday silence, the early fall silence, lay over all. With a big smile, Richard plunged into the brush.

Within twenty minutes, he had rediscovered the shimmering pool. He came upon it almost unexpectedly, after a last turn in the apple orchard. He had thought it was farther on, and to find it there, so close, was a shock.

There was no unicorn that he could see. But he hadn't expected to find it at once. That would have been too lucky, and Richard didn't believe in that kind of luck for himself. He was going to have to remain, in the words of the hunting book, "still and silent." It might be a long wait.

He found an inviting spot not far from the wild apple tree. He settled himself on the ground, sitting on the extra sweater to keep out the cold. Taking the sandwiches from his pocket, he found the cards, too. He spread them around where he could see and read them over and over but would not have to pick them up. He forbade himself any movement.

Today he would just *see* the unicorn. He would think about the rest later. But as he sat still, his thoughts began to drift to next week and beyond. Without a book to lead him on, for once he let himself be led by his own desires. And what he really wanted—he was beginning to understand it now—what he really wanted was to capture the unicorn. Not to hurt it, of course. Not to cage it. Just to tame it to his hand. His. His very own hand.

But from his reading, Richard knew that the unicorn could be a dangerous beast. Its horn, its hooves, were lethal. So Richard had a problem to solve. In this time of still waiting, he would devise several plans.

One book—he found the card with his eye—told how to catch a unicorn by provoking the animal to charge. Then the hunter would dodge behind a tree and the beast's horn would become lodged in the tree. Once held fast that way, the unicorn was said to be easy to capture. Richard remembered the picture some ancient artist had made; it had been in the book, too. It was an interesting plan, to be sure. But he was not positive such a trick would work. For one thing, what if he couldn't outrun an angry unicorn? Or for another, what if it merely came 'round the tree? More important, a friendship shouldn't begin in anger. And he wanted the unicorn—rare and magical—to be his friend.

Another card caught his eye. He translated his code with practiced ease: "A pure Maid need only sit in the wood and the unicorn would come and place its head gently on her lap. Then she would secure it with a golden bridle and lead it like a pet out of the forest."

Richard was dubious. It might work. But there were two problems. The gold bridle was one. And the pure Maid. That was the other.

Richard puzzled over this and other problems for about two hours. Then the lack of sleep, the fresh air, and dreams overcame him. He fell asleep, still sitting backed up to the tree by the shimmering pool.

Six

Heather could barely sit through the church service. Usually she enjoyed the movement, the singing, the feeling of community, and especially the color. The light filtering through the stained-glass window where the lion and the lamb lay beneath Christ's feet always filled her with a special joy. But this Sunday was not like other Sundays. She didn't want to be enclosed in the church. Today it seemed airless, the dwelling place of men and not God's house.

The lion and the lamb kept reminding her of the woods outside. Her woods. She had always considered them so, ever since she was little. And especially Five Mile Wood, the meadows and the valley across from the state forest. Her brothers used it, bent the paths and trees and animals to their own needs. But she never *used* the woods. She let the woods become a part of her. And so she believed she and the woods were one, in some mysterious way. It was, she thought with sudden guilt at the blasphemy, a true Eucharist. Body of my body, blood of my blood. My woods.

And outside in her woods, she knew, the white deer was waiting. Her deer.

"And he *is* mine," she thought fiercely. No one had ever mentioned the deer before, so no one else knew. It was that simple, that clear. And since keeping secrets was so difficult for Heather, for they always seemed to spill out of her, this secret had to be sworn in church.

She knelt down with the rest of the congregation but did not listen to their responses. She was repeating her own prayer over and over. "Please let me keep the secret. Please let me keep *this* secret."

She mumbled it loud enough for her brother Ian to knife her with his elbow. She shut her mouth and eyes and ears to the rest of the service and dreamed of the woods.

By the time the Fieldings returned to their home, it was lunch. Heather gulped her sandwich down so quickly she got the hiccups. Not wanting to ride while hiccupping, she had to waste precious minutes eating a teaspoon of sugar (her mother's idea), holding her breath (her father's idea), drinking a glass of water with a pencil clenched in her teeth (Dylan's contribution), and then nearly dying of fright when Ian jumped out at her from behind the staircase. Whether it was one or all of them together that worked, the hiccups were gone by the time she came out of the house.

"The message still stands," she had called back over her shoulder to Brian, who was going out of the barn. He would interpret her shout to the rest of the family: The note on the bulletin board was the same for today. So they all knew that Heather was going to be in Five Mile Wood, but they didn't know just where.

Heather got Hop from the barn and mounted him bareback, as usual. She resisted the temptation to kick him into a canter, for she knew that such a change from her usual slow, easy pace would bring a bevy of questions at the dinner table that evening. Then, deciding she must already have made them suspicious by her hasty exit from the table, she pressured Hop's broad ribs with her knees.

Once on the macadam road, she relaxed, and smiled at the thought of the albino. Her deer. Given enough time, quiet time, she could tame him. Of that, there was no doubt. She knew she was good with animals. Her horse followed her everywhere. She had a dog, now too old to go far from home; three cats; a guinea pig; and two rabbits about to become more. She had, in turn, tamed a raccoon, a family of chipmunks, and surprisingly, even a black snake. And she had entertained her family in the evenings with tales of her progress. Taming the deer might take longer. Or shorter. You never knew with a wild animal. But the challenge called to her.

She turned Hop into a path lined with Sweet Everlasting, the white flower clusters still fragrant despite the cold fall. The path led through the old apple orchard and into the heart of Five Mile Wood.

When they got to the pool, sooner than she had expected, Heather slid off Hop's back. Holding his halter, she led him around the water. Today she wanted to tie him in one place, where he could graze quietly but would not frighten the deer when he came. For the white deer would come back. She knew this for sure. As the only non-hunter in a family of hunters, Heather knew that deer had special eating and drinking and sleeping habits. They rarely went more than a mile or two away from their own territory.

She led Hop silently, looking up at the sky to check the time and weather. That was why she did not notice the sleeping boy until she tripped over his outstretched foot.

Straightening herself quickly, she looked down at him. "Who are you?" she demanded, louder than she meant. "What are you doing at my pool?"

Richard woke with a start to see a skinny girl standing over him. Behind her was a spotted horse. Framed against the sky, they looked enormous.

"What? I mean, who are *you?*" he shouted in return, his voice breaking on the last word as he jumped up to face her. Once on his feet, he could see she was actually small, smaller than he by half a head.

"Who are *you?*" she flung back at him.

"You first."

"I asked first."

"What does that matter?" He suddenly stopped shouting and added, in a hissing whisper, "Shhh."

Heather quieted, too, suddenly remembering the deer. "It matters because . . . oh, damn you." Tears started in her eyes. The white deer secret, so beautiful and special and hers alone, was spoiled. She made a face to help control the tremble of her mouth, but the anger shaking her would not go away. Bending down, she picked up a forked stick and flung it savagely into the underbrush. It fell, with a soft thud, by the apple tree.

Seven

The white hart could hide no more. He started up with a shrill whistle and leaped away.

All either child saw was his white tail and legs as he disappeared into the thicket.

Once away from the danger, the white hart began a browsing search for food through a piney wood. All that afternoon, he kept well below the shoulder of the hills. His instincts were good, for his outline would not show up against the sky.

Occasionally he stopped by a stream to drink deeply of the cold, clear water. Mostly he followed the barely discernible trails that he had worn away over five years. They were his paths, often running parallel with, but not touching, the trails that had been known and followed by generations of other deer.

The afternoon was closing down, making shadows dance in the feathery pines. Yet the shadows did not frighten the white deer as he moved purposefully through the woods.

He paused at the last line of trees, grown many branchless feet high, their tops full, and green. The needles were soft underfoot and silent, but occasionally he crunched a tiny pinecone as he made his way to the wood's edge.

Beyond the pine forest lay a meadow, quite brown and sere, for the fall had been exceptionally dry. At evening, the hart could make out the movements of a herd of does near the far side. There were seven, and with them five fawns and several yearlings. Close by and yet not too close were four bucks, in pairs. It was no longer the time of rut, and so the pairs of bucks remained together, apart from the herd. Each pair consisted of an older male with a younger. They regarded the does with only a mild interest and then passed them by. They would seek their own food farther on.

From the forest edge, the white hart watched the slow-paced ritual of does and bucks. That he was a deer made him part of them, yet he was separate. He did not seek any of them; they did not accept him.

The setting sun went down entirely behind the mountains and the meadow was suddenly dark. The white hart moved his head, sniffed the air, turned, and was gone.

Not one of the other deer remarked his leaving.

Eight

"Now you've done it," said Richard angrily.

"*I've* done it?" Heather's body was rigid. "You've done it. Shouting like that. You've scared my white deer away."

"You were the one who threw the stick. You were the one who came clomping in here while I was quietly waiting. I've been waiting since this morning. And what do you mean *yours?* And what do you mean *deer?*"

It was a long speech for Richard, and made to a stranger. The effort seemed to exhaust him. He sank back down again on his sweater, chin between his knees.

"Hold on," said Heather. She was used to dealing with boys who shouted and stood up to her. She was not sure what to do about one who started collapsing after the very first encounter. "Okay. I admit it. I was pretty noisy. And I admit I threw the stick, too. But what are you doing here, anyway? You weren't waiting. You were sleeping. And what do you mean 'what deer?' Why, the white deer, of course. The albino. The one that just jumped up and ran off. You saw him, too. Don't try and tell me you didn't." It seemed suddenly important that the boy not deny this, though moments before she had wanted the deer all to herself.

Richard looked up at her warily. She was an intruder. She was a loud, angry intruder in this place of peace. But still, she had seen it. And called it a deer. He had to tell her what it really was. She knew about it anyhow, that it existed. She had to know its true name.

"It's not a deer," he said. "It's something more beautiful. It's a unicorn."

"You're crazy," she said and started to walk away.

"No, wait." He jumped up again and came over to her. "Don't go away. Let me explain. I know it seems strange. But I've been studying about it, the unicorn."

"Unicorns don't exist," said Heather. "And maybe you don't exist either. Sleeping on sweaters with . . . with . . ." She noticed the cards fanned out around the apple tree. "With litter all over the place. You're crazy."

"Wait, please," he said. The last word came out as a special request, for Richard seldom said "please" to anyone. He either did something or he didn't. But he hardly ever asked, for asking always seemed to lead to more questions. "Did you see a rack? I mean antlers. If it was a deer, you would have seen them."

"I know what a rack is," said Heather. "And of course I did." Then she stopped and looked down. Her braids swung back and forth. Lying was something she just couldn't do. Her honesty was what made her an easy target for her brothers, though she didn't realize it and couldn't have changed if she did. Her hesitation made Richard bolder.

"You didn't, did you?"

"Well . . ."

"Well, did you?"

"I never saw him slowly. Or closely," Heather admitted. "I mean, he was mostly just a bunch of white. And the antlers would be dark, anyway. So maybe I wouldn't have seen them with all the white." It sounded lame, even to her.

"So you can't say for sure it was just a deer," Richard said.

"Of course it was a deer; what else could it be?"

"I *told* you," Richard answered. "It's a unicorn."

"You're crazy."

"But you didn't see any antlers."

"You're crazy."

"And deer aren't that white, that gleaming, that . . . that beautiful."

"Oh, they're beautiful, all right." Heather was definite. "There's nothing more beautiful than a deer in the wood."

Richard went on as if he had not heard. "And the pool where a unicorn drinks is clear and blue and quiet. It is free from all poisons, because the unicorn dips its horn there. And all little animals are safe there. But if the unicorn leaves, or is driven away, the pool turns bracken. Like a swamp."

"You *are* crazy."

Richard turned then and looked straight at her. "This pool and that animal we both saw were different from any we have ever seen." He ached to explain it in just the right way. "Just to look at the pool and the beast, you knew how different."

"Well . . ."

"And it made *me* feel different, too. Important. No, *special*. Because I was allowed to see it when no one else did."

"I saw it."

Richard ignored her. "And inside me, it was like something that had been holding me had burst, like a chain had snapped. And something else, too. I felt . . . I felt I had always been a puzzle with pieces missing and now the pieces were all there, had been given to me, and all I had to do was put them in the right places. Only just when I was going to put them together, *you* came." He looked up at her again, but not with bitterness. It was just an assessment he was making, painstakingly judging each word before dealing it out. It was as if nothing was true until he spoke it aloud, and then it *became* true.

Heather responded immediately, for his hesitation seemed to beg for a response, and she was moved by the plea. "Yes," she said. "I know."

It was all the encouragement he needed. Almost wildly he said, "You know!"

"But it couldn't be. They aren't real. It couldn't be."

"It was," said Richard. "It is."

"A unicorn," Heather whispered, and then was still.

Nine

"Tell me more about unicorns," said Heather, finally, flopping down beside Richard. She landed half on, half off his spread-out sweater. One of her sneakers scuffed at a card and left a dirty mark on it.

Richard hesitated a moment. He felt a great thudding in his chest and hoped he wouldn't be sick.

"Unicorns are *ughm*." He cleared his throat of his voice, which had suddenly begun to squeak. "Unicorns were *ughm*." The throat kept doing funny things. It was better when the girl had been an enemy. He took a deep breath and said, "I'm Richard Plante." As he spoke he moved away a bit.

"I know. The boy with the broken heart. You've just come to school. I've heard about you and seen you between classes. I'm Heather Fielding. We're almost neighbors."

"It's not broken. Just . . . just bruised a little." It was a feeble joke, but Heather suddenly burst into great gales of laughter as if she thoroughly enjoyed it. Her laughter was contagious and Richard joined in. They both laughed until they were exhausted, and then Heather suddenly rolled over on her stomach, full on the sweater, her braids coiling on the ground. Richard, in an awkward scramble, was pushed onto the cold grass.

Heather looked over at the boy. He seemed suddenly so uncomfortable—prickly or shy, like a wild animal unused to a human touch. She folded her hands together and was very quiet, as if to show him she wouldn't try to hurt him. Then she said again in a very tiny voice, "Tell me more about unicorns."

Richard checked her out from the corner of his eye. She had said the last with such obvious sincerity. He sighed. He would try his voice again. "The books all say the unicorn is a mythical beast." He looked down at her.

Heather continued to stare quietly at her hands. At last she said, "Is there only one of it?"

"I don't know," said Richard, at once bewildered at her leap and comforted by her interest. "I could look it up."

"Okay. But not now." She smiled, but the smile went into the ground, not toward Richard. "Now finish telling me about unicorns."

"I haven't begun yet."

Heather didn't say anything, and her silence encouraged him.

"The books say the unicorn is as old as Greek or Roman myths at least."

"At least," agreed Heather.

Richard looked over at her to see if she was mocking him. But she was just nodding and waiting for him to go on, plucking at some dry grass.

"It's supposed to look like a horse. Or a goat. Or maybe a deer. And it has this one golden horn in the middle of its head. A horn with a spiral twist."

"I like that," Heather said. "The twist, I mean."

"The name 'unicorn' means 'one-horn.'" Richard said it suddenly, almost triumphantly.

"I know that!"

"You do?"

"I'm taking Latin," said Heather.

This so surprised Richard that he didn't know what to say. Yet he didn't know why he should be surprised. So he ignored it and went on. "Some unicorns seemed to have goat's beards or lion's tails." He reached out to finger the card with the smudge on it.

"So there are—I mean is, or do I mean are?—more than one in the world."

Richard was puzzled again at this leap. Then, just as suddenly, he understood the way her mind had gone. He said thoughtfully, "I think it's just the difference between one storyteller and another. One added a tail. Another a beard."

"Okay," said Heather, plucking at the dry grass again, "but it might be important." She noticed the sandwiches wrapped up and lying on the ground. She sat up then and picked them up, offering one to Richard and taking the other herself. She began to munch, and then, with a mouth full of peanut butter and apple jelly, said, "You see, we have to know everything we can about it if we're going to tame it. If there's a herd, or if it's male or female, or what it likes to eat or . . ."

"But how did you know?"

Heather looked at him. "Know what?"

"That I want to tame it."

"*I* want to tame it."

"But it's my . . ."

"*Our* unicorn," said Heather. "So we will have to do it together. What do the books say about taming unicorns?"

"Well," admitted Richard, "they mostly say the unicorn can only be captured with a golden bridle by a pure Maid."

"We've got one of those at home," said Heather excitedly.

"A golden bridle?" asked Richard.

"No," said Heather. "The maid. Well, maybe not a maid, but a cleaning lady."

"Oh my God!" said Richard.

"What's wrong?"

"A Maid, a pure Maid is . . ." He suddenly stopped talking.

"Did I say something wrong?" asked Heather.

"A Maid is a maiden."

"Oh," said Heather, without thinking. "You mean a virgin."

They were both so embarrassed then, they flopped simultaneously on the grass, and their shoulders almost touched.

"Well," said Heather at last, "we do have one of those." She looked down steadily at the ground as if summoning up the courage to say what had to be said next. And then suddenly she sat up on her knees and looked at Richard, her eyes and mouth smiling. She drew in a deep breath. "Then *I* could capture it. It would still be mine. You couldn't, could you? I mean, I am. I am a Maid. And I can get the unicorn."

"It might be scary."

"I'm not afraid. Animals don't scare me. I've tamed a raccoon and a whole family of chipmunks and a snake."

"You have to sit in the forest and let it put its head in your lap."

"I'm still not afraid."

"Horn and all?"

Heather bit her lip. She had forgotten about that. Then she looked at Richard, who was watching her carefully. She nodded. "Horn and all."

"All right," he said.

They got up as if by mutual consent. Richard picked up the cards and the sandwich wrappings and stuffed them into his pockets. He tied his sweater carefully around his waist.

While he got ready, in silence, Heather mounted Hop, leaping onto him with a light quick movement that surprised Richard.

Richard walked over to the horse and girl. Cautiously he put his hand to the horse's flank. It was warmer than he expected. The muscles under the skin flinched at his touch, but otherwise the horse did not move.

Heather squeezed Hop with her knees and he started his long, slow, rolling walk. Richard kept his hand on the horse and they walked that way until they got to the road. Then Richard went toward his house and Heather turned Hop around and went home.

Ten

The hart came home, too, to his bed of fern by the pool, but he did not come home until morning.

It was a strange pool, crystalline and blue, like a piece of polished sapphire. And it was strangely quiet, too, for birds did not call out idly there, nor did little animals scratch and scrabble wildly in the undergrowth.

The white hart settled himself down, nose to the ground. In the summer, his ears kept up a constant twitching as he tried to rid himself of the tormenting flies. But this late in the fall, the flies were mostly gone. So the white hart lay absolutely still.

He looked asleep, but he was alert. His eyes and ears and nose worked silently for him. The November night was cold. Soon there would be rims of ice on the lake and ponds, a snowfall of light powder to dust the trails. But until the deep snows of winter, when he would seek the sheltered creek bottom or the southern slope of Little Sugarloaf Mountain, this clear, strange pool was his special home.

The white hart sniffed the air again. The wind brought him the sweet pungence of pine and fern, and the late-blooming gentian, the sharper smell of several small animals upwind. But there was no danger his nose or ears warned him of.

He closed his eyes and slept.

Eleven

By mutual assent, though neither had said a word about it, Richard and Heather did not talk to each other at school. They did not show, by the flicker of an eye, that they even knew one another's names.

For Richard, this meant no difference in his outward habits. He spoke to no one in his classes beyond answering direct questions or giving page references. As for Heather, her lighthearted talkiness just remained directed toward the crowd of girls that milled about her.

Once, as he passed by her that week in school, Richard was startled to hear her say, "But I saw the deer . . ." and he stopped, unable to move farther down the hall, an emotion that was part anger, part fear, and part pure horror seething inside him.

An older boy bumped into him at that moment, and Richard was thrown off balance. As he recovered, he heard the rest of the sentence: ". . . down in the far meadow by the piney woods. I hope my brothers don't find out. If they knew there are a lot of them, they'd be all over Five Mile Wood."

Richard felt the steel band around his chest snap, just like Faithful John in the fairy tale. Only he hadn't been faithful, he thought. He had thought Heather guilty of betraying their secret. Just because the word "deer" is both singular and plural. He couldn't wait until school was over and he could meet Heather at the shimmering pool. He wouldn't, couldn't, tell her what happened, but he would be extra nice to her to make up for his suspicions.

They had been meeting at the pool every afternoon. Some afternoons, because she had lessons of one sort or another, Heather did not get there until late. But get there she did.

The first day, Monday, Richard had gone back on his own, fighting his fears and anticipations in equal measure. He had rehearsed the scene so often, it was as if it had already happened. Yet when it came, it was different from all he had imagined.

He had barely settled down when he heard some branches snap and the breathing of a large animal. It was too heavy and earthbound for the unicorn, of that he was sure. It had to be Heather's horse.

He jumped up in greeting. Heather waved gaily in return and slid from the horse's broad back. She tied the reins to a tree branch and came over. She would have taken Richard's hand, but he drew away and gestured awkwardly to the old army blanket he had spread on the ground. Heather shrugged and sat down, sitting cross-legged.

Richard sat down carefully on the far edge. "I hoped you would come," he began. It was how he had begun every scene in his mind.

"Couldn't keep us away."

"Us?" Richard was disconcerted, for in his rehearsals she had never said anything like that.

"Hop and me." She nodded at her horse.

"Do you go everywhere on that horse?"

"On Hop? Of course. Oh, he won't scare the deer, I mean unicorn, away if that's what's worrying you."

Richard looked down. "You don't really believe in it, do you," he said. It was a statement, not a question.

"No, I do. I really do. It's just . . . it's just it takes some getting used to. I mean, I've seen loads of deer, but I've never seen a unicorn before. And yesterday, when it was here—the unicorn—it seemed right. That it was a unicorn. I believed the whole thing. But today—today it seems harder, somehow, to believe."

"It takes practice."

It was Heather's turn to look bewildered. "What?"

"Believing. It takes practice."

"That's a weird thing to say."

"Well, actually, I didn't invent it. The White Queen said it."

"But that's Wonderland. And this is here." Heather said it softly. She didn't sound angry or unbelieving or anything negative. She just sounded as if she wanted to be convinced.

"Wait till you see the unicorn again," Richard said. "You'll believe it. I know you will."

"I know I will, too," said Heather.

"If your horse doesn't scare it away." Richard didn't know why he added that.

"Look," said Heather. She was clearly annoyed. "I told you he wouldn't scare it away."

"You said 'deer.'"

"Well, I meant 'unicorn.' And what do you have against my horse, anyway?"

Richard shrugged and looked over at the horse that was quietly cropping the brown grass. Occasionally the horse took a cautious step toward Heather and was stopped by the halter reins looped and knotted around the tree. "I don't . . . it's . . . his spots, I guess. Like measles. Or chicken pox. You know, diseases. Not white like the unicorn, but diseased. That's it. He looks diseased."

"Oh no," said Heather.

"You asked," Richard said defensively.

"But he's not spotted like a disease," she said. "You've got it all wrong. He's dappled like trout and finch's wings and freckles." She closed her eyes and recited: "Glory be to God for dappled things."

"But that's a poem," said Richard. "That's Gerard Manley Hopkins."

At his name, Hop lifted his ears and twitched them back and forth, whickering softly.

"Of course," said Heather. "Do you think you're the only one in the whole world who reads?"

Before Richard could begin to frame an answer, Heather reached into the pocket of her blue jeans and pulled out a crumpled piece of paper. "I was hoping I would see you today. No, I *believed* I would see you today." Her attempt at sarcasm fell flat and made them both uneasy, so they pointedly ignored it, and Heather went on. "I copied this down. We have a book at home on the unicorn tapestries. I'll bring it tomorrow if you like."

Richard was eager to please her. "Yes, I'd like that," he said rather more formally than he intended.

Heather smoothed out the paper with fingers that still bore signs of her afternoon painting class. "It says that 'wealthy kings and bishops owned unicorn horns, long and whorled and white.' What's 'whorled'?"

"Twisted." He made an upward spiral motion with his hand.

"'Five feet or more in length. These horns were beyond price, for they changed color when brought into contact with poisoned food or drink.'" Heather cocked her head to one side and thought a minute. "There must have been an awful lot of unicorns around."

"I don't know," said Richard. "Maybe then. But I like to think that there's just one in the whole world now."

"Yes," said Heather. "Ours."

Suddenly Richard had a horrifying thought. "How do you suppose the kings and bishops got all those horns?"

"I don't want to think about that."

"Could be the unicorns shed their horns every year like deer, and the kings and bishops just found the horns lying around under trees."

Heather grinned. "Medieval litter," she said.

"I used to call it," Richard said, trying out a joke of his own, "I used to call it the Middle Evils."

Heather clapped her hands delightedly.

Richard relaxed and allowed a grin to pull itself across his face. "What else does *your* book say?"

"Just the other stuff you said yesterday. About the Maid . . . maiden. Except . . ." Heather hesitated.

"Except what?"

"Except if she had any stain in her—the maiden—the unicorn would rip her open with its horn. I think that means if she isn't pure any more. But I'm not really sure how far . . . what a stain is. I kissed Henry Castlemain at his birthday party. It was just a game. Is that a stain?"

"Oh, I don't think so," Richard said quickly, furious at the thought.

"But then, you aren't a unicorn."

"Are you afraid?" Richard asked.

Heather considered the question a long time. She was remembering Henry Castlemain and trying not to think about the horn. It was some time before she spoke.

"If you were there with me, I wouldn't be afraid."

Richard smiled. "Of course I'll be there," he said.

Twelve

Each subsequent meeting at the pool was a discovery. They discovered they both liked poetry, though Richard liked to read it silently and Heather to recite it aloud. They discovered they both liked fall better than spring—Richard for all the things that were being covered and hidden, Heather for the colors and the raucous calls of the birds flying south. They discovered they both liked secrets, though Richard had always known it and Heather had just learned it. And they discovered each other.

It happened on Friday, that final discovery, when Richard was walking Heather to her horse. "I never talk to anyone, and now I'm talking to you."

"Oh, I talk *to* a lot of people. And a lot of people talk *at* me," Heather answered. "But you're the only one I talk *with*!"

They were both silent a moment. Then, as Heather climbed onto Hop, they both started again in a rush.

"Why do you suppose we haven't seen . . ." Richard began.

"Do you think you might come to dinner tonight?" Heather asked.

The invitation was overriding. Not only was Heather's voice louder, but in the confusion and excitement, they both forgot Richard's question, which was the more important. For they hadn't seen the white hart since the previous Sunday when they had started him from his soft ferny bed.

Richard was alarmed at the idea of going to Heather's house for dinner, to face the barrage of questions she had promised him would come from her boisterous family; yet he blurted out "yes" without hesitation. His tongue was simply not listening to his cowardly heart.

Heather shouted, "Great! See you at six. Only white house on Hunt's Lane," and kicked Hop into a lazy canter before Richard could change his mind. Indeed, she could hear him shouting after her, "Wait, Heather! Maybe I shouldn't." She refused to hear any more.

Richard was so afraid of telephoning the Fieldings to say he couldn't come that he went. In fact, his Uncle Hugh drove him over and didn't stop talking the entire way, so there was never any time for Richard to voice his fears.

"Never really met the Fieldings," Uncle Hugh was saying. "But know them by sight. Good family. Stick together. Great hunters, too, you know. Been here generations, not newcomers like us. Own a lot of the town, or used to. Understand she paints. Pretty woman. You meet the girl in school?" It went on like that for some time. So when they finally arrived at the only white house on Hunt's Lane, Uncle Hugh carried his monologue right into the house and finished it up on Mrs. Fielding.

She didn't seem to recognize it as one-sided. Presumably she had participated in many similar ones before. She invited him in for a drink.

Heather and Richard stared at each other for a long, horrible moment, suddenly strangers, and Heather ran back into the kitchen, where she attacked the salad with a paring knife. Richard wanted to follow her in and he wanted to run out to the car and he wanted to sink into the carpet. Instead he stood where he was, feeling sure that every time Heather's brothers, unseen in the family room, laughed at the television show, they were really laughing at him.

At last, his uncle's drinks and his uncle's jokes were finished. Uncle Hugh clapped him on the back and said, "I'll be back at ten for you," and disappeared out into the fresh night air.

At that point, dinner was served.

If dinner was good or bad, Richard did not know. He barely ate it. Heather watched him turn alternately white and pink as the conversation eddied and flowed around him. She pitied him and was angry at him for not being as funny and dear and sweet and serious as she knew he was. Her brothers seemed especially loud in their jokes. Yet they also seemed lively, while Richard seemed dead or turned to stone.

"Richard and I," Heather said, "have known each other for ages. In school. But we never spoke until last week. Did we, Richard?"

"*Ughm*," Richard said, the horrible noise rising again in his throat. The questions had started, and Heather herself had started them. He felt like an animal at bay.

"Richard, dear, you've scarcely touched your plate. Is anything wrong with the food?" That was Mrs. Fielding.

They were going to be on him now for sure, Richard thought. Why? Why? Why? There was no hope of avoiding the questions.

"Are you in Heather's class?" asked Mr. Fielding.

"A grade ahead, actually," said Heather, slipping in with answers to rescue him. He threw her a thankful look. "He was tutored and is ever so much smarter than the rest of us, aren't you, Richard?"

It was the kind of question that needed no answer, and they both knew it.

Ian looked up from his plate, where, until now, most of his attention had rested. He tossed his dark hair out of his eyes. "Richard? Or Dick? Or Rich? Do they really call you the whole thing—Richard?"

Brian, across the table, laughed. "Richard the First, Richard the Second, or Richard the Third?"

"Oh, don't be beastly," said Heather, grimacing across at him.

"Well, which is it?" asked Dylan. A natural athlete, he fancied himself a scholar as well, and was actually close to brilliant at history. "Richard the Third was a humpback, so that can't be it. You're tall but straight. And Richard the First was lionhearted, brave, and outspoken. Or so they say. Whoever *they* is. They always say *they* when they don't have any real facts.

But you don't seem very outspoken. How about lionhearted and brave? And Richard the Second was . . . well, he was a bit of a problem, he was. He had an overbearing uncle and a rebellion and a flag with a white deer on it. Which . . ."

"A white deer? Oh, Richard, then that one's you. It's our . . ." Horrified, Heather stopped herself by clapping both her hands over her mouth. She stared at Richard, who suddenly couldn't take his eyes off the table. He turned absolutely white himself and started to choke on his food.

"Hit him on the back," cried Ian.

Mr. Fielding, sitting at the head of the table, reached over and began to pound Richard while the boy kept on sputtering.

"Not so hard, dear, he has a bad heart."

"Only bruised, Mother," said Heather, but it didn't sound like a joke at all.

Brian, though, was not to be diverted. "What's this about a deer, Heath? Have you spotted one for us?"

Ian took it up. "Where'd you find it, Heath?"

Heather, her hands back again on her mouth, shook her head, imperceptibly at first, then harder and harder. But the boys would not let up.

"Heath's a great little spotter, Rich," Dylan said. "She and Hop find all our deer for us on their travels. She never wants to tell us where they are, but she never can keep a secret. We always worm it out of her in time."

"She has this peculiar problem, you see," Ian added. "She cannot tell a lie." He put his hand up as if pledging allegiance. "So it's all a matter of asking the right questions."

Brian came in then. "The Famous Fielding Finder, we call her, don't we?"

"Boys," warned Mr. Fielding, who realized that this time the teasing had gone too far.

But Ian did not pay attention. Like a dog on the scent, he was unable to stop. "Hey, I know where you went this week. Bet it's in Five Mile Wood. Come on, Heath, is he big? Is he a nine-pointer? Don't forget, tomorrow's Opening Day."

Heather ripped her hands from her mouth and cried out, starting like a small animal from a bush, "It's a secret! I can't tell you. I can't. I can't. *Richard.*"

Richard pushed his chair away from the table and stood up. His arm brushed Mr. Fielding's wineglass, and the glass overturned on the table, staining the cloth. He hissed at Heather, "Traitor. Traitor. You've just told them. You've just told them everything."

His voice had barely risen above a whisper, yet it could be heard clearly by everyone at the table.

Heather couldn't answer him. She felt he was right and yet he was wrong. She couldn't think what to do, and so she tried to buy time by reaching over with her linen napkin to sop up the spilled wine.

But Richard didn't wait for an answer. He ran to the door. He looked one more time at Heather, his mouth twisted with anger, but his eyes brimming with tears. Then he opened the door and ran out of the house into the dark.

Heather couldn't move except to turn the napkin over and over, running her finger across the wine-colored stain. Suddenly her mother was standing by her chair with Richard's coat in her hands. "Best run after him, dear," she said. "He's very upset about something." And she handed Heather the coat.

"Oh, Mother," Heather said, snuffling, and then the sobs came in earnest. She let the coat slip through her fingers to the floor. Then she got up, went over to the door, and closed it.

Thirteen

The white hart slipped along the path, ever windward, between his bed and the feeding grounds. The path he chose was an old Indian trail through an orchard long gone to seed. Apples, sweet even without man's cultivating hand, could be found there in season. In season, too, wild blueberries lined the tumbled stone walls.

The hart's toes were still quite sharp. Age had not yet rounded them. They left small, precise prints in the soft parts of the path that a hunter might have followed.

This night, in the full moon, a keener hunter than man was on the hart's trail. The blue-gray Scottish deerhound was out tracking. Not one to go by scent, the rough-coated hound had glimpsed a shadowy movement through the moonlit trees and was on the hart's trail at once.

The dog had no real need of food. He ran home each evening for a dish set out by the door. But hunting wild deer was what he had been bred for. And the old blood called to him.

Usually the deerhound led a pack of farm dogs. But this night the others had remained home, chained or sleeping, content, their bellies filled with canned food. So the hound tracked the hart alone. A foolish joy, but one the dog could not deny himself.

The hart stopped in a small turnabout and sniffed the air again. He heard a crackling of twigs behind him. Instead of bounding away in swift leaps, the hart turned and set himself for a fight. He lowered his head slightly and pawed the ground.

The hound was not ready for such a trick. He bounded into the tiny clearing that was full of the overwhelming musk of deer. He nearly galloped right onto the hart's horns. The paleness of the animal, gleaming white in the half-light of moonshine, confused the dog for a moment.

That moment was all the hart needed. He scooped his head down and lifted the silent dog up upon his horns. The weapons of bone struck home.

Like a ghostly pantomime, gray and white in the wood, the deadly dance concluded. Speared, the dog was lifted into the air on the hart's rack. Only then, when he was in the air, did the dog begin to scream. He continued screaming as he was flung over the albino's back. He stopped only when he hit the ground, blood staining his gray coat.

The white hart paused a moment to pound the dog's crumpled body with his hooves. Then he turned and leaped off to find the shimmering pool—the fight, the death of the dog, already forgotten.

Fourteen

Richard felt a pain in his chest, but he did not stop, and he barely noticed the dark. He knew he could not possibly run all the way home, but to keep warm he jogged slowly, willing the pain to go away. The rhythm, the pace, finally eased the ache, and it went, a little at a time. He was left with a feeling of exhilaration that surprised him. He guessed it was a combination of the crisp night air, the full moon, and the thought of what was to come. What had to come. People lay behind him; only the unicorn lay ahead. He would have to take action, something he had never really done before. It was like a quest, an adventure, a heroic journey. He could count on no one else in this, certainly not on Heather, who had betrayed them at their first real trial. He could count only on himself.

It pleased him that this time, he, Richard Plante, would be doing this. Not reading about someone else in a book, hiding his fears in silent retreat from the world and its questions. He had the answer, and he was giving it loud and clear.

As he thought, planned, what he had to do in the dark night ahead, a car flashed past him, the light suddenly blinding. Then the car turned and cruised up beside him.

Of course, it was Uncle Hugh, phoned by the Fieldings. Richard slipped gratefully into the car's warmth. This was no compromise. He could do nothing until near midnight, when everyone was asleep.

Uncle Hugh did not speak, not when Richard got into the car, and not later, when Aunt Marcie enfolded him in a hug calculated to drive out his demons.

For once, Aunt Marcie was silent, too, except for her eyebrows, which worked up and down overtime. But Richard did not start any conversation, though he knew they were waiting for him to do so. Wordlessly, he went upstairs to bed.

He heard Uncle Hugh say, as he went up the dark stairs alone and totally unafraid, "He didn't say a thing. You'd think he'd have some explanation. I guess we'll wait till tomorrow and then we'll try and get his side of it." Richard could only guess at Aunt Marcie's eyebrows as she snorted in return "Young love!" and dialed the phone.

But none of it touched Richard as he marched up the stairs slowly and deliberately. He paused at the top landing and saluted the ghosts of his mother and father, who he knew must hover somewhere in the house. Then he went into his room, closed the door firmly, and went to bed.

But not to sleep. No, not to sleep. For many long minutes, Richard waited for his aunt and uncle to go to bed. They would turn in early tonight. Uncle

Hugh had never missed an opening of deer season yet, or so was his boast. The creak of the stairs, the shuffling in and out of the bathroom, the slight sighings and whisperings, the click of the closing door, were the signals Richard waited for. And after the noises ceased, he waited some more—twenty times sixty heartbeats—before he got out of bed.

He got up cautiously in case anyone was still awake. But his every move was ritual. He dressed in his good blue trousers and his blue jacket with the crest on it that Uncle Hugh had brought back from England. He put on his heaviest socks and boots. And for warmth, since he had left his coat at the Fieldings' house, he tossed his navy blue blanket around his shoulders like a cape. It hung in graceful folds to his ankles. Then he tiptoed down the stairs and out into the night.

The night was cold and crisp but windless. Richard walked briskly toward the path where he would turn off into the orchard. No cars passed by him as he walked, nor could he hear any of the usual night noises. There was just darkness and silence, heavy, palpable, and real.

In the daytime, coming down the path, he had often stumbled. But he did not stumble now. He walked with authority. And even the brambles, dried and stiff, did not catch his makeshift cape. He made not a single wrong twist or turn or misstep, and he came at last to the shimmering pool watched only by the moon, which hung like a blind eye in the blue-black socket of sky.

Fifteen

Heather leaned her back against the oak door. She looked straight ahead but could see nothing through her tears. No one in the family spoke to her, or if they did, she couldn't hear them. Snuffling faintly, she went up to her room.

She lay down on the bed and stared at the bright yellow canopy. When she had been much younger, she had played at being a princess in her room. But now it was as if the sky had fallen and was waiting, old and yellow, to crush her utterly. She turned over on her stomach and put her hands under her head.

It was then that she discovered she was still clutching the wine-stained dinner napkin. She raised up on her elbows and looked at it thoughtfully. She was still thoughtful when she took off her clothes and climbed into her nightgown. It was long and white, with a shirring of lace and a yellow ribbon woven about the neck and a yellow tie at the waist.

Slowly she unplaited her braids. Her hair, so long bound, fell over her shoulders in dark shining waves and reached down to the small of her back.

Heather sat down again on the bed and smoothed the damask napkin on her lap. The red stain in the soft light of her room looked black, but it still had the sickly sweet smell of wine.

Heather shook her head vigorously, as if to shake off her imaginings, and turned off the light. Then she lay down on the bed, tucked the napkin into her bodice, and remained unmoving in the dark.

A knock sounded on her door. Her mother came in. "Heather, dear, do you want to talk? Is there anything I can do?"

Heather willed her voice to calmness, firmness. "No, Mother. I'm all right. Really I am. We'll talk tomorrow. Please."

Mrs. Fielding knew her daughter well enough to leave then. Heather could hear whisperings in the hall. Her father and then the boys cursed Richard for a coward and a fool and asked about her. She knew her mother would make them leave her alone. At least until morning. Even so, that would barely be enough time for what had to be done.

For Heather knew that she and she alone had to act. And she had to act that night if she were to save the unicorn from the hunters—from her brothers and her father and all the rest. She could not count on Richard; he *was* a coward and a fool, just as her brothers had said. A coward not to back her up, a fool to think she had let the secret slip on purpose. That she had, indeed, let the secret out was a pain she would have to bear alone. As penance, she would have to save the unicorn alone, too. So she waited out the ticking of her bedroom clock and kept herself awake.

The clock was barely touching eleven when the silence in the house told her everyone else was asleep. The boys and her father, she knew, always went to bed early the night before Opening Day. They had to rise before dawn.

And her mother would be rising with them to fix them breakfast. It was a tradition never broken.

Heather got up and slipped her feet into boots. She moved silently downstairs, grabbed her heavy school cape from the closet, and was gone before the dog had time for more than a sleepy, growling yawn.

She did not take Hop out of the barn. He would hate to be disturbed for a night ride. And the heavy clopping of his hooves might alert someone in the house. Though she had to be back before one of the early risers noticed she was gone, silence was no less important than speed.

She ran down the road, her dark cape floating behind her like bat's wings, the white gown luminous in the dark. She was lucky that no cars passed as she ran. And when, out of breath and trembling slightly from the cold, she came to the path through the apple orchard, the moon came out from behind a cloud. It was full and bright, and in the shadows it cast, the linen dinner napkin tucked in her bodice glistened both white and black.

Heather was careful not to make a misstep as she went down the path toward the pool. She stepped on nothing that might crackle or snap. And when she came at last to the clearing where the pool was set like a jewel in a ring, Richard was there before her.

"You!" they said together. But in the single word was both surprise and forgiveness.

Richard hesitated, then took the blanket off his shoulders and spread it on the ground under the wild apple tree. They both sat down, hands folded, silent and waiting.

Sixteen

And then it came.

White and gleaming, stepping through fragrant sweet violets, the unicorn came.

It was high at the shoulder, with a neck both strong and thick. Its face was that of a goat or a deer, like neither and yet like both, with a tassel of white hair for a beard and eyes the color of old gold. Its slim legs ended in cloven hooves that shone silver in the moonlight. Its tail was long and fringed at the tip with hair as soft and fine as silken thread. And where it stepped, flowers sprang up, daisies and lilies and the wild strawberry, and plants that neither Richard nor Heather had seen before but knew at once, the cuckoopint and the columbine and the wild forest rose.

But it was the horn that caught their gaze. The spiraled, ivory horn that thrust from the unicorn's head, that looked both cruel and kind. It was the horn that convinced them both that this could be no dream.

And so it came, the unicorn, more silent than night yet sweeter than singing. It came around the shimmering pool and knelt in front of the children as they sat breathless on the blanket. It knelt before them, not in humility but in fealty, and placed its head gently, oh so gently, in Heather's lap.

At the unicorn's touch, Heather sighed. And at her sigh, the silent woods around suddenly seemed to burst with the song of birds—thrush, and sparrow, and the rising meadowlark. And from far off, the children heard the unfamiliar jug-jug-jug of a nightingale.

Suddenly, it was spring and summer in one. Richard looked around and saw that within the enclosure of the green meadow, ringed about with a stone wall, encircled in stone arms, was a season he had never seen before. The glade was dappled with thousands of flowers. He could see, from where he sat, pomegranate and cherry trees, orange and apple, all in full bloom. The smell of them in the air was so strong that he was almost giddy.

But Heather seemed to notice none of this. She had taken the yellow ribbon from her waist and bound it about the unicorn's head like a golden halter, over the forehead and around the soft white muzzle. Her fingers moved slowly but surely as she concentrated on the white head that lay on her lap, the horn carefully tucked under her arm. She stroked the unicorn's gleaming neck with her free hand and crooned over and over, "You beauty, you love, you beauty." And the beast closed its eyes and shuddered once and then lay very still. She could feel the veins in its silken neck under her hand, pulsing, surging, but the great white head did not move.

Richard looked over at the beast and the girl, and on his knees he moved across the blanket to them. Hesitantly, he reached his hand out toward the unicorn's neck. And Heather looked up then and took his hand in hers and placed it on the soft, smooth neck. Richard smiled shyly, then broadly, and Heather smiled back.

As they sat there, the three, without a word, a sudden harsh note hallooed from afar.

"A horn," Richard said, drawing his hand away quickly. "Heather, I heard a hunting horn."

But she seemed not to hear.

The horn sounded again, nearer. There was no mistaking its insistent cry. "Heather!"

"Oh, Richard, I hear it. What shall we do?"

The unicorn opened its eyes, eyes of antique gold. It looked steadily up at Heather, but still it did not move.

Heather tried to push the heavy head off her lap. "You have to go. You *have* to. It must be near day. The hunters will kill you. They won't care that you're beautiful. They'll just want your horn. Oh, please. *Please.*" The last was an anguished cry, but still the unicorn did not move. It was as though it lay under a spell that was too old, too powerful to break.

"Richard, it won't move. What can we do? It'll be killed. It'll be our fault. Oh, Richard, what have you read about this? Think. *Think.*"

Richard thought. He went over lists and lists in his mind. But he did not recall it in any of his reading. And then he remembered the unicorn tapestries Heather had found in her mother's art books. She had brought the book for them both to see. The unicorn had indeed been killed, slaughtered by men with sharp spears and menacing faces. What could he and Heather do about such evil?

Heather was leaning over the unicorn's neck and crying. "Oh, my beauty. Oh, forgive me. I didn't mean you to be killed. Before I saw you, really saw you, I wanted to tame you. But now I . . . we want to save you."

Richard watched her stroke the neck, the head, her hand moving hypnotically over the gleaming white, tangling in the yellow ribbon.

Suddenly Richard knew. "Heather," he shouted, "the yellow ribbon! It's the golden bridle. Take it off. Take it off!"

Heather looked at the ribbon and in that moment understood. She ripped it from the unicorn's neck. "Go!" she said. "Be free." The ribbon caught on the spiraled horn.

The minute the ribbon was off its neck, the unicorn got up heavily from its knees. It flung its head abruptly backward and the golden band flew through the air.

The ribbon landed in the middle of the pool and was sucked downward into the water with a horrible sound. The birds rose up mourning from the trees as, in a clatter of hooves, the unicorn circled the pool once, leaped over the stone wall, and disappeared.

In an instant it was November again, brown, sere, and cold.

And the pool was no longer crystal and shimmering but a dank, brackish bog the color of rotted logs.

Seventeen

The horn sounded again, only this time it was clearly a car horn. Loud, insistent, it split the air over and over as the sun rose, shaded in fog, over the far mountains.

"It's day," said Richard heavily. "Opening Day."

"But it's all right," said Heather, soothingly. "The unicorn is gone. It's gone forever."

"How do you know?"

"I know because I believe. Even without much practice, I believe." Heather put out her hand to Richard, and he took it. Then they curled together for warmth and fell asleep in the dawn.

They were found two hours later, still sleeping, by Brian and Ian, who signaled with three shots fired in the air. They had to be shaken awake, for somehow the gunfire did not disturb them. Wrapping themselves in cape and blanket, Heather and Richard stumbled groggily to their feet and followed the boys out to the road. The boys were rough with them, as if to punish them for the scare they had inflicted on the family and for the fact that they had ruined Opening Day.

When they got to the road, there was a long row of cars waiting, for hunters and police had joined in the search.

"Mom was worried and checked on you about midnight," Brian explained. "And when you were gone, she called Mrs. Plante."

Ian interrupted. "And when your aunt found out *you* were gone as well," he said to Richard, "that's when we really got worried and called the police."

Dylan added, "Well, you can imagine the scene."

Heather and Richard could, indeed, imagine the scene. But they didn't speak. They just looked at each other, smiles hidden behind serious faces.

Mrs. Fielding came over and enfolded them at once. "It was silly to run away," she said to them both. "What happened at the table was nothing."

She smelled of talcum and early-morning coffee, and she seemed both angry and relieved. Richard breathed deeply, and for the first time since they had been found, spoke. "It wasn't 'nothing,' Mrs. Fielding. It was actually the beginning of something."

Mrs. Fielding did not answer. Perhaps she hadn't heard. Or perhaps she was afraid to ask what he meant, since they had been found sleeping together in the woods, Heather in her nightgown. But she was silent and just gathered them both in again, as she gathered all the arguments at her house, without judgment.

Heather allowed herself to be gathered in for a moment. Her chin went down on her chest, and the napkin tucked in her bodice tickled. She pulled it out and stared at it for a moment. It was no longer stained. It was white and fresh and gleaming.

"Look, Richard, look!" she cried, holding it up to his face. As it came close to him, Richard could smell the sweet scent of crushed violets, and faintly imprinted on the linen napkin he saw a pattern of swirls as if something spiral had lain there.

He sucked in his breath, and Heather tucked the napkin back into her gown, and without a word more they all went home.

There were explanations, of course. For a swamp doesn't appear and children disappear without them. But none of the explanations mattered to Richard and Heather. And they, alone, offered none in the general clamor that followed their midnight transfiguration. For indeed, how could they explain about the unicorn? It was, after all, a mythical beast. Or the shimmering pool that had become a bog? Or the wine-stained table napkin now gleaming and white as the unicorn itself? They could think of no explanations that anyone would believe, and so they smiled and gave none.

But they kept the napkin safe, first in one drawer and then another, to remind them both, as if they needed reminding, of that moment in time when autumn became summer and now became then and what was logical and what was magical became one.

Eighteen

It was just dawn. The sun rose, shrouded in fog, and fog covered the valley.

The white hart ran swiftly and purposefully out of the woods. In the distance, he could hear guns and the occasional bleat of a car horn.

He came to a wide macadam road which smelled sharply of men and machines and was covered with a rolling mist. He hesitated a moment, then clattered onto the hard surface.

The deer traveled east, toward the sun that burned behind its mask of fog. He ran for several miles, passed only by a single slow-moving car, but in the white fog he was almost invisible.

Suddenly, he plunged into the brush on the opposite side of the road, turned around for just a moment, and sniffed the air. His ears twitched forward and back. Then he moved into the low briars and disappeared.

The woods on this side of the road covered thousands of acres and were part of a protected reserve.

The white hart was never seen again.

UNICORN SERIES

Nancy Springer

[I]

I am not unlike the unicorn,
Shy wanderer of a mystic solitude,
Serene as ignorance, yet keenly drawn
To seek the lap of truth. You'll think me puffed
With pride to set myself beside the faery
Form of sorrow. Yet I too have known
The traitor virgin, the mocking hunters, the sharp
Teeth of the hounds. I too have felt the hard
Encircling boards. Only I lack a white
And supple body and a soaring horn,
Their passion lost in unity of loves,
To dream completion for the half-made world.

[II]

Solitude
    is a vast sea
        a vast sand upland

the high wild mountains
    the high wild wind in the sky
  the high wild wind
    among the strange trees
      where hidden one with white mane
        lank and stirring on his withers
        and a wide seeking eye
          scans sea and mountain and sky

Solitary
  is the unicorn
    from the day it is born

[III]
Snow shuts down
    the highway, street lights
    lets the stardark in.
The wild things cry in the wind.
White in the nightout
    Nearer than the stars
    The unicorn is standing
    In the snow.

[IV]
Moonglow unicorn
Son of the moon
Of pearl is your horn
Stars fall from your mane
And your flank is as white
As the white winter light
Of the moon.

[V]
Tell me, fair unicorn,
How, like a young woman
World knew its own wonder
Those days of creation
With the one mystic eye.
Great god-eye of sky,
Clear eye of awareness
By which as in mirror
Of bright mountain water
A fair cloud-white unicorn
Or a young woman
Might if they saw truly
Yet see self divine.

[VI]
The unicorn leaps on the mountains.
    The unicorn couples amid the mountains
        Under a crescent moon.
            The horn is as hard as the mountains,
                Singular as the horns of the moon.

Where the sunrise is,
        There is the silver unicorn.

Where the sunset is,
        There is the golden unicorn.

Where the moonlight is,
        There is the unicorn of shining horn.

The unicorn leaps on the mountains.
    The unicorn flies in the far dark sky
        Unseen, between as the stars spin by
        On their rounds of mystic omen.

[VII]

The waves arch their white crests,
    The waves leap in moonlight.
        The unicorn lives in the waves.

The moon is a bright curve
        Whose two horns are one.
           The unicorn lives in the moon.

The moon is crescent,
        Full, decrescent, dark
           The waves leap in darkness.
        The unicorn lives.

[VIII]

The mist is rising.
The unicorn is walking in the meadow.

See the soft grass,
The silver tufts of grasses by the river?
The unicorn is silent.
Softly it walks through the wish light,
Through the pearl gray light of dusk

The flowers are folded.
Who has seen the unicorn?

ABOUT THE EDITOR

Peter S. Beagle

Peter Soyer Beagle is the internationally bestselling and much-beloved author of numerous classic fantasy novels and collections, including *The Last Unicorn, Tamsin, The Line Between, Summerlong*, and *In Calabria*. He is the editor of *The Secret History of Fantasy* and the co-editor of *The Urban Fantasy Anthology*.

Born in Manhattan and raised in the Bronx, Beagle published his first novel, *A Fine & Private Place*, at nineteen, while still completing his degree in creative writing. Beagle's follow-up, *The Last Unicorn*, is widely considered one of the great works of fantasy. It has been made into a feature-length animated film, a stage play, and a graphic novel.

Beagle has written widely for both stage and screen, including the screenplay adaptations for *The Last Unicorn* and the animated film of *The Lord of the Rings* and the well-known "Sarek" episode of *Star Trek*.

Beagle is the recipient of the Hugo, Nebula, Mythopoeic, and Locus awards, as well as the Grand Prix de l'Imaginaire. He has also been honored with the World Fantasy Life Achievement Award and the Inkpot Award from the Comic-Con convention, given for major contributions to fantasy and science fiction.

Beagle lives in Richmond, California, where he is working on too many projects to even begin to name.

ABOUT THE EDITOR

Jacob Weisman

Jacob Weisman is the publisher at Tachyon Publications, which he founded in 1995. He is a World Fantasy Award-winning editor and is the series editor of Tachyon's critically acclaimed, award-winning novella line, including the Hugo Award-winner, *The Emperor's Soul* by Brandon Sanderson, and the Nebula and Shirley Jackson award-winner, *We Are All Completely Fine* by Daryl Gregory. Weisman has edited the anthologies *Invaders: 22 Tales from the Outer Limits of Literature*, *The Sword & Sorcery Anthology* (with David G. Hartwell), and *The Treasury of the Fantastic* (with David M. Sandner).

Weisman lives in San Francisco, where he runs Tachyon Publications just a few blocks from the house he grew up in.